Sacred Wind
The Complete Trilogy

Andy Coffey

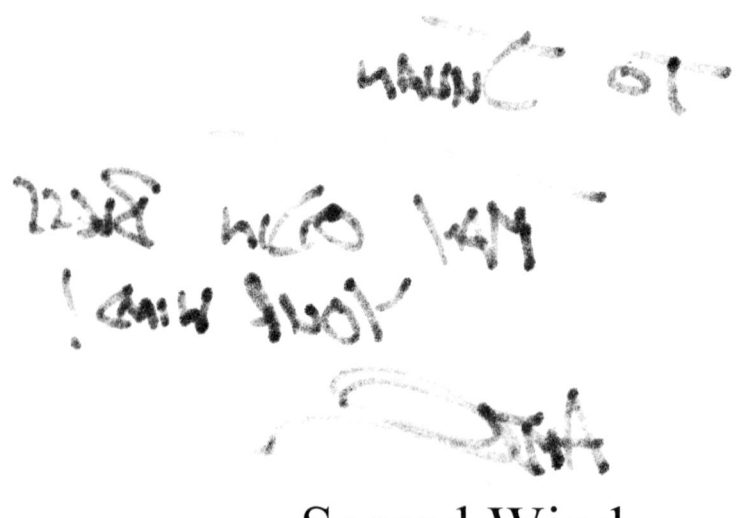

Sacred Wind
The Complete Trilogy

Copyright © Andy Coffey 2014

The right of Andy Coffey to be identified as the author of this work has been asserted in accordance with sections 77 and 78 of the Copyright Designs and Patent Act 1988.

All characters in this book are fictitious, and any resemblance to actual persons, living or dead, is purely coincidental.

1st print edition

ISBN-13: 978-1500682866

ISBN-10: 1500682861

Printed by CreateSpace

Available from Amazon.com and other retail outlets

Available on Kindle and other book stores

Illustrations by Joe Latham joe@lookhappydesign.com

'Quantum computing is…a distinctively new way of harnessing nature…It will be the first technology that allows useful tasks to be performed in collaboration between parallel universes.'
David Deutsch – Centre for Quantum Computation, University of Oxford.

'There are vibrations of different universes right here, right now. We're just not in tune with them. There are probably other parallel universes in our living room – this is modern physics. This is the modern interpretation of quantum theory, that many worlds represent reality.'
Dr Michio Kaku - Theoretical Physicist and Bestselling Author.

'In infinite space, even the most unlikely events must take place somewhere.'
Professor Max Tegmark - Dept. of Physics, MIT.

'This is a victory for life, a victory for common sense and, ultimately, recognition that consciousness is pervasive in our abundant and wonderful universe.'
Dr Lamb Dopiaza-Pilau Rice – following the 1968 legislation by the Welsh Parliament recognising curries as conscious entities..

Other books by Andy Coffey

Sacred Wind: Book 1
Sacred Wind: Book 2
Sacred Wind: Book 3
Sacred Wind: The Appendices
Sacred Wind: Songbook

Sacred Wind – The Album

Possibly the finest debut album by a Welsh Viking Flatulence Rock band from an alternative reality… Available at all good download stores!

www.sacredwind.co.uk

CONTENTS

1	There's something in the air	1
2	The Cheese of Pleasant Dreams	8
3	Be good for Mrs Perriwinkle	17
4	That explains everything…	23
5	It may be linked to The Prophecy	28
6	Is there a bank around here?	34
7	I'm still getting dressed, darling	39
8	She may be the last of her kind	43
9	We'd like a room, please	47
10	Would sir like a cravat with that?	51
11	Metal and Curry	54
12	The name of vengeance is Sacred Wind!	58
13	My Sword is my Sword	65
14	Ooh, can I have your autograph, please?	76
15	I've heard your sausages are to die for	82
16	You allow them to enter if they pay a bond	87
17	Have you looked in the mirror lately?	93
18	Hello and welcome to 'Rock your Deity'!	100
19	Do you think they'll put out bunting?	108
20	I see you've brought your trumpet	115
21	Has anyone seen the Queen?	124

22	So it would appear that the outcome is not decided	131
23	Do you think people will sing songs about us in the future?	136
24	I had no idea you had such a fondness for old condiments	143
25	May Odin bless their wind	147
26	Perhaps you can help me, I'm looking for someone	157
27	Have you prepared the room for the press conference?	161
28	Follow that cab!	169
29	Are the troops ready?	176
30	It seems our cover is blown	185
31	Prepare to be boarded	190
32	I believe I'm feeling slightly peckish	196
33	Cover your ears, ladies	202
34	The most noble of sheep	210
35	The proportions look slightly understated	215
36	We'd better stick close together	218
37	Hope always finds a way	226
38	There has been a massacre!	234
39	Just think of the merchandising sales later!	239
40	It's a full house, my Lord	247
41	May the best contestant win!	252
42	Do we turn left or right at the city gates?	258
43	Stand firm! Stand firm!	264
44	It looks like you've been usurped	271

45	Show no mercy!	279
46	Is this part of the act?	285
47	Odin blesses your wind	294
48	Dragon Ships and Women's Hips	301
	Epilogues	311
	Appendix 1 – A Quick Guide to Quantum Computing	315
	Appendix 2 – The Bi-Millennial Deity Conference	318
	Appendix 3 – The Frothy Ale Tsunami of '87	326
	Appendix 4 – History of the Cestrian Music Tournament	329

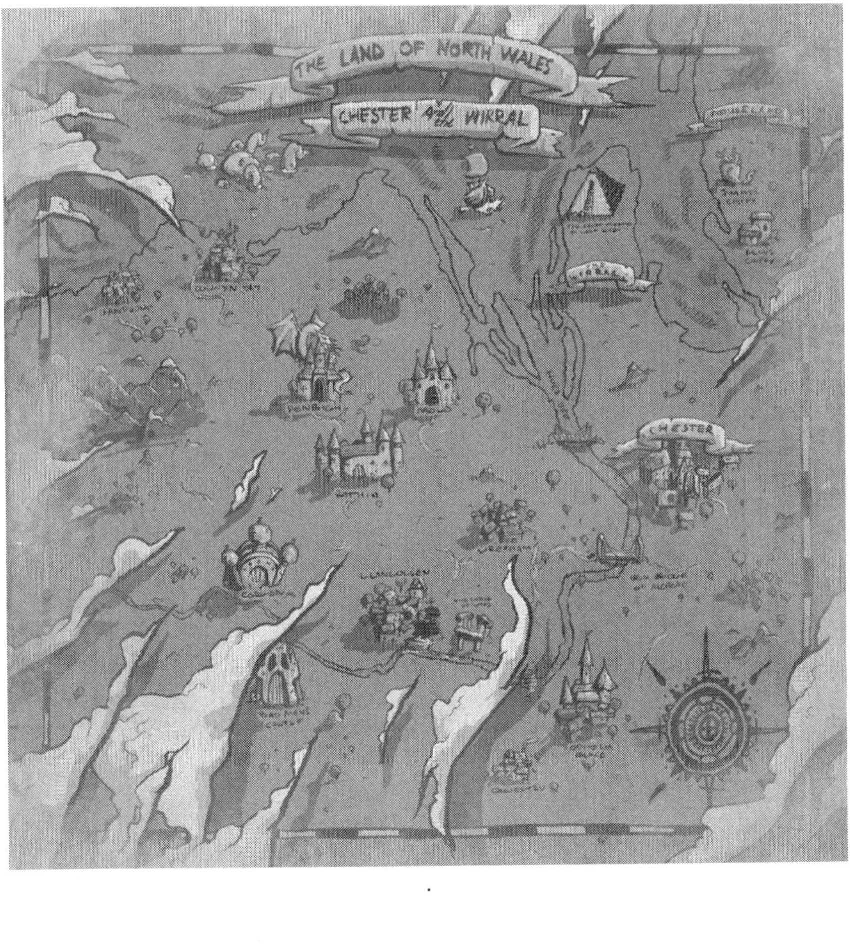

CHAPTER 1 – THERE'S SOMETHING IN THE AIR

Baron Bartholomew Vincent Blacktie sat slumped on his sizeable gold and marble throne, scratching his chin. His bejewelled coronet lay slightly to one side on his head and he nonchalantly stroked his pet ferret, Velvet, who was sat on his knee. Looking out at the opulent great hall in front of him, he sighed.

He had been the Supreme Ruler of Chester and the surrounding areas of North Wales and the Wirral for a little over five years, and things had never been better. Tax revenues were high, the people were obedient, cheese production was under strict control, and instances of unauthorised flatulence were at an all-time low. But, irrespective of all this, he was troubled.

'Pimple,' he said to his Chief Courtier, who was standing in one of the decorative stone arches that surrounded the throne room, 'am I a benign and noble leader?'

'Only on Thursday's, my Lord, after you've had a good helping of Ma Chesterton's dumplings, a piece of Cheshire Blue and a goblet or two of port.'

The Baron shook his head, disconsolately. 'Really, Pimple? Oh, I must make more of an effort. For I wish the people to love me, to be inspired by me, and to think of me as someone who has their best interests tattooed indelibly on his benevolent and egalitarian heart.'

'I thought you simply wanted power and wealth beyond all imagination, my Lord?'

'Oh, how little you know me, Pimple,' the Baron sighed again. 'Although my actions make it appear that I seek only omnipotence, subjugation of all beings before me and wealth beyond measure, do you not realise that I also long to be loved?'

'Er, it hadn't really crossed my mind, my Lord.'

'Nevertheless, it is true, Pimple. I desire to exude bonhomie and joy, so that the people will wish to cling to my metaphoric breasts like suckling kittens.'

Pimple raised a solitary eyebrow and continued to listen attentively.

'And, to be frank, I also want to exhibit a more positive image in the run up to the next election.'

'But the next election is forty-five years away, my Lord, based upon the amendments you made last year regarding tenure.'

'Ah, true, but I do so hate leaving things to the last minute. Time waits for no man, Pimple. You should remember that.'

'I will, my Lord.'

'And I need to ensure that all of the electorate are completely behind me. Do you remember what percentage of the vote I received last time?'

'99% my Lord.'

'And who received the other 1%? Was it not Lord "Goody-two-shoes" Nobleheart?'

'It was my Lord.'

'And have you seen him recently?'

'Yes, my Lord.'

'And…?'

'He's in the canal where you left him, my Lord.'

'Ah, how fares he?'

'Well, he's lost a lot of weight, my Lord… and some life.'

The Baron looked forlorn, raised a weary hand to his forehead and continued to stroke Velvet. 'Nevertheless, Pimple, I feel an obligation to convince this 1% of my subjects that, at the next election, they should allay their fears and cast their votes for me. I wish them to see that I am truly their humble servant and offer them succour in their time of need, and protection from our enemies.'

'I'm not sure you'll be able to achieve that, my Lord,' Pimple said, taking a tentative step forward.

'And why, pray, do you think that will be?' the indignant Baron asked.

'Because they're in the canal with Lord Nobleheart, my Lord.'

The ceremonial fanfare of trumpets blared out and the ostentatious doors to the throne room opened inwards. A troop of armoured men, in full military regalia, entered and saluted en masse, the clang of steel arms on steel breastplates reverberating around the room.

'My Lord,' a weasel-faced steward shouted with an air of self-importance, 'I announce General Ramases Darkblast, who seeks audience to inform you of progress regarding the Scouseland Crusades.'

General Ramases Darkblast, the Supreme Commander of the Knights of Flatulence, the Baron's Imperial Guard, was an imposing man and a lifelong soldier. Although he was dour and serious, to the point where any sense of humour he had possessed had long since headed off to seek a more fulfilling life elsewhere, he was loyal to the point of stupidity. It was this quality, plus his considerable prowess on the battlefield, that endeared him greatly to the Baron.

'General Darkblast, your presence is most welcome,' the Baron said, rising from his throne and depositing Velvet on the floor. 'Pray, how did you find Scouseland?'

'Still heavily populated by chip shops, my Lord.'

'And the local populace, did they show any form of resistance to your incursion?'

'Someone threw a kebab at us on one occasion, my Lord.'

'And was your response measured and appropriate?'

'Yes, my Lord, we threw it back.'

'A wise move General,' the Baron commented, 'there's no need for unnecessary violence at this stage of the diplomatic procedure. Tell me, though, did you attempt to converse with the indigenous people?'

'We did, my Lord. At first we tried to parley with them in their own tongue, but we were met with blank stares. Our interpretation of their dialect still needs work, I'm afraid. So we tried an alternative approach.'

'And this was?'

'We sang them a medley of songs by The Bertles.'*

'And was this demonstration of musical affinity well received?'

'Not really, my Lord, that's when they threw the kebab at us.'

'However,' the General added quickly, sensing the Baron's growing unrest, 'we did succeed in obtaining a few volunteers to join the palace guard. A sort of exchange deal, if you will.'

'Excellent,' the Baron responded, 'and perhaps when we have instructed them in our ways they can be sent back as emissaries, to spread words of enlightenment to the masses.'

'Indeed, my Lord.'

'Or, of course, we could torture them, brainwash them and send them back as spies.'

'Well, yes, there is that option, my Lord.'

The Baron walked clockwise around General Darkblast, in a manner similar to a cat circling an injured bird. 'But enough of business in uncharted lands, my good General, I have needs of a more local nature that require urgent attention. Tell me do you know the whereabouts of Hob and Nob?'

'Yes, my Lord, they were last spotted in Mold, disguised as Vagabond Acupuncturists.'

The Baron turned and walked slowly over to the large bookcase that stood against the wall to the right of the throne. He pulled out one of the great tomes from the middle shelf and gently stroked its dusty, leather cover. His eyes sparkled and a smile that contained no joy appeared on his lips. 'Despatch some of your men to bring them to me,' he ordered. 'I have a task for them.'

The Bertles, or Bert, Saul, Marge and Gringo as they were affectionately known, were the most successful musical band to come out of Scouseland. At one time they topped the charts simultaneously in twenty eight countries. In fact, the ruler of Latvargravia-Crustia, the Grand Emperor Igor Rocakovich, was such a fan that he passed a law forcing citizens to buy a copy of their most famous song, 'She Loves Me All Night Like A Walrus', every week to ensure its continuing position at the top of the Latvargravia-Crustia charts. He was eventually overthrown in a bloodless coup that actually involved quite a lot of blood.

***

The ancient stones in the Circle of Wind stood firm against the elements, as they had for millennia. A fierce wind cut through the icy air, while above spears of lightning cracked the sky; vast tendrils of light acting as the harbinger for the thunder that was to follow.

In the distance the sound of hooves grew ever closer, their pounding rhythm providing a rumbling counterpoint to the storm overhead. Then, as sheet lightning turned night into day, they appeared over the nearby hill; four giant horses, and on their backs four mighty warriors, their weapons drawn, challenging the elements to meet them in battle.

One held a giant broadsword, its steel blade shimmering as it reflected the storm's light. One held a mighty axe, its worn edges bearing the hallmark of many battles. The third whirled a spiked ball and chain above his head which, if he wasn't careful with it, could take somebody's eye out. And the last wielded a huge war hammer… which he nearly dropped as the spiked ball and chain nearly took his eye out.

'Will you please watch what you're doing with that thing, Agnar,' Grundi the Windy screamed.

'Sorry,' shouted Agnar the Hammered, 'the old spiked club was much easier to handle.'

'Perhaps it was,' Smid the Merciless (né Pig Herder) yelled, 'but this looks so much better, you just need to keep practicing. You'll soon get the hang of it.'

'That's easy for you to say,' Grundi shouted, 'you're not riding next to him in constant fear of accidental decapitation.'

'Look, if it's causing that many problems why don't you swap with him, Grundi,' Olaf the Berserker interjected.

'You mean I can have the hammer? Aw, that'd be great!' Agnar said. 'Please, Grundi, I'd love the hammer.'

'Oh, go on, then,' Grundi said, 'You can have the hammer, for health and safety as much as anything else.'

'Aw, thanks Grundi!' Agnar shouted. 'I'll take good care of it.'

As they entered the stone circle, the four warriors reared their horses and clashed their weapons together, sending sparks fleeing into the darkness. They swiftly dismounted, each of them taking a ceremonial position in front of one of the large, moss-dappled stones. And then, in silent salute to the gods, they raised their weapons skyward once more.

'Smid, would you do us the honour of saying the words?' Olaf said.

'I would be honoured indeed, Olaf.'

'Odin I beseech thee, accept my gift of wind,
It's from the heart of my bottom,
It's a gift I won't rescind,
I fart for all your glory; I fart for all your might,
Give me the strength to not follow through,
And I'll fart for you; I'll fart for you all night.'

'Well said, Smid,' Olaf observed, nodding appreciatively.

The four warriors pulled their pants down, pointed their bottoms to the sky and methane mingled with the cold night air. 'Someone's a bit fragrant tonight,' Agnar said.

'Ah, that'll be me,' admitted Grundi. 'I ate the Curry of Worry at the Diner earlier and I've felt something nasty brewing for a while.'

'Right, let's head off to rehearsal,' said Olaf. 'We need to work on the set list for tomorrow night, and sort out the timing to the new ending of "My Sword is my Sword". It isn't quite there yet.'

'Agreed,' said Smid.

And so, they pulled their pants up, mounted their steeds and rode off into the night. Overhead, the storm began to recede, either of its own volition or perhaps propelled by Viking flatulence.

Meanwhile, less than a hundred yards from the Circle of Wind lay the boarded-up entrance to the ancient cheese mine of Hairy Growler. Hardly anyone had ventured inside its dark tunnels and stalactite-encrusted caves for many years; that, however, was soon to change.

***

The hour was late and Merlin Crackfoot yawned, as he began clearing up the cutlery, crockery and glasses that littered the tables in Cracky's Diner. Outside all was now still, and in an inky, star-speckled sky a baleful full moon illuminated the street, casting shadows where you'd expect shadows to be cast and not doing anything un-moon like.

All in all the first 'Cuisine de la Terreur' night had been a resounding success. The Beefburger of Dismay and The Fish of Fright went down extremely well with his clientele (and thankfully stayed down). True, sales of the Pork Sausages of Panic and the Beans of Apprehension weren't quite what he'd hoped for, but he could live with that. And a minor complaint about the Pasta of Disaster was simply down to his exuberance with the garlic and pineapple sauce. But, overall, people had left with full tummies and happy hearts. And so, it was with a deep feeling of satisfaction that he began the washing-up.

However, as the fruity aroma of bubbling washing-up liquid wafted up his nostrils, his contented scrubbing was interrupted by a knock on the front door. 'Who is it?' he shouted, without lifting his head up from the sink.

'Cracky, it's me, Taff; Taff Thomas. We need to talk,' the voice from behind the door replied, barely above a whisper.

'Wait one minute, I'll just leave these to soak,' Cracky said, removing his rubber gloves.

The glass front door of the diner was now resplendent with its new logo of a wizard clutching a frying pan. Cracky opened it and Taff Thomas rushed in. 'What's spooked you?' Cracky said, quickly closing the door behind Taff.

'I've heard a rumour that Blacktie's going to be clamping down on cheese smuggling,' Taff said. 'I thought you should know that next week's delivery may be the last for a while, so if you want to add anything to your regular order now's the time to do it.'

'Ah, yes, I had heard the rumours. In which case, can you please add a couple of pounds of Purple Caerphilly; only the good stuff, mind, not that rubbish that causes your bowels to move in a rhythmical fashion. And I'll take a pound of Spitchcock's Tintern.'

'That Tintern could be very, very difficult to obtain at such short notice,' Taff said.

'Go on, then, how much?' Cracky said, with a sigh.

'Well an extra £20 should cover the sundry expenses.'

'£20! That's extortion. I'll not pay more than an extra ten.'

'I couldn't possibly do it for £10, Cracky, what with all the bribery, back scratching and philandering that's involved.'

'Philandering?'

'Oh, yes. Old Gwyneth Evans strikes a pretty hard bargain you know.'

'Well, £15 and I can't go a penny more.'

'Call it £16.50 and I'll throw in a nice piece of Wolfman's Acorn.'

'Deal,' Cracky said. 'Next Wednesday as usual?'

'Aye, no problem,' Taff said, opening the front door and stepping out into the cobbled street.

'You know, Taff, there's something in the air,' Cracky said, as he stood in the doorway, bathed in the full moon's light.

'Yeah, I can smell it! Have those bloody Vikings been in tonight? I hope your farting license is up-to-date, otherwise Blacktie'll shut you down… and more! Remember what happened to Owen Jones, the confectioner. He's a shadow of the man he once was, and his cola balls have never been the same since.'

'No, Taff, I mean I can sense change coming. Can't you feel it? ' Cracky said, looking up into the sky and sniffing the air. 'Mark my words, Taff, change is coming. And nothing and no-one will be able to stop it.'

'Well,' Taff said, as he skulked off down the street, 'the only way we'll get change around here is if someone gets rid of bloody Blacktie. And who's mad enough to try that?'

CHAPTER 2 – THE CHEESE OF PLEASANT DREAMS

The alarm clock jingled and danced its merry morning dance, before being silenced by a well-aimed slap from Aiden Peersey's left hand. He sat up, yawned and rubbed his bleary eyes, trying to accept the banishment of sleep and the onset of another day. It had been a particularly late night and he was feeling the effects of a lack of sleep, a tad too much to drink and an overindulgence in pizza. Humphrey stood at the side of the bed looking at him disapprovingly.

'Okay, I'm sorry I got back so late. But if it's any consolation I'm suffering for it now,' Aiden said.

Humphrey said nothing and continued to gaze straight at him, his brown eyes meeting Aiden's with a stony stare, conveying both his lack of sympathy and his obvious disgruntlement.

'Look, I'll make it up to you. We can go out tonight, take a walk down to the canal.'

Humphrey continued to stare in silence. 'And we could get something to eat on the way back, from the chip shop?'

More silence, although accompanied by a raised eyebrow. 'And I'll let you have a swim in the canal?' Aiden said, raising his eyebrows quizzically.

'Woof,' said Humphrey, jumping onto the bed.

'Good boy, now go and get your lead and we'll have a quick walk around the block.'

'Woof,' said Humphrey again, grabbing the lead off a nearby chair and throwing it unceremoniously on the floor.

Outside, Aiden was greeted by blinding early morning sunlight and a garden that needed mowing. 'A lovely morning isn't it, Mrs Perriwinkle,' he called over to his elderly neighbour, as he and Humphrey made their way down the short, gravel path to the gate. 'How are you today?'

'I'd be feeling much better if I hadn't have been woken up in the middle of the night by your noisy friends dropping you off,' answered Mrs Perriwinkle, waving her garden rake in his direction.

'Oh, I am sorry, Mrs Perriwinkle. I'll make sure they're quiet in future. We'd all had a bit too much to drink, I'm afraid. It was a very good gig, you see.'

'Well, I know it doesn't happen very often,' Mrs Perriwinkle said, lowering the rake, 'and I know you young people love your "gigs". And, since you're such a polite young man, I'll forgive you on this occasion.'

'Thanks, Mrs Perriwinkle.'

'I used to love a good gig when I was younger, you know,' she went on. 'Mr Perriwinkle was very good at it. In fact, we'd often be at it for several hours at a time without a break. We'd be covered in sweat by the time we finished.'

'Really,' Aiden said.

'Oh, yes. People would stand around watching and applauding. We'd often have a big crowd around us while we were doing it. And then, after about ten minutes, a lot of them would join in and we'd all swap partners for a bit.'

'And that was quite common when you were younger?' Aiden said, shifting his stance uncomfortably.

'Very much so; I often had over ten partners a night. It was quite tiring and you get a bit sore after a while, but it was very satisfying. We were the Flintshire Foxtrot Champions five years in a row, you know.'

'Well I never knew that,' Aiden said, somewhat relieved.

'Oh, Mrs Perriwinkle,' he added as he opened the gate, 'I'm going to be out for most of the day, so are you still okay to nip in and check on Humphrey later?'

'Of course, not a problem; he's a lovely little dog, aren't you Humphrey?' Mrs Perriwinkle said, smiling at Humphrey and adopting a particularly silly face. 'What kind of dog is he, again?'

'He's an English Cocker Spaniel,' Aiden replied, patting him on the back.

'Oh, we'll have a great time later, won't we Humphrey,' she said, her voice rising in pitch. 'I'll bring some sticks from the garden and you can fetch them for me. And then we'll play ball.'

Humphrey gave Aiden a withering look but remained quiet. 'Thanks very much. I'll see you later, then,' Aiden said.

Aiden and Humphrey went for a walk every morning and every evening. Humphrey loved his walks and was fascinated by the conversations of people they'd pass on their way. 'They lead such simple lives,' he'd think to himself, interrupting his general thoughts on metaphysics and chasing cats.

Today, Aiden had decided they'd only have a quick stroll down Watery Road and across the bridge towards the hospital, before retracing their steps back to number 22 Bright Street, their home.

This area of Wrexham was generally tranquil, and the rows of semi-detached or detached houses had neat gardens and an interesting mixture of trees. Humphrey liked trees, and actually thought they made better conversationalists than humans; at least they could understand him. The old elm on Watery Road just before the bridge was his favourite. He was an absolute hoot and told some splendid stories. Humphrey invariably cocked his leg and watered him by way of thanks every day. This morning, however, there was only time for a brief 'hello, how are you' and a very quick leg-cock before they had to head back home. Aiden had plans for today.

For the last ten of his thirty-five years, Aiden Peersey had worked for Parmesan Systems, an IT company that specialised in innovative telecommunications products. After a series of promotions, he now found himself with the title 'Head of Design', a role he thoroughly enjoyed. He was also popular for a geek, mainly because he was affable, performed almost legendary vocal impressions of celebrities and didn't really show off his intellect too much in social circles. The girls in HR also liked him quite a bit too. 'Woo hoo, Aiden!' they'd shout as he walked past their office in the morning, usually followed by something like 'Oh, isn't he adorable. He's so handsome and clever.' He liked that.

His house phone rang. It was Bob. 'Hey, lanky, how's your head this morning?' Bob said, his voice bristling with far more energy than it had any right to have after last night.

'I think it's still on my neck, but it's difficult to tell at the moment.'

'Hah! Have you had a chance to listen to the tape from the gig yet?'

'No, but I'm going out later, so I'll stick it on in the car. Then when I get back I'll digitise it, look at the equalization, stick some limiters on it, add some suitable compression and then normalise it before transfer.'

'You lost me after "car",' Bob said.

'I mean I'll put it on a CD for you.'

'Thanks mate, catch you later then. Let's hear it for the Swingers, yee hah!'

His other passion was music. Not that he could play any instruments or sing, but he listened avidly and found himself ineluctably drawn to music technology. His ambition was to eventually own his own recording studio, but in the interim he had amassed a reasonable collection of music-related equipment in his house which he enjoyed playing with. He liked mixing live music too.

'The Hefty Swingers' were a good-time rock band, and although they hadn't made it past the first rung on the ladder of stardom yet, they had a strong local following and were very entertaining to watch. Aiden's friend, Bob, was the lead singer and Aiden was in command of the sound system and the mixing desk. Last night's gig at the 'Randy Parrot' nightclub had been one of their best; three encores and they actually got paid.

Aiden gulped down a glass of water and grabbed the tape. He needed to clear his head this morning, and fortunately he felt somewhat more human after his walk with Humphrey. Today was the day he'd decided to operationally test his new innovation, which was based on an idea that had sprung into his mind last year.

He'd always been fascinated by quantum physics, so when the first forays into the exploration of quantum computing* became public knowledge he saw the potential immediately. His own investigations to harness this new technology had resulted in the design and production of the 'QC Operating System' for Smart Phones and Tablets, the first of its kind. The simulated tests all appeared successful, with startling increases in processor speed and memory capacity. But it had now reached the stage where he needed to try out the system practically.

Humphrey looked at him intently, his tongue lolling about in his mouth, and offered Aiden his paw. 'Ha, good boy,' Aiden said, patting him affectionately on the head. 'Now, I'm going to be popping out for a while. I'm having a drive to Llangollen, not been there for ages. And this little baby,' he said pointing to his new phone, 'is going to do the navigation for me. Isn't that cool?'

'Woof, woof, woof… woof, grrr, woof,' said Humphrey.

And it was a real pity Aiden couldn't understand him, otherwise he'd have known that 'Woof, woof, woof… woof, grrr, woof,' when translated, means 'I really wouldn't do that if I were you.'

*See appendix 1

***

'My Lord, Hob and Nob are here, as you requested yesterday,' Pimple announced, as he walked into the throne room.

'Ah, very good, Pimple; bring them in and leave us. I wish to speak to these gentlemen in private,' Baron Blacktie said, rising from his throne.

Hob and Nob had been spies for as long as anyone could remember. No-one knew where they originated from, nor indeed where they lived; they were an unusual looking pair and people tended to keep out of their way. There always seemed to be an atmosphere of malevolence and subterfuge around them, which was only amplified by their regular apparel of matching wide-brimmed black hats and knee-length brown leather coats. The fact they were so recognisable could be considered a serious disadvantage, given their profession, except they were both masters of disguise. Hob was the taller of the cadaverous pair by several inches, and he carried a black briefcase with him at all times.

'Good day, Baron. I hope we find you in high spirits,' Hob said, his dark eyes barely visible under the rim of his hat.

'You do indeed, my dear Hob. I am feeling most exhilarated about some forthcoming events that you, my friends, will play a part in. But, firstly, pray tell me what have you learned from your little trip to Mold?'

'There are murmurings within the curry community, my Lord,' Hob replied, putting his briefcase on the floor. 'There is talk of revolution in the air.'

'Well, as long as it stays in the air and doesn't make it onto the ground that should be fine,' the Baron said, chuckling.

'This is a serious matter, Baron,' said Nob. 'They are talking about an alliance with the Wrexham Curries.'

'Hmm, that could indeed be a problem we could do without,' said the Baron, twiddling his moustache. 'A mixture of Mold and Wrexham curry is potentially a recipe for disaster.'

'Indeed, my Lord,' said Nob.

The Baron continued his twiddling and threw in a touch of musing for good measure. 'This is something that does need addressing, gentlemen,' he eventually said, 'but for the moment it will have to wait. There are more pressing matters at hand, not least the task I have for you now.'

'More pressing than quashing a curry rebellion? I am intrigued, Baron,' Hob said, loftily. 'Your ruthless reputation for nipping these things in the bud before they bloom would appear to be somewhat awry at present.'

The Baron walked purposively over to Hob and stood face to face with him, their noses almost touching. Hob shuffled backwards, recognising and regretting the impertinence of his last statement. 'Never, EVER, question my decisions,' the Baron whispered, in a way that sent a chill down Hob's back, 'else you will feel, and smell, the power of my wind, which given what I had for breakfast will be most potent. Now, we will deal with the curries when the time is right, but that time is not yet at hand. Do I make myself clear?'

'Absolutely my Lord,' Hob said, the deference and fear in his voice tangible.

'Good. I'm glad that's settled,' the Baron said, walking back towards his throne. 'Now, what know you of cheese lore?'

'I would consider myself well-versed in that area,' Nob answered.

'Excellent. Then what can you tell me about Ceridwen's Cheese?'

'Why it is a myth, my Lord. It was known as "The Cheese of Pleasant Dreams", for it was reputedly not only the finest-tasting cheese ever mined, with the most exquisite texture, but was also said to give one a sense of great serenity.'

The Baron sauntered over to the bookshelf and affectionately stroked the spine of the large book he'd been reading during General Darkblast's visit. 'Oh, it is no myth, my friends. Your famous omniscience is perhaps wanting here, as it would appear there are things that even the great Hob and Nob do not know.'

'Last year,' the Baron continued, 'a man was found wandering the streets of Chester in a sorry, yet very happy, state. My guards noted that he was raving about "the lost cheese of the ancient's" being found and how its discovery would lead to the deliverance of the people. Naturally, most took him for a simple drunken fool, but my curiosity was piqued and I bade my guards to bring him to me for an audience.'

The Baron picked up a large scroll from the bookshelf and unrolled it onto the impressive marble table, to the left of the throne. The parchment sparkled as the light hit it, creating an eerie glow on the face of the Baron as he examined its contents. 'He had this map with him. It is an old map; a very old map.'

Hob and Nob sidled over to the table and stood either side of the Baron. 'Do you recognise the map?' the Baron said.

'It cannot be,' Hob said in disbelief. 'Surely, this is a fake.'

'It's no fake, I can assure you. It is the only one of its kind.'

Nob was visibly trembling as he looked at the map. 'This is treasure beyond all treasure, Baron. Do you really know what you have here?'

'Oh, I do, my good Nob. This is indeed the ancient map of Scratchy Crotch.'

The Baron walked over to the bookcase again and removed one of the smaller books from the third shelf. There was an ornate leather and gold bookmark placed inside it. He opened the book and began to read.

"Let it be known that Scratchy Crotch was the first of the Evil Wizards of Bala. His power transcended all and he was thought to be invincible. His beard was black and his codpiece firm. No-one knew how he acquired such might and he did not reveal his secret. It was rumoured that all creatures of evil bowed before him, both in this world and in the dark realms; for he regularly communicated with unearthly beings and people from Prestatyn. He lived to be 534 years old and had 77 wives, 43 concubines and 12 barmaids during this period. He fathered only one son, to his 76th wife, the Lady Clarissa of Rhyl; a witch of high repute, great beauty and extraordinarily malodorous armpits. The child mysteriously disappeared before his second birthday, along with Clarissa, and this broke his nefarious heart. Subsequently, he became a recluse, shunning contact with all, until his marriage to Buxom Betty of Betws-y-Coed, the daughter of a local cobbler with plaited nostril hair. During his life, Scratchy Crotch maintained the largest collection of cheese in the land. He would relax by feasting on suckling pig, drinking malt whisky, singing sea shanties and playing the bongos."

The Baron licked his index finger and turned the page. 'There's a lot more here, including his battle with the Dragons of Denbigh, the destruction of the Parsimonious Wizards of St. Asaph, his fear of embroidery and his obsession with esoteric hair brushes, but I'll skip to the bit about the map.'

"He amassed many powerful mystical treasures during his time, and shortly before his death he told his servants to bury each of these in secret places. When they returned from their task and told him where each of the items were buried he had them all killed, meaning only he knew of their whereabouts. This knowledge he allegedly put into a map, written on sacred parchment and inked with the timeless ink of Gringlegore. However, the map has never been discovered and the veracity of this particular tale is thus questionable."

The Baron closed the book with aplomb. 'Questionable until now, my friends; for as you can see the map does indeed exist and is in my possession.'

Hob turned to look at the Baron, shaking his head. 'Unbelievable, my Lord. Yet, if it is written that he was invincible how did he meet his demise?'

The Baron flicked past a couple of pages before locating the necessary passage. 'The book says *"the townsfolk, at the end of their tether with his wicked ways and harsh rule, confronted him at his castle. They carried flaming torches and were protected by a variety of cross-stitch shawls, wrapped around their shoulders. The sight of so much embroidery caused him to convulse uncontrollably and he summoned a dark spirit to repel the people. But, in his weakened state, he had not the strength to control the demon and he was devoured entirely, apart from his left foot which was hurled skywards and remains lost to this day"*. He was never seen again by mortal man; which is a great pity as he sounded like an absolutely splendid chap.'

'My Lord, this map details the whereabouts of the greatest and most powerful artefacts known to the black arts,' said Nob. 'Whoever could manage to bring these treasures together would surely be able to rule the world. If this is the task you would have us complete, simply say the word and we will get you the Aphrodisiac Dragon Horn of Jiggery, the Fragrant Sword of Pokery, the Magical Preserved Left Buttock of King Peculiar-Uliar and even the Mysterious Unknown Book of Ambiguous and Seemingly Useless but Actually Very Dangerous Evil Spells.'

'All in good time, all in good time,' the Baron said, waving his hand in a calming motion. 'Firstly I would draw your attention to this section of the map here, do you recognise it?'

'Yes, it is just south-east of Llangollen, near the Circle of Wind. There is nothing of interest there, Baron,' Hob replied.

'Look closer, my dear Hob, what do you see?'

'It is a representation of a cheese mine, my Lord. But the only recognisable structure in that vicinity is the disused mine of the dead eccentric Hairy Growler. It used to contain a rich vein of Red Cheekfizzler, but that has long been exhausted.'

'Indeed, but that was only on the upper levels,' the Baron said. 'The lower levels, I am very reliably informed, contain possibly the richest vein of Ceridwen's Cheese ever to be discovered. It is also where the Ancient Map of Scratchy Crotch has been hidden for the past several centuries, until its timely unearthing last year.'

'With all due respect, Baron, why this interest in a simple cheese?' said Nob. 'There are things of value beyond wealth that can be regained here.'

'Accepted, my good Nob. Nevertheless, I wish you to infiltrate Llangollen and find out who owns this mine. I can find no record of ownership since the passing of Hairy Growler some twenty years ago. Although I could simply claim the mine as my own, I wish to be circumspect here. There may be other powers at large and I will not take risks unduly. As part of this mission, I also wish you to secretly break into the mine and search for the green and gold cheese of Ceridwen in the lower levels. I have no doubt you will find this, and then you must obtain a small sample.'

'But beware,' the Baron continued, 'I hear rumours there are things that dwell in the mine that are so terrible even Trolls avoid them. Ensure you are appropriately armed, my friends, for I would not wish you ill... at least not until you have completed your task.'

Hob and Nob exchanged glances and nodded to each other. 'If this is what you desire, my Lord, then we will fulfil your request... for the usual fee... plus 50%,' said Hob.

'You drive a hard bargain, gentlemen,' the Baron replied, smiling, 'but I agree. You will be paid when I have the sample in my hands. Now, I will despatch some of my men to meet with you in three days to ascertain your progress. Have you a place earmarked as your base for this endeavour?'

'I think it prudent if we mingle as much as we can with the locals, my Lord, so we will seek residence at a place called "The Sheep's Stirrup". It is a harmless and nondescript tavern,' replied Nob.

'Good. Now, I'm assuming you will be transforming yourselves into something less conspicuous during your quest, so how will my men recognise you?'

Nob reached into his pocket and produced a small, leather-bound book. He flipped through the pages, with Hob looking over his shoulder. After a few seconds he stopped and pointed at a particular page. A short whispered conversation between the pair ensued before they raised their heads.

'We will be disguised as Vagrant Vacuum Cleaner Exorcists, My Lord.'

'And you deem this disguise appropriate?' the Baron said.

'Yes, my Lord. By all accounts vacuum cleaner possession is rife in the area.'

'Very well, good luck to you. The rewards for success will be great, gentlemen. And failure, as you well know, is not an option.'

Hob picked up his briefcase and they bowed to the Baron, before heading off to encounter some experiences they were definitely not prepared for..

CHAPTER 3 – BE GOOD FOR MRS PERRIWINKLE

The little, red MG sports car had been Aiden's vehicle of choice for five years. He loved the old styling and liked nothing better than driving with the top down, when the often precarious North Wales weather allowed. Humphrey watched out of the window as Aiden got in and fired the engine up. 'See you later boy, I'll be back in a few hours.'

'Woof, woof, wuf-wuf,' said Humphrey, which translated meant 'I very much doubt it'.

'Be good for Mrs Perriwinkle.'

The Nova QC phone was a very chic device; ultra-slim, with an extra-long-life battery, touch screen control and Aiden's new 'Voiceotronic' guidance system. He pressed the little 'on' button and the screen instantly fizzed into life, playing a classic eighties guitar riff in the process.

'Navigation,' Aiden said, which immediately initialised the navigation app.

'Llangollen, North Wales,' he added, somewhat over dramatically, but it was that sort of day and he had that sort of feeling.

'In one hundred yards, turn left into Llys David Lord, you sexy beast,' the phone said in the sultry female voice Aiden had programmed in.

'Oh, you flirt, Natasha,' he replied, using the name he'd given to the phone.

'You better believe it, now just drive, darling,' Natasha said.

He cruised up Bright Street feeling in high spirits, his hangover now easing but with pizza occasionally repeating on him. The wind coursed through his hair and his sunglasses became a graveyard for flies.

'In two hundred yards, at the roundabout, take the second exit onto the A483… and then head over to my place big boy,' Natasha said, followed by a 'grrr'.

It was after about five miles of smooth travelling that the car began juddering every so often. 'Bloody tracking again,' Aiden thought to himself, as he'd had the same problem before. Out of the corner of his eye, though, he noticed the Nova QC phone. The Navigation app map had disappeared and the whole screen was pulsating with a powerful white light. He moved into the inside lane of the dual carriageway and was just about to pull over when there was a blinding flash… and he found himself heading straight for a traffic jam; which was odd, as several seconds earlier there had hardly been a car on the road.

'You better put that top up, mate,' a man in a modern-looking blue car shouted out of the window, 'the traffic wardens will be along any second now.'

'Pardon, did you say traffic wardens?' Aiden said. 'I wouldn't think we need to worry, we're on a dual carriageway in a traffic jam; I hardly think that's classed as a parking offence.'

'Don't make any difference to those beggars,' the man said, 'since the deregulation of 2024 they don't care. My old mum was driving in her little hoverchair last week and stopped to exchange pleasantries with a friend. In a second they were all over her like flies. Twenty two tickets they gave her. Terrible, it was.'

'But that's ridiculous, can't she complain, or simply refuse to pay,' Aiden said, before adding 'hang on, did you say hoverchair?'

'What, and get shot?' the man said, startled. 'You mean you've never seen one of their firing squads in action? Where've you been, mate, Scotland?'

It started as a low rumble, just behind a hill to the left of the carriageway. Aiden strained his ears trying to identify the source of the noise, which was steadily increasing in volume. The other drivers started to panic, seeming to know the fate that was about to befall them; many were crying and some were praying. As the noise drew closer, Aiden turned his eyes towards the hill. He had no idea what to expect, but it's safe to say he wasn't expecting five hundred heavily-armed traffic wardens to appear, their faces resplendent with yellow and black war paint.

'Hells bells,' shouted the man in the blue car, 'it's the Wrexham Posse! We better run for it, they don't take prisoners.'

The Wrexham Posse charged down the hill towards the congested highway, roaring and holding their weapons aloft. By now many of the drivers and passengers had left their vehicles, running in blind panic in search of an escape. But it was too late, and the Posse poured over the two lanes of traffic like a monstrous tidal wave of yellow and black.

Screams began, followed by gunshots and the sound of tickets being indiscriminately slapped onto glass. 'Have mercy, have mercy!' someone shouted from nearby, only to be met with maniacal laughter and the blood-curdling cry of 'You're illegally parked, say your prayers.'

One of the more vicious-looking members of the Posse closed in on

Aiden's car, ticket in one hand and Kalashnikov rifle in the other. He was a tall, burly man, probably somewhere in his forties, although with his face painted it was difficult to tell. Thankfully, Aiden managed to get the roof and windows up just before the traffic warden slammed into his car. He pressed his face against the passenger side front window, salivating and staring at Aiden with bloodshot eyes. His identity badge said his name was Mr Peter Twatt.

'Get out of the car, now. You're illegally parked and you're going to get a ticket, you bastard,' Mr Twatt spat, the saliva running down the window like little rivulets.

'Now, look, er, Mr Twatt,' Aiden said, noting the name on the badge, 'I'm sure that being in a traffic jam doesn't actually count as illegal parking, you know.'

Mr Twatt's eyes narrowed and his mouth twisted into a sneer. 'Don't you "Mr Twatt" me, nobody calls me that anymore, and if I say you're illegally parked you're bloody well illegally parked, you toe rag.'

'Well what should I call you?' said Aiden, hoping the small talk might buy him some time.

'Spine-splitter,' spat Mr Twatt.

'Ah, yes, a splendid name,' Aiden said, in a conciliatory tone, 'and why have you adopted that particular moniker?'

'On accounts of me record of breaking the backs of people that won't pay,' replied Mr Twatt.

'And just how many would that be?'

'One hundred and six, at the last count,' Mr Twatt/Spine-splitter said, proudly. 'I'm looking to make it one hundred and seven today, maybe more.'

Another tortured scream attacked his ears and Aiden jumped out of his seat, as a second face pressed against the driver side window, yellow teeth grinning maliciously. 'This one's mine, Bogpaddler. I saw him first,' Mr Twatt/Spine-splitter shouted to the second traffic warden, whose badge identified him as Mr Frank Todger.

'Now, there's nothing wrong with sharing, Spine-splitter. Let's just cut him straight down the middle,' Mr Todger/Bogpaddler said, producing a large, blood-stained cleaver from beneath his jacket.

'Bugger off and get your own. I ain't sharing with nobody, not least a toilet-breathed, wee-wee panted fart like you.'

For a few seconds an uneasy silence fell, as both men stared at each other over the top of Aiden's car. 'Wee-wee panted?' said Mr Todger/Bogpaddler.

'Yes, wee-wee-panted,' replied Mr Twatt/Spine-splitter.

'Toilet-breathed?!'

'Yes, toilet-breathed.'

'Fart?!!'
'Yes, fart.'
'Wee-wee-panted?!!'
'Yes, wee-wee-panted… with stains!' shouted Mr Twatt/Spine-splitter.
'With stains?!!!' Mr Todger/Bogpaddler yelled.
'Yes, with stains!!'
'Nobody calls me 'wee-wee panted with stains' and lives!!!' screamed Bogpaddler, vaulting over the bonnet of the car.

Aiden watched dumbstruck as the two men grappled, hands around each other's throats, whilst all around was chaos, blood and an exorbitant amount of parking tickets. A scream came from the side of the car and Spine-splitter stood up, bits of flesh dripping off his blood-stained teeth. 'Your turn,' he said to Aiden, banging on the window with his gun.

Aiden had never thought about meeting his maker before, but at this moment in time he began to give serious consideration as to what he would say. However, even before he could decide on the proper form of address, the QC Nova phone sent out another blinding flash of light and he found himself on a clear road, driving at about sixty miles per hour. 'In one hundred yards take the slip road to the A539, you naughty boy,' purred Natasha.

Had he momentarily fallen asleep at the wheel? That had to be it; there was no other logical explanation. He laughed out loud and shook his head. A dream, and how ridiculous; traffic wardens with painted faces acting like merciless, roving criminals, gunning people down for not paying. It was preposterous. Although he did admit he could see them going in that direction in the future, if left to their own devices.

As he approached the slip road he recognised the turn off for the A539, and could see the sign that read 'Llangollen'. 'At the roundabout take the second exit and I'll tell you what I'm wearing,' Natasha said.

Aiden had driven down this road many times and had a reasonable memory of the region. Landmarks were thankfully familiar and he recognised the old pub coming into view. 'Stay on the A539 for five miles,' Natasha said as the Nova phone began to glow once more. 'I'm wearing stockings but I'm not wearing any…' and then she went silent for a second. 'Data connection lost. See you later darling,' she said, as the phone flashed and the road turned from smooth tarmac into a narrow dirt track.

The car bumped and shuddered over the rough terrain. Aiden grasped the steering wheel tightly and hit the brake, narrowly avoiding one of the larger water-filled pot holes that were scattered about. The car scraped along the hedge on the right hand side of the road, scattering little twigs and leaves into the air. Applying the brake even firmer he stopped the car, turned off the engine and breathed a very long sigh of relief.

There was a bottle of water in the glove compartment and he drank deeply as his mind continued to race. He checked the Nova phone. No signal, no GPS. Outside it was peaceful. The narrow lane was flanked by high hedges on both sides, regularly interspersed with tall oak trees. A rabbit scuttled across the road, giving him only a passing look before diving through the hedge. He got out of the car and looked around. There was no sign of any traffic at all. Behind him the lane stretched for at least a mile, its contours and scenery consistent with what lay in front of him. 'But that's impossible,' he thought.

He couldn't have driven more than a hundred yards since the road changed dramatically, and that meant he should easily have been able to see the A539 from where he was standing. Yet the only visible roadway was the narrow, hedge-flanked lane stretching off into the distance. There was also no sign of the old pub.

Perhaps he'd underestimated the distance he'd actually covered? That could have been a possibility, so he locked the car and began to walk back to where the A539 should have been. After about half a mile he stopped. 'There's no way I could possibly have covered this distance,' he said aloud, as the peaceful lane continued to wend its way into the bright countryside.

Back at the car, the little rabbit had reappeared through the hedge with one of his friends. Both were sat upright, looking at Aiden as he opened the car door. Then, without any warning, they both scuttled away again, followed by a large congregation of sparrows who had been perched in the nearby trees. That's when Aiden heard the roar and looked up into the sky.

He estimated it must have been at least fifty feet long, its wing span perhaps half as much again. Enormous flames poured from its nostrils, its red, scaly skin looked thick enough to withstand bullets, and its talons appeared sharp enough to cut through anything in their way. And in their way currently were Aiden and his car.

'What the bloody hell is that!' he shouted, as the huge beast sailed overhead, missing him by no more than a few feet (and ironically those were the exact words that Dave the Dragon was thinking as he soared by). Aiden started the motor and drove as fast as the road surface and pot holes would allow. He didn't look back.

Now, interestingly, Aiden wasn't the only person whose morning wasn't quite going as planned. Half-blind Ron was having a bad day. His attempts to steal a chicken from Farmer Pigwhistle's coop had been thwarted by the farmer's fat, but persistent, Labrador dog, which had chased him all the way to the edge of Flopmarsh Lane. Fortunately, the dog refused to cross the boundaries of the farmer's land, which allowed Half-blind Ron to nip through the hedge and fire off some choice insults at his potential assailant. 'Fat git! I'll have your bloody ears off next time, you flea-ridden, mush-for-brains, lardy mutt!'

So, with fresh chicken off the menu, a new strategy was required to ensure lunch would be obtained with minimum fuss and minimum danger. However, as he wandered down the lane, a variety of cunning plots forming in his head, his train of thought was rudely interrupted by a noise from behind.

Aiden spotted him at the last minute, as the car hurtled round a bend. He slammed on the brakes, skidded and stopped with little room to spare between the car's front bumper and Half-blind Ron's backside.

'Oh, you're alright, puss. Thank god for that,' Aiden said, as he watched the scruffy grey and black tabby scamper off to the side of the road.

'Yeah, I'm bleedin' alright, you flippin' idiot. Watch where you're going with that thing, you almost had me tail off!'

Aiden heard the words as clear as day in his head and looked at Half-blind Ron with disbelief, noticing the cat's eye patch for the first time. 'Pardon?'

'Pardon?!' screamed Half-blind Ron. 'You nearly squash me old nuts and chop me bloody tail off, and all you can say is "Pardon"!'

'Er, I'm very sorry.' Aiden said, contritely.

'Oh save it, you prat,' Half-blind Ron said, his thoughts reaching angrily into Aiden's mind. 'I suppose you haven't got any chicken have you?'

'No, sorry again,' Aiden replied.

'Well bugger off then, you scruffy-haired, monkey-brained, lanky git. I'm off to find me some lunch, and me day'll be all the brighter for not seeing you again.'

And with that, Half-blind Ron darted off down the lane in search of lunch.

CHAPTER 4 – THAT EXPLAINS EVERYTHING…

As Aiden continued to drive, the lane eventually widened and the surface became more conventional. Feeling slightly more relaxed, he tried to assess his recent experiences logically.

Maybe he was still groggy after falling asleep and had accidentally missed his original turning? That made perfect sense. The dragon was probably part of some air display, a customised aircraft of some description. And as for the telepathic cat with the eye patch? Well, the trauma of thinking he'd hit the poor creature must have been playing on his mind, and his overactive imagination must have kicked in. Up ahead he saw a sign that said 'Welcome to Llangollen'.

The place was as picturesque as he remembered, but it seemed unusually quiet. There were no other cars on the roads, although the occasional horse and cart could be seen, which he thought was quaint. As he drove down the main street towards the bridge that crossed the River Dee, he passed the rows of pretty little shops displaying their wares. It was like a throwback to the days before supermarkets and multi-national stores dominated the high streets of most towns. Simpler times, he thought.

For all his love of modern technology, he was invariably happy in places where time had not moved on as much as it could have. He was attracted to historical documentaries and secretly longed to own a broadsword. As a child, and to this day if truth be told, his favourite films involved ancient soldiers, monsters, mysterious creatures, magic and, importantly, scantily clad ladies. Basically, anything that allowed him to escape to a world that was more exciting and with a greater sense of nobility at its heart.

He turned left just before the bridge and parked his car, stepping out and breathing deep from the clean air. On the other side of the road was a lady with two small sheep dressed in children's clothing. They had pirate hats on their heads and were waving little plastic swords.

'Come on children, we don't want to be late,' the lady said to the sheep, looking over and smiling at Aiden.

'Great costumes,' Aiden said. 'Very unusual.'

'Thanks! They love dressing-up, and they've been excited about the festival for the past week. I had no trouble getting them out of the barn this morning,' the lady said, laughing.

'Well, I hope they have a good time,' Aiden replied.

'We will! Goodbye, sir,' one of the sheep said. And off they walked towards the park by the river.

At the end of the bridge, Aiden spotted a charming old pub. He remembered he'd been there once before and had found it to be a particularly friendly place, filled with a potpourri of slightly eccentric locals, unusually normal locals and a smattering of tourists. He couldn't remember the pub's name, but as he got closer the letters on the sign outside came into focus. They read 'The Sheep's Stirrup', and in smaller letters underneath, 'Proprietor: M Fluffywool'.

He turned the handle of the weatherworn, oak door and was met by the musty aroma of beer. The sun was streaming through a far window, creating an atmospheric haze above the rustic, wooden tables and chairs dotted about the room. On the whole it looked pretty much as he remembered... apart from the short man standing behind the bar in a sheep costume.

'Good afternoon, sir. It is a pleasant day, is it not?' the man in the sheep costume said.

'Hi, yes, a lovely day,' Aiden replied. 'Is there some kind of festival going in the town?'

'Indeed there is, did you not see the signs on the way in?'

'No, it looks like I came via an alternative route today,' Aiden replied, honestly.

'Oh, it's the "Grand Carnival of Shearing and Hoof Waxing", so most folks are in the park. There's a fair and all kinds of stalls and amusements. It's the most important sheep-sponsored event of the year; you should have a look later.'

'I will,' Aiden said.

'By the way, the name's Maurice, Maurice Fluffywool,' the man in the sheep costume said, extending a hoof over the bar. 'I'm the landlord of this fine establishment.'

'Aiden Peersey,' Aiden replied, shaking Maurice's hoof. That explains the costumes, he thought.

'Can I offer you a drink?' Maurice said.

'Yes, thanks, just a half of lager please,' Aiden replied, putting his hand in his pocket to take out some money.

'No, no, put your money away. The first one's on the house.'

'Thanks. That's very kind of you.'

'Think nothing of it; it's a courtesy I like to extend to new customers. Mind you, the place will be full tonight, so I'll turn in a tidy profit.'

Maurice pulled on one of the brass pump handles behind the bar and waited until the frothy, amber liquid filled the glass. Then he picked it up with both hooves and placed it on a fresh beer mat on the bar.

'So, whereabouts do you hail from, Aiden?'

'Not too far away, Wrexham,' Aiden said, taking a sip from the glass.

'Ah, my good friend, Bill Plumprump runs one of the most popular pubs in Wrexham, The Flopsy Fleece. You must know it?'

'Can't say I do, actually,' Aiden answered.

'Oh, well, that is a surprise. What about "The Lamb and Saddle"?'

'Er, no.'

'The Frisky Flock?'

'Afraid not.'

'The Black-faced Ram?'

'Not come across it.'

'The Frolicking Ewe?'

'Nope.'

'Well surely you must know the Mutton Dressed as Lamb nightclub, it's the hottest club in the area?'

'Sorry, never seen it.'

'Are you sure you're from Wrexham?' Maurice quizzed, with a look of suspicion.

'Not as sure as I was about five minutes ago,' Aiden said.

As he looked more intently at Maurice, the sun of understanding seemed to rise in his mind, its glorious rays firing little beams of comprehension in all directions. 'You're a sheep!' he exclaimed, his eyebrows doing their utmost to make contact with his hairline.

'Well, you may not be sure where you're from, young man, but there's nothing wrong with your eyesight, I see,' Maurice replied.

'Sorry, it's just that I'm from the real outskirts of Wrexham and we don't get many sheep running pubs in that area,' Aiden said, thinking on his feet.

'Ah, still a bit sheepist there, are they? Well we're a lot more liberal here, if you don't mind, we've fully embraced the Ovine Equality Act of 1952.'

'Oh, so around here sheep have been running pubs since 1952?' Aiden said casually, as he leant on the bar.

'No, no, don't be daft,' Maurice replied. 'A lot of us started out as glass collectors and worked our way up'.

Aiden swiftly finished his drink and put the empty glass on the bar. 'Well, thanks very much for the conversation and the drink,' he said, moving slowly to the door, 'but I think I'll go for a little walk now, while it's so nice outside. One last question, though, well two questions really. Am I actually in Llangollen and what year is this, please?'

'My lad, are you sure you've not been on the old Cheshire Black or something. Yes, this is Llangollen, and it's 1987 of course'.

Was he hallucinating? Was he dreaming again? Had he wandered into some bizarre genetic experiment? Was it an invasion of alien sheep landlords? Or was he simply cracking up? Two sheep on the opposite side of the road, carrying balloons, shouted 'hello' and waved. Aiden slowly raised his hand and politely waved back.

'It's a lovely day for it, isn't it?' said one of the sheep.

'Yes, it is indeed,' replied Aiden, still waving. And then his phone rang.

The ringtone blared out 'What's New Pussycat' and the name on the screen said 'Tom'. Aiden didn't know anyone called 'Tom'… and he hadn't actually programmed any numbers into the phone. 'Hello,' he said, clicking the 'Receive Call' button and tentatively putting the phone to his ear.

'Oh, hi, I thought I'd better give you a quick call as you're probably a bit disorientated right now. And you'd probably like an explanation of what's going down, so to speak,' a voice in a comforting Welsh brogue said.

'Yes, thank you, that would be great,' Aiden said, as he watched the sheep with balloons skipping down the road. 'And you are?'

'Well, I'm Tom. I think you'll find it said that on the phone.'

'And have we met before? I don't recall programming your number into my phone?'

'Well, we've never actually spoken, as such. But I've sort of been keeping an eye on you for all of your life.'

'Well, "Tom", I'm not sure how you got hold of this number, but I'm having a pretty strange day here. I've had a dream where I'm being attacked by traffic wardens carrying Kalashnikovs, I've been strafed by what appeared to be a large red dragon, I've been insulted telepathically by a cat, and to top it all I've been served rather good lager by a talking sheep. So, "Tom", I'd appreciate it if you'd just bugger off and leave me alone.'

'Look, now, there's no reason to be like that, is there,' said Tom. 'Would you like me to shed some light on the events of the day?'

Aiden removed the phone from his ear and took a sharp intake of breath. He looked at the phone's screen and realised there was no network coverage. So how was he receiving this call? His natural curiosity knocked on the door of his conscious mind… so he let it in and offered it a biscuit.

'Very well, "Tom". If you have any information as to what is causing my apparent mental implosion will you please let me know, because it's reaching the point where I'd just like to go and sit under a tree for a while.'

'Well, okay,' Tom said. 'I'm actually your higher self, or your intuition, if you like. Normally, I can only communicate with you via thoughts or feelings, helping you on your way, so to speak. But, since you've managed to cross a dimensional barrier and have now physically manifested in an alternative reality, I can speak to you on the phone now. How cool is that?!'

Aiden took the phone away from his ear again and looked at it for a few seconds. He went to press the 'End Call' button and hesitated. Then he slowly put the phone back against his ear. 'Ah, yes, that explains everything, thank you.'

CHAPTER 5 – IT MAY BE LINKED TO THE PROPHECY

Prince Theo of Corwen was sat on the bed in his royal chambers, licking his private parts, when Captain Marmaduke entered. 'Sorry, Your Highness, have I come at an inconvenient time?' the Captain said, removing his helmet.

'No, I'm just finishing off,' Prince Theo replied, licking his paw and wiping it over his face. 'What's up?'

'We have just received word that an unusual event has occurred close to Llangollen, on Flopmarsh Lane. I suspect Your Highness will wish to hear more detail.'

'Sounds interesting, Captain. Where does your information come from?'

The Captain coughed uncomfortably. 'From Half-blind Ron, Your Highness.'

'Oh, not that mad old moggy again,' the Prince said. 'Let me guess, he's been drinking Meow's Extra Strong Catnip and he claims we're being invaded by singing pink goblins.'

'If that were simply the case I would not be attempting to grant him audience with Your Highness,' the Captain replied.

'What, you've brought him here? Captain, you are one of my most trusted advisors, and also one of my closest friends. I respect your judgement ordinarily, but I'm at a loss as to why you feel I should devote some time listening to a semi-ratted old puss like Half-blind Ron. You must admit that the dear old cat is slightly puddled.'

'Agreed, Your Highness, but in this instance he assures me he was a model of sobriety, on account of the fact that he needed to have his wits about him for chicken hunting at Farmer Pigwhistle's. Also, the encounter he claims he had does not appear to be one of his fanciful, catnip induced stories. It may be linked to The Prophecy.'

Prince Theo sat bolt upright. 'Go on.'

'It would be better for you to hear it from Half-blind Ron himself, Your Highness.'

'Alright, Captain, my interest is sufficiently aroused. Show him in.'

The Captain opened the door, made a beckoning gesture and Half-blind Ron ran in. 'Your Gracious Majesty, Royal Highness, Princeness, I am ever your humble servant and am honoured to be in your divine presence,' he said, supplicating himself on the floor.

'Please, stand and face me,' Theo said, waving his paw upwards. 'My Captain tells me you have a tale to tell.'

'Oh, I does, your Princeness. Just this morning I was minding my own business walking down Flopmarsh Lane—,'

'— Er, my Captain says you were attempting to steal chickens, from Farmer Pigwhistle,' Theo interrupted.

'A minor misunderstanding, Your Majesty, Highness, I was merely looking to borrow one for educational purposes.'

'Anyway,' Half-blind Ron continued, 'I was walking down Flopmarsh Lane when all of a sudden this big, red horseless carriage appears behind me, almost flying it was. It headed straight at me and I thought I was goner, Your Princeness. It stopped just before it crashed into me back end. I thought me old jewels were gonna be history.'

'And who was in charge of this "horseless carriage"?' Theo asked, his eyes narrowing.

'Some lanky, human git, Your Majesty, Highness. A right weirdo if ever I met one. I reckon he was a wizard or a musician or sumfin.'

'Why say you so?' Theo asked again.

'He had strange clothes, Your Princeness, and very scruffy hair, and he was carrying this little box which lit up. If you don't believe me have a word with Fiery Dave from Denbigh, he saw him too.'

'Is this true, Captain, is there corroboration to his story?'

'We have sent word to Denbigh to request this information,' the Captain answered. 'We hope to hear back from them shortly.'

Theo jumped off the bed and placed a paw on Half-blind Ron's shoulder. 'Thank you for informing us of this. You can trust that we will seek to track this stranger down. We will be in touch shortly.'

'You mean I may get to meet Your Majesty, Highness, Princeness again?' Half-blind Ron said, with wide-eyed wonderment.

'Indeed, for we may wish to speak further when we have ascertained some more of the facts. Your testimony today has been very valuable.'

'Thank you, thank you, Your Gracious, Magnificent Princeness. Will you perhaps have a bit of chicken on hand next time?'

'We'll see what we can do.'

Captain Marmaduke led Half-blind Ron through the door and turned back to Theo. 'Can you see why I thought you should see him now?'

'I can indeed Captain. Once again you serve me well, my friend. Do you recall the exact words of The Prophecy?'

'Not quite, Your Highness, but from my recollection of the text there undoubtedly appears to be a connection.'

'Yes, it would seem so. The actual passage reads thus,' Theo said, staring out of the window. *"One day a stranger will arrive from a land beyond distance and beyond time. He will bring with him strange gadgets and strange ideas. He will tell tales of his home and people will gain strength from his words and his strange ways, although no-one will copy his hair style. He will join a group of heroes and set off on a quest that will deliver the people from fear and suppression. Evil will be vanquished and peace among the lands will follow."*

There was a knock on the door.

'Captain, we have word from Denbigh,' said one of the guards.

'Go on, man. What do they say?'

'Fiery Dave reported seeing a red, horseless carriage being piloted by a scruffy-haired human this morning, sir. It was heading towards Llangollen.'

'Well, Captain,' Theo said, 'it would appear that a trip to Llangollen needs to be added to my itinerary.'

***

'So, let's see if I've got this straight,' Aiden said to Tom. 'Because the QC operating system on the phone works on the uncertainty principle related to quantum mechanics, it does all its computations in parallel universes. So, instead of the Navigation app navigating me to Llangollen in my reality, it navigated me to another Llangollen in an alternative reality, where cats are telepathic and sheep serve rather good lager.'

'You're getting there now,' said Tom.

'And all this happened because the app selected the most appropriate Llangollen in the Multiverse for me by analysing my subconscious, which, like everything else in the Multiverse, is intrinsically connected consciously on a quantum level. So, to allow me to be navigated to this other Llangollen, the energy frequencies of my physical body and car were readjusted and aligned to this reality.'

'Yep, that's about the top and bottom of it.'

'And you seriously expect me to believe you?'

'Why would I lie to you? I'm not some smartarse, little demonic prankster, infiltrating your mind and tempting you to stuff your face with another slice of pizza. I'm your higher self for god's sake.'

'Demonic possession, oh come on, I suppose that happens a lot does it?' Aiden scoffed.

'All the bloody time, to varying degrees. Sometimes it's murder chasing the little monsters off; your drunken visit to the Pizza Plaza last night being a good example. How many slices did you have in the end?'

'Well, I was only going to have one, but... I felt tempted to have more... so I ended up having three. And I was going to go for a fourth but then changed my mind.'

'That was me after I smacked the little sod's metaphorical butt!' exclaimed Tom. 'Pesky little blighter.'

'You make it sound like I'm not in control of my own mind!'

'Well, there's a good element of truth in that. You have to understand that the human mind is a big mish-mash of things. There's you, that's your conscious mind, and then there's a whole host of other elements and hangers on, all vying for control at certain points in time, dependent upon the circumstances. Like your emotions, for example. They're a right bunch of whining beggars, I can tell you.'

'But,' Tom continued, 'and this is the key, you're living in a free will universe; so the choices you make are still down to you, your conscious self. The other elements of your mind and the infiltrators can only influence, although sometimes those influences can be pretty potent. It's my job to guide you and try to ensure that you do what's best. So, whenever you've followed your gut feeling or instinct, that's generally me nudging you to take the best path at that time. Remember, always listen to me.'

'Right,' Aiden said, scratching his chin. 'So when I felt the urge to chat up Rebecca Clark at the work's party, as I really felt she fancied me, that was you pointing me in the right direction?'

'No, that was your ego, Roger. He's a complete prat. You should never trust that pillock. Now me, I was screaming at you not to go anywhere near her because I knew she was a bloody fruit loop. Do you remember what happened the following week?'

'Er, yes, she chained herself to the old elm tree in my garden and claimed that she'd been sent by the wood nymphs to save it from satanic hair conditioner and inappropriate hieroglyphics. I had to get the police to move her after a couple of days.'

'See, there you go,' replied Tom.

'Excuse me my good man, but do you happen to have the time, please?'

Aiden pulled the phone from his ear and turned to look at a well-dressed sheep, wearing small, rounded spectacles and carrying a trumpet. 'Pardon,' he replied.

'Do you happen to have the time? I fear I may be late for the concert. I get a bit absent-minded these days, and I was so engrossed in a conversation about waistcoats with Mr Ruffle, the sheep tailor, that I've lost track of time completely.'

'Oh, it's half past two,' Aiden said, looking at his watch.

'Thank goodness and bless my clacky hooves,' the sheep said. 'The concert doesn't begin until three, so I have plenty of time. Thank you.'

'You're welcome.'

'Oh, I'm forgetting my manners. I'm Charles Corriedale, trumpet player with the Oswestry Sheep Orchestra,' Charles said, extending a hoof.

'Aiden Peersey,' Aiden said, swapping the phone to his other hand and shaking the extended hoof.

'Have you ever seen the OSO play?' Charles asked.

'No, I don't believe so.'

'Well, if you have time, why not pop along to the park by the river later. We're playing a sterling set today, including one of my favourites, "Where Sheep Safely Graze" by Baach. That always gets a great reception, and it's a really lovely tune.'

'I'll try my best to,' Aiden said, politely.

'Please do,' an enthusiastic Charles said. 'Anyhow, I must be on my way. It was very nice to meet you, Aiden, but I'll bid you adieu, good sir.'

'Nice to meet you too, Charles.'

And with that Charles Corriedale turned and headed over the bridge, trumpet in hand and with a spring in his stride. Aiden swapped the phone back to his right hand and placed it against his ear. 'So this isn't simply a bizarre dream?' he said to Tom.

'No.'

'And I'm not hallucinating because I'm having a reaction to something Stoner Steve from the Hefty Swingers may have put into my drink last night?'

'No.'

'And it's not some genetic experiment?'

'No.'

'And we've not been invaded by alien sheep landlords?'

'No.'

'And I'm not having a breakdown.'

'No'

'And in this reality, the composer Bach is actually Baach and is a sheep?'

'Yes.'

'And you really are my intuition/higher self?'

'Yes.'

'So, Everett's Many Worlds interpretation of the universe, which states that every choice that is made creates a copy of the universe where the actions resulting from that choice are then perpetuated, is actually correct?'

'Pretty much, yes.'

'I think I need to sit down.'

'You do that, then.'

Aiden grabbed one of the solid, wooden chairs at the front of the pub and slowly eased himself into it, keeping the phone pressed against his ear. He gazed blankly over the bridge into Llangollen town centre. 'How do I get back?' he said.

'I'm not sure, yet. This is a very unusual event, you know, not everyone goes dimension hopping. You're going to have to hold up for a time while I do a bit of investigative work. Look, I've got a conference call in a couple of days with the Higher Self Union, so I'll have a chat with a few well-versed souls and see what I can find out.'

'A couple of days! But what am I supposed to do? Where the hell am I going to stay? Can I drive back to my house?' Aiden asked, slightly exasperated.

'Well, you could. But I'm afraid it's not quite as you remember it.'

'Meaning?'

'Well, the building is there… but it's used as a nursing home for senile bingo callers.'

'Great. Do you have any suggestions, then?'

'Why not get a room in the pub here. It looks quite nice.'

'Well, for a start I haven't got any money on me and I doubt very much that they'll accept my credit card.'

'But you do have your wallet and bank card, don't you?'

'Yes, but how on earth is that going to help me here. Do you suggest I just wander to the nearest ATM and make a withdrawal?' Aiden said, with a touch of sarcasm.

'Actually, yes,' Tom replied. 'Look, you know the theory that the force of gravity is much weaker than it should be because it permeates all dimensions?'

'Yes…'

'Well, believe it or not, it's the same with banks. Trust me on this. Find a bank, use your normal pin number and you'll be fine.'

'That's scary,' Aiden said. 'But somehow I'm not that surprised.'

CHAPTER 6 – IS THERE A BANK AROUND HERE?

Merlin 'Cracky' Crackfoot was not quite his usual cheery self today, despite the success of the previous night. Today was the 30th anniversary of his father's death and he still missed him greatly.

Morgan Crackfoot was the last of the great wizards of Llangollen. He was also a kind and patient man who used his powers to help others, and Cracky had always wanted to emulate him. When he was young he would practice magic every day, sitting on his father's knee, whilst the attentive Morgan watched and guided him with wise and loving words. Sadly for Cracky he was what could be described as 'magically dyslexic'. He understood the principles of magic, but he simply couldn't get to grips with it in any kind of practical perspective. That's not to say he couldn't perform any magic at all, it's just that it never quite went as he intended. His first real attempt with fire spells provided a clue to his unfortunate condition.

It all started fine, as he adopted the correct posture, thrusting his arms out and concentrating on the freshly-chopped wood piled high on the log fire. It was only when he opened his mouth that things went slightly awry, with the words 'Inflamus Logs' somehow being translated by his will into 'Inflamus Rocks'. Sadly, the large log fire in the cottage remained unlit, whilst the cat with the flaming testicles made a very swift exit into the nearby stream.

However, Cracky discovered that he did have a natural aptitude for cookery, after imaginatively embellishing a recipe he found one day in his mother's cookbook. He assembled all of the listed ingredients, seemed to know intuitively what to add to enhance the texture and flavour, and created what both his mother and father agreed was a delicious steak and raspberry soufflé.

From this point onwards there was no stopping him, and, if anything, his prodigious talent for creating gourmet masterpieces from mixing together the most unlikely ingredients was the equal of his father's gift for wizardry. However, as gratifying as it was to see his parents so proud of his culinary achievements, he still longed to follow in his father's magically altruistic footsteps... so the cat kept out of his way most of the time.

'Excuse me,' Aiden said, from the doorway of Cracky's Diner, 'but is there a bank around here at all?'

'What?' Cracky said, snapping out of his thoughts. 'Oh, yes, about ten minutes' walk, just on the outskirts of the town centre.'

'Thanks. Er, what's the branch called?'

'The Black Bank, of course,' Cracky replied. 'They're all Black Bank branches now, sadly.'

Cracky looked Aiden up and down, noting his hair, clothes and general demeanour. 'I sense that you're a stranger to these parts, Mr...?'

'Peersey, Aiden Peersey.'

'Well, Mr Peersey, my instincts tell me you are quite a ways from home. And, I would add, not too familiar with this area?'

'You could say that,' Aiden replied. 'But please, call me Aiden.'

'Aiden it is then,' said Cracky. 'I can accompany you, if you like. I need to head down to the bank myself. By the way, the name's Merlin Crackfoot, but please call me Cracky, everyone else does.'

'Thanks, Cracky. I'd appreciate that.'

Aiden found Cracky to be very good company. In the ten minutes it took to walk to the bank, he told him all about his Diner, all about Llangollen and its inhabitants, and he strongly recommended 'The Sheep's Stirrup' as a place to stay. He was particularly scathing about Baron Blacktie, who, he said, ruled North Wales, Chester and the Wirral with an iron fist, and had introduced many unpopular laws.

The sign in the window of the Black Bank said 'Bank with the Black Bank and Your Money is Safe.' In smaller letters underneath it read 'After all, it's not as if you have a choice'. Aiden could see another poster on the wall behind the counter which read 'Your Money is Our Money... and we like to keep it like that'.

'Right, I'm going to see Mr Grabitall, the manager,' Cracky said. 'Unless he wants a fight again, I shouldn't be more than five minutes. There's the ATM in the doorway.'

Aiden tentatively inserted his card and fully expected it to be eaten by the machine, no doubt followed by alarm bells, armed guards and god knew what else. Instead, the screen asked for his pin number. He entered his pin and was given the option of how much cash he wished to withdraw. Having no idea what things were likely to cost, he opted for the maximum, which was £200. A few seconds later his card was returned and a little metal flap opened, providing him with a mixture of ten and twenty pound notes. He breathed a sigh of relief, placed the card back in his wallet and examined the money.

All the notes bore the image of Baron Blacktie. On the front of £10 note he was dressed in military regalia, looking out to sea; on the back he was seen playing with children, laughing (although Aiden noticed that the children didn't look so cheery). On the front of the £20 note he was sat on a throne with a ferret on his knee; on the back he was in serious pose reading from a book.

For all his vanity, and there was a great deal of that, Baron Blacktie was as astute with money as he was devious and treacherous. After he was elected Supreme Ruler, he decided to merge all of the independent banks under one banner, 'The Black Bank.' Now, not all the banks were keen to simply throw in their lot with the Baron, irrespective of his promises of higher interest rates for loans, lower interest rates for savings, and the introduction of harsh penalties for unauthorised overdrafts. The Baron didn't take too kindly to any dissenting voices and made personal visits to see the concerned parties. He was always accompanied to these meetings by his personal bodyguard, Grunt.

Now, Grunt may have been a troll; he may have been the missing link between man and Neanderthal; he may have been abandoned by his parents because he'd never be in a successful boy band; or he may simply have come from Rhyl. Nobody knew, but nobody asked and nobody argued with him. The dissenting voices became assenting voices when they met Grunt.

'Now, come on, Mrs Muncher, you know the rules,' an armed bank guard said, as he escorted a little old lady out of the bank's front door.

'But I'm only 10p overdrawn,' protested Mrs Muncher, 'and that's because I didn't think the direct debit for my new subscription of "Tai Chi Bingo for Beginners" would come out until next week, and that's when I pay my pension in.'

'That's too bad, I'm afraid,' the guard said, as a second guard handed him a large hammer. 'Now, if you'll kindly lie down here so I can get a good swing at those knees, please.'

Mrs Muncher lay down and the second guard grabbed her ankles. 'Now keep still, this will only take a second.'

'What on earth do you think you're doing?' Aiden said, standing in the way of the guard with the hammer.

'Move out of the way, sir, please. This is a bank matter, I'm sure you understand.'

'No, I bloody well don't understand. The lady said she's only 10p overdrawn and you're going to kneecap her. That's barbaric!'

'Well, overdraft punishment is overdraft punishment, and she drew straws to see which one she'd get after all,' the guard said. 'She could have got nostril stretching or severe ear twisting, but she got kneecapping. That's just the way it goes, I'm afraid. Rules are rules.'

Aiden weighed up the situation. He wasn't exactly small, but he figured that the two guards would be able to overpower him easily if he physically intervened. Plus, if this ritual was in some bizarre way accepted in this reality he was in danger of exposing himself as an outsider, and the last thing he wanted was any kind of brush with the authorities, particularly if this is how they dealt with overdrafts.

'So, do you actually want to break her kneecaps?' he said to the guard with the hammer.

'Er, no, not really, sir. But, as I said, rules are rules.'

'But, if you do break her kneecaps it's pretty likely she won't be able to walk again, particularly given her age, would you not agree?'

'Oh, there's no way she'll walk again after this, sir. Not a chance.'

'In fact, it's possible that she could die from shock, or from a heart attack?'

'I'd say that's a very likely possibility, sir.'

Mrs Muncher was still lying on the ground listening intently. So was the second guard. 'And,' Aiden continued, 'if that happened she'd still be overdrawn and wouldn't be in a position to be able to clear the overdraft.'

'I never really thought about it like that, but I believe you'd be right, sir.'

A small crowd was beginning to gather, and Aiden felt he was on a bit of a roll. 'So, you'd actually serve the bank better if you didn't kneecap her, as that way she'd still be a regular customer.'

'Are you suggesting that we stretch her nostrils or twist her ears severely instead, sir?'

'No, no. I'm suggesting that you, Mr…'

'Tenderhands, Albert Tenderhands,' the first guard replied.

'I'm suggesting that you, Mr Tenderhands, make an executive decision to delay her punishment, thereby allowing her to collect her pension next week and pay it into the bank.'

'And then we kneecap her?' said the second guard, who was still holding Mrs Muncher's legs.

'No, you won't have to, because then she'll have cleared the overdraft and there'll be no reason for any punishment.'

'Doesn't sound right to me, Albert,' the second guard said.

'Executive decision, eh,' said Albert. 'I've never had to make an executive decision before. Why it would almost feel like a promotion.'

'Yes, it would,' Aiden said. 'Now, Mrs Muncher, can you promise that you'll come in next week, as soon as you get your pension, and pay it into the bank to clear your overdraft?'

'Too bloody right I will,' Mrs Muncher said, nodding frantically.

'Well, then, Mr Tenderhands, are you going to bend the rules and make that executive decision, thereby doing the bank a great service?'

'Bend the rules. That's a new one, I'll say,' Albert said, and you could almost see the wheels of his mind turning... slowly.

'Right then, Mrs Muncher,' he said after some serious chin rubbing, 'I've made an executive decision. I hereby grant you a delay in your overdraft punishment, thereby allowing you to clear said overdraft next week when you pick up your pension. Do you agree?'

'Oh, yes. Thank you, thank you,' said Mrs Muncher, as she was helped to her feet by the second guard.

'If you don't, of course, your kneecaps are forfeit,' Albert added.

The small crowd broke into a round of applause and Mrs Muncher stretched up to plant a kiss on Aiden's cheek. Cracky walked out into the street just as the crowd started to disperse. 'What's all the commotion here, then?' he asked.

'That young man just saved Mrs Muncher from a kneecapping,' shouted a small, portly gentleman with a red face and matching cardigan.

'Did he now?' Cracky said, raising an eyebrow, as Aiden simply shrugged. 'C'mon, then, I'll walk you back to the Diner and then lunch is on me. After that we'll sort you out a room at The Sheep's Stirrup.'

'By the way,' he added, as they set off down the street, 'do you happen to like rock music, by any chance?'

'Yes, as a matter of fact I do.'

'Well, you're in for a treat later. It's live music night at the Stirrup and Sacred Wind are playing. They're actually very good.'

'Oh, right,' said Aiden, blissfully unaware of what the night would bring.

CHAPTER 7 – I'M STILL GETTING DRESSED, DARLING

'C'mon, Tikky we're going to be late,' Vindy shouted to his wife, from the sumptuous surroundings of the Wrexham Grand Palace morning room. 'What are you doing?'

'I'm still getting dressed, darling, I won't be too long,' Tikky, shouted back.

'Just a little more around the edge and a slight sprinkle on top and then I think we'll be done, Your Majesty,' Tikky's hand maiden, Greta, said. 'You look absolutely delicious and I think there'll be gentlemen drooling when they see you today.'

'You're very kind, Greta. Let's just hope the King appreciates all the effort. The people expect us to set an example and the least I can do is to look my absolute best when we go on walkabouts.'

'Is it Your Majesty's intention to travel straight to Llangollen, following the parade?' Greta asked.

'Indeed it is. The King and I haven't had a good night out for ages, and I do so enjoy the music at The Sheep's Stirrup. I'm ever so glad Maurice invited us over. But please remember, not a word to anyone. We want to keep this strictly under the radar,' Tikky said, as the two of them began to make their way down the main stairway to where the King and his man servant, Harold, waited.

'My dear, you look absolutely divine. I'll be the envy of every curry in Wrexham,' King Beef Vindaloo-Boiled Rice III said. 'That touch of parsley and sprinkling of coriander really beings out your flavour, and you smell scrumptious.'

'You don't look so bad yourself,' Queen Chicken Tikka Masala-Coconut Rice said. 'I love the mango chutney, it makes you look sweet. Was that

Harold's idea?'

'Of course, I don't know what I'd do without him,' the King replied.

'Your Majesty is too modest, in this instance.' Harold said, 'Although the idea may have been mine, the choice of placement on the plate was His Majesty's.'

'You look very nice too, Harold,' said Greta. 'That jacket really sets off your eyes.'

'And you look as radiant as ever, Greta. It is my honour to walk at your side, as well as to carry my King.'

'I think there may be love in the air, Vindy,' Tikky whispered to her husband.

'Heh, heh. I think you might be right, my darling. I can hear the sound of wedding bells already.'

Wrexham had been a 'Currydom' since 1979, following the hardship the people had suffered during the Risotto Wars'. Prior to this, men and curries had lived in peace and harmony for many years, respecting each other's cultures and sympathetic to each other's needs. However, following the 1968 legislation by the Welsh Parliament officially recognising curries as conscious entities, dark forces sought to infiltrate the curry community, spurring on insurgency, sabotage and acts of terrorism. Suddenly, eating in a curry house was no longer the peaceful, gastronomic experience it once was. Attacks by suicide Naan breads became common, overly hot poppadoms became the norm, and many curries sought to make themselves unpalatable by ingesting copious amounts of cinnamon.

The self-proclaimed leader of the rebel movement, 'El Currieda', was Bishop Chicken Biryani-Onion Bhaji, a mad zealot who believed the words written in 'The Holy Recipe Book of Curry' should be taken literally. He blamed men for the corruption of the 'pure' curries, and so began his campaign of terror and watery rice. His second in command was the evil genius Dr Prawn Balti-Naan, who desired to create the 'super curry', conducting hideous genetic experiments involving turmeric powder and strawberries.

However, not all curries viewed the actions and ambitions of Bishop Chicken Biryani-Onion Bhaji as representative. This group, 'Curry Action for Culture and Knowledge', or 'C.A.C.K.' for short, at first sought a diplomatic path with the mad Bishop. Their leader, Colonel Pork Pasanda-Chapati, tried in vain to convince him that his crusade of wanton curry-led violence was tearing the community apart. A series of meetings proved fruitless, largely due to the Bishop's increasing megalomania but also due to a dearth of sultanas. Draft treaties were torn up and the curry community of Wrexham effectively found itself in a state of civil war.

All this chaos let the Italians in, with the head of the Wrexham Risottos, Luigi Risotto Alla Milanese, sensing it was time for them to make their move for power. Spurred on by the division in the curry ranks, the Risottos opened many new restaurants and also took over previously established curry houses. As the ruling council of El Currieda watched the madness of their leader accelerate, and witnessed their rapid decline as the dish of choice, they realised there was only one course of action that could be taken.

Bishop Chicken Biryani-Onion Bhaji met his grim end during a parade through the centre of Wrexham on a cold November morning. The Chapatis came out of nowhere and many suspected it must have been an inside job to get past all the security. Some said they only saw one, others said it was at least two, and many more swear that the last Chapati came from behind a grassy knoll. Nevertheless, the Bishop's plate was wiped clean and only a lone Chapati was caught, and he was killed shortly afterwards by a rogue Samosa. The conspiracy of who killed Bishop Chicken Biryani-Onion Bhaji continues to this day.

With the Bishop gone, Colonel Pork Pasanda-Chapati and his brave second in command, Lieutenant Beef Vindaloo-Boiled Rice III, galvanised the curry populace and took the battle to the Italians. The final showdown took place in Fabio's Pizzaria, with curries and Risottos on the same table for the first time. Bedlam ensued, but the Risottos had bitten off more than they could chew and the curries emerged triumphant… but it took weeks to get the rice out of the carpet.

However, although victory was theirs it came at a heavy price, when an errant Italian waiter knocked Colonel Pork Pasanda-Chapati to the floor. Faced with certain death due to a severely smashed plate, the Colonel passed over command to the young Lieutenant who had served him so well, and who promised to make his wish that men and curries would live in peace once more a reality.

The people of Wrexham, endeared by the bravery and morals of the curries, recognised that their own rulers in the council were actually a bunch of idiots who cared more about attending fetes, filling out expenses forms and erecting statues of themselves rather than governing effectively. So, following a request that they all bugger off, an independent poll was held and it was decreed by the people that Lieutenant Beef Vindaloo-Boiled Rice III be crowned King.

The royal monthly walkabouts in Wrexham were always joyous occasions, and Vindy and Tikky would always make a point of greeting everyone who queued up patiently to see them. As usual, the press were there and the royal couple were also equally gracious to them, always posing for photographs. They understood all too well the advantages of having a good relationship with the media.

'Over here, Your Majesty,' a skinny fellow with odd eyes from the Wrexham Gazette said, to Tikky. 'If you can just turn slightly sideways, please, so I can get a good shot of your bay leaves.'

Back at the palace, the preparations were being made for tonight's undisclosed visit to The Sheep's Stirrup. As the King and Queen returned they were greeted by the head of their Imperial Guard, General Lamb Korma-Saffron Rice.

'Good day, Your Majesties. And can I just say that you both look splendid.'

'Why thank you, Saffy,' the Queen said, using the informal name that both she and the King addressed the General by. 'And you look as dashing as usual. Is everything prepared?'

'Yes, Your Majesty. Your unmarked carriage awaits, and I will accompany you for the trip, if Your Majesties are in agreement.

'I'm not surprised you're not letting us out of your sight, Saffy, and it is appreciated,' said the King. 'I must say, though, I would have thought you'd have insisted on some form of armed guard for the trip.'

'Well, ahem, although we may be travelling effectively alone, we will be followed by a battalion of elite Tandoori Naans. However, they are under orders to keep their distance and only to move on my command,' Saffy replied.

'Oh, one more thing, Saffy,' Tikky said, as they were carried into the carriage, 'are we still to meet with you know who?'

'We are Your Majesty. I have received communication that both parties will be present this evening.'

'Ok, then, what are we waiting for,' said Vindy. 'Let's hit the road, cause I'm in the mood for dancing!'

'Calm down, dear, you'll make your rice go sticky,' Tikky said.

And with that the carriage sped off to Llangollen and their date with destiny.

CHAPTER 8 – SHE MAY BE THE LAST OF HER KIND

Aiden thought the food at Cracky's Diner was rather good, as he quickly polished off a healthy portion of Chicken of Catastrophe and Scallops of Shock, with some Peas of Dread on the side. This was washed down with one of Cracky's excellent home-brewed ales.

'I have to say, Cracky, I'd never have guessed that melon, garlic and chicken would work so well together. That was one of the best meals I've had in ages.'

'You're welcome,' said Cracky. 'One does one's best. Now, I'm not due to open again until 5:00 pm so, if you'd like, I'll walk over to the Stirrup with you. I can have a quick catch-up with Maurice.'

'Thanks, but I was going to have a walk down to the park first to have a look at the fair. I believe there's a sheep orchestra playing and that's something I'd like to see.'

'The OSO, yes, they're very good. Would you mind if I joined you?'

As they began the short walk to the park on the banks of the River Dee, Aiden thought he'd better check on his car. 'Well, bless my soul, you don't see many of these old things anymore,' Cracky said.

'Oh, yes it is a bit of a classic,' said Aiden, proudly. 'I didn't see any other cars on the roads when I arrived, so parking was pretty easy. Is this because of the fair?'

'No, not at all,' Cracky said, 'hardly anyone drives these machines these days. They went out of fashion about forty years ago. I don't think I've ever seen one in such good condition.'

Aiden's look of surprise didn't escape Cracky's notice, and as they walked to the park an uneasy silence decided to hang around to see what was going to happen next.

'I think, my friend, that you are, shall we say, quite a long way from home. Would that be fair?' Cracky said, after about a minute.

'It would appear so,' Aiden replied. 'It's a bit of a long story.'

'Well, I tell you what, then. Tomorrow, after you've had an enjoyable night at the Stirrup and perhaps feel a bit more settled in, why don't you come to the Diner for lunch. I'm cooking a new special, The Salmon of Panic. I think you'll like it; the bananas really bring out the flavour. And perhaps afterwards we can have a chat.'

Aiden smiled and agreed with a silent nod.

The Grand Carnival of Shearing and Hoof Waxing was a kaleidoscope of colour and sound, wrapped up in an intoxicating blend of aromas. People and sheep bustled hither and thither, meandering between the many stalls that were selling a variety of produce. There was certainly plenty of hoof waxing and shearing going on, with the vendors competing vigorously with each other for customers.

'Get your hooves waxed here! Only the finest Welsh hoof wax used. Ten pence a hoof for ewes, fifteen pence a hoof for rams, and its buy one get one free!' a large man in a trench coat and a straw boater hat yelled.

'Free hoof waxing for lambs!' another man wearing white overalls shouted. 'And free lollipops too. We use the same hoof wax as the OSO; it's the finest English Shimmy Shine.'

The stalls offering shearing were equally as assertive with their advertising strategy. 'Ewe, madam, yes, ewe!' a rather dashing-looking young farmer shouted to a giggling group of sheep. 'Look at the styles we've got on offer today. Tight perms, loose perms, why we'll even perm round your udders. C'mon, the rams won't be able to resist ewe!'

'Latest cuts from the City,' a stocky man with shorts and very hairy legs proclaimed. 'Want to look like a celebrity? Well you've come to the right place. Get the fleece you've always dreamed of. Shampooed, cut and blow dried to perfection. Go on, you know you're worth it!'

Aiden and Cracky watched the OSO perform a couple of well-executed pieces of music to an appreciative crowd. He may have been in a completely different reality but Aiden actually felt quite at ease, thoroughly enjoying the music and festivities. And then he spotted something on the river that made his heart skip a beat. It was a replica Viking long ship, complete with a mighty wooden dragon at the prow and another at the helm.

'Come on,' Cracky said, walking towards the ship, 'there's someone I'd like you to meet.'

As they got closer, Aiden could see a huge man in a Viking costume standing proudly with his arms crossed on the prow, watching over the throngs of people and sheep on board. 'Five minutes until we sail!' shouted the Viking. 'For Odin, for glory and for Sacred Wind!' Then he uncrossed his arms, lifted his huge broadsword into the air… and farted loudly, which was met by cheers from the crowd.

'See him,' said Cracky, pointing at the Viking. 'He's the lead vocalist and guitarist in the band you'll be watching tonight.'

'You're not serious?' Aiden said, with a smile.

'Oh, yes. Fantastic voice and a pretty good guitar player.'

'My, my and how is my good friend Mr Crackfoot today,' a small man with a very long, grey beard said.

'I'm very well, Mr Olafson. Nice to see you again,' Cracky replied, warmly shaking the bearded man by the hand. 'And this here is Aiden Peersey.'

'Oldfart,' the bearded man said, extending his hand towards Aiden.

'Pardon,' Aiden replied.

'Mr Olafson… Oldfart Olafson,' the bearded man said, keeping his hand outstretched. 'But please call me Oldfart.'

Aiden couldn't help but smile again. 'Pleased to meet you, Oldfart,' he said, accepting the handshake.

'Are the band well-prepared for tonight's gig at the Stirrup?' Cracky asked.

'Well, that's what they tell me,' Oldfart said. 'They're trying out a couple of new numbers tonight, so we'll have to see how they get received. It's a very strong set list now, though, and I reckon they're ready to move on to the next level.'

'Oldfart's the manager of Sacred Wind,' Cracky said to Aiden.

Aiden was continuing to eye the Viking ship on the river, which didn't go unnoticed by Oldfart. 'Would you like a trip on the boat? I'm sure we can squeeze you two in somewhere.'

The man in the Viking costume released the anchor, whilst another equally large Viking untied the thick hawser that moored the boat to the old, wooden jetty. The craft then moved silently out into the river, steered manfully by Oldfart Olafson. The passengers cheered again and Aiden felt rather splendid. The sun was shining and the river glistened as it reflected the warm rays. 'Isn't this exciting!' said one of the little sheep that Aiden had met earlier, still dressed in its pirate costume.

'Yes, it is rather,' he replied, truthfully.

It was after about five minutes that Aiden started to think about propulsion. He couldn't detect a motor, there was nobody rowing, and even though the huge sail was raised there didn't really seem to be enough wind for the ship to be travelling as effortlessly as it seemed. The big wooden dragon that towered over Oldfart, as he navigated the ship, stared silently ahead, like an immense, unmoving guardian. Then, only for a split second, it moved its eyes and looked sideways at Aiden.

'Cracky, did you see that? That dragon's eyes moved, I swear to you.'

'Really?' Cracky responded. 'You're very honoured, she normally doesn't give most folks the time of day.'

'She?'

'Ethel,' Cracky said. 'That's her name. She's very rare, you know. In fact she may be the last of her kind. It's her ship. Well, essentially, she is the ship.'

Aiden stared up at Ethel, but her eyes were now unblinking, focussed on the river ahead. 'Would you like to hear the story?' Cracky said.

'I'd love to.'

'Okay, then. Legend has it that long, long ago a fleet of Viking ships set sail in search of adventure and treasure. They sought a magical island that was thought to be lost, yet which had been sighted on several occasions by sea farers. After many weeks of searching, they finally sighted the island; but then, from nowhere, a mighty tempest erupted around them. The storm claimed all but two of the ships, but both were badly damaged, although they eventually managed to reach the island. Now, Odin, who as you may know is the King of the Norse Gods, watched these events from on high and was impressed by the bravery of the men who had managed to steer their ships through the violent storm. Many, though, had died and those that were left were close to death. So, the legend says, he gave them the Blessed Bottom Breath of Life, thus reviving and repairing their bodies, and enriching their souls. Also, in order for them to safely return home, he gave the same gift to the two ships, infusing them with life... and a soul. This is one of the reasons that Vikings regard the passing of wind as sacred. They believe every fart is a blessing.'

'Oh, I see,' Aiden said, with a barely-concealed smile.

The dragon once again turned its eyes slightly towards Aiden and winked. 'I really have seen everything now,' he said, as the ship turned and began the journey back to the fair.

'Actually you probably haven't,' chuckled Cracky. 'Anyway, let's head for the Stirrup when we get back on shore. We'll get you sorted out with a room and then I need to open the Diner.'

CHAPTER 9 – WE'D LIKE A ROOM, PLEASE

'I am Mr Breezy and my partner here is Mr Waft,' the tall man holding the briefcase said. 'We'd like a room, please,'

'Yes,' said the shorter man, 'preferably one with a view of the river.'

'It's your lucky day, good sirs,' said Maurice Fluffywool. 'We've only two rooms left but they both have a lovely view of the Dee.'

'We'll only need one, thank you,' Mr Breezy said.

'Oh, I see,' Maurice said, winking. 'Well, we're very enlightened around here, so that's not a problem.'

'Ah, I fear you may be incorrectly assessing our status,' Mr Breezy said, his face reddening. 'Ours is purely a business relationship. There is, I assure you, no impropriety of any nature. We share a room so we can keep our costs low and so that we may discuss and plan our business strategy.'

'Indeed,' Mr Waft added, 'we sometimes sit long into the wee hours discussing the ins and outs of things.'

They both wore long, green coats and had matching black, bowler hats. Maurice thought they looked a bit shifty so he decided to probe. 'What kind of business are you gentleman involved in, then?'

'These are strange times, Mr Fluffywool,' Mr Breezy said, dramatically. 'We are here on matters of extreme sensitivity. Our clients do not always like to wash their dirty linen in public, so to speak.'

'Ah, so you two are spies are you?' Maurice replied.

'Er, no, no, of course not,' Mr Waft said, slightly agitated. 'What makes you think we are spies?'

'Well you do have the look of spies about you gentlemen, and I've met a few in my time. Also, isn't that black briefcase a spy kit?'

Mr Breezy and Mr Waft looked at each other and laughed. Then they looked at Maurice and chortled. Then they tittered… and ended with some 'tee, hee, hees.'

'No, Mr Fluffywool, we are purely Vagrant Vacuum Cleaner Exorcists, trying to earn an honest crust,' Mr Breezy said.

'Oh, I had no idea vacuum cleaner possession was an issue these days,' Maurice said. 'I've certainly not heard of anything of that nature in these parts of late.'

'Ah, you would be surprised, Mr Fluffywool,' said Mr Breezy. 'We have just crossed the border from England and the situation in some villages there was horrendous.'

'Horrendous,' echoed Mr Waft.

'Indeed,' said Mr Breezy. 'Sadly, we got to one village too late and they had already begun burning vacuum cleaners at the stake, fearing this was the only method they could employ to stem the evil tide. It was a terrible sight.'

'And a dusty one,' Mr Waft added.

'We hope that the special blessings we can bestow on your town will perhaps prevent you from witnessing the horrors we have seen. This is our goal, this is our purpose, this is our quest,' Mr Breezy said, grandly.

'Here, here!' shouted Mr Waft.

'Well, in which case, I can only wish you gentlemen good fortune,' Maurice said. 'And I'll certainly sleep more soundly in my bed knowing that my vacuum cleaner is far less likely to indulge in projectile-vomiting and speaking in tongues when I try to get into those tricky corner areas. Right, the room will be £10 a night, including our rather delicious Welsh breakfast. How many nights will you be staying?'

'I would envisage just two,' Mr Breezy said. 'Although this will obviously be dependent upon when we feel our mission, and your safety, is assured.'

'Well, if you can just sign here, please, Mr Breezy,' Maurice said, passing him the guest book. 'And here's your key to Room 13. Go up the stairs and it's the last room on the right, at the end of the corridor.'

'Thank you, Mr Fluffywool,' Mr Breezy said, as he and Mr Waft walked towards the stairs. 'Oh, one more thing,' he said, turning back to Maurice. 'We have a passing interest in ancient structures and we noticed a fascinating old cheese mine near a large group of standing stones as we travelled here. Do you perhaps know anything of this mine and who it belongs to?'

'Oh, that's been closed for many years. It used to be owned by a quaint old chap called Hairy Growler, but he transferred ownership to the McSvensson clan just days before his death.'

'The McSvensson clan!' Mr Waft said, somewhat alarmed.

'Yes, have you heard of them?'

'We have,' Mr Breezy replied, as he and Mr Waft exchanged nervous glances. 'They are the most feared warriors in the land.'

'Yes, indeed,' said Maurice. 'But Angus McSvensson bequeathed it to his cousin as a birthday gift, on the understanding that he takes care of it from time to time. As you can imagine, the McSvenssons don't tend to travel to these parts much.'

Mr Breezy and Mr Waft relaxed visibly. 'And would you know the whereabouts of this cousin at all?' Mr Breezy said.

'His name is Agnar the Hammered and he plays drums in a quite excellent band by the name of Sacred Wind. They are performing in this establishment this very evening, so I'm sure I can introduce you.'

'Thank you, Mr Fluffywool, that information is much appreciated,' said Mr Breezy, as they went up the stairs.

'I thought he was onto us for a minute there,' Nob said, closing the door to room 13 behind him.

'Yes, but I feel our supreme acting skills have once again ensured that our disguises remain intact,' Hob replied, putting his briefcase down next to one of the two single beds.

'Quite,' Nob agreed.

Hob went over and stared out of the window at the pleasant view of the town and river below. 'So, it belongs to a drummer,' he said. 'This could make our task easier than we thought.'

Virtually as soon as Mr Breezy and Mr Waft had disappeared upstairs, Aiden and Cracky walked thought the door. Aiden was still smiling. 'You seem very happy, Mr Peersey,' said Maurice. 'And good day, Mr Crackfoot, I believe that the "Cuisine de la Terreur" went very well last night.'

'Good day, Maurice. Yes, it did, thanks,' said Cracky. 'I just need to take it easy with the garlic and pineapple sauce next time.'

Maurice immediately began to fill up two glasses for them. 'And I do feel much better now, Maurice,' Aiden said, as he and Cracky leaned on the bar. 'I was feeling a little odd before, but the visit to the carnival has cleared my head a bit.'

'Cheshire Black,' Maurice whispered to Cracky.

'Aiden would very much like a room, if you have any spare,' Cracky said. 'Although we're not sure how many nights this would be for.'

'You're in luck, Aiden,' Maurice said, 'I've only one left, but it's very nice with a lovely view of the Dee. Mind you, it's a good job the two spies who've just checked in only wanted one room.'

'Spies?' Cracky said.

'Well, they said they were Vagrant Vacuum Cleaner Exorcists, but I'm pretty sure they're spies. I can smell them a mile off. They want to chat to Agnar about that old mine of his. I suspect they're probably harmless but I'll keep an eye on them.'

'I knew a lady whose vacuum cleaner became possessed once,' Cracky said. 'It used to drive her up the wall... and even onto the ceiling sometimes. I'll check out these two "spies" tonight, as well.'

Maurice placed their drinks on the bar and Aiden produced his wallet, only to be waved away by Maurice's hoof. 'No, this one's on the house, gentlemen. First drink is free for guests and as Mr Crackfoot kindly recommended my establishment as your abode of choice, he can have one too.'

'Very kind of you, again,' Aiden said.

'Yes, cheers, Maurice,' said Cracky.

'So, did you enjoy the OSO today?' Maurice asked, bringing out the guest book from under the bar.

'Very much so,' Aiden replied.

'My brother, Henry, is their conductor and musical arranger, you know. He'll be around tonight, as he tends to stay over when they're playing in the area. If you'd like I'll introduce you to him. He can be a bit snooty but he has a good heart really.'

'I'd be delighted,' said Aiden.

'Right then, the room will be £8 a night, including breakfast. And just wait until you've tried my Blanche's sausages! I swear you'll never want to taste any other sausages again. Sign here please.'

Aiden signed his name and Maurice handed him the key to room number 11. 'Up the stairs to the left and it's the third room from the end of the corridor, on the right hand side.'

'Thanks, Maurice. I'll have a quick look now, but then I need to go back into town to try and buy some spare clothes. Can you recommend anywhere?'

'Well, you could try Ruffles Garments,' Maurice said, 'although he tends to specialise in sheepwear. There's also Chez Viking, but I'm not sure if their styles would suit you.'

'Yes, I think Aiden requires something a little more contemporary,' Cracky interjected. 'I would have thought that Mr Kneepatcher's Trouser and Jacket Emporium may well fit the bill.'

'Now, why didn't I think of that!' exclaimed Maurice.

'Right, then, if you walk with me back to the Diner now, I'll give you directions. It's literally around the corner,' Cracky said. 'But watch out he doesn't try and sell you his entire stock. He's a nice chap but he can be pretty pushy.'

CHAPTER 10 – WOULD SIR LIKE A CRAVAT WITH THAT?

'So what is it that sir is looking for exactly?' Mr Kneepatcher quizzed, his tape measure draped around his neck and his glasses perched on the end of his long nose.

'A couple of pairs of pants, jeans preferably, some t-shirts, socks, underwear, a shirt, a pair of boots and perhaps a jacket,' Aiden replied, as the pound signs began to light up in Mr Kneepatcher's eyes.

'Of course, sir, of course, absolutely-dutely,' Mr Kneepatcher gushed, as he pulled the tape measure from around his neck. 'Please come this way so I can take sir's measurements. Has sir had a good day?'

'It's been interesting,' Aiden replied.

'Is sir going to the concert at The Sheep's Stirrup tonight, to see Sacred Wind?' Mr Kneepatcher said, as he took Aiden's inside leg measurement. 'Ooh, I do love those Viking costumes. They make me go all of a dither!'

'Yes, I am, as a matter of fact. I've heard they're very good.'

'Oh, they are, sir,' Mr Kneepatcher said, putting the tape measure around Aiden's chest. 'That Olaf, the singer, he gives me goosebumps when he sings the high notes in the big ballads. Mind you, I'm not surprised when his trousers are that tight. I swear I just go to putty.'

As Aiden was being measured up for just about everything, he looked out of the shop window. The Hefty Swingers had used many different methods of transporting equipment to gigs in the past; vans, cars, even by train once. However, he was pretty sure they'd never used a horse and cart.

'Watch out for that pothole, Smid, my right bass drum nearly jumped out of the cart last time,' Agnar the Hammered shouted, from the back of the cart.

'We'll be fine, Agnar, Smid the Merciless said. 'The suspension's been fixed and old Bertha's calmed down a bit now that stallion's not in the field next to the pub anymore.'

'I do hope Roisin will be there tonight,' Agnar said, with a dreamy look.

'Oh, you're not still trying to woo her, are you?' said Grundi the Windy. 'She's out of your league.'

'Aw, now c'mon, Grundi,' Agnar said. 'She smiled at me the last time we played here.'

'I think that may have been wind, my friend,' Smid laughed. 'Anyway, didn't she say she was happy just being friends? That's what girls say when they don't fancy you. I mean, how many times have you asked her out?'

'Twenty-four,' said Agnar. 'But they do say that Odin loves a trier.'

'Well, maybe you'd have more luck asking Odin out,' said Grundi.

'Knowing my luck he'd be washing his bloody hair as well!'

The three band mates laughed heartily as the cart pulled up outside The Sheep's Stirrup. 'Whoa, Bertha,' said Smid, pulling on the reigns.

'What time did Olaf say he'd be here, Grundi?' Agnar said, as he grabbed one of the large PA speakers from the back of the cart.

'Anytime now, I would think. He went round to see Ophelia earlier this afternoon. She'd promised to shine his helmet again.'

'Maybe I should ask Roisin to shine my helmet,' Agnar suggested.

'I really wouldn't,' Smid advised.

Mr Kneepatcher was also very keen on helmets, particularly selling them, and he passed one to Aiden. 'No, thanks, I don't really think it's me,' Aiden said, looking at the cone-shaped, metal headwear.

'Oh come now, sir, I think you'd look very dashing. Just give it a quick go,' he enthused, trying to place it on Aiden's head.

'Honestly, no thanks, but I would like to have a look at that jacket, though,' Aiden said, pointing to a thick, brown leather coat that had more pockets than one would ever really need.

Mr Kneepatcher flamboyantly threw the helmet onto a handily placed sofa and smiled the smile of a shopkeeper whose customer had asked to see something expensive. 'Of course, sir, your taste is divine,' he said.

'Now,' Mr Kneepatcher cooed, 'this princely garment has been fashioned from only the finest Scottish leather. It was tanned by an ancient family of Scottish tanners, who ate only haggis for supper and whisky porridge for breakfast during the process. The leather was ripened in the glens of the highlands and then taken over foggy lochs in rowing boats, where seagulls would sing to it. Then it bore witness to the sacrifice of a virgin haggis and the ceremonial burning of the boots of Old Charlie McSniffysoles. Finally, it was serenaded by a lone piper in the light of the full moon before being tanned to perfection. It's easy on the eye, comfortable as the warmest faerie's bed and tough as sheep's hooves.'

'How much?' Aiden asked, as Mr Kneepatcher helped him put the jacket on.

'To you, sir, £40.'

'Well, I am buying quite a few other items,' Aiden said, feeling the need to haggle, 'so why don't we say £25?'

Mr Kneepatcher developed a nervous twitch in his right eye and a few beads of sweat appeared on his forehead. 'Did I tell you the lining has been blessed by the Avuncular Monks of Lothian, and that it has been stitched with the finest thread by the Uncanny Old Ladies of Inverness.'

'£25,' Aiden said again.

'£35 and I'll let you have a free pocket knife.'

'£30, but I'll still take the pocket knife.'

Mr Kneepatcher shook his head with the look of a man who had actually got the price he really wanted. 'You drive a hard bargain, but £30 it is.'

'We have a deal,' Aiden said, shaking Mr Kneepatcher's hand.

'Wonderful!' Mr Kneepatcher said, clapping his hands together. 'Now, would sir like a cravat with that?'

As Aiden walked back to The Sheep's Stirrup he was thinking about Humphrey. He knew that Mrs Perriwinkle would look after the little dog until he could return home, and she'd give him a hard time for leaving Humphrey alone for so long. A nice box of chocolate gingers would probably soften the level of Mrs Perriwinkle's scolding, and he'd make it up to Humphrey by taking him on a really long walk, including canal swimming, and buy him some serious doggy treats, maybe even some steak.

And so, feeling slightly better, Aiden crossed the road in front of the pub, just as the sun began to set. In the clear sky above, the first speckles of starlight appeared, like the distant lanterns of faraway travellers. He drew in a long breath from the clean, crisp air and smiled; blissfully unaware that this was actually the calm before the storm.

CHAPTER 11 – METAL AND CURRY

As Aiden walked into the pub he was greeted by the sight of one of the biggest drum kits he'd ever seen; two huge bass drums, eight concert toms, a huge floor tom, a very deep, steel snare drum, at least ten cymbals of varying sizes, and the obligatory peddle-operated hi-hat cymbals. A couple of side-lights on the wall shone down, highlighting the polished chrome fittings, in stark contrast to the gloss black finish of the drums themselves.

Maurice was behind the bar, watching the band set up and cleaning glasses. 'Would you like a drink, Aiden?'

'No, thanks, I'd better take this lot up to my room,' he said, pointing at the large bag of clothes he'd purchased from Mr Kneepatcher.

Room 11 was pretty much as Aiden had pictured it in his mind. It was scrupulously clean with two very neatly made single beds, both with little bedside tables and accompanying lamps. There was a writing desk and chair by the window, and a large, oak wardrobe stood ominously in the far corner next to the television. The adjoining bathroom was bright and immaculate, plus it even had a little cupboard stocked with toiletries, including a new toothbrush and toothpaste.

Aiden was quite surprised to see a television, and he made a mental note to ask Cracky more about the history of this reality after they'd had their conversation tomorrow. As there didn't appear to be a remote control, he simply pressed the 'On' button.

'Good day, you're watching the Blacktie News channel,' a man dressed in a dark suit with a flamboyant cravat said. 'Welcome to the news at six. Today, our glorious leader, the revered, ennobled, handsome, clever, artistic, charming, well-endowed and virile Baron Blacktie announced that all entries for The Cestrian Music Tournament 1987 have been received and that the tournament will take place this Wednesday at the Grand Gateway Theatre, Chester. On this year's judging panel will be none other than Colin

Mowsel, the Head of Dee Records. As this year celebrates the tournament's 100th anniversary, Mr Mowsel has kindly agreed that the winner will receive a one-album international recording deal. As usual, the entries have been wide and varied, covering the entire spectrum of musical styles... apart from heavy rock and metal, which, of course, the Baron has banned. In other news, a local hair salon had its flatulence license revoked after being reported for exceeding its allocated number of farts per hour. The owners of the salon blamed the events on the accidental inclusion of Bishop's Bowel Bubbler cheese in the selection of hors d'oeuvres being offered to customers. Also, a local man stands accused of the heinous crime of cheese sniffing without consent. Witnesses say that whilst in the Pandemonium of Cheese outlet store, he blatantly sniffed cheese already purchased by Mr Douglas Crumbly-Texture. An angry mob gave chase and eventually cornered the man, who was then handed over to the authorities. If found guilty, he will be sentenced to the maximum penalty of extreme forced teeth flossing and fifteen years of community service...'

Aiden shook his head and switched off the television, and then the floor began to rumble. 'Can I have a bit more bass in the monitors,' Agnar shouted to Oldfart, who was manning the mixing desk situated at the back of the room.

'Okay, try that,' Oldfart said, twisting one of the little knobs on the desk. Smid played a few notes and Agnar gave Oldfart the thumbs up.

As Aiden wandered up to the bar, drawn to the sound check like a moth to a flame, the front door of the pub was flung open and the huge Viking he'd seen on the ship earlier in the day walked in, with a guitar case and a ridiculously shiny helmet.

'May Odin bless your wind!' Olaf the Berserker shouted, followed by a loud fart.

'May Odin bless your wind!' the other members of Sacred Wind shouted back, responding with farts of their own.

'Where've you been, Olaf? Assuming you are Olaf,' Smid said, shielding his eyes. 'I can't really make out your face because of the glare coming off your helmet.'

'Well, you know what Ophelia's like,' Olaf said. 'She wants me to look my best so she just kept on rubbing!'

'Was that after she'd finished shining your helmet?' Grundi said, laughing.

'Very funny, Grundi,' Olaf said, with a grin. 'And I know that I've gotten out of carrying any gear in, but I'll make sure do plenty of humping after the show.'

'We can imagine,' said Smid.

'Is Roisin coming to the gig with Ophelia later on?' Agnar asked.

'She is,' Olaf replied, 'but you're not going after her again, are you? I fear you'll have no luck there, my friend.'

Agnar looked slightly crestfallen and gave his snare drum a good whack. 'We've already had this conversation,' Grundi said to Olaf.

Olaf took his guitar out of its case and plugged it into his amplifier, which was sat on top of two large speaker cabinets. He checked the tuning and then walked up to the microphone, perched high on its stand in front of him. 'One, two, one, two,' he said, checking that it was actually switched on. 'Right, shall we have a run through *"Metal and Curry"*?'

'Why not,' Agnar replied, counting them in. 'One, two, three…'

The first thing that struck Aiden was how good they were. If truth be told he was expecting a bit of a train crash. However, they were all more than competent musicians and Olaf's voice was superb.

'Hello there, Aiden,' Oldfart shouted, as Aiden joined him behind the mixing desk. 'Glad you could make it. What do you think?'

As Aiden listened closely to the band's sound, it quickly became obvious that he could radically improve it. Oldfart's experience at mixing appeared to involve pushing the little slider controls for the levels to create a balance, but didn't extend to tweaking the equalisation and other knobs on the mixing desk to enhance the sound. Not wishing to be rude, but itching to make the changes he knew would make a drastic improvement, he decided to combine diplomacy with fact.

'Pretty impressive, I have to say, but the bass guitar sounds a little muddy.'

'You sound like you have some experience here, my friend.' Oldfart said.

'It's a hobby of mine, actually,' Aiden replied.

Oldfart could see that Aiden was like a dog waiting patiently to be told he could now have the bone being held in his master's hand. 'To be honest, this isn't really my area of expertise. So, if you wish, I'm quite happy to let you take the console, so to speak. Our last mixing engineer had a bad experience at his bank, I'm afraid, and we've not been able to find a replacement.'

'Was he overdrawn by any chance?' Aiden asked.

'Sadly, yes,' Oldfart answered, 'it may take some time for his ears to recover.'

Aiden went at the knobs on the desk like a man on a mission, tweaking and twiddling away. He gave the bass more punch and tone, gave the drums more crack and sparkle, gave the guitars a much more defined and powerful sound, and stopped Olaf sounding like he was singing through a sock.

'That's incredible,' Oldfart said. 'I've never heard them sound as good as that before. You, my young friend, are a genius.'

The band stopped playing and Oldfart waved them over. 'This is Mr Aiden Peersey,' he said, introducing Aiden to the band, 'and, if he has nothing better to do this evening, I think we should ask him to mix the sound for us. It's powerful enough to stir Odin's bowels, trust me.'

'I'd love to,' Aiden said. It seemed like the natural thing to do.

Agnar gave Aiden a friendly smack on the back, which nearly pushed most of his internal organs through his rib cage. 'Well done, my scruffy-haired friend! This place is going to be rocking tonight!'

CHAPTER 12 – THE NAME OF VENGEANCE IS SACRED WIND!

'Are we nearly there, Saffy?' King Beef Vindaloo-Boiled Rice III said, bubbling with excitement.

'Honestly, Vindy, you're acting like a young curry whose rice has just been boiled for the first time,' Queen Chicken Tikka Masala-Coconut Rice said affectionately to her husband.

'I know, I know, Tikky. But it seems like ages since I've been able to loosen up and just let everything slide around my plate.'

'We're just coming into Llangollen now, Your Majesty,' Saffy shouted, from the driver's seat at the front of the carriage. 'I can see The Sheep's Stirrup from here.'

Within a minute or so they pulled into the carriage park next to the pub and the driver tethered the horses, before disappearing inside, carrying Saffy.

It was now 8:00 pm and The Sheep's Stirrup had transformed from a quiet country pub into a heady mix of chatter, laughter, music and dancing. People and sheep mingled happily together and conversation was light and joyful, the perfect end to a day of celebration. Two members of the OSO, Oriana Oftsheared (flute) and Cliff Corriedale (cello, and nephew of Charles) were performing a lively impromptu duet in the corner, and a small congregation of children and lambs were showing their appreciation through traditional dance.

'Hello, General, lovely to see you again,' Maurice said as the driver placed Saffy on the increasingly busy bar. 'Are the "special guests" outside? I have a table prepared for them.'

'They are indeed, Maurice, and it's equally pleasant to be in your company once more,' Saffy said. 'The King is very excited; I thought he was going to lose his chutney at one point during our trip.'

'Typical! It'll be good to see Vindy again,' Maurice laughed. 'Is Her Majesty still looking as delectable as ever?'

'She is, and although she's a bit more composed than His Majesty, I know that she's really looking forward to the evening. Are the two rooms ready, by the way?'

'Yes. The King and Queen are in the deluxe suite in Room 1 and you're right next door in Room 2.'

'Excellent, and thanks again, Maurice. I'll go and escort them in,' Saffy said, beckoning the driver to pick him up. 'Is there any sign of the other "guests" as yet?'

'I'm assured that the good Doctor and the General will be arriving at around 10:00 pm. I've reserved a room for them too.'

Upstairs, Aiden was just finishing his bath. Given all the trials, tribulations and shocks of the day so far, it was nice to soak peacefully in warm water and suds, letting the stress just drain away. Oldfart had treated him to a quite excellent bar meal of steak and chips, and he was genuinely looking forward to the evening's events. After he'd dried himself with one of the sizeable, fluffy towels in the bathroom, he started to get dressed and overheard voices in the corridor.

'Now remember, let's simply mingle in with the crowd and try not to attract too much attention,' Mr Breezy said.

'Understood,' replied Mr Waft.

'Let's see what we can find out about the mine from this Agnar, but let's not be too pushy and make him suspect we have any ulterior motives.'

'Good plan,' Mr Waft agreed.

Aiden opened the door as Mr Breezy and Mr Waft were making their way down the stairs. Although he couldn't quite make out what they'd been saying, he had an uneasy feeling about them. As he made his way to the bar he saw Cracky chatting to Maurice. 'Hello, Aiden. How's your room then?' Maurice asked.

'It's lovely, Maurice, really welcoming.'

'Would you like a drink?' Cracky said.

'I would, thanks. Just an orange juice though, I'm mixing the band later.'

'Are you now? My, you are full of surprises. Orange juice it is then, and can I have another pint of Riggley's Piddle, please, Maurice.'

As Maurice poured the drinks, Aiden turned and saw three of the most beautiful women he'd ever seen in his life walking towards him. They were all quite petite, and he almost felt himself physically melt as they noticed him and collectively smiled. There was a stunning blond girl in a green outfit, a sultry brunette, dressed in black, and a gorgeous redhead, whose exquisite face was set off by a mass of copper-coloured curls. She gave Aiden another smile, as they stood at the bar next to him, and said 'Hi, fella,' in a lilting Scottish accent. They all had quite extraordinary green eyes, curvaceous figures and very shapely... gossamer wings.

'Queen Ophelia, what a delightful pleasure to see you and your charming friends again,' Maurice said. 'To have my establishment blessed by the sight of such beauty is a gift beyond price.'

'Oh, you smooth talker, Maurice,' Ophelia replied 'Are you flirting with me?'

'I might be Your Majesty,' Maurice said, smiling. 'Would the Queen like her customary gin and tonic?'

'Yes, please, Maurice. Roisin, what would you like?' she said to the raven-haired beauty.

'Ooh, let me see, can I have a vodka and lemonade, please,' Roisin replied, in a beguiling Irish brogue.

'What about you, Mara?' Ophelia asked the lovely redhead.

'I'd like a whisky and blackcurrant please,' Mara replied. 'Not too heavy on the blackcurrant, though, Maurice.'

Cracky gave Aiden a quick dig in the ribs. 'If you don't close your mouth soon, my lad, you'll be letting flies in.'

'Oh, right,' Aiden said, tearing away his open-mouthed gaze and trying to regain his composure.

'I gather you've not seen too many faeries before,' Cracky said, smiling

'Er, no, not really.'

'The blond girl there is Queen Ophelia,' he explained. 'She's engaged to Olaf, believe it or not. Her two friends are actually her hand maidens. I think Mara has her eye on you.'

'Hey, Cracky, who's the new eye candy?' Mara said, pointing at Aiden.

'This splendid chap here is Aiden Peersey,' Cracky said, putting his arm on Aiden's shoulder. 'He's visiting these parts, although somehow he's managed to get himself a job mixing the band tonight.'

'Nice to meet you Aiden,' Mara said, winking at him. 'Perhaps we can have a chat later on.'

'Mara, you're such a flirt,' Ophelia said, giggling. And with that the three girls grabbed their drinks, waved at Aiden and were escorted to an awaiting table by Maurice.

'It's quite a night for royalty, you know,' Cracky said, taking a long slurp from his tankard. 'Do you see that table over there in the corner? Well, believe it or not, that's the King and Queen of Wrexham. They visit every so often, but always unannounced.'

Aiden looked over at the two young people sitting at the table, with three plates of curry in front of them. 'They look so normal,' he remarked.

'Well, as I said, they don't like to draw attention to themselves on trips like this, so they tend to dress down a bit. Would you like me to introduce you?'

The closest Aiden had ever got to meeting royalty was when the Queen of England waved and smiled at him on one of her visits to Wales. He was only three-years old at the time and dropped his ice cream in the excitement. As he'd already had the pleasure of meeting one queen this evening, and given that he didn't have an ice cream in his hand…

'Yes, I'd be happy to.'

'Okay, I'll pop over to say hello and ask if I can introduce you.'

Cracky wandered over to the table and shook the hands of the two young people whose smiles and easy manner indicated they'd met him before. After a brief conversation, Cracky beckoned Aiden over with a wave.

'Very pleased to meet you Your Majesty,' Aiden said to the young man, bowing slightly and keeping a firm hold on his drink. 'And also you, Your Majesty, and you look radiant, if I may be so bold,' he said to the beautiful young woman.

'Oh, he's very charming, Cracky. I see why you like him so much,' the young woman said, without moving her lips.

'Indeed, he seems like a splendid fellow. Pleased to meet you Aiden,' the young man said, also not moving his lips.

Given Aiden's previous experience with telepathic cats, he remained completely at ease with this new-found form of communication. He even tried it himself by thinking 'thank you, Your Majesty.'

'Am I to understand that you are meeting some "friends" later?' Cracky enquired.

'We are,' the young woman said, again without moving her lips. 'The good Doctor and General should be joining us around 10:00 pm. It's about time we got together to talk.'

Then the young man actually spoke. 'Pardon me, Your Majesty, but some of your mango chutney is about to slide off your plate, shall I take care of this for you?'

'Oh, yes please, Harold,' King Beef Vindaloo-Boiled Rice III said.

Aiden dropped his glass on the floor *(see appendix 3)*.

'Are you alright, young man? You look like you've seen a ghost,' General Lamb Korma-Saffron Rice said to him.

Aiden realised that this new voice seemed to be coming from the third plate of curry on the table, bubbling ever so slightly as the words hit his ears. 'Yes, I'm fine, thanks. My glass just slipped that's all, I'll go and get a cloth.'

Maurice had already heard the noise and appeared armed with a cloth and a small dustpan and brush. 'Sorry, Maurice,' Aiden said.

'Oh, don't worry about it these things happen all the time in here. It won't be the last broken glass this evening.'

'Anyway,' Cracky interjected. 'We'll take our leave at this point and let your Majesties drink up the atmosphere, and importantly the music. The band should be arriving shortly.'

'I'm really looking forward to seeing them,' Tikky said, bubbling. 'They play such great songs. I'll just have to watch that my husband here doesn't get too carried away.'

When they returned to the bar, Cracky gave Aiden a look which suggested he already knew the answer to the question he was about to ask. 'So, I'm guessing that you've not seen too many curries either?'

'Oh, I've seen plenty of curries before, Cracky, I've just haven't come across any with the power of speech.'

Cracky laughed. 'Well, as we said, let's have a chat tomorrow. I'm beginning to think the more I understand of your situation the more I'll be able to help.'

Aiden ordered them another drink and it was at this point that he noticed a large plaque behind the bar.

'The Sheep's Stirrup is hereby granted a license to permit flatulence in this establishment under the following conditions – Monday to Saturday inclusive:

1) No more than a total of ten farts per hour from the hours of 12:00 – 2:00 pm.
2) No more than twenty farts per hour between the hours of 6:00 – 9:00 pm.
3) No more than thirty farts per hour from 9:00 – 11:00 pm.

A special dispensation is also granted, thereby permitting a "happy hour" of unlimited farts at the proprietor's discretion on a twice weekly basis. Flatulence is not allowed on Sundays under any circumstances.'

It was signed *'B V Blacktie'*.

The atmosphere in the pub was building nicely and Aiden was enjoying himself. Mr Kneepatcher had arrived feeling 'all of a dither', wearing a bright blue shirt and cravat, and Maurice introduced Aiden to his brother, Henry Fluffywool. Henry was delighted at the compliments Aiden paid to the OSO. 'You have sublime taste, young man,' he'd said.

Mr Breezy and Mr Waft were sat at the end of the bar being generally cordial, without getting involved in any meaningful conversations. They had asked Maurice if he would let them know when Agnar arrives, to which Maurice had cryptically replied 'oh, you'll know when he gets here'.

Aiden was wondering where Oldfart had disappeared to when he arrived at the front door, with a strangely dressed companion; a very short man with a floor-length black cloak. The hood of the cloak covered the majority of his face, with the remaining features obscured by a tightly-wound, black scarf. His hands were barely visible at the end of the sleeves and he seemed to be wearing ill-fitting gloves. He was holding a large notepad in one hand and a pen in the other. Oldfart led him over to the table next to the mixing desk and then headed straight for Aiden.

'The band will be here any minute,' he said. 'Let's go and get ready.'

Next to the mixing desk was a cassette deck. Oldfart produced a tape out of his jacket pocket, inserted it into the deck and pressed play. He also pressed a button on the console adjacent to the desk and dry ice started to fill the room. Maurice switched the pub's main lights down low and Oldfart flicked a couple of switches on the lighting console. Four strategically-placed spotlights lit up and shone through the atmospheric fog. A low rumble emanated from the PA speakers and then erupted with the sound of thunder.

'Today, four great warriors will take to the battlefield. They have been sent by Odin himself to vanquish the foes of freedom, to conquer the enemies of valour, and to triumph over those who repress our right to fart freely.'

The crowd cheered.

'For vengeance has a name, and let this name strike fear into the hearts of all who seek to follow the path of injustice, tyranny and persecution; for the name of vengeance is SACRED WIND!'

The crowd cheered again.

Anthemic orchestral music started to blare through the PA as the narrator said *'Can you hear the sounds of battle? Can you feel the thunder stir your bowels? They have the power of wind and metal coursing through their veins, and they have come to free you from fear and destruction. Behold, they are here!'*

Oldfart ran over to the front door of the pub. 'Prepare for Sacred Wind. Your salvation has arrived!' he exhorted, opening the door and pointing outside.

The crowd didn't need that much of an invitation and the vast majority ran out into the street. The air was still and all was silent, apart from the faraway hooting of a solitary owl, a melancholy lament echoing wistfully in the night. And then the silence was broken by the sound of hooves, distant and indistinct to start with but growing closer by the second.

Coming over the bridge in front of the pub were two giant, black horses, their riders twirling their weapons above their heads. On the road to the left another black horse and rider could be seen, and then another on the road to the right. They were equidistant from each other and approaching at breakneck speed. They screeched to a halt in front of the pub and the riders reared their horses, clashing weapons in a show of solidarity. 'For metal, for glory, for honour and for Odin!' Olaf the Berserker shouted, twirling his huge broadsword around his head. 'May Odin bless your wind!'

'May Odin bless your wind!' the crowd outside shouted.

'Right,' said Oldfart, 'let's get the flashbombs ready.'

CHAPTER 13 – MY SWORD IS MY SWORD

Aiden reckoned he got his sight back after about twenty seconds or so and really wished he'd listened to Oldfart when he told him not to look at the stage. By this time, Sacred Wind were blasting out the instrumental overture to their first song and the atmosphere in The Sheep's Stirrup was crackling with anticipation. The overture ended with a mighty crescendo, followed by some very impressive guitar, bass and drum interplay. A crunching guitar riff and lead solo then set the scene for eight bars before Olaf burst into song…

We drop our pants for Odin
And climb upon our steeds
We pass the Sacred Wind
Until our bottoms bleed
It's all in praise of Odin
We feel him in our hearts
For he gives us our power
And we give him our farts

Fart for Odin, Fart for Odin
Raise you bottom to the sky
Fart for Odin, Fart for Odin
Spread your cheeks, spread them wide
Fart for Odin, Fart for Odin
Let your bottom burp with pride
Fart for Odin, Fart for Odin
To the circle of wind we ride

The Sheep's Stirrup was indeed 'rocking'. The crowd were obviously familiar with the song and sang along enthusiastically to the chorus. Mr Kneepatcher had fainted as soon as Olaf had started to sing and was being revived by Roisin. 'Ooh, have you seen how tight his pants are. I'm all of a dither again!' he said, fanning himself with his hand.

Aiden adjusted the sound and equalization levels slightly, to account for the fact that the place was now filled with people and sheep. It was sounding pretty good; loud, but clear as a bell.

We hail the mighty Asgard
With fire in our veins
In all its strength and majesty
In flatulence it reigns
Oh hear this mighty Odin
From one who is so true
My rear end shakes like thunder
As I let one go for you

Fart for Odin, Fart for Odin
Raise you bottom to the sky
Fart for Odin, Fart for Odin
Spread your cheeks, spread them wide
Fart for Odin, Fart for Odin
Let your bottom burp with pride
Fart for Odin, Fart for Odin
To the circle of wind we ride

A symphonic mid-section had the crowd waving their hands in the air and Henry Fluffywool turning his nose up disapprovingly. Grundi the Windy then launched into a screaming guitar solo and Aiden was treated to the sight of some sheep playing air guitar... quite well, actually.

It was at this point that he noticed the strangely-dressed, small man that had arrived with Oldfart. The little chap was scribbling away on his notepad, hardly ever looking up and actually watching the band.

'Fart for Odin' reached its rip-roaring finale and The Sheep's Stirrup exploded with cheers and applause. 'It's good to be back,' Olaf shouted, with a huge grin on his face. 'So, are you people ready for metal?'

'Yes!' screamed the crowd.

'Are you people ready for curry?'

'Yes!' the crowd screamed again, and General Lamb Korma-Saffron Rice looked around nervously, raising one of his mini poppadoms in the air protectively.

'Well, if you're ready for metal and you're ready for curry, what are you ready for?'

'Metal and Curry!' roared the crowd.
'I can't hear you!' Olaf screamed back.
'Metal and Curry!' roared the crowd again, much louder.
'Metal and Curry!' screamed Olaf, and off they went.

Another town, another pub
Another place where I can get my grub
My axe is honed
It's in fine fettle
My pants are tight
And I'm ready for metal

Metal and Curry, Metal and Curry
Give it to me now 'cause I'm in a hurry
Metal and Curry, Metal and Curry
Pile my plate high and there'll be no worries

'Try not to listen to the words, Your Majesty,' Saffy said to Tikky. 'They may upset you.'

'Oh, don't be so prudish, Saffy. It's only a song,' Tikky replied. 'Anyway, I like this one, it really tenderises my chicken.'

'Tikky!' Vindy cried. 'You shouldn't say such things in public... you should wait until we're alone afterwards,' he added, simmering ever so slightly.

Another night, another gig
Another table
And my plate is big
The crowds are wild, they don't want no crock
They're primed for metal
And they're ready to rock

Metal and Curry, Metal and Curry
Give it to me now 'cause I'm in a hurry
Metal and Curry, Metal and Curry
Pile my plate high and there'll be no worries
Metal and Curry, Metal and Curry
Give me poppadoms too cause I want a full tummy
Metal and Curry, Metal and Curry
Make my plate big, don't be a dummy

Olaf and Grundi then executed a scintillating guitar dual, with Smid and Agnar hammering away in the background. Mr Kneepatcher was at the front of the crowd continually supplicating himself in front of Olaf.

As the band continued with classic songs such as 'Warriors of Asgard' (which contained quite a few references to buxom damsels in distress), 'Rock, Rock, Rock, Rock Ragnarok' (which told of the doom of the gods when 'all things will go boom') and 'The Power of Cheese,' (which paid homage to… cheese), Aiden was convinced that Sacred Wind were one of the best live bands he'd ever seen, even if the lyrics did seem slightly ridiculous on occasion.

'What do you think, then?' Oldfart said.

'They're fantastic, Oldfart. I can't believe I've not come across them before.' And then he remembered where he was.

'This one's for all the ladies, ewes and chicken tikkas in the audience,' Olaf shouted, to the screams of ladies, the high pitched baaing of ewes and the hysterical yelp of delight from Queen Chicken Tikka Masala-Coconut Rice. 'This is called *"Sail with Me"*.'

I was just a fool
Playing by the rules
Ravaging and pillaging
And trying to look cool
Then you made me see
All that life can be
Now you are inside my heart
I want you here with me

Stay by my side
Make my life complete, baby
You are the one, you're my light
Now you've made my helmet shine

Sail with me
Now I've found you I never wanna let you go
Hold my oar
Forever more
Sail with me
Now I've found you I never wanna let you go
Hold my oar
Forever more

Mr Breezy and Mr Waft stayed glued to the bar while the band continued to play. They sipped their drinks politely but looked increasingly uncomfortable. 'How long is it until they finish?' Mr Breezy asked Maurice.

'Oh, well they're due off stage at about 10:00 pm, so I guess about another fifteen minutes or so. Are you enjoying the concert, gentlemen?'

'It's an experience we'll always remember,' said Mr Waft, with a deadpan face.

'It's just a pity they can't play in the Cestrian Music Tournament next week,' Maurice said. 'I'm sure they'd have a great chance of winning.'

'I'm sure they would indeed light up that particular event,' Mr Breezy said, with barely concealed sarcasm.

Henry Fluffywool was stood next to them and couldn't help overhearing. 'Of course it's not real music,' he said. 'I'll grant they can play their instruments and sing, but where are the nuances, the subtle counterpoints, the soft adagios, the delicate pastorals, the exhilarating allegros?'

'Yes, it's not really our cup of tea either,' said Mr Breezy. 'Our tastes are more, how shall we say, quieter.'

'I couldn't agree more, my good man,' Henry said. 'Give me a nice flute concerto any day and I'm happy as a ram in mating season.'

'This next song is for the Viking on my left,' Olaf said, as he and Grundi picked up acoustic guitars. 'For a long time now, Grundi the Windy has been in love.'

'Aah,' said the crowd.

'But this is a love that is unrequited,' continued Olaf.

'Aah,' said the crowd again, and Grundi looked genuinely downcast.

'For he is in love with a goddess; and not just any goddess, but the wife of our Lord Odin himself.'

'Ooh,' sighed the crowd.

'Long has he yearned for her beauty, long has he yearned for her touch, long has he yearned to smell her armpits, but alas this is something that can never be.'

Grundi shook his head, dejectedly.

'And so, in honour of our friend's love we have written this song about the goddess of his dreams. This is called *'Frigg'*.'

Aiden panicked a bit, because there hadn't been any sound check for the acoustic guitars. Fortunately they both sounded crisp and tuneful through the PA. Olaf's voice was tender and mellow, and several members of the audience held little lanterns aloft. Dry ice drifted out from the stage area, creating a soft and wispy blanket that went up to everyone's knees.

In times of silence
I think of you
You're in my dreams when I sleep
And my heart when I wake
You are my goddess
And my sword is yours

*Your beauty shines like the sun
As my tears fall like rain*

Then Oldfart hit the flashbomb button again as the chorus erupted.

*Frigg… your face is eternal
Frigg… your body is divine
Frigg… your mouth speaks only wisdom
Frigg… your armpits smell of wine
I wish I could be your lover
Odin's such a lucky bugger
Frigg*

Another heartstring-pulling verse followed and things really took off after the second chorus, when the guitar solo kicked in. Grundi played as though his life depended on it, hitting soaring notes, ripping through blindingly fast arpeggios and ending up on his knees with his head thrust backwards. The audience went crazy and Mr Kneepatcher was in tears. 'I love you Grundi,' he shouted, waving his tear-soaked hanky.

One of the other bar staff whispered something in Maurice's ear and he nodded in understanding. He picked up his cleaning cloth and walked over to the King and Queen's table. 'Your Majesties, I am informed that the other "guests" have arrived. They are presently awaiting your company in the room I have prepared upstairs. I have taken the liberty of telling them it would be better to wait until the band have finished before having discussions.'

'Thank you, Maurice,' Vindy said. 'That makes sense. And, as much as I'm looking forward to meeting our esteemed guests, it would be a pity to miss the end of the show.'

'I second that,' said Tikky.

As the noise of the crowd died down, Olaf held onto the microphone stand with two hands, letting his guitar hang loose on its strap. 'I'm afraid that this is our last number for this evening.'

'Aw,' the crowd cried.

'But, I'd just like to say that when we play our next gig, the audience there will have a lot to live up to, because tonight you've shown that Llangollen is the most rock 'n' roll town in the land!'

The crowd went completely wild, whooping and hollering. 'This is for all of you. It's called *"Sacred Wind"*. Now let me see some hands!'

And so the band launched into their theme tune with virtually the entire pub clapping along. Even General Lamb Korma-Saffron Rice was clicking his mini poppadoms together.

I can feel it building
From deep down inside
Can you see my cheeks tremble
As the gases start to rise
It's the breath of Odin
And it's forever hallowed
You better head for the hills now
Cause it's about to explode!

You can run
And you can hide
But you're never gonna last
Cause you'll be felled
By my sword
And a blast from my ass!

Feel the power of my wind
Sacred wind
Feel the power of my wind
Sacred Wind
Sacred Wind

See my foes as they scatter
As they flee from the smell
With my sword and wind with me
I'll send them straight to hell!
And they'll take a message
To tell to far and near
About the power of my sword
And of my bottom of fear

'Sacred Wind' ended with more flashbombs, dry ice and the stage area awash with strobe lighting. Then everything went black and when the lights came up the band were gone.

'More! More! More!' yelled the crowd, apart from the sheep who yelled 'Baa! Baa! Baa!'

A minute or so of wild applause passed and then the lights went down once more. A single spotlight shone and Olaf the Berserker appeared. 'Thank you so much. We love you all!' he roared. 'Now, we do have one more song for you.'

'Here we go,' said Oldfart. 'This should be pretty spectacular.'

'Many years ago there were men who wished to keep both people and sheep in a state of fear. They were bad men. What were they?' he asked the crowd.

'Bad men!' shouted the crowd.

'When we saw the deprivation these men had wrought, we knew we had no choice but to intervene. So, this song is based on a true story. It's called *"My Sword is my Sword".'*

The crowd went potty as Olaf, Grundi and Smid played the opening notes. Agnar battered a fast drum fill and then they were off; a galloping double-bass drum beat supported scything guitar and bass, with Grundi playing an emotion-filled guitar solo.

When we came to this land
There was evil in the fields
The trees had no leaves
And the sheep were in trauma
So we made a solemn vow
And gathered up our arms
And rode past all the farms
And the people were waving
(We said)

Have no fear
Help is here
And we ride now to bring you salvation
This is our song
It will make us strong
It will free you from fear and destruction

My sword is my sword
My shield is my shield
Together we ride
Into the battlefield
And our foes will fall
At our feet
As we fight
For honour
And glory

The audience sang along joyously to the chorus and even Aiden felt compelled to join in. The little fellow with the cloak was getting very giddy, trying to clap along while holding his notepad and pen... which he dropped on the floor.

'Bless my clacky hooves,' he said, as he picked it up. It was a voice Aiden found vaguely familiar.

*So we polished our steel
And rode to the bad men's castle
We said there would be no hassle
If they left the people alone
But they laughed at us and swore
And showered us with spears
But we did not show fear
And that's when we got our swords out
(We said)*

*You will fall
Death will call
He waits now in anticipation
We will not fail
Yes, we will prevail
So for death now you should make preparation*

    A second uplifting chorus was followed by yet another virtuoso guitar solo from Grundi… and that's when the two armed warriors burst through the door.
    The crowd parted so the two warriors could get to the stage area, where they began clashing swords and hammering away at each other's shields. The sound of metal on metal was audible above the PA as the music died down to a whisper. Then Olaf sang again, accompanied only by a dulcet bass line from Smid.

*The battle was fierce
But we stood our ground
And their shields broke
As our swords crashed down*

Then the band came in with crushing staccato bursts.

*And so they got scared
And they ran away
So we sang our song
We had won the day*

    Somewhat inevitably there was an audience participation section, with more singing, baaing, clapping, poppadom clicking and lanterns, before the final chorus and massive flashbomb-littered finale. The band left the stage to thunderous applause and, after acknowledging the appreciative crowd, went straight over to the large table Maurice had reserved for Queen Ophelia, Roisin and Mara. Ophelia jumped up and gave Olaf a big kiss before sitting down on his knee.

'Right, then,' Oldfart said to Aiden, as he switched off the PA and lighting rigs. 'I don't know about you, but I need a drink.'

As they walked over to the table, Aiden looked around to see if the little fellow in the cloak was joining them, but to his surprise he was nowhere to be seen.

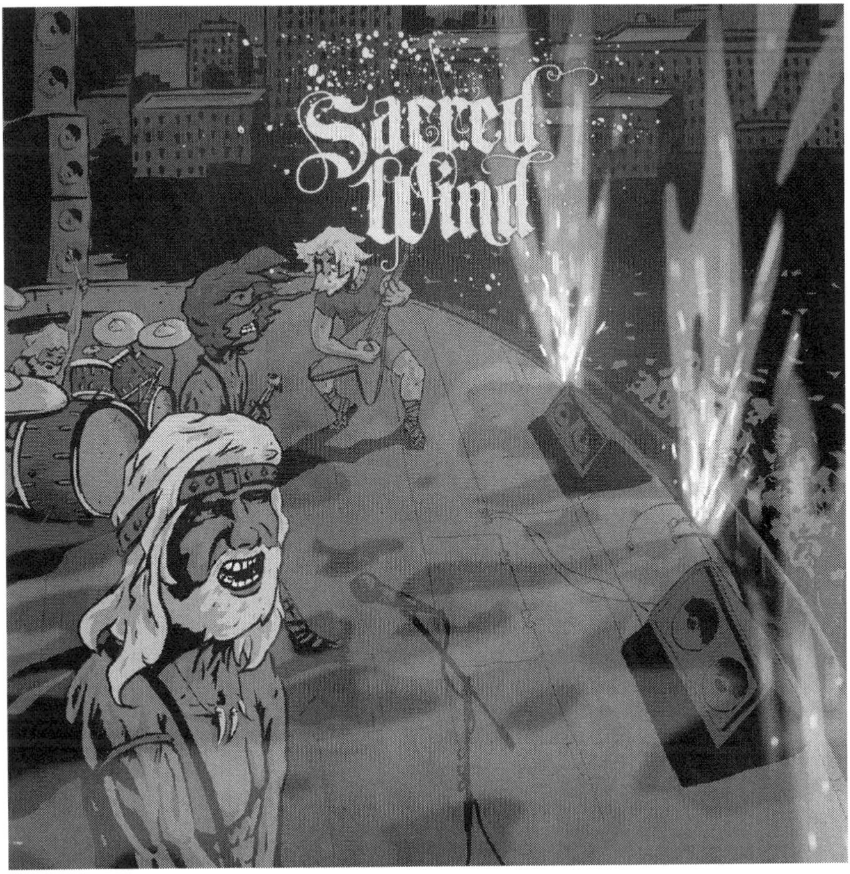
Sacred
Wind

CHAPTER 14 – OOH, CAN I HAVE YOUR AUTOGRAPH, PLEASE?

'To good health, to Odin and to all of you, my friends,' Olaf said, raising his tankard high, before farting loudly. 'And you, Aiden Peersey, gave us the best sound we've ever had on stage, so… to Aiden,' he added, raising his glass again.

'Yes, the sound was fantastic,' Mara said to Aiden, smiling invitingly. 'You were wonderful.' Then she turned to Ophelia and whispered 'I'm going to kiss him afterwards.'

'Do you have to kiss every nice boy you meet?' Ophelia whispered back.

'No, of course not… only the really good looking ones!'

Agnar was sitting next to Roisin, trying to look as appealing as a puppy. 'Did you enjoy the gig, Roisin?'

'You were excellent, Agnar. One of your best shows ever.'

'In which case could I possibly have a celebratory kiss?'

'No, don't be so cheeky!' she said, smacking his hand.

Agnar's face dropped and he took a dejected slurp from his tankard. 'He is very sweet, Roisin. And he obviously really likes you,' Ophelia said to her. 'Maybe you should give him a chance.'

'He is sweet, Ophy, but he's not really my type.'

Unsurprisingly, Sacred Wind were the centre of attention and they were quite happy to shake hands, sign autographs and chat to everybody. 'Let me through, let me through!' Mr Kneepatcher shouted, squeezing his way through the throng of people surrounding the table.

'Ooh, can I have your autograph, please?' he said, stuffing a photo of the band and a pen into Olaf's face.'

'Of, course,' Olaf said. 'Who do I make it out to?'

'To my good friend Gilbert Kneepatcher,' said Mr Kneepatcher.

Olaf wrote the message on the photo and signed it with a flourish. 'There you are, and thank you, Gilbert.'

'He called me Gilbert! He called me Gilbert! Mr Kneepatcher screamed. 'Ooh, my heart, my heart, I'm all of a dither.' And then he fainted again.

As the celebrations continued, Aiden noticed the two odd-looking men from room 13 making their way over to the table. 'I don't like the look of these two, Oldfart. I think they're up to something.'

'My good fellows,' said Mr Breezy. 'Firstly, we'd like to congratulate you on a most excellent show.'

'Indeed,' added Mr Waft. 'It was an experience to live long in the memory.'

'Thank you,' said Smid.

'But for us, the piece de resistance…' said Mr Breezy.

'The piece de resistance…' echoed Mr Waft.

'…was the drumming of Agnar the Hammered. Sir, we salute you.' Mr Breezy said, doffing his hat and bowing.

'We salute you,' echoed Mr Waft, mimicking Mr Breezy's doff and bow.

Agnar seemed quite taken aback. 'Well, thank you, gentlemen. Did you like my paradiddles?'

'Superb,' said Mr Breezy.

'Sublime,' said Mr Waft.

'And did you notice the snare drags in the verses of "Frigg"?'

'Almost poetic in their execution,' Mr Breezy gushed.

'Poetic indeed,' gushed Mr Waft.

'In fact, it would be a great honour if we could possibly spend some time in your company to discuss the finer merits of your playing,' Mr Breezy said.

'An honour,' said Mr Waft.

'I don't see why not,' a particularly flattered Agnar said. 'Grab yourself a couple of chairs and let's chat.'

Mr Breezy and Mr Waft listened patiently as Agnar talked them through drum tuning, double-bass drum playing, accidentally hitting your nose with a drumstick, and how he once thought he was having a spiritual experience during a drum solo.

'Mr the Hammered you are inspiring,' Mr Breezy complimented. 'It is surely a rarity to find a drummer who speaks with such intellect, erudition and passion. Why it's almost intoxicating.'

'Intoxicating,' said Mr Waft.

'But, may we be so bold as to ask you a non-drum related question that pertains to some information we received earlier today?'

Agnar was now very feeling very relaxed in their company, plus the three tankards of ale he'd drunk greatly assisted in loosening his tongue… which needed little encouragement on most occasions anyway. 'Fire away,' he said.

'We are men of many interests, Mr the Hammered.'

'Many interests,' Mr Waft echoed.

'One of these just happens to be a fascination with ancient structures, and we were told that the cheese mine near the Circle of Wind is in your possession now?'

'That old thing, oh, yes, it was a present from my cousin Angus McSvensson a few years back. Well, I say a present; it was more a request to take care of it.'

'So you do not actually own the property?' Mr Breezy said, with a worried sideways glance at Mr Waft.

'Oh, it's my mine alright,' Agnar said. 'I've got the paperwork somewhere. Mind you, I've only been inside once and I got chased out by bats.'

Mr Breezy rubbed his chin, feigning being in deep thought. 'Hmm, it could be that we may be able to help out here,' he said. 'A client of ours may be very interested in taking it off your hands, for a good price of course.'

'Oh, I couldn't sell it, Angus would kill me,' Agnar said. 'Although, I've not seen him for a bit so I could always ask him.'

'No, no,' Mr Breezy and Mr Waft said together, holding their hands out as if to avert an invisible danger.

'That will not be necessary,' Mr Breezy continued. 'We would not wish to be the cause of any potential family disagreements.'

He looked at Mr Waft and nodded. Mr Waft nodded back. 'Well, the hour is getting late and we must be up early tomorrow as we have a long journey ahead of us. So, if you don't mind we'll take our leave and retire to our room and into the arms of Morpheus.'

'Oh, well don't let me keep you, gentlemen,' Agnar said, winking. 'Is she a bit of alright, then?'

'Who?' Mr Waft said.

'Morpheus.'

'You misunderstand, Mr the Hammered,' Mr Breezy said, laughing. 'We are simply going to sleep.'

'Of course, I understand,' Agnar said, with another wink. 'Goodnight my friends and may your night be full of pleasure, naughty dreams and fragrant wind.'

'Good night, Mr the Hammered, it has been a joy to meet you,' Mr Breezy said, standing up and shaking Agnar's hand.

'A joy,' said Mr Waft. And with that they retired to room 13.

'What a complete idiot,' Hob said, as he sat on the bed. 'This complicates matters a great deal.'

'I agree,' said Nob. 'If he is unwilling to sell the mine, then the Baron may have to take it by force.'

'I doubt he'd want to do that, the McSvenssons are not people you would wish to cross. However, there may be another solution but we will need to talk to the Baron first.'

'Would this have anything to do with the tournament?' Nob said.

'It would, but we'll need more information. Let's get out of here after breakfast tomorrow morning and pay the Baron a visit.'

Down the corridor in room number 4, another conversation was taking place that would also have an impact on the momentous events to come. 'Your Majesties, it is good that we meet at last,' said Dr Lamb Dopiaza-Pilau Rice. 'And may I introduce you to the head of our armed forces, General Beef Madras-Wholegrain Rice.'

'Yes, it has been too long in coming,' Vindy replied. 'And I am delighted to make your acquaintance, General.'

'The honour is all mine,' the General replied.

'Indeed, my good Doctor,' Tikky said. 'We meet as friends with a common goal and I hope we will also leave as friends.'

'If I may,' the General said, 'I would like to share some information that has come to light that may force our plans to be expedited.'

'Go on, General,' Tikky said.

The curries were placed strategically on a large table near the window. Greta and Harold sat silently by. 'Harold, will you please check there is no-one eavesdropping outside the window?' Vindy said.

'Yes, Your Majesty,' Harold replied, pulling back the curtains and looking out the window. 'It looks clear, Your Majesty.'

'Please continue, General,' Vindy said.

'Mold has been subject to infiltration by two of Blacktie's spies. We fear they have already informed the Baron of our potential alliance.'

'That's not good,' said Tikky.

'Indeed,' continued the General. 'We may need to move sooner than we would have wished. As we speak, I have four battalions of our finest Spiced Chapatis, three battalions of Garlic Naans, four battalions of Samosa Commandoes, and our own Rogan Josh Imperial Guard ready to move. We could be at Chester within the day. If you could provide a similar force I feel we could take the city.'

'General, I do not doubt the quality and bravery of your forces, or of ours,' Saffy said, 'but to simply attempt to take the city in this way at present would be currycide.'

'Why so? We're led to believe that the Knights of Flatulence are engaged in the Scouseland Crusades. The city's defences are severely weakened by their absence.'

'Who told you that, General?' Saffy said. 'The Knights returned to Chester last week. If I were you I'd check your sources more carefully, and if I didn't know better I'd say you may have a saboteur in your ranks.'

'Did the information come from the Brotherhood, by any chance?' Dr Lamb Dopiaza-Pilau Rice asked.

'Yes,' replied the General.

'You suspect someone, Doctor?' Vindy said.

'Sadly, yes. Not all view this alliance of ours as salubrious. There is one in particular who has been most vocal in his opposition. He also holds supreme influence over the Brotherhood, and he advocates conflict with Wrexham as opposed to unity. If this is part of some subterfuge of his creation then I would guess that Your Majesties' safety may also be in jeopardy.'

'Whom do you speak of, Doctor?' Saffy said, angrily crunching a mini poppadom. 'I would seek words with this insolent and no doubt tasteless curry.'

'He was once a holy curry, a member of the Order of Dhansak. These were curried monks pledged to live the simple life. They gave up their spices, dispensing with fineries like Basil, Sage and Chives, and sought solace in prayer and meditation. Brother Vegetable Jalfrezi-Basmathi Rice was once a shining light in the Order, but something or someone turned him against the holy ways.'

'So now we have enemies within our own community,' said the General. 'These are sad times to be a curry.'

'At least we seemed to have foiled this particular plot,' Tikky said. 'And I'm sure you gentlemen will be doing your utmost to have a talk with this "monk" when you return.'

'I think Your Majesty can rely on that,' said the Doctor.

Downstairs, things were starting to wind down. Most folk had now left the pub and Aiden was beginning to feel very tired and slightly tipsy. He hadn't drunk that much, but the drink had gone straight to his head and he felt it was time to retire.

'Oh, you can't leave so soon,' Mara said, grabbing his arm as he got up off the chair.

'I'm sorry, Mara. You've all been delightful company but I'm absolutely beat. I'm sure we'll all meet again soon.'

'Well, here's something to remember me by,' she said, pulling him towards her and placing a lingering kiss on his lips. By the time she'd finished he was bright red and the table was full of smiles.

'Mr Aiden Peersey, you may consider yourself to be an honorary member of Sacred Wind,' Olaf said, raising his tankard again. 'So, to Aiden, the finest scruffy-haired mixing engineer we've ever had.'

'To Aiden,' everyone on the table said, raising their glasses and tankards in salute.

'Goodnight, Aiden. I wish you sweet dreams,' Mara said, waving as he walked up the stairs to his room.

And so, as he climbed into bed and fell asleep almost immediately, the strangest day in Aiden Peersey's life so far came to an end. He didn't know at the time, but as strange as this day had been, there would be even stranger days ahead.

CHAPTER 15 – I'VE HEARD YOUR SAUSAGES ARE TO DIE FOR

Bright sunlight sneaked surreptitiously through the curtains, as the sound of a cock crowing heralded the start of a new day. Aiden woke up with a start and looked at the little clock on the bedside table. It said 8:05 am. The delicious aroma of bacon and sausages infiltrated his nose and he sat up, stretching. He looked around the quaint room, his eyes blinking as the rays of the sun danced across his face.

He took a quick shower, brushed his teeth and felt considerably more awake after his morning ablutions. His stomach was imploring him to stop ignoring the smell of breakfast, so he got dressed and wandered downstairs.

The Sheep's Stirrup had a small restaurant area, in a room adjacent to the bar, and several guests were already availing themselves of the early morning fare.

'Good morning,' Mr Breezy said, through a mouthful of toast.

'Good morning,' said Mr Waft, gesticulating with a sausage skewered on his fork.

Aiden nodded to both of them and sat down at a table near the window.

'It's a beautiful day out there today,' said a small sheep, wearing a bonnet. 'What can I get you for breakfast, young man?'

'Well, I've heard your sausages are to die for,' Aiden replied, with a smile.

'Oh, I see Maurice has been singing my praises again, bless him,' Blanche Fluffywool said.

'He has,' said Aiden. 'I'm guessing that you're Blanche?'

'That's right, and I'm guessing you must be Aiden,' Blanche said, placing a tray of toast on the table. 'He spoke a lot about you last night. You've obviously made a good impression on him.'

'The feeling's definitely mutual,' Aiden said.

'Well, then, we've got my speciality sausages, smoked bacon, both locally farmed of course, mushrooms, hash browns, poached eggs, fried eggs, the finest drippydizzle beans, and fried bread,' Blanche said, taking a small notebook and pen out of her pocket. 'What would you like?'

'Would you think it greedy of me if I asked for a bit of everything?'

'No, of course not, I'd take it as a compliment. Now would you like any tea?'

'Yes, please.'

When breakfast arrived, it was indeed the feast Aiden's stomach had been hoping for, and he wasted little time in cleaning the plate. 'Blanche, that was possibly the finest breakfast I've ever tasted,' he said, as she came to take away the used cutlery.

'Ah, I bet you say that to all the ewes,' she said, giggling.

At that moment a panic-stricken Maurice ran into the restaurant, puffing and blowing liked he'd just been chased by a herd of rabid dogs who fancied some lamb cutlets. 'We have an emergency,' he said, catching his breath between the words as he spoke. 'Mr Breezy, Mr Waft, I fear we may need your expertise.'

'Er, whatever for, Mr Fluffywool,' Mr Breezy said, with a worried look.

'It's Mrs Ripsnorter, the handkerchief vendor's wife. She's claiming her vacuum cleaner is possessed.'

'Oh, dear,' said Blanche, 'that's terrible.'

'It is indeed,' said Mr Waft, with a nervous glance at Mr Breezy.

'Quickly, gentlemen, she's outside now with the infernal machine. We may not have much time, it's started levitating.'

Mr Breezy and Mr Waft exchanged more nervous glances and Mr Waft shook his head. 'I'm afraid we may not be able to assist, Mr Fluffywool,' said Mr Breezy, feigning disappointment. 'If a vacuum cleaner has reached the levitation stage, there's not really anything we can do. Also, we have urgent business in Chester that we must attend to.'

'Yes,' added Mr Waft. 'There have been several substantiated reports of vacuum cleaners reciting the black mass and shaping their hoses into inverted crucifixes. We must make haste, lest we fear the worst.'

'Or you could just be scared,' Aiden said, as he stood up from the table.

'Scared? Scared?!' Mr Breezy said, defensively. 'Don't be so insolent my good fellow.'

'How dare you!' added Mr Waft. 'Why would we, of all people, be scared of confronting a possessed vacuum cleaner?'

'Of course, how silly of me,' Aiden said, his mind whizzing. 'You gentlemen obviously laugh in the face of fear and would no doubt banish the foul demon in a second. It's just a pity that in situations like this, scurrilous rumours of cowardice can spread. But I'm sure your reputation is such that people would never believe them.'

Everyone in the breakfast room looked at Mr Breezy and Mr Waft, whilst outside an eerie howl was followed by the sound of high-powered suction. 'Perhaps we can take a quick look, then,' Mr Breezy said, with a nervous smile.

'Are you mad?' Mr Waft whispered. 'We may be found out.'

'It will look far worse if we don't,' Mr Breezy whispered back. 'We may need to use this disguise again. Look, let's just say a few incantations and get out of here.'

Mr Breezy stood up and grabbed his briefcase and Mr Waft finished the last piece of toast on the table. 'You are right, my good fellow. It would indeed be remiss of us to not assess the situation and to offer our services in this time of dire need. Come, Mr Waft, we have work to do.'

Outside, a distraught Mrs Ripsnorter was being comforted by a friend as her vacuum cleaner span in the air. Its hose was flailing about and it seemed to be moaning in at least three different voices. Mr Breezy raised his hands in a grand gesture and started to speak.

'Oh foul demon of the netherworld, we command you to leave this poor vacuum cleaner. Be gone and do not return!'

'Yes, be gone, dark spirit!' added Mr Waft, dramatically.

The vacuum cleaner stopped spinning and pointed its hose at Mr Breezy and Mr Waft. 'And who the bloody hell do you think you two are, then?' it said, in a rasping voice.

'Er, we are highly-trained Vagrant Vacuum Cleaner Exorcists,' said Mr Breezy. 'And we have come to send you back to where you belong.'

'No you're not!' the vacuum cleaner spat. 'You look like a right couple of plonkers to me. Bugger off, I ain't going anywhere.'

'I can assure you we have banished many of your kind back to their dark holes, where they now fester for all eternity,' Mr Breezy lied. 'Now, by all that is holy, by all that is cheesy, and by all that is held sacred by the Philosophising Priests of Penrith, may you be discombobulated, eviscerated and rusticated!'

'You're making this up, aren't you?' said the vacuum cleaner.

'I am not,' insisted Mr Breezy.

'You, are!' the vacuum cleaner said, chortling. 'Look, I've been exorcised loads of times and you're not saying any of the right words.'

'What do you mean?' said Mr Waft.

'Well, for a kick off, I'd expect something along the lines of *"We who stand before you have tickled our armpits, have drunk the holy sweat of Tipsybugger and have danced naked through the frozen wastes of Holywell. So, shoo, shoo, shoo, oh nasty one. Get thee hence before we reveal our underwear."* And then you'd bounce on one leg, clapping vigorously. That normally does it.'

'Ah, yes, of course,' said Mr Breezy, 'but we were hoping we would not have to resort to incantations of that potency. It now appears you leave us little choice.'

Mr Breezy stood on one leg and Mr Waft followed suit. 'We who stand before you have tickled our armpits, have drunk the holy sweat of Tipsybugger and have danced naked through the frozen wastes of Holywell. So, shoo, shoo, shoo, oh nasty one. Get thee hence before we reveal our underwear!' Then they hopped up and down, clapping vigorously.

The vacuum cleaner stopped spinning. Then it pirouetted. Then it gasped and emptied most of the contents of its bag on the ground. Then it gave out an anguished cry and fell to the floor with a bang... and then it started to laugh hysterically. 'I can't believe you two fell for that. I mean, I've come across some real idiots in my time but you two take the bloody biscuit. Absolute quality, that was!

Mr Breezy was incandescent. Mr Waft was puffed out.

'Oh, hang on,' said the vacuum cleaner, 'I've got a message coming through from the other side. Oh, yes, from the darkest pits of the nether regions this stems; a lost soul trying to get through to her loved ones. Here it comes.'

All went momentarily dark and the vacuum cleaner span faster. 'It's here, the message is here..."Oh, my dearest, please help me. I am forced to boil hosiery all day, and then when I am finished I have to garnish them with pepper and eat them. Oh, the torment, the torment. For this I must do for all eternity"...'

The vacuum cleaner went silent and stopped spinning. Then it pointed its hose right into Mr Breezy's face and cackled hysterically. 'You mother cooks socks in hell!'

'I think it is about time we made our exit,' said Mr Waft.

'Agreed,' said Mr Breezy.

'Yeah, bugger off before I get the urge to stick this hose up your trousers,' the vacuum cleaner said.

And with that, they turned on their heels and ran off into town. 'I think we must give more cogitation to our choice of disguise before our next assignment,' Hob said, puffing as he ran.

'Drifting Feng Shui Practitioners?' Nob suggested.

'My thoughts exactly, my good Nob.'

'Had enough, boys?' said the vacuum cleaner, triumphantly, as Hob and Nob disappeared from sight. 'Vagrant Vacuum Cleaner Exorcists my arse. Now, then, who's next?'

People and sheep backed away in fear and the vacuum cleaner looked smug, or at least as smug as a possessed vacuum cleaner can look. It randomly span to and fro, giggling gleefully and twirling its hose. 'Why don't you see if you have any messages for me?' Aiden said, stepping forward.

The vacuum cleaner stopped spinning with a jerk and pointed its hose at him, moving it from side to side and applying a mild suction action, as if it were sniffing. 'That's funny,' it said. 'I'm getting nothing from you at all.'

It repeated the process, but more frantically. 'You're weird. Where are you from?'

'I'm from a place where vacuum cleaners don't have bags,' Aiden said.

'Bagless vacuum cleaners? You're not serious,' the vacuum cleaner said, startled.

'Oh, yes. And they never lose their suction.'

'Oh, come on now, you can't expect me to believe that,' the vacuum cleaner said, dismissively. 'You'll be telling me next they don't get possessed.'

'Never,' said Aiden. 'We worked out how to stop all that.'

The vacuum cleaner looked concerned. Its hose began twisting slightly and bits of dust started coming out of the seam of its bag. It moved back several feet. Aiden threw his arms up in the air, theatrically, and spoke in a booming voice.

'I call upon the power of our Lord Dyson…'

'Now, let's not be hasty,' the vacuum cleaner said.

'… to rid the Multiverse of this entity…'

'Can't we talk about this?'

'… for all time and…'

'Sod this, I'm off,' the vacuum cleaner said, dropping to the ground and switching itself off. A rush of wind was felt by all and in the distance a shrill cry could be heard, fading softly in the morning mist.

Mrs Ripsnorter tentatively approached the inert vacuum cleaner and prodded it with her walking stick. 'It's been cleansed!' she shouted, and burst into tears.

For the second time in as many days Aiden found himself receiving a round of applause, just as Cracky was wandering over from the Diner. 'You know,' Cracky said, smiling, 'if I didn't know better I'd swear you were just an attention seeker, Mr Peersey. Now, would you like to join me for that chat we planned?'

CHAPTER 16 – YOU ALLOW THEM TO ENTER IF THEY PAY A BOND

Velvet the ferret had the mouse cornered in the throne room. She was looking at it with a sadistic smile and kept tapping at it with her paw, as the little thing trembled.

Velvet enjoyed torturing small creatures, and she considered herself to be quite adept at it. She also craved attention, sulked if she couldn't have her own way and would do anything to get what she wanted, not caring how she did it or who got hurt in the process. If she were human, her ideal career would be a TV reality show contestant. She really wasn't a very nice ferret at all.

'Hmm,' she said, 'shall I kill you now, or wait for later?'

The little mouse cowered pitifully, holding its front legs across its face. 'I'd rather you didn't kill me at all,' it said, with a quivering voice.

The door to the throne room opened and Baron Blacktie marched in, with Pimple in close attendance. His bodyguard, Grunt, followed, looking menacingly around the room. 'Looks like it's your lucky day,' said Velvet, smacking the mouse with her paw, causing it to fall on its side. And then she ran off and sat in her basket next to the throne.

'What did they say exactly?' the Baron asked, as he sat down imperiously.

'They left a message with Stacey on reception saying that they urgently needed to see you and that they'd be here in less than an hour,' Pimple replied.

'I hope for their sake that it's good tidings,' the Baron said, looking straight at Grunt. 'Otherwise it may be necessary for chastisement of some description.'

'Grunt crush?' said Grunt.

'Not yet,' replied the Baron.

'Grunt rip?'

'No, not yet.'

Grunt smiled, raised his huge hands and made a snapping motion. 'Grunt break?' he said, somewhat hopefully.

'Perhaps later,' the Baron replied.

'Oh, Grunt plop,' said Grunt, looking a bit embarrassed and feeling the back of his tattered trousers.

'Oh, for heaven's sake, I've told you if you need to go to the toilet just go!' the Baron yelled. 'You don't have to wait for permission. Do you want to be put back in nappies again?'

'Grunt sorry,' said Grunt, bowing his head.

'Get him cleaned up, Pimple. If that smell gets out the throne room will be off limits for days.'

'Do I have to, my Lord?' the horrified Pimple said.

'Yes, you do. Now get him out of here.'

'Yes, my Lord,' said Pimple, reluctantly taking hold of Grunt's hand.

As Pimple and Grunt left the throne room General Darkblast entered, flanked by two of his imperial guard. 'You summoned me, my Lord?'

'Yes, General. It would appear our two spies are returning early on a matter of some urgency. I thought it best that you be in attendance when they arrive.'

The doors to the throne room swung open and Hob and Nob rushed in, unannounced. They were both breathing heavily and were drenched in sweat. After bowing courteously, Hob placed his briefcase on the floor. The Baron stood up in anticipation. 'So, gentlemen, I believe you have news that demands my ear?'

'We do, my Lord,' said Hob.

'Did you manage to obtain a sample of cheese, as agreed?' the Baron questioned.

'Not yet, my Lord,' Nob said. 'We encountered complications and thought it best to impart the news we have gleaned. You can rest assured we will return and acquire the sample of cheese you desire.'

The Baron's mood darkened and his eyes became like slits. He walked around the throne, picked up his imperial mace and placed the tip into Hob's left nostril. 'You are lucky that my friend Grunt cannot control his bowels, otherwise your physical appearance would be altered quite radically.'

'Please, hear us out, my Lord,' Hob pleaded. 'We know who owns the cheese mine that was once Hairy Growler's, and we have a plan as to how you can make it yours.'

'Go on', said the Baron.

'The mine is now in the possession of one Agnar the Hammered. He is a drummer in a band called Sacred Wind.'

'My Lord, this is good news indeed,' interrupted General Darkblast. 'Given that he is a drummer, he would surely let you the have this mine for a bag of sweets or some shiny trinkets that would keep his small mind occupied. And if he were to refuse this legitimate route, why we can simply take it by force before he can get his drumsticks out.'

'If only it were that simple, General,' Nob said.

'What do you mean?' the Baron asked, removing the mace from Hob's nostril and placing back behind the throne.

'Although he owns the mine it was a gift from his cousin, who has bade him to take care of it,' Hob said.

'And this "cousin" may prove to be difficult if the mine were somehow spirited from this Agnar's grasp. Is that what you are saying?'

'Yes, my Lord. For the name of his cousin is Angus McSvensson.'

The Baron reeled backwards as if he'd been hit by something quite big that didn't have protective padding. 'He's related to the McSvenssons! Yes, now I see what you meant about complications.'

General Darkblast stepped forward, putting his hand on his sword in a gesture that implied he wished to use it quite urgently. 'Come, now, Baron, we should not be deterred by some cousin from a realm that is quite distant. Why, we could appropriate the mine with minimum effort before any word reached his tartan ears.'

'General, am I right in thinking that your men have encountered the McSvenssons before?' the Baron said, walking over to a filing cabinet and sifting through the contents of the top drawer. 'Ah yes, I believe I have the report right here.'

The Baron removed the file and read the first page. 'So, it was a reconnaissance mission to Arbroath, is that correct?' he said, passing the file to the General.

'It was, my Lord.'

'And would you say it was in any way successful?'

'Well, in the sense that the men performed reconnaissance, yes.'

'But you didn't get too much information, would that be correct?'

'It's true the information we received was not what we had hoped, my Lord.'

'And in what form was this information?'

'It was in the form of a letter from...' the General opened the file and located the letter '... from a Morag McSvensson.'

'And it said?'

'It said *"Go to hell ye Sassenach bastards. If ye send any more men up here ye'll get them back as a collection of mini haggis without the trimmings"*.'

The Baron dusted off one of his sleeves and sat back down on his throne. 'And what would you say you learned from this information?'

'That they're not very keen on the English but they do like haggis,' the General replied.

'Indeed,' said the Baron. 'So, General, how many men did you send?'

'Seventy-two were sent, my Lord.'

'And how many returned?'

The General skipped through the report before replying. 'Seventy-two returned, my Lord.'

'Let me stop you there for a second and I'll rephrase the question, so that we can perhaps get an answer that is both more specific and more accurate. How many men returned intact?'

'Er, none, my Lord.'

Baron Blacktie rose, walked back over to the General and grabbed the file off him. He flicked to page six and passed it back 'Could you please read out the inventory of what was actually returned?'

'Of course, my Lord. It reads *"Seventy-two men despatched, seventy-two parts returned as follows – twelve legs, nine arms, eight heads, ten hands, eleven toes, four thumbs, five testicles, three livers, seven ears, two fingers, one small penis and a bag of hair of indeterminate origin"*, my Lord.'

'Quite,' said the Baron. 'So, General, I wish my plans to be executed with the minimum of fuss. This has to be a low risk exercise and the last thing I need are hordes of very angry, psychopathic, kilt-wearing maniacs ravaging through the palace looking to cause as much dismemberment to my person as is humanly possible. Do I make myself clear?!'

'Yes, my Lord,' the General replied, nodding frantically.

Hob put his hand to his mouth and cleared his throat. 'My Lord, we believe we may have a solution to this dilemma, but we need some information first.'

'What do you wish to know?' the Baron said, his rage dissolving into curiosity.

'The Cestrian Music Tournament takes place in three days, is that correct?' asked Nob.

'Correct,' replied the Baron. 'How is that relevant?'

'Have the band Sacred Wind applied to be in this year's competition?'

'I've no idea,' the Baron said. 'This is the band you say Agnar the Hammered plays drums for?'

'It is my Lord. If we could trouble you to find out if they have entered the tournament it would be appreciated.'

The Baron looked at Hob and Nob quizzically, before picking up the phone on the small table by the throne. He dialled a number and a polite lady answered. 'Stacey, get the contestants for this year's music tournament out for me and check to see if we have an entrant called Sacred Wind.'

Some seconds passed and the Baron drummed his fingers on the table impatiently. 'A band called Sacred Wind did apply to enter the tournament, but they were rejected, my Lord,' Stacey eventually said. 'In fact, they've applied for the last four tournaments and have been rejected every time.'

'Why is that?' the Baron asked.

'They are a heavy rock band, my Lord, and are therefore banned from playing in the city.'

'Ah, of course,' the Baron said, putting the phone down. 'They have applied, gentlemen, but were rejected due to the fact they play heavy rock.'

'That is excellent news,' said Hob.

'It is indeed,' said the Baron. 'I cannot bear to have my ears stained by that grotesque racket. Heavy rock has been banned for several years now and I have no intention of lifting the ban. General, what happened to the last heavy rock band that tried to play in the city?'

'We informed them that if they continued to play then they would be decapitated. However, this threat was not successful.'

'Why so?' the Baron said, with incredulity.

'I believe they said that it was a great idea and would provide an excellent addition to their stage show.'

'How, then, did you make them see the error of their ways?'

'Oh, we decapitated them anyway, my Lord. But this led to them getting an encore from the audience.'

'How, pray, did they manage to play an encore with their heads separated from their bodies?'

'Not too successfully, my Lord. The audience got restless after two minutes and began a slow handclap, until the lead singer's body convulsed and sprayed blood into the crowd. This was very well received.'

Hob marched over to the Baron, intently. 'You must let Sacred Wind enter the tournament, Baron.'

'Are you insane, Hob? I cannot be seen to rescind this law. It could be construed as a weakness by any enemies I have left who are not in the canal. And anyway, how would this assist in gaining possession of the mine?'

'You allow them to enter if they pay a bond, say £10,000,' Hob said. 'As it is extremely unlikely they could raise that kind of money, you ask for collateral instead; for example, property... or a cheese mine.'

The Baron smiled and patted Hob on the shoulder. Hob visibly winced from his touch. 'Interesting, very interesting. Go on.'

'You say that the mine will still be theirs if they win the tournament, but if they lose then the mine is forfeit. And this applies not only if they do not win, but also if they fail to participate in the tournament... for example if some mishap should occur which would lead to them being unable to reach the city in time.'

The Baron's chilling smile grew wider.

'You could spin the fact that you were letting them enter as a sign of your great benevolence and your wish to expand horizons and create equality,' added Hob. 'The people would not only believe this, but your popularity would soar.'

'Yes, yes!' the Baron said, walking over to the large bookcase and, again, stroking one book in particular. 'Obviously, we ensure that this Sacred Wind do not get to the city, and that should be easy to arrange. And as the agreement between Agnar and I will be a legitimate transaction, Angus McSvensson would direct any wrath at the loss of the mine to his cousin and not towards me.'

'Exactly,' said Nob.

'You have done well, gentlemen,' the Baron said. 'I fear Grunt will have to wait a while for his exercise.'

Hob and Nob exchanged glances and looked visibly relieved.

'We will need to speak to the band to initiate this most excellent plan. Who is their contact?' the Baron asked.

'They are managed by a man called Oldfart Olafson,' Hob said.

Baron Blacktie twirled dramatically, his leather cape sweeping out in an arcing motion before settling back into place. He placed one foot on the throne and stood flamboyantly with his hands on his hips. 'General, let it be known that I wish to speak to this Oldfart. We will travel to Llangollen tomorrow. Prepare your men.'

CHAPTER 17 – HAVE YOU LOOKED IN THE MIRROR LATELY?

'So, now you probably think I'm either mad or inventing the whole thing,' Aiden said, after recounting yesterday's eventful trip to Llangollen.

Cracky looked at him thoughtfully, a wry smile on his lips. Growing up with a wizard for a father had certainly provided him with an open mind. He also paid great heed to his intuition, and at the moment his intuition was telling him that Aiden was telling the truth. 'I must admit it's a pretty amazing story, but I've no reason to disbelieve you. I mean, let's look at the evidence. For a start there's that old car you arrived in, I've never seen one quite like that. It's also obvious that you've not encountered too many sentient sheep, conscious curries, faeries or telepathic cats on your travels. I'm a good judge of character and you can't feign the kind of surprise I've seen on your face on several occasions. And then, of course, there's your scruffy hair style.'

'Why does everyone keep going on about my hair?' Aiden said.

'Have you looked in the mirror lately?'

Cracky poured them both a drink of orange juice and passed a glass to Aiden. 'I am most interested in looking at this phone of yours,' he said. 'That certainly sounds like something that would completely confirm your story.'

'Of course,' Aiden said, as he took the QC Nova phone out of his jacket pocket and passed it to Cracky. 'You just touch the screen,' he added, reaching over and prodding the screen to initialise the phone.

'My, my, now this is something,' Cracky said.

'Yes, it's a cool piece of kit,' Aiden said, proudly. 'You can play games on it, go on the Internet at super-speed bandwidth, download apps by all the major manufacturers, access all the social networking sites and even read eBooks that you already have on your computer at home. It's got the fastest processor on the market and its speed and memory are radically enhanced using quantum computing technology.'

'You lost me after "games",' Cracky said.

'Sorry, Cracky, I should have realised that you probably haven't seen a computer.'

'Oh, I've seen computers,' Cracky said. 'But they're obviously not quite as advanced as those where you hail from. The screens are normally just black and white, or more commonly green and black.'

'That's how ours were about twenty years ago,' Aiden said. 'You know, for all the differences between our two realities there would appear to be a reasonable number of parallels.'

Aiden thought for a second before continuing. He had so many questions. 'What about science,' he said. 'Have you heard of the theory of relativity, for example?'

'Oh, yes,' Cracky replied.

'And it was Albert Einstein who formulated it?'

'Albert Einstein? You mean Alfred Einstein,' Cracky said.

'Alfred Einstein?'

'Yes, his twin brother. Albert Einstein was a charlatan of the highest order. He was a playboy, a gambler and an inveterate cheese sniffer. It was one of the scandals of the century. Albert used to keep his twin brother locked up in a tower, telling him the outside world was controlled by monsters and ogres who tortured anyone who could do quadratic equations. Alfred used to discuss all his ideas and research with Albert, little knowing that Albert was passing these off as his own. Albert was eventually found out by the screen actress Martina Monroe, whom he was having a well-publicised affair with. She began to suspect something was awry when one night, after sex, she quizzed him on the Unified Field Theory and he began to talk about "knocking down fences and letting all the grass mingle together." At first she thought this to be just some clever metaphor… until he explained how this would allow the cows to roam freely. While Albert slept, she found the locked room in the tower and freed Alfred. Albert was thrown in prison for ten years, barred from cheese sniffing for life and was given twenty stern twists of his left ear. Alfred went on to win the Nobbly Peace Prize and marry the luscious Martina. Am I to gather this is not the way things transpired where you're from?'

'Not quite,' Aiden said.

Cracky turned the sign on the diner door so that 'Open' faced outwards. 'You're welcome to hang around for a bit,' he said. 'It may not be that busy today. Sunday's are normally quiet until later in the afternoon.'

'Thanks, Cracky, but I think I'll have a walk around town again. I may drop in for a drink later, if that's okay.'

'Absolutely, my door is always open for you.'

Aiden was just about to leave when a thought popped into his head. 'Cracky, I've been meaning to ask ever since last night, but you obviously have electricity here?'

'Yes, of course.'

'But I've not seen any overhead power cables, so does that mean they're all underground?'

'Well, the electricity does come from underground,' Cracky said. 'Come on, I'll show you.'

They walked out of the back door and Cracky pointed to a silver-coloured pole that was sticking out of the ground. It was about ten feet tall and had a series of small cables that stretched from its top into what appeared to be a fuse box, fitted to the outside wall.

'There you go. That's my EET.'

'EET?' said Aiden.

'Earth Electricity Transducer. You just put it in the ground, attune the frequency and it's ready to go.'

'Are you telling me that you simply get all your electricity from the earth?' Aiden said.

'Yes,' Cracky replied, looking surprised at the question. 'Where do you get yours from?'

'We make it, using large power stations the size of small towns. We have big generators, some of which even use nuclear power.'

'Dear me, that sounds expensive; and a bit impractical, if you don't mind me saying.'

'Well, electricity prices are quite high, so I suppose you're right in that sense.'

'You mean you pay for your electricity? How odd.'

***

As Aiden ambled along one of the quiet country roads that led out of town, he was reminded how extraordinarily clean the air smelled here, and that was something he'd noticed as soon as he'd arrived. On the right hand side of the road, tall hedges provided a jagged barrier to lush, verdant fields that stretched for miles. He also noticed that the grass seemed to be a much darker shade of green here, as if it were also cleaner, more alive.

Managing to work his way through a hole in the hedge without ripping his clothes, he bent down and laid his hand on the grass; it was warm and soft to the touch, its smell fresh and vibrant in his nose. There was a large oak tree nearby and its leafy branches reached out wide from its huge trunk, offering a protective canopy for anything that wished to nestle below.

'That's the beggar, over there,' Half-blind Ron said, from behind the tree. 'He's changed his clothes but I'd recognise that bloody hair anywhere. What's he thinking Your Highness, Princeness, Majesty?'

'Your Highness, are you sure it was a good idea to bring him with us?' Captain Marmaduke said, with a pained expression.

'He's already proven his worth, Captain. And I'm sure if we tell him he can have an extra chicken as a reward, if he keeps quiet, he'll comply completely, won't you Ron?'

'Mmm, mmmm!' said Half-blind Ron, nodding his head and putting his paw over his mouth.

'Right, then,' Theo said, as they peeped around the large oak tree, 'please be still and I'll try and reach into his mind.'

Prince Theo had the rare gift of being able to go beyond simple telepathic conversation and could actually probe deep into the minds of other creatures. He could not only read their thoughts but could also sense their emotions and moods. The gift became apparent when he was a kitten and it was cultivated through teachings by his mother, the sadly departed Queen Tiddles, who had been blessed with the same talent. She had instructed him how to master and control his gift, how to access thoughts without being detected, and how to create permanent connections for short periods of time. The wise Queen also taught him how to protect himself against any malevolent forces that he may encounter when using his gift. Theo loved her very much and always listened, knowing that someday a need may arise where it would be necessary to put those lessons into action.

'His mind is full of strange things,' he said, as he concentrated. 'He's not from this world, and he's not from this time. The place he's from is similar, but also very different. He's a good man, very clever. He likes music and… there are lots of images of females, including one who he met in The Sheep's Stirrup last night. There's something about food… breakfast at the pub and something called "pizza". I'm also picking up images of possessed vacuum cleaners, some very scary men in black and yellow, something called a Nova phone and a love of swords. He really is most unusual.'

'But is he the one mentioned in The Prophecy?' the Captain said.

'I do believe that he may be, Captain. Although he's out of place here, he doesn't feel out of place, if that makes sense. His mind is unique… but he has a dog.'

'A dog!' Half-blind Ron exclaimed. 'I told you he was a weirdo. If the bloody thing comes near me I'll scratch its knackers.'

Theo concentrated again and probed a little deeper. 'He's already made quite a few friends, including Cracky, so I think we should pay a visit to the Diner later.'

'Agreed, Your Highness,' said Captain Marmaduke.

'Wait a minute, there's something disturbing here,' Theo said. 'I can see two figures. He met them yesterday in the pub. They were in disguise but

I'd recognise them anywhere.'

'Go on,' said the Captain.

'It's Hob and Nob. They were staying in The Sheep's Stirrup yesterday. He had a bad feeling about them.'

'Well, he's a good judge of character,' said the Captain. 'They'll be on Blacktie's business, that's for sure. But what could be so pressing that it called for him to despatch his two top spies to Llangollen?'

'I've no idea, Captain. But I think we better go and find out.'

***

As Aiden made his way back into town he spotted a fallen tree trunk, which lay lifeless near the hedge. He sat down and stared up into the clear sky as a couple of magpies fluttered by, no doubt in search of treasure or perhaps worms. It was now late afternoon and his thoughts began to turn to home once more, mainly because he was missing Humphrey; although the really weird thing was that even after only two days he actually felt he somehow belonged here. What was it Tom had said, 'all this happened because the app selected the most appropriate Llangollen in the Multiverse for you by analysing your subconscious.' He took a deep intake of the crisp afternoon air and then he felt his phone buzzing.

His immediate reaction was that it must be Tom with some news. But when he produced the phone from his pocket the ringtone was distinctly different, almost like heavenly angels singing. He looked at the name being displayed on the screen. It said 'Odin', so he answered it.

'Hello.'

'Oh, hello. Now you'll have to excuse me, as I don't tend to use these things much, but Tom asked me to give you a call.'

Given what he'd witnessed over the past couple of days, Aiden had decided that he'd keep an open mind to anything he encountered from now on. He still needed to ask what seemed to be a perfectly reasonable question, though. 'So you're actually Odin of Asgard?' he said, with a completely straight face.

'You mean you know another Odin?' replied Odin. 'Well, I shouldn't be too surprised. I have a cousin who called his dog Odin. A right feisty little bugger it was. Whenever we'd visit him — that's me and the wife, Frigg — I used to get a bit confused at meal times. "Odin, Odin, din dins" they'd shout, and up I'd get and wander into the kitchen. Don't get me wrong, dog food isn't normally my thing, but to be honest some of the stuff was actually quite tasty.'

'Sorry,' Aiden said. 'I meant are you Odin, King of the Norse Gods.'

'I am indeed, young man. Now, Tom said he's a bit tied up but told me to tell you not to worry and that he'll be back in touch on Thursday.'

'Ah, okay, and thanks for letting me know.'

'My pleasure, young man, I've heard some good things about you. And your wind's been blessed on several occasions already.'

Aiden remembered the tale Cracky had told him when he was on the boat trip yesterday; that the Vikings believe every fart is a blessing. 'So all those "blessings" actually get to you?'

'Oh yes. If a fart is done with feeling and the thoughts that go with it are pure and noble, then it'll find its way up my holy nostrils. It's no different from praying, you know. It's the positive energy that counts. Unfortunately for me, I often receive the positive energy surrounded by the most ungodly smells!' Odin said, with a booming, hearty laugh that was so infectious Aiden couldn't help but join in.

'I will say this, though,' Odin continued. 'One of the biggest pains we gods have is this whole "freewill" thing. I mean, it was our idea and it did make perfect sense at the time. Allow life forms the opportunity to make their own decisions and keep interference to a minimum, provide a few basic rules and then just let it roll. That's what we all agreed. Now, don't get me wrong, by and large it works perfectly well, but you do sometimes get a bit frustrated when things get misinterpreted.'

'Misinterpreted?' Aiden said.

'Yeah, it's happened quite a lot. I'll give you an example; I was speaking to God, the big guy, at the last Bi-Millennial Deity Conference* and he was talking about this very subject. "Ods," he'd say, as that's his nickname for me, which is much better than some of the other nicknames I have. "Ods," he'd say, "never trust a scribe, because it doesn't matter what you say, they'll make up their own version anyway. Look at what's been written about me in the Bible. One minute I'm a kind and loving god and the next thing I'm smiting this and smiting that. I've never once told anyone to smite bloody anything! I mean, how hypocritical would that be. I set out the Ten Commandments, without caveats bear in mind, and all of a sudden it's as if I've said 'well, yes, but obviously they don't apply to me, particularly if I think that someone needs a bloody good smiting.' What kind of example would that be setting?" He was really miffed about the whole thing.'

'You know, I've never thought about it like that,' Aiden said.

'And the other thing that does get to me, on occasion, is the boredom,' Odin continued. 'Again, don't get me wrong, Asgard is a wonderful place and some of the goddesses do provide very welcome distractions, if you know what I mean. But it can all get a little bit tedious. I mean, you can only create so many planets, stars, mammals, suit-wearing giraffes and four-eyed, fire-breathing, chest-beating gnomes before it starts to feel a bit samey, can you understand?'

'Well, why don't you get yourself a hobby,' Aiden said, 'something completely different.'

'You know, that's really not a bad idea. Have you any suggestions?'

'Oh, er, I don't know. How about hosting a radio show?' It was the first thing that jumped into his head, and he had no idea why.

'Hey, what a great idea, I really like the sound of that! I could do music, interviews, competitions, phone-ins. Brilliant. Thanks very much, young man.'

'You're very welcome,' Aiden said, surprised and slightly relieved.

'Right, then, I must be off. I need to get hold of some deities to interview on my new show. Very exciting. Take care, Aiden Peersey, I reckon I owe you a favour.'

'Thanks. Goodbye, Odin.'

*See appendix 2

CHAPTER 18 – HELLO AND WELCOME TO 'ROCK YOUR DEITY'!

'Hello and welcome to Rock Your Deity!'(female choir jingle) 'Rock Your Dei-i-tyyyy'
'Yes, you're listening to Rock Your Deity and I'm your host, Odin. We'll be playing some of your gods' favourite tunes today, and we'll be having a live phone-in later. So, it'll be your chance to get loose with Loki, get down with Dionysus, and get amorous with Aphrodite! I'm also interviewing the big guy himself; yes, God will be here to talk us through his top ten songs of all eternity, including such classics as "Hallelujah", "God Gave Rock 'n' Roll To You", "Let There Be Rock", "Knocking on Heaven's Door" and, perhaps surprisingly, "Bat out of Hell".'

'What's that on the radio?' Aiden said, as he walked up to the bar.
'I'm not sure,' said Maurice. 'I just switched it on for some background music while I'm cleaning up. Has anyone told you the news yet?'
'No, I've been on my own most of the day... apart from one unusual conversation... what's happened?'
'Baron Blacktie is paying a visit to Llangollen tomorrow. He's actually coming to the pub, and he wants to meet with Oldfart and Sacred Wind. Apparently it's something about the Cestrian Music Tournament.'
'I saw a news article about the music tournament on television last night,' Aiden said. 'It mentioned that rock music was banned, from what I can remember.'
'Indeed,' said Maurice, putting down his cleaning cloth. 'The Baron is very fond of New Romantic music and can't stand heavy rock or metal. For some reason I'm sure we'll find out about tomorrow, we're told he's had "a change of heart", but it sounds suspicious to me. That man never does anything unless it's in his own interests.'
On the table in the corner, a heated debate was taking place between

Vindy, Tikky and Saffy. 'But Your Majesties are supposed to be holding court tomorrow. There are several matters that will require your approval,' Saffy said.

'We're quite aware of that, Saffy, but a visit from Blacktie is something we need to stick around for,' said Vindy. 'He's up to something and I want to hear about it first hand; and, given our new-found alliance with Mold, I believe that we'd be remiss in our commitment if we didn't take a hands-on approach here.'

'Vindy's right,' Tikky said. 'I'm sure that First Minister Prawn Karahi-Onion Rice can look after things in our absence. Kara's a very capable politician and I think we all know we can trust his judgement.'

Saffy bubbled, cracking one of his mini poppadoms in frustration. He knew his king and queen were correct, and that this was too important an opportunity to let pass. 'Very well, I can see that I'm not going to be able to talk you out of this.'

'No you're not, Saffy,' Tikky said, 'and we appreciate your concern. You're our most trusted advisor, and one of our dearest friends. But in this instance the King and I will be staying to find out just what infernal plans the Baron may be hatching that involve Oldfart and Sacred Wind. We wish no harm to come to them and we will do everything in our power to assist where we can.'

'You realise that I'll have to leave some of your armed guard behind,' Saffy insisted.

'I'd expect no less, Saffy,' Vindy said. 'But please ensure that they keep their distance. If Blacktie spots any Tandoori Naans he's bound to get suspicious, particularly as Llangollen doesn't have a curry house. Tikky and I will try to blend in with the background.'

'Are you talking about disguising ourselves? Now that is exciting,' Tikky said, wobbling her plate.

'I could always cover you both in tin foil and we could pretend that you are part of a buffet?' Maurice called over, from the bar.

'Excellent,' said Vindy. 'That sounds absolutely splendid.'

'I can't wait to see you in metal, Vindy. Why, my bay leaves are curling now at the thought,' Tikky said, giggling.

'Now, now, dear, please try and control yourself in front of our friends. But, if we ask nicely, maybe Maurice will let us take the costumes home afterwards!'

'Ooh, Vindy, you saucepot!' Tikky smouldered.

Over at the Diner, Cracky was just about to close for the evening. He enjoyed his quiet Sunday nights, liking nothing better than to get lost in a good book, aided and abetted by a couple of flagons of his home-brewed ale. He was just about to head upstairs when he noticed five little shining eyes looking at him through the window… followed by a voice in his head.

'Nice to see you again, Cracky, it's been a while. If you can spare the time I think a chat may benefit us all.'

'Your Highness, as usual it would be a pleasure,' Cracky said, as he opened the door and the three cats ran in.

'First thing's first,' Half-blind Ron said, sending his thoughts into Cracky's mind, 'have you got any chicken?'

Cracky supplied the cats with some of his special melon chicken and some saucers of milk. Despite the protestations of Captain Marmaduke, Theo insisted that they eat off the floor so as not to arouse suspicion.

'That was excellent, Cracky,' Theo said, washing his paws with his tongue.

'Best chicken I've ever tasted, Mr Crackpot!' exclaimed Half-blind Ron, purring away.

'Actually, it's Crackfoot,' said Cracky, 'although I've been called worse.'

'Can we get down to business, Your Highness?' Captain Marmaduke said. 'Although I must say that the chicken was indeed superlative, Cracky.'

'You're all very welcome,' said Cracky. 'Now what brings Prince Theo of Corwen and his Captain of the Guard to my humble Diner?'

Theo told Cracky about Half-blind Ron's encounter with Aiden and what he discovered when he probed his mind. He also explained his reasons as to why he felt Aiden's sudden appearance was linked to The Prophecy. And this was one piece of the current jigsaw of events that hadn't crossed Cracky's mind, up to this point.

The Prophecy was allegedly written several centuries ago by a personage or personages unknown. It was a book of portents and predictions, many of which had come to pass. Theo, as a student of esoteric literature, was well-versed with its contents and interpretation. Cracky's father had also studied the book.

'It's been many years since I've looked through my father's copy, I must admit,' said Cracky. 'But it would seem that Aiden's appearance in our world does fit some of the criteria.'

'I'm actually convinced, Cracky,' said Theo. 'I've studied this work too closely and I can read the signs. Don't forget, there's a complimentary prophecy supposedly set to occur at the same time which says "Four great warriors will face a challenge from an evil baron in a city far away." Now if we can find some correlation between current events and this section of the book... well, we could really be onto something.'

Cracky poured some more milk into the three saucers on the floor, just as Oldfart knocked on the door. 'Are you coming over to the Stirrup later on, Cracky?' Oldfart said, walking in and completely ignoring the three cats lapping at the milk

'I wasn't going to, why?'

'Because Blacktie's coming here tomorrow.'

Captain Marmaduke spat out some milk on the floor and started to choke. 'Is that cat okay?' asked Oldfart.

'Oh, I'm sure it's just a fur ball,' said Cracky, eyeing the Captain, 'please go on.'

'I received a call from his secretary and she said it's something to do with "a change of heart" and the Cestrian Music Tournament.'

'Blacktie hasn't got a heart to change,' Cracky said. 'So you need to be very careful, here. Without wishing to pre-empt anything he has to say, he either wants something or he wants to use you all for something.'

'I'll be willing to bet this is related to whatever Hob and Nob were in town for recently,' Theo said.

Oldfart looked around the Diner trying to find the location of the voice. 'Cracky did you just say that without moving your lips?'

'No,' said Cracky, sighing. 'Can I introduce you to Prince Theo of Corwen, Captain Marmaduke and Half-blind Ron. The voice in your head was Theo's. He can communicate with thought.'

Each of the cats nodded to Oldfart, who stumbled backwards and sat down heavily on a chair. 'Nice to make your acquaintance, Oldfart,' Theo said. 'I've heard a lot of good things about you.'

Oldfart's eyes were wide, although he stood up and managed a clumsy bow. 'And I you, Your Highness, but I must admit to be slightly taken aback. Please accept my apologies.'

'There is no need,' said Theo, waving his paw.

'Unless your apologies come with some more chicken,' Half-blind Ron said.

Cracky passed Oldfart a cup of tea, which he gratefully accepted. 'Your Highness was talking about Hob and Nob,' Oldfart said. 'I've never met them but from what I know they're Blacktie's eyes, and wherever they go trouble tends to follow.'

'You're right on both counts,' Theo replied. 'When I reached into Aiden's mind earlier today I saw them. They were in disguise, but it was definitely them. They were in The Sheep's Stirrup last night, and this morning.'

'Hmm, methinks that perhaps Mr Breezy and Mr Waft were not quite the Vagrant Vacuum Cleaner Exorcists they'd have us believe,' Cracky said. 'It looks like Maurice's hunch about them being spies was correct. But what, in Odin's name, would they be after here, of all places?'

Oldfart stood up and walked to the back of the Diner, cup of tea in one hand and stroking his long beard with the other. 'Last night, after the band had finished, they spent a good deal of time talking to Agnar. At first they were complimenting him on his drumming, which should have aroused suspicion anyway, but I recall overhearing the end of the conversation and it made no sense to me at the time.'

'Go on,' said Captain Marmaduke.

'Well, they were asking him about the old cheese mine that his cousin Angus gave him a few years back; you know, the one that used to belong to Hairy Growler. Agnar said something about a client of theirs would be most interested in taking it off his hands. He told them that he couldn't really sell it because he'd be worried about what Angus may say… and do. When he explained who his cousin was they seemed to get very twitchy.'

'There's got to be a correlation here,' Theo said, looking at Cracky.

'I would agree,' Cracky replied. 'But I find it difficult to believe that Blacktie would be interested in that old thing, its cheese veins are virtually empty, from what I know. And, anyway, Red Cheekfizzler wasn't exactly a delicacy, had no special qualities and played havoc with your bowels. If anyone dedicated any farts to Odin after they'd eaten that stuff I reckon they'd have to evacuate Asgard.'

'It could be a coincidence, Your Highness,' Captain Marmaduke said. 'Perhaps Hob and Nob were working for another client. They're not completely beholden to the Baron.'

'True, but I think we all need to be circumspect,' said Theo. 'If Blacktie is after the mine I doubt it's for its previous reservoir of cheese. There must be another reason.'

'Well then, 'said Oldfart. 'I guess we'll just have to wait and see what tomorrow brings.'

***

Ophelia Palace was situated just across the river Dee, near the Bridge of Faeries and was very, very pink. Several local farmers did a roaring trade providing sunglasses for anyone visiting. Word of Baron Blacktie's visit and its potential consequences had been seized upon by Ophelia, Mara and Roisin as an excuse to arrange a party… not that they normally needed one.

'So, who else have you invited?' said Mara, as Ophelia scrolled through the invitation list.

'I've asked most of my aerobics class, they'll definitely be up for it.'

'In more ways than one, from what I've heard,' laughed Roisin. Ophelia gave her a withering look and continued.

'I'm going to invite Mr Kneepatcher, because he's hilarious, and I'm going to ask Cracky to come and bring some nibbles. Then there's that lovely Charles Corriedale and his nephew, Cliff. Oh, and Oriana Oftsheared as well. I think she and Cliff are becoming a bit of an item.'

'And?' said Mara.

'Oh, and I'll ask those nice boys who sing on the farm. I think one of them has his eye on you.'

'Which one?'

'You know, the short one with the mousey hair and the funny nose.'

'Walter Muddywellies? You can't be serious!' Mara said, aghast. 'He picks his nose and eats it. Now, are you absolutely sure there isn't ANYONE else you should be inviting?'

'No, I think that's about it,' Ophelia said, smiling.

'Ophy, you know who I mean!' Mara screeched.

Ophelia pretended to scroll through the invites once more, ticking everyone off on her list. 'Oh my, how could I be so forgetful?'

'At last,' Mara said.

'I'll ask Vindy and Tikky to come along as well, while they're in town.'

Mara looked her straight in the eye and fluttered her wings in a threatening fashion. '… and I'll invite Aiden,' Ophelia sighed.

Mara's smile was both beautiful and very wide. Then the doorbell rang.

'Hello, my name is Mr Ping and this is my assistant, Mr Pong,' the man with the briefcase said, when Roisin opened the door. 'We are Drifting Feng Shui Practitioners seeking to offer our expertise to only the most exclusive households.'

'Yes, no riff raff,' said Mr Pong.

'We are told that there is a need for cleansing in this charming palace, which we will achieve by aromatic furniture arranging, spurious Tai Chi and clandestine Tao Te Ching narrating,' Mr Ping said.

'And don't forget the cushion-puffing,' reminded Mr Pong.

'Of, course,' said Mr Ping. 'Cushion-puffing is a prerequisite of any attuned abode. We puff cushions like you've never seen.'

'We're indeed champion puffers,' added Mr Pong.

Roisin looked closely at the two men, feeling some vague sense of recognition. They both wore large top-hats and had matching round glasses. 'Haven't we met somewhere before?' she said.

Mr Ping showed no sign of concern at this announcement and produced a card, handing it to Roisin. 'It is a possibility, my dear lady. Mr Pong and I have Feng Shui'd quite a bit in this area in the past.'

'Yes, we've been positively rampant,' said Mr Pong. 'Some of clients can't get enough of it.'

Roisin examined the card, eyeing the two of them with more than a hint of suspicion. 'Wait here, please. I need to speak to the Queen,' she said, walking back to the drawing room.

'Ophy, there are two odd-looking men outside claiming to be Drifting Feng Shui Practitioners. Do you know anything about this?'

'Oh, yes. I remember asking Filbert, the accountant, to hire someone to give the place a new look last week. Are they expecting to stay for a few days?'

'I'm not sure, Ophy, I'll ask them. Shall I arrange rooms if they are?'

'Yes, thanks, Roisin,' the Queen said, 'they can make a start first thing in the morning.'

'It appears you are expected,' Roisin said, as she approached the front door. 'The Queen wishes to know how long you will be staying.'

Mr Ping looked at Mr Pong and smiled. 'Our work in a palace of this grandiosity would take at least two days by my reckoning, would you not agree, Mr Pong?'

'Two days? Yes, I would have thought so.'

'Well then, I'll get the butler to arrange appropriate accommodation,' Roisin said, still feeling slightly uneasy. 'Will you be starting first thing in the morning?'

'Why that would be most excellent, dear lady. First thing in the morning is fine by us, isn't that so, Mr Pong?'

'Fine, indeed,' agreed Mr Pong.

'Well, then, I'll go and get Jarvis to show you to your rooms.'

'Oh, we will only require the one room,' said Mr Pong.

Roisin smiled for the first time in the conversation. 'I see,' she said, winking. 'Well I hope you gentlemen have a pleasant night together.'

Mr Ping looked at Mr Pong, as both of their faces reddened appreciably. 'Ah, I think you do not understand our situation, dear lady,' said Mr Ping. 'Ours is a purely professional relationship. Cohabiting simply allows us to discuss the finer arts of our trade. We will often stay awake until the wee hours going through the ups and downs.'

'And the ins and outs,' added Mr Pong.

Jarvis escorted them to one of the more luxurious guest rooms, carried in their bags and bade them goodnight. 'Well, that was easy,' said Nob.

'You have to remember we are dealing with simpletons, way below the level of our intellect,' Hob replied. 'It is indeed child's play to weave our insidious schemes in such circumstances.'

Hob placed his briefcase into a nearby pink wardrobe and went over to the drinks cabinet. 'Shall we indulge in a glass of champagne, as a toast to our skill, endeavour and genius?'

'Why not,' Nob said. 'Tomorrow we shall gain entrance to the mine, obtain the cheese and collect our sizeable fee from the Baron.'

'Although we may have to puff a few cushions first,' Hob said, popping the cork of the bottle.

He poured the champagne into two large flutes and passed one to Nob. 'So, to us, my good Nob,' he said, raising his glass.

'To us,' Nob said, raising his glass to chink with Hob's. 'I am supremely confident that the task ahead will prove to be one of simplicity and minimal effort.'

'Quite,' Hob agreed, drinking the rest of the champagne from his flute. 'I foresee no problems whatsoever.'

***

In the lower levels of the cheese mine of Hairy Growler, Boris and Barry were hanging upside down discussing the poor quality of rat's blood.

'Let's face it, all the good rats have buggered off,' Boris said, stretching out his little black wings. 'This lot that are left have blood as thin as gnats wee.'

'Yeah, and there's hardly any of it,' Barry said. 'You know I drained one dry in less than a minute yesterday.'

'What I wouldn't give for some lovely, thick, human blood,' Boris sighed.

'Oh, yes, that'd be wonderful. You know I can still remember the taste, the texture and the smell.'

'Well, I suppose we can dream, my friend,' said Boris. 'But unless a complete pair of idiots pay a visit to this godforsaken place, we've got no chance.'

CHAPTER 19 – DO YOU THINK THEY'LL PUT OUT BUNTING?

The sun was doing its utmost to break through the dense cloud that hung over Llangollen, but was meeting with little success. Aiden checked the time on the little alarm clock on his bedside table. It said 9:20 am. He went downstairs, ate a breakfast to rival the gastronomic delight of yesterday and then wandered into the bar, where Maurice and Oldfart were already deep in conversation.

'Word has spread very quickly, you know,' Oldfart said. 'I think there'll be quite a crowd when he arrives. Although saying that, there's a lot of folk who've told me they're going to shut all their doors and windows and stay inside.'

'Well, I'll be honest, he scares the living jibbery-pibberies out of me,' Maurice said. 'And I've heard he has bad wind. Some say his bottom-burps are so ghastly that they make hardened men weep and cry for their mothers.'

'Where's Vindy and Tikky, I thought they'd be down here already?' Aiden said, joining them at the bar.

'They are,' Maurice said. 'They're over there in disguise.'

Maurice had prepared a long table, adorned with a variety of foodstuffs, including fresh bread, fruit, a mixture of pastries and some cold meats. At the end of the table were two plates covered with tin foil. 'Good morning, Aiden,' said Tikky, rustling the tin foil slightly.

'Yes, good morning my good fellow,' Vindy said, mimicking his wife's rustling. 'Do you think these disguises will fool the Baron? I think Maurice has done a splendid job.'

'Definitely,' Aiden said, with a smile. 'As long as the Baron doesn't try and eat you.'

'Oh, that would be horrid, Vindy. Can you imagine going through that awful man's bowels?'

'It doesn't bear thinking about, my dear.'

'Don't worry, I'll be keeping a close eye out,' Maurice said. 'If anyone is tempted to uncover your tin foil, they'll have a plate of Blanche's sausages pushed under their nose. That'll certainly provide a distraction.'

The large, black carriage moved purposely towards Llangollen centre. Both of its metal doors bore the Blacktie crest of a black crow on a red shield, circled by the Blacktie motto, 'Arcum et cedat aut ventum liberari' (Bow and yield or my wind will be freed). Flanking the carriage were two heavily-armed members of the Knights of Flatulence, while in front General Darkblast rode proudly, holding the banner of Blacktie aloft. At the rear were six more knights, swords unsheathed and shields held close to their chest.

Despite the Baron's authority and influence, he was very aware that certain factions may be audacious enough to attempt an assassination. You didn't achieve the level of power and wealth he had without making lots of enemies, so he took no chances when he embarked on any journey outside of the city walls. The entourage surrounding his carriage was backed up by forward reconnaissance troops, crossbows at the ready, and a battalion of infantry brought up the rear.

'Do you think they'll put out bunting?' the Baron said to Pimple, who was sat next to him inside the carriage.

'I wouldn't know, my Lord. Did you order them to?'

'No. I suppose I should have really. I do like bunting.'

'Grunt go get bunting for Baron,' said Grunt, who was sat opposite them, his head pressed against the roof.

'No, that won't be necessary, Grunt,' the Baron sighed. 'And you did go to the toilet before we left, didn't you?'

'Grunt had big plop,' said Grunt. 'All plop gone.'

'No need for details,' said the Baron, with a grimace. 'Just so long as there are no accidents on the way back.'

'Grunt look for more plop in bum before go home,' Grunt said, earnestly.

As the carriage began its slow passage through Llangollen, people and sheep watched silently on the walkways, some averting their eyes as it passed by. Curtains in windows twitched every so often, the eyes of the occupants occasionally visible through the gaps.

Cracky stood by the door of the Diner, with Theo, Captain Marmaduke and Half-blind Ron out of sight under a table, but able to observe through the side window. 'Stop here for a second,' the Baron shouted. The horses whinnied as the driver pulled harshly at the reins.

'Well, well, Merlin Crackfoot. It's been a long time, has it not?' the

Baron said, leaning out of the window.

'Not long enough for me,' Cracky replied.

'Ah, so I see you're still not willing to let bygones be bygones.'

'You know I'll never be able to do that, Baron.'

The Baron shrugged and pulled the curtain back across the window. 'Onwards,' he commanded.

'What was that all about, Cracky?' Theo said, emerging from under the table.

'It's a long story, Your Highness. But it's a story for another time.'

The Blacktie entourage stopped outside the front entrance of the pub and General Darkblast swiftly dismounted. He opened the carriage door and the Baron stepped out onto the cobblestones, raising his arms and yawning.

Inside the pub, Oldfart, Sacred Wind and Aiden were stood at the bar. Behind them Maurice was frantically cleaning glasses, trying to stop his hooves from clacking.

General Darkblast entered first, flanked by two Knights of Flatulence. Then the Baron strode in, with Pimple and Grunt in close attendance. 'Olaf,' Darkblast said to Olaf, nodding in recognition.

'Darkblast,' Olaf responded, also nodding his head, but demonstrating disdain as much as respect.

'You two know each other?' Smid whispered to Olaf.

'We go back quite a long way, but let's just say there's no love lost between us.'

The Baron sniffed the air in a haughty manner and walked over to the bar. 'I'd very much like a glass of your finest port, that's assuming you are actually civilised enough to stock it,' he said to Maurice.

'Coming right up, my Lord,' a quivering Maurice said, grabbing a bottle from behind the bar and filling up a large wine glass.

Maurice handed it to the Baron and he sniffed it gingerly. 'Would you like me to taste it first, in case of poison, my Lord?' General Darkblast said.

'No need, General. I think Mr, er, Fluffywool,' he said, reading the sign behind the bar, 'wouldn't attempt anything of that nature. Isn't that right, Mr Fluffywool?'

'Oh, absolutely, my Lord,' Maurice said, nodding while his hooves clacked together.

The Baron took a sip and raised his eyebrows in pleasant surprise. 'This is actually rather good; not quite up the standard in the palace, but perfectly palatable.'

'Thank you, my Lord,' Maurice said, relaxing visibly.

The Baron turned to face the pub, resting both his elbows on the bar behind him. 'So, to business, then; which one of you is Oldfart Olafson?'

'I am he,' Oldfart said, stepping in front of the Baron.

'Ah, delightful to meet you, Oldfart,' the Baron said, extending his hand. 'And I trust that these good folk are Sacred Wind?'

'They are,' Oldfart replied, slowly taking the Baron's hand.

At that moment Ophelia, Roisin and Mara rushed in, followed by two of the Baron's guards. Darkblast and the guards inside the pub unsheathed their swords. 'Keep your filthy hands off me and show some respect,' Ophelia said, pushing away one of the guards who attempted to grab her arm.'

'My apologies my Lord,' the guard said, 'we told them they could not enter but they refused to listen.'

'My, my, and what have we here?' the Baron said, admiring the three beauties. 'I certainly wasn't expecting to see such a pleasant sight on this visit, I can tell you.'

'I am Queen Ophelia and these are my hand maidens,' Ophelia said, running over to Olaf and linking his arm. Mara sidled over to Aiden and Roisin stood next to Agnar.

'Ah, Queen Ophelia, I've heard so much about you,' the Baron said. 'And it would appear it's all true. Your beauty is legendary, and I see not exaggerated.'

Ophelia stared straight at him but said nothing. She tightened her link with Olaf's arm. 'In fact, you and your hand maidens should really pop along to the palace one day,' the Baron continued. 'I host some very extravagant parties and I'm sure you'd thoroughly enjoy yourselves.'

'I'm not sure that the Baron would enjoy our company as much once my knee had connected with his groin,' Ophelia said.

'Ooh, you are a feisty one. I like that!'

'And to be honest, Baron,' she continued 'I'd rather be locked in a dingy cell with rats and deprived of my comb for a week then attend one of your "parties".'

'Well that can easily be arranged,' the Baron said, with a wicked smile that made Olaf reach for his sword.

'Not now, Olaf,' Grundi said, putting his hand on Olaf's sword arm.

'Anyway, enough of pleasurable activities, let us discuss the matters at hand,' the Baron said. 'I'm assuming that my secretary made you aware of the reason for this visit?'

'I was only told you wished to speak me about the Cestrian Music Tournament and that you'd had a "change of heart",' Oldfart said.

'Indeed,' the Baron said, sighing. 'Times are changing, ladies and gentlemen, and even I must acknowledge this, lest I lose touch with the common people.'

Blacktie moved over to the table were the food was displayed and started to look from platter to platter. 'If he even attempts to lift your foil he's going to get an eyeful of chutney,' Vindy whispered to Tikky.

The Baron stopped short of the two disguised curries and picked up a sausage roll. 'Mmm, this is very good too,' he said between bites. 'Anyway, as I was saying, for too long now I have allowed my own musical proclivities to both influence and control matters. It is now time to loosen up, so to speak, and relinquish some of that control. As much as I still cannot abide rock music in any of its deplorable forms, the people should be allowed to make their own minds up. Wouldn't you agree, Oldfart?'

'Absolutely,' Oldfart said.

'To this end, then,' the Baron continued, 'I hereby invite Sacred Wind to take part in the Cestrian Music Tournament, to be held in two days' time in the Grand Gateway Theatre, Chester.'

Agnar punched the air, yelling loudly and Oldfart clapped his hands together. 'Er, there is one proviso, though,' the Baron said, with a cough. 'I cannot be seen to allow this late change without receiving something in return from the entrants. I'm sure you understand; fair play and all that.'

'Here we go,' Grundi said, looking at Smid.

'So,' the Baron continued, 'you will be obliged to pay a bond, which you will get back if you win the competition.'

'What kind of bond?' Oldfart said.

'A bond to the value of £10,000,' the Baron replied.

'£10,000!' Olaf exclaimed. 'We haven't got that kind of money. I knew there'd be a catch.'

'It doesn't have to be money, Gentlemen. It could be a property, say a house or an old cheese mine or something?'

'I've got a cheese mine,' Agnar shouted, putting up his hand as if he'd been asked a question at school.

'Oh, have you now? That is fortuitous,' the Baron said, feigning surprise. 'Which cheese mine is this then?'

'It's the one that used to be owned by Hairy Growler, near the Circle of Wind. The cheese is nearly all gone, and it was bloody rubbish anyway, but it's still a cheese mine.'

'Hmm, you're not doing a very good job of selling this to me, you know,' the Baron said.

'But it does have potential,' Agnar added, thinking quickly. 'You could use it as a tourist attraction for, oh, I don't know, under-privileged Trolls who could wallow in its murkiness, licking the dank water off its walls while singing songs about how wonderful it is to be a troll.'

Grunt smiled and looked at the baron appealingly. 'Grunt like sound of that.'

The Baron shook his head and started to walk towards the door. Then he stopped dead in his tracks, turned around and put his hands out. 'Well, okay. Call me an old softy but it's a deal,' he said. 'Pimple, pass me the contract.'

Pimple produced a sealed scroll from his inside pocket and handed it to the Baron, who unfurled it and placed it on the bar. 'Just sign here,' he said, handing a pen to Agnar.

'Now, wait a second, Agnar,' Smid said. 'Angus will use your innards as cake decorations if you lose that mine. Think about this for a second.'

'I agree,' Aiden said. 'There's more to this than meets the eye, Agnar.'

The Baron seemed to notice Aiden for the first time, and looked him up and down warily. 'And who, pray, might you be?'

'This is Aiden Peersey, he's our sound engineer,' Oldfart said, before Aiden could answer.

'I see,' the Baron said. 'Well I would advise the scruffy-haired fellow that this deal is straight up. If Sacred Wind win the competition, they keep the mine.'

'Pardon me for speaking, my Lord,' Aiden said. 'But this deal appears to be heavily weighted in your favour. Could you not see fit to also grant another concession if the band win?'

'Like what?' the Baron replied, his curiosity piqued.

'Well, like extending the flatulence license so that people can fart freely,' Aiden said, with no idea why that had come into his mind.

The Baron looked Aiden up and down once more and pursed his lips. 'Very well, I agree,' he said. 'If Sacred Wind are successful I hereby declare that The Sheep's Stirrup will be a "no limit fart zone." Now, if you'll just sign here and then we can all be off.'

Agnar scrawled his signature on the parchment, which was then hastily retrieved by the Baron and handed back to Pimple. 'A wise move, my good man,' the Baron said, turning towards the door. 'So, I bid you all farewell and look forward to our next meeting at the tournament on Wednesday.'

Outside, General Darkblast felt it necessary to voice his concern. 'Do you not think you are taking a risk here, my Lord,' he said, as the Baron was about to step back into the carriage. 'What if this band were to actually win the tournament?'

'Well, you have to be in it to win it,' the Baron said. 'And that means they'll have to successfully navigate their way to Chester. That trail can be fraught with danger, General. Who knows what terrors they may encounter.'

The General smiled.

'Now, as soon as we return, get hold of Taffy Tuffy from the Tan-Y-Lan Tuffies,' the Baron continued. 'I wish to speak to him as a matter of urgency.'

The General looked shocked. 'My Lord, I would advise you not to deal with those pirates. Do you know anything of their nature?'

'I have heard they roam the seas fuelled by super-strength ale and surrounded by prodigious body odour, and that they mercilessly assail their victims with unrelenting violence and inverse aromatherapy,' the Baron replied.

'Yes, er, that would be accurate,' said the General.

'In which case, they sound ideal. Get word to Taffy that he and his hordes should set sail for Chester immediately. I will make it well worth his while. Tell him he needs to be in the palace by tomorrow morning.'

'Yes, my Lord.'

'Oh, General, one last thing before we depart,' the Baron said, as he stepped onto the carriage steps. 'Have Hob and Nob been successful in their infiltration?'

'I believe so, my Lord. I am told that they will be able to obtain the sample of cheese you require by tomorrow.'

'Good. However, send word to them that there is a slight change of plan. I will be in contact with the details later.'

'As you command, my Lord.'

CHAPTER 20 – I SEE YOU'VE BROUGHT YOUR TRUMPET

'You've done what!' Cracky shouted at Oldfart, putting his flagon of Riggley's Piddle down heavily on the bar.

'We've put Agnar's old cheese mine up as a bond. It was a bit of a no-brainer really.'

'Doesn't this strike you as ever so slightly suspicious, Oldfart?' Cracky continued, his reddened face portraying his annoyance. 'I wish you'd have spoken to me first. Blacktie doesn't do anything unless the outcome favours him. He must want the cheese mine for a reason we have yet to fathom.'

'I would agree with Cracky,' said Tikky, now out of her tin foil disguise. 'There's something not quite right here and we should really try to get to the bottom of it.'

Agnar decided it was time to voice his opinion. 'Look, it's my cheese mine and I've made a decision that it's worth a gamble. This could be our passage to the big time after all.'

Theo had listened long enough and also decided it was time to enter the debate. He knew intuitively that he was with friends. 'Good Agnar,' he said, allowing his thoughts to be heard by all within the immediate circle. 'I have no doubt that you have acted in the best interests of your friends by agreeing to this deal, but you must be aware that there could be forces at work here that have another agenda. I apologise for being silent until this moment, but now is the time for cooperation and openness.'

All eyes looked around to see where the pleasant and sagacious voice was coming from, until Cracky pointed downwards towards Theo. 'I am Prince Theo of Corwen,' he said. 'And my friends and I are at your service, wherever that may now lead.'

'Hello you lanky git,' Half-blind Ron said to Aiden.

'I thought it was you,' Vindy said to Theo. 'I just didn't want to blow your cover. But we have met before, haven't we?'

'Indeed, Your Majesty,' Theo said. 'And it is a delight to see both you and the Queen looking so well. I believe I was a tad younger when we last met in Wrexham.'

'You were,' said Tikky. 'And you were delightful. Have your "gifts" continued to bloom?'

'That would be a true statement, Your Majesty.'

Tikky looked more sombre, her colour fading slightly, as she asked the next question. 'How is your father?'

Theo's head dropped momentarily and then he proudly composed himself. 'He ails, Your Majesty. He is very old and weak. I fear he may not see out the next winter.'

'Please tell him he has the best wishes of the people and curries of Wrexham,' Vindy said.

'Thank you, Your Majesty.'

Tikky turned one of her bay leaves upwards, as if using it as a magnifying glass. 'You've grown into a very wise and royal cat, Theo. Your mother would be so proud. Are you aware that she and I were great friends?'

'Yes, Your Majesty. She spoke of you a lot and with great affection.'

'Well, this is a turn up for the books,' Olaf said. 'Who'd have thought that a simple music tournament could generate so much interest and attract such royal and prestigious guests. I think I speak for the entire band when I say we are very honoured that we have your support.'

'And, of course, you'll all have to come to my party later,' Ophelia added.

***

Ophelia's parties were always one of the highlights of the social calendar, and anyone who was anyone just had to attend. To not be invited was construed by some as tantamount to being ostracised from society. Only last year, Lady Monica Slackpants, who failed to make the cut for Ophelia's birthday party, was so distraught that she dyed her hair maroon, became an persistent clog-wearer and announced that she was taking on a new career as a speech therapist for disadvantaged budgies.

'Hello, oh, I do hope we're not too early. Bless my clacky hooves, I don't think I've been so excited for years.'

'Of course you're not too early, Charles, please come in. And you too, Cliff,' Ophelia said, with a warm smile. 'I see you've brought your trumpet, how splendid. Now, promise me that you'll not have too much to drink before you play for us later. I still remember last year when you lost your balance trying to reach that high note after several glasses of Roisin's special cider.'

'Oh, dear,' said Charles, 'that was embarrassing. But at least I had the pleasure of you and Mara catching me!'

Upstairs, in Ophelia's royal bedroom, Mr Ping and Mr Pong were busy puffing cushions, under Roisin's watchful eye. 'I didn't realise that Feng Shui involved so much cushion-puffing,' she said, still feeling very unsure of the odd pair.

'My dear lady, gratuitous cushion-puffing is a vital part of the preparation process for any successful Feng Shui exercise,' said Mr Ping.

'Indeed,' added Mr Pong, 'we have forged our career and reputation by the level and quality of our puffing.'

'But aren't you suppose to place things strategically to generate positive Qi?' she asked.

'Of course, the essence of Qi is channelled through the puffing of the cushions,' said Mr Ping. 'But, now we have puffed enough and it is time to embark on the serious matter of furniture placement. Mr Pong, please pass me that small ottoman.'

Mr Pong picked up a pink ottoman at the end of Ophelia's luxurious bed and handed it to Mr Ping, who stared up into the air and began to turn his head in a circling motion. 'Ah, I can feel it now. The Qi is strong over here,' he said, placing the ottoman by the window. 'Can you feel the Qi, Mr Pong?'

'It's making my toes curl as you speak. I can feel it going up my trousers.'

'Well, I'll leave you gentlemen to it for a while,' said Roisin. 'The Queen is expecting guests this evening and I should really make an appearance. I'll come and check on your progress shortly.'

And with that she exited the room and made her way downstairs to the party. 'Thank goodness she's gone,' said Nob. 'She's a nosey one.'

'Indeed,' said Hob. 'But once again, our superior thespian skills and improvisational abilities have allowed us to successfully perpetuate our masquerade.'

There was a knock on the bedroom door and Hob and Nob looked at each other with alarm. 'Come in,' said Mr Ping.

'Pardon me, my good sirs, but this letter has just arrived for you,' said Jarvis, holding out the sealed envelope.

'Ah, er, that will no doubt be from our agent, informing us of our next engagement. Thank you so much,' Mr Ping said, as he took the letter from Jarvis.

'Who on earth would be sending us a letter?' Nob said. 'Nobody even knows we are here.'

'It's from the Baron,' Hob replied, unfolding the letter and reading its contents. 'It would seem there is to be a slight change of plan.'

Downstairs, Charles Corriedale was indulging in two of his favourite pastimes; drinking cider and talking music. 'Of course, I'll be playing with the OSO in the tournament,' he said, with a glass of cider between his hooves. 'But I would like to say that I'll still be cheering you fellows on. I'm actually quite a fan.'

'Are you really?' said Grundi. 'I wouldn't have thought our style of music would be your thing at all.'

'Nothing could be further from the truth,' Charles said, between hiccups. 'I adore the power and the passion of your songs. In fact, the musicality and compositional structure isn't that far removed from classical music. I tell you, I've had quite a few evenings when I've just let my fleece down and rocked out. Isn't that right, Cliff?'

'Hah, my uncle speaks the truth,' Cliff said. 'I have borne witness to his uncommonly accurate air guitar playing. However, he shouldn't bang his head so much now that his years are advancing.'

'Fiddlesticks!' Charles retorted, to the laughter of Grundi, Smid and Aiden. 'You're as young as you feel. Or as young as the ewe you are feeling,' he added with a wink.

'Uncle, you are incorrigible,' Cliff said, smiling.

'Oh, yes. I do hope so, my nephew. I do hope so!'

As Charles wandered off in search of another drink, Cliff watched him and shook his head. 'You know he really is one of a kind.'

'Absolutely,' Grundi agreed. 'You obviously love him very much.'

'More than my own life, Grundi; I'd do anything to protect that old sheep.'

Vindy and Tikky were given a starring role on a table in the middle of the ballroom, but far enough away from the buffet to avoid confusion. 'Would you two like anything?' Ophelia said.

'I think I could go for a little lime juice, thank you,' Vindy said, chuckling. 'Not too much, though, it goes straight to my beef these days.'

'Just a touch of pineapple juice for me, please, my dear. If Vindy's going on the lime I better make sure I keep my wits about me in case he starts trying to dance again,' Tikky said.

'What do you mean "trying to dance"? I seem to remember that at the last party we attended I was being praised for my "twirling plate boogie"!'

'Yes, dear, that's true. And then Harold had to intervene before you nearly fell off the table after attempting that pirouette.'

'Ah, yes,' Vindy admitted, 'but it would have looked spectacular if I hadn't have bumped into that large pepper pot.'

The party was now in full swing and Aiden had been introduced to that many people that names were no longer sticking in his memory. He had also met the faeries from Ophelia's aerobics class, who had all flirted with him outrageously, much to Mara's chagrin.

'Are all faeries as beautiful as this?' he'd said to Cracky, who had been smirking away at him in the corner of the room, talking to Mr Kneepatcher.

'Well put it this way,' Cracky had said. 'I've never met one yet that didn't make my knees turn to jelly with a smile.'

In Ophelia's bedroom, Hob and Nob were peering at the contents of the open briefcase. 'I wouldn't recommend that one,' said Nob.

'Why not?'

'It's Yellow Nostrilflarer. It does indeed render a victim immobile, but the common side-effect of increasing the size of the nostrils fivefold can take days to wear off.'

'I see,' said Hob. 'What we need is just a simple tranquilizer cheese that will put a faerie under for, say, two hours. The Baron is sending us a swift carriage so the dose must not be too great.'

'Aha,' Nob said, picking up a small cube, wrapped in pink paper. 'This is what I was looking for. This is Pink Sleepybobos and it has never been known to have any adverse side effects. A couple of crumbs of this in her drink and she'll be out like a light.'

'Perfect,' Hob said, as Roisin knocked on the door. 'Come in,' he said, closing the briefcase, as Nob put the small cube of cheese in his pocket.

'I just thought I'd check and see how you are getting on,' Roisin said.

'My dear lady, we are making excellent progress, but we have hit a stumbling block,' said Hob.

'What kind of stumbling block?'

Mr Ping put his hand to his head, feigning exasperation. Mr Pong followed suit. 'We will need to complete an incantation for the carpet here,' Mr Ping said, pointing at a lush, pink rug near the window. 'We fear it has been subject to undue negative Qi for a considerable period of time, possibly influenced by that particularly recalcitrant chest of drawers. But we will need assistance from the Queen. For we are certain that only her royal and calming nature, amplifying the words we need to speak, will facilitate a successful operation. Would you be so kind as to ask her to join us, if she is free?'

'Does it have to be now?' Roisin said. 'She is in the middle of hosting an important party.'

Hob approached Roisin and adopted the most earnest façade he could muster. 'My dear Roisin, if I may be allowed to call you by name. The stars are aligned at this very moment and I fear that if we delay, this poor carpet could become a permanent victim of "insensitive chest of drawers syndrome". This is a particularly odious negative energy that can cause fraying at the edges and underlay exposure. I have seen it before and it is best to be preventive in these situations.'

'Preventive,' echoed Mr Pong.

'Okay,' Roisin said, reluctantly. 'I'll go and ask her if she can spare you a few minutes and then I'll bring her up.'

Mr Ping shared a quick glance with Mr Pong and they both shook their heads in unison. 'It would be better for the incantation if only the Queen attended,' Mr Ping said. 'The balance we must strike is quite delicate and we must ensure that the flow of Qi is well controlled, else the situation could exacerbate.'

'Indeed,' said Mr Pong. 'We not only wish for a successful outcome, but neither I nor Mr Ping wish to be known as people who exacerbate unnecessarily.'

'Very well,' Roisin said, 'I'll go and speak to her.'

Ophelia was feeling a tad tipsy. She was sat on Olaf's knee having an in-depth conversation with Mr Kneepatcher about cravats. 'Of course you've got to tie them right,' said Mr Kneepatcher. 'Otherwise you just don't get the effect.'

'Do you think Olaf would suit a cravat?' she asked, in a slightly slurred voice.

'Oh, darling, he'd look wonderful!' Mr Kneepatcher gushed. 'I've got a beautiful blue one in stock that would set his eyes off perfectly. I'll bring it around tomorrow.'

'Thanks, but I may give it a miss,' Olaf said.

'Ophy, the two Feng Shui gentlemen have asked if you can pop upstairs for a minute to help them with an incantation or something,' Roisin said, sitting down next to Olaf.

'Will it take long, do you know? Charles is due to play at any minute and we may need to catch him again!'

'I wouldn't have thought so. But they insist on seeing you alone,'

Olaf shifted in his seat uncomfortably. 'Are these "gentlemen" trustworthy, Roisin?'

'They seem harmless enough, even if they are a bit odd,' she replied.

'Oh, I'll be fine, Olaf,' Ophelia said, nearly falling over when she got up off his knee. 'I'll be back shortly.'

Cracky and Oldfart watched as Ophelia staggered up the heavily-carpeted grand staircase, both of them poised to catch her if she fell backwards. 'By the way, where are Theo and the cats?' Oldfart asked Cracky, once Ophelia had safely reached the top of the stairs.

'They stayed back at the Diner. Even though he revealed himself to us today, he still wants to stay behind the scenes for the time being.'

Ophelia managed to successfully navigate her way down the long corridor to the royal bedroom, using the walls for balance on several occasions. She placed her half-full glass of champagne delicately on to the carpet outside the door, telling it to 'shush' as she placed a finger in front of her mouth. 'Yoo hoo,' she said in a high pitched voice, as she leaned against the bedroom door. 'I believe you gentlemen wish to see me.'

Mr Pong opened the door and the Queen fell through and landed at the feet of Mr Ping. 'Well, hello there, how can I be of service,' she said, giggling, as Mr Ping helped her to her feet.

'Your Majesty, thank you for agreeing to see us,' Mr Ping said. 'We are sorry to have to drag you away from your party, but this matter is most urgent.'

'Most urgent,' agreed Mr Pong.

'We are required to perform an incantation to save this beautiful carpet of yours,' Mr Ping continued, pointing at the large pink rug near the window. 'We require you to simply stand on the rug and think positive thoughts.'

'That all? Shouldn't be too hard,' Ophelia said, swaying.

'But first, we must drink this sacred water that Mr Pong has prepared. It will provide balance for our bodies and souls,' he said, passing a goblet of water to the Queen.

'Oh, I could definitely do with something to help my balance at the moment!' Ophelia giggled, as she eventually took the goblet off Mr Ping at the third attempt.

She drank deeply and dropped the goblet unceremoniously on the floor. 'Oops, sorry. Now shall we all sing this incant-, incatash… song of yours…?'

And then her eyes began to close and she fell into the arms of Mr Pong, who was standing behind her. 'Simplicity itself, my good Nob,' Hob said, rubbing his hands.

'How do we get her out of the palace?' Nob asked, laying the Queen on the pink rug.

'Oh, I already have a plan for that,' said Hob. 'Now, roll her up into the carpet and let's be on our way. We will exit via the stairs used by the servants, and hopefully we'll encounter one as we leave.'

'You want us to be seen?' Nob said, with surprise.

'Indeed, I am counting on it.'

The plush, pink rug was easily big enough to accommodate Ophelia's tiny frame completely, and Hob and Nob had little trouble carrying it down the stairs and into the kitchen, where Jarvis was drinking a cup of tea. 'Oh, hello sirs, is everything alright?' he asked.

'Ah, Jarvis, I'm glad we caught you,' Mr Ping said, feigning relief. 'We have just come from the royal bedroom, where Her Majesty has now taken to her rest. She asked us to pass on a message that she is very weary, but that the party should continue in her absence. She also requested that she is not disturbed until morning.'

'Has Her Majesty perhaps had a little too much champagne?' Jarvis said, with a smile.

'Indeed,' replied Mr Pong. 'She has also asked us to help this carpet here by providing our special Moonlit Feng Shui treatment. We fear it has been subject to negative forces and, if not dealt with appropriately, may begin to infest other furnishings in the palace.'

As if on cue, the rug let out a small groan. 'See it begins already.' Mr Ping said, shaking his head.

A shocked Jarvis ran to the back door and slid open the bolts. 'Thank you,' said Mr Pong, as Jarvis opened the door. 'I just hope we've not left it too late. We will return, hopefully, within the hour.'

'Good luck, sirs. May the gods be with you,' Jarvis said, as Mr Ping and Mr Pong headed out into the night.

At the end of the dark lane behind the palace, a black carriage was silhouetted in the moonlight and enveloped in silence, save for the occasional snorting of its horses. As Hob and Nob approached, one of the doors swung open.

'Do you have the cargo?' Pimple said.

'Let us just say that we do not think the Baron will be displeased,' Hob replied, as they climbed inside with the carpet.

'Driver!' shouted Pimple, and the carriage pulled away at speed.

Sacred Wind: The Complete Trilogy

CHAPTER 21 – HAS ANYONE SEEN THE QUEEN?

Oriana Oftsheared was a very gifted flautist, even by sheep standards. She had been a member of the OSO for just over a year and had cemented her place due to her technical dexterity and superb musical interpretation. She had also struck up a firm friendship with Cliff Corriedale, often performing flute/cello duets when the occasion arose. Their relationship, though, was now turning into something more.

Cliff was a very handsome sheep, in a rugged-ram kind of way, and attracted the attention of the younger ewes at the OSO's concerts, to the point where many of them would throw their udder-garments at him on stage. Oriana was considered to be his female equivalent and even had her own fan club. There had also been several offers to appear in some of the more racy magazines, such as 'Playsheep' and 'Sheep Parade', but she politely turned them all down. Music was her first love and she was very dedicated to her craft, and she was quite happy to spend her personal time out of the limelight. As Cliff was of a similar mind, their mutual appreciation of each other's talents, complimentary personalities and the fact that they fancied each other to bits meant that the inevitable was only a matter of time.

'Charles is beginning to look very wobbly,' Oriana observed to Cliff, as she linked hooves with him.

'I know. I may have to take him home soon, bless him. He's started to flirt with the faeries, particularly the two that caught him when he lost his balance playing… again. I'm sure he does that on purpose, you know.'

'Hello you two, are you enjoying yourselves?' Roisin asked, finally managing drag herself away from Agnar.

'Oh, we're having a wonderful time,' Oriana said, with a sideways glance at Cliff that made Roisin smile. 'I was hoping to chat to the Queen before we left but I've not seen her for a while.'

'Oh, damn,' Roisin said. 'I completely forgot that I was supposed to call her before Charles played. Although why she's been gone so long, I'm not sure. I better go and see if everything's okay.'

As Roisin was just about to walk up the grand staircase, Jarvis appeared, newspaper tucked under his arm, preparing to retire for the night. 'Have you seen the Queen recently?' Roisin asked.

'No, ma'am, I've not. But I was told she was feeling weary and had retired for the evening. She sent a message that everyone was to continue in her absence.'

'Who passed on the message?'

'Why, it was those two Feng Shui gentlemen. They were on their way out to perform a Moonlit Feng Shui treatment on the Queen's pink rug, from the royal bedroom. Actually I thought they'd be back by now. They've been gone for well over an hour.'

Roisin's intuition was something she always relied on and it rarely failed her. She bolted up the stairs, leaving an open-mouthed Jarvis in her wake. The bedroom door was closed. 'Ophy, are you awake?' she shouted, knocking loudly on the door.

Silence was the reply, and Roisin could feel panic welling up inside her. 'Ophy, Ophy, wake up!' she said, increasing the volume of the knocking. 'If you don't come to the door in ten seconds I'll have to enter uninvited. I'm worried about you.'

She was greeted with the same silence as before, or it may have been a different silence, it was difficult to tell. All silence tends to sound the same after a bit.

'One... two... three... four...' And then she burst in, impatience and concern cutting the count short.

The bedroom was empty and the pink rug was gone. She rushed around the room looking for Ophelia in the most improbable of places; under the bed, behind the curtains, in the wardrobe. But the Queen was nowhere to be seen.

Jarvis had made his way up the stairs and appeared at the bedroom door. 'The Queen is gone, Jarvis,' Roisin said.

'Perhaps she's simply gone outside for some fresh air?'

'Maybe, but I've not got a good feeling about this. I'll go and ask if anyone's seen her.' And with that she ran down the stairs, almost tripping on a couple of occasions. 'Has anyone seen the Queen?' she shouted, to the crowded main ballroom.

The response was a mixture of blank stares, a few 'noes' and several shakes of heads. She ran into the drawing room, which was acting as an overspill area by a few of the guests, and repeated the question, but received the same set of responses.

Jarvis had now come downstairs and was looking concerned. 'Jarvis, when you saw the two men with the rug did you see or hear anything unusual?' Roisin said.

'Well, come to think of it, there was something rather odd. As the two gentlemen were taking the rug through the kitchen, it groaned.'

'The rug "groaned"?'

'Yes, ma'am. They said it was because of negative forces in the rug and that they had to get it outside as soon as possible before anything else got infested.'

Roisin ran back into the main ballroom and headed straight for Olaf. By now she was almost in tears. 'Olaf, I think Ophy's been kidnapped.'

**

Ophelia was enjoying watching the squirrels in the garden. They were ever so playful and cute, with their big brown eyes and bushy tails. 'Now then, Mr Squirrel, if you come over here I'll tickle your chin and you can have this nut,' she said to one of the more curious squirrels, holding the nut out in her tiny hand.

'Is it a nice nut?' asked the squirrel. 'It's not going to send me to sleep or anything is it?'

'Of course not. These are very fine nuts. Only the best for you because I love you all,' she said, smiling widely.

The squirrel came over to her, took the nut and immediately started nibbling on it. Several other squirrels came over, followed by a little deer and some birds. She was soon surrounded by a loving throng of cute animals.

Then two black rats appeared. 'She's not what she seems, you know,' one of the rats said. 'You animals should be careful.'

'Well you're very rude and completely wrong,' Ophelia said to the rats, as the cute animals started to back away from her.

'I've heard she likes squirrel stew, with deer dumplings and bird fritters,' said the other rat.

'I do not!' Ophelia shouted. But it was too late, the cute animals scattered and the two rats just laughed… and then started to grow. Soon they were bigger than Ophelia and they began to walk towards her, grinning and salivating.

'You're coming with us, my dear Queen,' one of them said as they picked her up, one holding her legs, the other her arms.

'Help! Help! The rats have got me!' she shouted, but there was no-one else around. She could see a black door up ahead, but it was very fuzzy and seemed to have a glow around the edges.

'Let's get her inside,' the rat holding her arms said. 'There's a special room prepared for her.'

'Good idea,' the other rat said. 'The Baron will want to speak to her when she wakes up.'

As consciousness grabbed a machete and began to chop its way through the thick undergrowth of her unconscious mind, Ophelia's eyes opened and closed intermittently. She could see walls and paintings, marble floors and pillars… and a big giant man coming towards her. 'Be careful with nice Queen or Grunt do big whacks on heads,' the giant man said. 'Baron said Queen not to be harmed.'

A door creaked open and she was placed on a comfortable bed. The big giant man looked at her and smiled, his crooked teeth appearing more like huge standing stones, defying the force of gravity by leaning against each other. 'Grunt make sure Queen safe,' he said. Somehow she found this reassuring.

And so, her consciousness dropped its machete and was swallowed by her unconscious undergrowth once more. She drifted off to sleep but this time there were no squirrels.

***

'Any luck yet?' Cracky said, rushing back into the palace after a futile search of the grounds.

'No, nothing at all,' Olaf said, his face etched with worry.

They had been looking for nearly three hours and it was now well after midnight. In the drawing room, Roisin was still tearful and was being consoled by Mara and Agnar. Aiden, Smid and Grundi had just reappeared after an equally futile search of the palace. Vindy and Tikky had been placed on a large, oak sideboard by the wall.

'Who's reported back?' Cracky asked.

'Oriana, Cliff and the lads from Mr Morningmilker's farm did a thorough search of the road from here to the bridge but found nothing. They've taken Charles home now, but they said they'd come back first thing in the morning,' Mara said.

'What about Oldfart and Mr Kneepatcher?'

'We haven't heard anything from them, and they've been gone for quite a while.'

'Harold and Greta?'

'They're still searching the south side of the palace and the grounds. They should be back shortly.'

As if on cue, they appeared at the door. 'I'm sorry, but we can't find a trace of her,' Harold said.

Roisin went to Olaf and embraced him. 'I'm so sorry. If only I'd listened to my inner voice. It was screaming at me that there was something wrong with those two.'

Olaf held her tightly and planted a kiss on top of her head. 'It's not your fault, Roisin; you have no reason to blame yourself. You weren't the only one who was fooled by them, whoever they are.'

'I strongly suspect that I know the identity of the Queen's abductors,' Cracky said. 'But I'll need to bring someone along in the morning to verify my theory.'

'What do you mean?' Aiden said.

'Prince Theo reached into your mind the other day, without you being aware, my friend. It turns out that Mr Breezy and Mr Waft were actually two of Blacktie's spies.'

All eyes turned to Cracky upon hearing Blacktie's name. Grundi drew in a sharp breath and Agnar crossed his arms defiantly. Olaf clenched his big hands into fists. 'So you think that the two "Feng Shui gentlemen" are Mr Breezy and Mr Waft?' Roisin said.

'Well, they aren't their really names, but, yes. If it's the two names mentioned by Theo then they are masters of disguise. We'll need him to probe your mind tomorrow, Roisin. Then at least we'll be able to confirm one way or the other.'

'I'll do whatever is necessary,' said Roisin, wiping the last of today's tears from her eyes.

***

Her Majesty Queen Ophelia Goldendwing had been Queen of all Faeries for just over two years, following the abdication of her mother Queen Hazel Goblinfly.

The race of faeries have no realms as such and just tend to make their homes wherever they are welcome, therefore the Queen's subjects are spread far and wide across the entire country. It should also be said that there is no such thing as a male faerie, so in order for a faerie to mate she must take a human lover. Given that all faeries are invariably stunningly beautiful this has never caused a problem, and in fact the queues are generally very long when a faerie advertises herself as 'available'. Every faerie is born with wings and although they are unable to fly as such, they can use them to hover for short periods of time.

Ophelia was a very popular queen. She was kind and giving and cared deeply for all living creatures. She brought joy and light with her when she entered a room, had a wonderful sense of humour, and also had quite probably the most beautiful smile in the cosmos. Her wings were considered to be flawless (a sign of great purity in faerie lore) and she was wise beyond her years. Like most faeries, however, she was very fond of handbags, shoes and combs.

She had been engaged to Olaf for six months and he had said that he wished to marry her as soon as Sacred Wind landed a major record deal. Although faerie wealth is legendary, as a proud Viking of semi-noble heritage himself, he desired to pay his way... or at least buy the shopping every week.

Ophelia awoke with a start, sitting up and peering into the near-darkness around her. As her eyesight began to grow accustomed to the low light, she went over to the door and turned the handle. It was locked and she wasn't really surprised. She felt around the walls for a light switch and found one.

The room was not unpleasant. The furnishings were clean and of very good quality, indicating that whoever owned this property wasn't short of money. There was a single window with curtains drawn across it at the far end of the room, so she pulled them back. The window was barred, so although her host or hosts wanted her to stay in relative comfort, they obviously didn't want her to leave. As her head began to clear she delved into her memories, trying to bring the most recent ones to the surface.

She remembered feeling tipsy and going upstairs at the palace. She remembered falling through the door of the royal bedroom and chatting to the two Feng Shui practitioners. She remembered the pink carpet and remembered being given a drink. After this everything seemed to be a blur; vague recollections of being carried and a giant man smiling at her.

As she looked out of the barred window she could see the tall spires of a massive cathedral nearby. There was only one cathedral of that size in the vicinity. She was in Chester.

The lock on the door clicked and it swung open. 'Hello there, Queen Ophelia. I hope you had pleasant dreams and find the room to your liking,' said Baron Blacktie, standing in the doorway with Grunt behind him.

'You'll be staying with us for a few days,' the Baron continued. 'I think you'll find I'm an excellent host... well most of the time. But I'm afraid it's past my bedtime now, so I will bid you adieu for this night and we can have a good chat in the morning, after breakfast. I'm sure you'll have lots of questions.'

'I have one now,' Ophelia said.

'Well, as long as it's quick. I really am rather pooped,' the Baron sighed.

'Have you seen my comb?'

***

Mr Kneepatcher and Oldfart were out of breath as they ran into the drawing room and all heads turned automatically in anticipation. 'We've found something,' Mr Kneepatcher said, attempting to get his breath back, bending down with his hands on his knees.

'What is it?' Olaf said, his eyes brightening with a glint of hope.

'This,' said Oldfart, holding out an ornate, pink comb. 'We found it a few hundred yards to the north, on Dark Lane. There were fresh footprints, made by two men, I'd say. And fresh carriage tracks.'

Mara rushed over to Oldfart and he passed her the comb. 'It's Ophy's alright.'

'So she has been abducted,' Smid said. 'And it would appear that Blacktie's spies are responsible.'

'We can confirm that in the morning,' said Cracky. 'What we do know for certain is that we have no idea where she's been taken, and wherever she is she won't be able to comb her hair.'

CHAPTER 22 – SO IT WOULD APPEAR THAT THE OUTCOME IS NOT DECIDED

As he began the long walk back to Llangollen, Cracky tried to piece together the events so far. Blacktie was obviously interested in the mine, and it did seem a little coincidental that he had a readily-prepared contract waiting for Agnar's signature. Claiming that he wished Sacred Wind to enter the competition for his own altruistic reasons was undoubtedly a lie. It was the mine he was after; but why?

The motive for kidnapping the Queen was less clear. Cracky had been told that she was certainly not overawed by the Baron when they had met at The Sheep's Stirrup. She had been typically courageous and had put in him in his place, following his lewd suggestions towards her and her friends. Blacktie certainly couldn't abide defiance, and there were many who had suffered quite ghastly fates for rubbing him up the wrong way. But this was the Queen of the Faeries we were talking about. No, this was more than simply taking revenge for an act of impertinence. Blacktie would know for certain that the band's plans to travel to Chester for the tournament would be thrown into disarray, with them potentially abandoning the trip. And then the mine would be his. But why take such a risk? Blacktie may have been many things but he wasn't a fool. The mine obviously held a secret of great import.

Theo was still awake when Cracky walked into the Diner, although Captain Marmaduke and Half-blind Ron were curled up fast asleep. 'You don't have to tell me what's happened, Cracky. I've been picking up your thoughts for the last five minutes or so. I hope you're not offended.'

'I thought as much,' said Cracky. 'I am still sensitive on occasions and I noticed your presence, but, no, I'm not offended in the slightest.'

As Cracky slumped wearily into a chair, Theo jumped up on his knee, much to Cracky's surprise. 'I'm still a cat, Cracky. If you stroke me it'll make you feel better, trust me.'

Cracky smiled and did as he was advised. 'We're missing something important and I can't put my finger on it, Theo. The mine is obviously a big part in this, but I sense there's something else.'

'I agree. The Prophecy is coming together and perhaps that is a good place to start, *"Four great warriors will face a challenge from an evil Baron in a city far away".*'

'What's the next line?'

'From memory I think it was *"because he desired their cheese".*'

'Well, let's go and confirm that,' said Cracky. 'I've not been in the loft in a long time and there are some very interesting books up there.'

Cracky returned from the loft with two very old books. One was a copy of The Prophecy, which was already open at a particular page, the other he simply placed on the table next to them. 'I think that you'll find this edifying,' he said to Theo, pointing at the page in question. 'Which version of The Prophecy do you have?'

'I believe it was one of the later editions. Why what do you have there?'

'This is THE 1st edition. It was my father's. Look at this paragraph here.'

He placed the book on the floor so both he and Theo could see more clearly in the light. 'It says *"The evil Baron will despatch his spies and capture the faerie queen, who will be betrothed to one of the warriors. He will challenge them to take part in a great tournament, lest she be left to suffer at his hands and be subject to his wind! And, if the warriors lose, the Baron will also win the right to their cheese. And, if this happens, he will gain power beyond imagining".*'

'I've never read that section,' said Theo.

'You won't have. For some reason it was removed from the 2nd edition onwards.'

'It's uncanny,' Theo said, scratching behind his ear. 'This passage seems to be describing the very times we are in.'

'Indeed,' replied Cracky. Now I'll read the next bit and then I need to show you something in the other book over there. Right then, *"They"*, which I think means the four great warriors, *"will gather with them friends willing to join their quest to win the tournament, to win freedom for the land, to save the faerie queen, to be able to fart freely, and to win the right to their cheese. Together they will be known as the Companionship of Wind!"*'

'Are you aware that Aiden actually asked the Baron to grant The Sheep's Stirrup an unlimited flatulence license?' Theo said.

'Yes, Oldfart told me. Now, listen, there's more. *"They will gather up supplies and weapons and set sail down the great river in a boat with a mighty dragon at the helm. They will face many dangers on the way, unspeakable terrors and some particularly dodgy curries, yet they will reach the city in time for the great tournament".*'

'How does it end?' asked Theo.

'That's it. There's no more.'

'So it would appear that the outcome is not decided,' Theo said. 'This is not the first time the passages in The Prophecy leave fate to write the final chapter.'

'So it would appear. Now, let me show you the other much older book.'

Cracky wiped a considerable layer of dust from the book's cover and put it on the floor. The letters on its ancient, leather cover were barely legible. 'This is possibly the most ancient book on cheese in the world,' he said, carefully turning the parchment pages. 'It once belonged to an evil wizard called Scratchy Crotch, and although there is no signature of authorship it is likely he wrote it. Look at this map here.'

Theo stared at the map, recognising the topography immediately. 'This is a map of North Wales, Chester and the Wirral.'

'It is indeed. Do you see these small circles dotted about?'

'Yes.'

'These are cheese mines. And beneath each mine is written the type of cheese contained within it. This one near Mold is Orange Tummywarmer; this one near Wrexham is Blue Bottomgrabber; this one near Chester is Green Kneetrembler... and this one near Llangollen...'

'That's near the Circle of Wind. It's Agnar's mine.'

'Yes. And can you make out the type of cheese written below it?'

'Does that say "Ceridwen"?' Theo said, turning and looking directly at Cracky.

'It does. You'd expect it to say Red Cheekfizzler, as that was the last known cheese mined there. But it clearly says "Ceridwen".'

'I've heard of that cheese, but I thought it had long since been extinct. I also remember reading that it was called something like "The Cheese of Pleasant Dreams".'

'Your education for one so young is noteworthy, Your Highness,' Cracky said, smiling. 'But, other than having soothing and pleasant properties, it has never been known to be particularly magical.'

'So why would the Baron be after a mine containing Ceridwen's Cheese, if all it's going to give him is a warm glow all over and some calming dreams?'

'He wouldn't,' Cracky replied. 'There's a missing piece of this increasingly enigmatic puzzle that we need to discover. But one thing is for certain, we've got to convince the band that, irrespective of the Queen's untimely abduction, they MUST travel to Chester for the music tournament, and they MUST go in Ethel.'

'Absolutely,' Theo agreed.

'Right,' said Cracky. 'We better get some sleep, Your Highness. There are only a few hours until dawn and I feel we'll need all the rest we can get, given what's likely to be ahead of us.'

***

'Are the eggs the way I like them?'

'Yes, my Lord. Over-easy with added pepper,' quaked Chef Buttonmushroom, the Baron's personal cook.

'And the bacon… crispy but not too crispy?'

'Exactly to your specifications, my Lord.'

The Baron looked around the plate and seemed satisfied. 'That will be all,' he said, waving him away with his hand.

'I don't know how you can eat that garbage,' the voice on the plate next to him said. 'It does not fuel the spirit.'

'It may not fuel the spirit but it fuels my wind,' said the Baron, 'and trust me, Brother, I know where my priorities lie.'

Brother Vegetable Jalfrezi-Basmathi Rice turned one of his tomatoes in contempt, but said nothing.

'Now, onto business,' the Baron said, crunching a piece of crispy bacon between his teeth. 'I require you and your Brotherhood to keep watch on Sacred Wind, whilst they attempt to traverse the hazardous journey they are likely to embark on. I have no desire to see those Viking noise-merchants anywhere near Chester, so I'll be relying on you and some other less-reputable types to ensure they are suitably delayed… or worse. Actually, worse might be better.'

'And what do we get in return, Baron?' Brother Vegetable Jalfrezi-Basmathi Rice asked, his onions moving like snakes swimming on water.

The Baron stuffed a fork-full of egg into his mouth and twirled the fork whilst he chewed. 'I need someone I can trust, or at least someone who understands the rewards of loyalty, to rule both Wrexham and Mold with an iron fist; or in your case a very hard carrot.'

'We think alike, Baron,' Brother Vegetable Jalfrezi-Basmathi Rice said, with a sneer of his shallots. 'I feel there is much we can accomplish together.'

'Well, there's much that I'll be able to accomplish by myself soon. But, I take your point. So do we have a deal?'

Brother Vegetable Jalfrezi-Basmathi Rice bubbled slightly. 'Let me discuss it with my compatriots,' he said, twisting towards the two other plates behind him. After several seconds of whispering and bubbling, he turned back to face the Baron. 'We agree. Do you know how they are travelling?'

'Oh, they'll be coming by boat. Of that I'm certain. But I should tell you that I'll be requiring you to work in tandem with another party, although they will be deployed first.'

As if on cue, Pimple entered the breakfast room with three very dirty and particularly vicious-looking men. 'My Lord, may I present representatives from the Tan-Y-Lan Tuffies.'

Brother Vegetable Jalfrezi-Basmathi Rice looked outraged and his tomatoes spat out little yellow seeds. 'You expect us to work with pirates! Perhaps you expect too much, Baron.'

The Baron rose from his chair and passed his stained napkin to Pimple. 'Oh, I think not. As I said, Brother, the rewards of loyalty will be great. But, rest assured, you would not wish the fate of those who are not with me.'

The Brother and his two compatriots wobbled nervously on the breakfast table. 'Now then,' the Baron said, moving closer to the three pirates, 'which one of you uncouth barbarians is Taffy?'

The three looked at each and shrugged their shoulders. 'I am,' they said in unison.

'Hmm,' said the Baron, eyeing each in turn, and then looking over at his Chief Courtier. 'This could be more problematic than I thought, Pimple. Very well, which of you three Taffies is Taffy Tuffy?'

Again, the three looked at each other and, again, shrugged their shoulders. 'I am,' they said in unison once more.

'Oh, this is ridiculous!' the Baron shouted. 'Which one of you is in charge?'

'Oh, that'd be me boyo,' said the smallest of the three. He had a large ring through his nose, a black hat that was at least two sizes too big for him and a disproportionately large cutlass.'

'At last,' said the Baron. 'Now, Mr Tuffy, do you know why I've summoned you here on this bright and, dare I say, glorious morning?'

'Is it something to do with mayhem, monstrous torture, murder and mutilation?' Taffy Tuffy enquired.

'Oh, I like your style, Mr Tuffy!' the Baron enthused. 'I can see your mind is so finely attuned that my instructions to you will be minimal.'

Taffy Tuffy smiled. It really wasn't a pleasant sight.

'Has General Darkblast told you of your reward for this edifying venture?' the Baron asked.

'Edif-what! Ay, boyo, he didn't say anything about any kinky stuff, just that you want some people sorted out, like. Good and proper.'

'My apologies for my loquacious verbosity,' the Baron said, holding both hands up. 'Your interpretation is correct. I want "some people sorting out, like. Good and proper".'

'Well that's alright then,' Taffy said, relaxing somewhat. 'We charge double for the kinky stuff, you know.'

CHAPTER 23 – DO YOU THINK PEOPLE WILL SING SONGS ABOUT US IN THE FUTURE?

It was not long past dawn when guests and party revellers of the night before returned to Ophelia Palace, in a more sombre mood. Cliff, Oriana and Charles had arrived first. Charles had insisted on coming and wished to help in any way he could. Cracky and the cats arrived last, with Cracky and Theo looking very weary from the night's investigations. Naturally, Half-blind Ron had asked if there was any chicken for breakfast, whereas Theo headed straight for Roisin. He was acutely aware of how important the information he may be able to obtain from her mind would prove to be.

'Just be still, Roisin, it won't hurt, I promise you,' he said, his eyes closed tight as he started to enter her mind. 'I can see two men in top hats.'

'That's them!' Roisin cried, 'That's Mr Ping and Mr Pong.'

Theo concentrated harder, trying to focus on the faces in Roisin's memory. He had once described this skill as akin to flicking through a photograph album; once at the desired location, you ceased turning the pages and simply looked at the photo in greater detail. After a protracted silence he turned back to the anxious faces in the palace drawing room. 'It's them alright. It's Hob and Nob.'

'So it is Blacktie's work after all,' Olaf said, smashing his fist on the table containing Vindy and Tikky, causing the plates to jump in the air. 'Sorry, Your Majesties,' he said.

'Yes,' said Cracky. 'We expected as much. Our studies last night threw up some surprising results.'

Cracky told them all what he and Theo had discovered last night; the challenge for the four mighty warriors, the kidnapping of the faerie queen, and the saga of the trip *'down the great river in a boat with a mighty dragon at the helm'*.

'And it would appear that Aiden is involved.'

'Me?' said Aiden. 'What do you mean, Cracky?'

Cracky had both books with him and he turned to the relevant section in The Prophecy. 'This is what it says. *"One day a stranger will arrive from a land beyond distance and beyond time. He will bring with him strange gadgets and strange ideas. He will tell tales of his home and people will gain strength from his words and his strange ways, although no-one will copy his hairstyle. He will join a group of heroes and set off on a quest that will deliver the people from fear and suppression. Evil will be vanquished and peace among the lands will follow"*.

'Well part of that is definitely true,' Smid said. 'No-one will ever copy your hairstyle.'

Olaf looked at him sternly. 'Now is not the time for jokes, Smid.'

'Forgive me, Olaf. I was just trying to lighten a mood which grows increasingly heavy.'

'You are forgiven, old friend,' Olaf said, clutching Smid's shoulder.

'But it says he will come *"from a land beyond distance and beyond time"*,' Tikky observed. 'Is there something young Aiden should perhaps be telling us?'

Cracky looked over at Aiden and raised an eyebrow, so Aiden told them. Unsurprisingly, Mr Kneepatcher fainted.

'It seems that momentous times are upon us,' Grundi said. 'Well, all I can say is that for someone who has come from beyond distance and time to assist in vanquishing evil from the land, you're a bloody good mixing engineer.'

'One thing we're not sure of, though, is if all the events outlined in this section of The Prophecy are actually in the same time line,' Theo said. 'This "quest" may not even be related to the other events, such as the Queen's kidnap and the great tournament.'

'Agreed,' Vindy noted, 'but you'd have to say that the propinquity would suggest this is likely to be the case.'

'That's a very big word, dear,' Tikky said. 'Don't be overstretching yourself or your meat will get tough.'

'Vindy's got a good point,' Cliff Corriedale said. 'There does appear to be a strong link.'

'So what on earth are we to do?' said Mr Kneepatcher, wiping his brow with his hanky. 'We've got to save Ophelia and give her back her comb.'

'And we have to get to the tournament,' Oldfart said.

The words seemed to come from inside, but Aiden wasn't sure where. In the same way he'd felt compelled to say certain things at certain times for no apparent reason since he'd been here, now it seemed that someone, or something, was feeding him an entire passage. He said it in his voice, and with full cognizance, but a part of him felt like he was being used as a vessel for communication from elsewhere.

'We've got to do both. From what I've seen so far we can't let Blacktie win. Even though we don't know what his endgame is, we can virtually guarantee he'll be seeking to increase his power and control. Nobody wants that. In the short time I've been here I've witnessed nobility of heart, empathy, kindness and friendship, and that is worth fighting for. So, if that means confronting Blacktie to allow these qualities to blossom, then I say we have to confront him. People's minds have been suppressed and controlled for too long. I'm sure there are many, many others that would support us if they see our courage, our conviction and our desire for true freedom.'

Mr Kneepatcher started a round of applause and was quickly joined by everyone else in the room. 'Where did that come from?' an admiring Cracky whispered in his ear.

'I've absolutely no idea,' Aiden said. 'But I actually meant every word.'

'Fine words from a fine fellow,' said Olaf, smacking Aiden on the back and nearly forcing his lungs through his rib cage. 'And he's absolutely right.'

'Fine words indeed, Aiden,' Theo said in his mind. 'And you've convinced me that your place in this is of supreme importance, although I don't think you realise it yet. Well done.'

A mood of hope now replaced despondency and despair. Eyes were brighter, hearts were lifted, and determination was etched on the faces of all... and steam rose from Vindy and Tikky with renewed purpose.

'So, how do we locate Ophy?' Mara said, linking Aiden's arm.

'We need to find Hob and Nob. If we can do that, I would say there's a strong possibility they'll lead us to her,' Cracky said.

'That makes a lot of sense, Cracky,' Oriana Oftsheared agreed. 'But given their penchant for disguise it could be like looking for a needle in a haystack.'

'It could be,' Theo said. 'But there may be a way that I can provide us with some direction, although I've never tried it before.'

Theo walked over to Roisin and rubbed himself affectionately against her legs. 'There's a possibility that I may be able to reach inside the minds of Hob and Nob through Roisin.'

'How does that work?' Agnar said. 'It's not dangerous, is it?'

'Not for Roisin,' Theo answered. 'But I'll have to be careful.'

Theo sat down and all eyes turned to him as he explained the technique he was about to attempt. 'Everything in the universe is connected. Without going into too much detail, these connections aren't always apparent in our conscious state, but our subconscious is aware of them and our unconscious mind actually has complete access to all information. It's a bit complicated, but within our subconscious minds connections are magnified by our emotions and experiences, and they can weaken and strengthen over time depending upon the circumstances. Is this making any sense?'

'I think so,' Roisin said.

'Anyway,' Theo continued, 'it may be possible for me to "jump" into the mind of either Hob or Nob via the connections that Roisin now has in her subconscious. This may only be for a few seconds, I simply don't know. But if I can, and if by doing so we can locate them, or manage to ascertain the whereabouts of the Queen, then I think we should give it a shot.'

'Are you putting yourself at risk?' Cracky asked him.

'I doubt it,' Theo lied. 'It may take a bit out of me, but that's about it.'

Theo asked Roisin to lie down on a couch, close her eyes and continue to think of Mr Ping and Mr Pong. He sat on her chest and closed his eyes, looking like a regular cat simply enjoying a sleep with its owner.

'It may be better if you left us alone for a few minutes,' Theo said. 'It would be easier for me if there's no-one here apart from Roisin.'

Everyone dutifully obeyed and left the room. 'Are you ready?' Theo asked.

'I am, and good luck, Your Highness.'

At first, all Theo could see were various images of Mr Ping and Mr Pong. He delved deeper, trying to draw out the sounds of their voices, their smells, the way they walked and their mannerisms from Roisin's mind. He knew that if he delved too deep there was a possibility that he could suffer from a temporary 'unbalancing.' His mother had taught him the technique and had explained the dangers. 'You won't lose your mind, but you'll need some time to regain your own mind-balance. It's risky, so only use it when absolutely necessary.'

Theo soon had complete recollection of every second that Roisin had spent with Mr Ping and Mr Pong, but he still hadn't made the 'jump'. He started to feel himself losing concentration; the effort of maintaining the connection was putting a strain on him like never before. Then, all of a sudden...

'So, we head to the mine today and get the sample?' Nob said.

'Yes. No messing about, no disguises. We simply get in, get the cheese and get out. And then we can rendezvous with the Baron,' Hob replied.

'What do you think he'll do with the Queen?'

'I'm not at all concerned,' Hob said. *'That's his business. I doubt it will be pleasant though.'*

'It's all coming together nicely, isn't it,' said Nob.

'It is indeed, my good Nob. Our artistry and intellectual efficacy is once again ensuring that we will be successful.'

'Do you think people will sing songs about us in the future?'

'How could they not, my dear Nob. How could they not.'

And then it was gone.

Theo jumped wearily onto the floor and lay down in a half slumber. 'Your Highness, are you alright?' Roisin said, as she sat up.

'I'll be fine, Roisin, thanks. Just give me a minute.'

The sound of voices was taken as a signal that the operation had ended, so everyone made their way back into the drawing room. Captain Marmaduke ran over to Theo, who was now motionless on the carpet.

'He asked me to give him a minute, Captain,' Roisin said. 'I think we should do as he wishes.'

'Very well, Roisin. But you can understand my concern.'

Mara went to the kitchen, filled a saucer with milk and placed it on the floor near Theo. He gingerly got to his feet and began to drink, much to the relief of everyone, but especially Captain Marmaduke.

'You had me worried there, Your Highness,' the Captain said.

'Me too, Your Highness, Princeness, Majesty,' agreed Half-blind Ron.

'Thanks, but my head's starting to clear now. Remind me not to attempt that too often.'

'I'm guessing that there was more danger involved in that little exercise than you led us to believe?' Cracky said, with a knowing look. 'I just hope that the effort was worth it.'

'It was,' said Theo, and then he told them all he had seen and heard.

'Then the plan is plain to see,' Olaf said. 'We make our way to the mine and accost them when they arrive. A few well-aimed blows with the flat of this,' he said, brandishing his sword, 'and they'll be squawking like hens.'

'I'm not sure that's the best approach, you know,' Aiden opined. 'Remember what Theo said about The Prophecy. You need to make sure that you reach Chester in time for the tournament.'

'Aiden's right, Olaf,' Tikky said. 'A more subtle approach may ultimately prove to be the right course of action.'

Olaf shook his head, but Smid and Grundi came over to his side and laid their hands on his shoulders. 'Her Majesty speaks sense,' Grundi said. 'If our role in all of this is to make sure we take our music and wind to Chester, then perhaps an alternative plan to ensnare these two sorry excuses for men should be looked at.'

'I suggest we form ourselves into two teams,' Theo said. 'One team will hide out and wait for Hob and Nob to reach the mine. Then we can follow them to their liaison with the Baron –'

'Then that's the team I'll be on,' Olaf interrupted.

'– while the other team travels to Chester in Ethel.'

'And that's the team you must be on, Olaf,' Agnar said, joining his band mates at Olaf's side. 'We have to stick together, you know.'

'Agnar's right, Olaf,' Oldfart said. 'We must put our faith and trust in others. I'm sure they won't let us down. They'll ensure that Ophelia's safe... and that she can comb her hair again.'

'I'd like to make a suggestion,' Cracky said. 'I think it makes sense if the team that travels to the mine is Theo, Captain Marmaduke, Half-blind Ron and me. A man and three cats aren't likely to raise any suspicion wherever we travel. We may also be able to utilise the talents of his highness along the way.'

'I'd like to go with you too,' Oriana said, which surprised everyone, not least Cliff.

'Oriana, I can't let you,' he said. 'It could be far too dangerous.'

'My dear Cliff,' she said, stroking his face with her hoof, 'there is danger everywhere right now from what I can see. But my intuition tells me that my part in this lies with Cracky and the cats, if they'll have me.'

'We'd be delighted,' Theo said, brushing himself against her leg.

'Well you can't go without me,' Roisin said. 'The Queen will need me.'

'That's very true, Roisin,' said Theo. 'But you are known to Hob and Nob. If you were spotted then our cover could be blown, and that's a risk I'm afraid we can't take.'

Roisin's head dropped and Mara put a friendly arm around her shoulders. 'He's right. We've got to think of what's best, you know.'

'Well, that's settled that, then.' Oldfart said. 'Olaf, Grundi, Agnar, Smid and I will travel in Ethel.'

'What about Aiden?' Smid said.

Oldfart looked over at Aiden, his gaze alive with anticipation. 'I'd be honoured,' Aiden said, as Cracky looked over at Theo and winked.

'Well there's no way that Mara and I aren't coming with you,' Roisin said.

'And that goes for me too!' shouted Charles Corriedale.

'Uncle, you cannot. We need to travel with Henry and the rest of the OSO; he's already bought the train tickets. And anyway you're far too delicate these days to be embarking on an escapade like this.'

'Now look,' Charles said, 'I know that you think I'm just an old sheep with clacky hooves and a fleece that needs shearing, but my heart is telling me to go. I've not had an adventure like this for more years than I care to remember. And anyway I can lift everyone's spirits with my trumpet.'

'Well, I'll have to come along as well,' Cliff said, 'You'll just get yourself into trouble otherwise.'

'Good!' Charles chuckled.

'And if you think we're going to let you confront Blacktie without us you'd be sadly mistaken,' said Vindy, puffing up his rice.

'My husband is right,' Tikky agreed. 'Saffy will probably have a fit when he finds out, but I feel we've got a part to play in this too. Harold and Greta can look after us, and there's plenty of room in that big boat of yours.'

Olaf's eyes were filled with tears as he spoke. 'You would all put yourselves at risk to help us? We cannot ask this of you.'

'You're not asking us, we're telling you we're coming with you!' exclaimed Vindy.

'Er, aren't we forgetting someone,' Mr Kneepatcher said, waving his hanky. 'You never know when you may need your clothes repairing.'

'You would also put yourself in danger?' Olaf said to him.

'Danger! I laugh in the face of it, darling,' replied Mr Kneepatcher, straightening his cravat.

'Well, then, Gilbert Kneepatcher, we would be proud if you would fart with us,' Olaf said, smiling.

'Ooh, dear, what an honour, and bless my cravat. I don't think I've ever been so dithered!'

'It looks like the *"Companionship of Wind"* is complete,' Cracky observed to Theo.

'Right,' said Oldfart, returning to business. 'I'd better get the press conference sorted out. I've already reserved some rooms at The Pig's Trotters pub, near the Iron Bridge at Alford. We'll be stopping there tonight.'

And so the mood of optimism gained momentum and the air was light with hope, but no-one was under any illusion that there wouldn't be perilous times ahead. It was unlikely the Baron would afford them safe passage on their journey down the river, but nobody could guess as yet how eventful that journey was to be.

CHAPTER 24 – I HAD NO IDEA YOU HAD SUCH A FONDNESS FOR OLD CONDIMENTS

'So, did Her Majesty sleep well?' the Baron asked, reclining on a plush chaise longue, as Ophelia was led into the palace morning room by Pimple and Grunt.

'As well as can be expected for one who was drugged, abducted and is now comb-less,' she replied, defiantly.

'Ah, I can see that you're not completely smitten with our hospitality yet. But fear not, we have a host of delights that will change your mind over the next couple of days. Ah, and I'm forgetting my manners, would you like some breakfast?'

'I'm not feeling very hungry at the moment, for some reason.'

The Baron waved his hand in a kind of shrugging motion. 'No matter, but do ask Pimple if you start feeling a bit peckish as the day goes on.'

'Look, Baron,' Ophelia said, between gritted teeth, 'would you do me the honour of explaining just exactly why I am here?'

The Baron stood up and straightened his cloak, before walking around behind the tiny queen. Then he stooped slightly and spoke over her shoulder. 'I would love to say that I've chosen you to be my bride and that you are to live here by my side for the rest of your days, forever enamoured and lost in matrimonial bliss.'

'I would rather die, or never see my comb and handbag again, than be at your side, you grotesque monstrosity! You have all the charm of a decrepit snake and all the sex appeal of an unsightly, pink-bottomed baboon.'

'I think that's almost a compliment,' Pimple whispered to Grunt, who nodded his agreement.

'Yes, I anticipated a response of that nature,' the Baron said, with a chuckle. 'Although I will admit that I was impressed by the imagination of the insults. But, as I was saying, I would love that this untimely abduction was perpetrated to whisk you away to be my bride… but I'm afraid I cannot. You will be relieved to know I have no intention of marrying you.'

Ophelia said nothing, but continued to view the Baron with disdain and loathing. 'No, my dear Queen Ophelia, you are here as leverage.'

'Leverage?'

'Oh, yes,' the Baron continued. 'Around about now, I would think, your tall, hairy boyfriend and his band of miscreant metal merchants will begin their voyage down the River Dee to Chester, to take part in the Cestrian Music Tournament tomorrow. Now, I have no intention of allowing them into the city and staining my tournament with that tuneless garbage they purvey as music —'

'That's unfair, they're really good,' Ophelia interrupted.

'— TUNELESS GARBAGE THEY PURVEY AS MUSIC!' the Baron screamed, his face red and contorted with rage.

'But,' he continued, calming down, 'I do wish to appropriate their cheese mine, which will legally be my property if they fail to win the tournament. So you see, if by some miracle they actually manage to get here in time to play, I need to ensure that they do not play to win, if you get my drift.'

'What's so special about this cheese mine that requires you to create this elaborate charade?' Ophelia asked. 'I mean, from what Agnar tells me, there's no cheese of any worth in there anyway.'

The Baron smiled a particularly wicked and knowing smile. Then he walked over to a picture on the wall and removed it. Behind the picture was the door to a safe. The Baron continued speaking whilst he fed in the combination.

'Ah, that's not quite true, you see,' he said, turning the dial and popping open the door. 'That mine contains a very special cheese. It is true that the cheese itself is little more than a pleasant, tasty morsel. But I have good reason to believe that when it is combined with this particular condiment, it will not only create a taste sensation but some of the side effects could be most interesting.'

The Baron reached inside the safe and pulled out a large, dusty jar with a yellow label. 'Have you any idea what this is?' he asked the Queen.

'Not at all, but I'd be surprised if it's still in date,' she replied.

'This is Mathonwy's Chutney, my dear Ophelia. It doesn't need to be in date.'

'Well, if it's full of preservatives you should steer clear of it,' Ophelia said. 'You should try more natural food, like nuts. I love nuts.'

'Grunt like nuts too,' said Grunt, as Ophelia smiled sweetly at him.

The Baron turned his eyes skyward in search of divine inspiration but the ceiling was in the way, so he kicked a well-placed waste basket instead.

'If I didn't need you in one piece, you would find that the reward for your irreverence would be extremely unpleasant,' he growled. 'And I can guarantee you will not be quite so flippant in your remarks two days hence. Now, as I was saying, this is Mathonwy's Chutney and it is, to the best of my considerable knowledge, the only remaining jar in all the land.'

'I apologise, Baron,' Ophelia said with a semblance of sincerity.

'Apology accepted.'

'I had no idea you had such a fondness for old condiments. It explains a lot about your personality, and your smell.'

'Don't push me too far, my little faerie queen,' the Baron said, giving her a stare that would freeze hot coals. 'If my patience wears thin, I may decide to concoct a different approach that finds you surplus to requirements, if you get my meaning.'

The Queen realised that overstepping the mark any further would not be wise, and would greatly diminish the chances of being successfully reunited with her comb. Or she could be killed, which would be nearly as bad. 'Okay,' she said, adopting a more congenial stance. 'Tell me about the chutney, I can see you're very proud of it.'

The Baron stroked the jar with genuine tenderness and held it tight to his chest. 'Many years ago there was a great wizard called Scratchy Crotch. Do you recognise the name?'

'Yes, from my lessons when I was younger. I seem to remember he was an evil wizard from Bala,' the Queen replied.

'Oh, not just any old evil wizard,' the Baron continued. 'He was the most powerful wizard who ever lived. Why if it wasn't for all the embroidery he may still be alive to this day.'

The Queen looked at Pimple and Grunt but they both shrugged, signalling that her ignorance was not singular.

'He never revealed the secret of his power, you know,' the Baron said, hinting that he may be about to do just that. 'Now, bear with me a second, I just need to go and get a book from the throne room,' he said, carefully putting down the jar on a table.

In less than a minute he returned, with a large and very old, leather-bound book, which he placed on the table next to the jar. 'Come over here, my dear. I'd like you to read something,' he said, with a grin that an egotistical and particularly sadistic snake would have been proud of. 'Firstly, can you read the title?'

Ophelia peered at the embossed letters on the front of the book. 'It says *"The Cookbook of the Damned"*.'

'Very good. Now open the cover and read the first page,' the Baron urged, walking into the centre of the room.

The Queen did as she was told, and the large cover threw dust into the air as it smacked heavily down on the table. 'Well?' the Baron quizzed as the

Queen studied the text.

'It says *"This book belongs to Scratchy Crotch. If found, please return to The Castle of Evil, 26 Darkstain Lane, Bala"*.'

'Not that page!' the Baron screamed, 'The adjacent page!'

'Oh, it says *"Rancorous Recipes for Really, Really Bad People"*.'

'It does, indeed. Now if you'll be so kind as to turn to page 224 and read aloud.'

Ophelia turned to the relevant page and stared hard at the faded words. 'It's difficult to make out but I'll try. It reads *"Wizard's Winkles. Take three freshly prepared testicles, cover in batter, apply a dash of cinnamon, place into an overproof dish, add two knobs of garlic butter and cook for an hour at gas mark 5, stirring occasionally"*.'

'Oh, sorry,' said the Baron, 'it's actually 226. I always get the pages mixed up.'

Ophelia turned the page. 'Is this the one, *"Cheese and Chutney Surprise"*?'

'That's correct, dear Queen. Read it for my pleasure.'

As Ophelia began to read, her eyes grew wide in tandem with the Baron's wicked smile. She finished the passage and closed the book, sending more dust up into the air, which shimmered in the light as it fluttered downwards. 'Th-this cannot be true!' she exclaimed, a look of horror on her beautiful face.

'Actually, I think you'll find it is, Queen Ophelia. And when my hirelings, Hob and Nob, return tomorrow with a piece of Ceridwen's Cheese, I think we can perhaps give this recipe a whirl.'

'You can't! We'll find a way to stop you, you monster!' the Queen screamed, rushing at the Baron, before being held back quite firmly by Pimple.

'I think it's time you went back to your room now, Your Majesty,' the Baron said. 'I'm sure all this excitement has made you weary. Pimple, Grunt, escort Her Majesty back to her quarters. Oh, and give her some nuts when you get there, there's much she needs to chew on.'

CHAPTER 25 – MAY ODIN BLESS THEIR WIND

As morning made a mad dash towards afternoon, a large crowd had gathered outside The Sheep's Stirrup. Word of the Queen's abduction had spread like wildfire and the air was full of murmurings, rumour, wild speculation and some speculation that was much better behaved. The crowd had also heard of the Companionship of Wind's quest to win the Cestrian Music Tournament, to save the faerie queen, to win freedom for the land, to be able to fart freely, and to win the right to their cheese. So they figured that anyone attempting that little lot needed a good send off.

Aiden trotted down the stairs into the bar carrying the black knapsack that Mr Kneepatcher had kindly given him, and he was wearing the leather jacket he had bought. Maurice, as usual, was behind the bar. 'What time is everybody rendezvousing?' he asked Aiden, pouring him an orange juice.

'Thanks, Maurice,' Aiden said, taking a sip from the glass. 'Oldfart said that we'd all meet here at 12:00 pm.'

As if on cue, Oldfart came through the front door. 'The lads will be along in a minute or so. Thankfully, Ethel has agreed to take us, so that's a relief,' he said.

'What would you have done if she'd refused?' Aiden asked.

'Well, generally she has a pretty common sense attitude to things, so I was hoping that the circumstances would make her choice academic. I did promise I'd polish her, though, and she'll probably hold me to that when we get back. Or should I say if we get back.'

'Now, don't be thinking like that!' Maurice cried. 'You've got the will of the people behind you, and I'm sure you'll get plenty of backing if Blacktie tries any rough stuff.'

'Actually, that reminds me,' Oldfart said, rummaging in his jacket pocket and producing a piece of paper, 'Cracky asked me to pass this on. He wants you to contact this person as soon as we've left, but please don't say anything to anyone.'

'Of course,' Maurice said, taking the piece of paper from Oldfart.

Maurice read the name and the message, and then his mouth dropped open. 'Not a word, please Maurice,' Oldfart said.

Harold and Greta appeared from upstairs with Vindy and Tikky. Both curries were steaming nicely, a sign they meant business. 'You have to remember,' Vindy said to Oldfart, 'we have friends in lots of places, including the Chester Stroganoffs, and you don't want to get on the wrong side of them.'

Cracky, Theo and the others had already left for the cheese mine without any fanfare, and all agreed that this particular part of the operation needed to remain as clandestine as possible. However, the members of the Companionship were afforded a reception like heroes when they arrived at the pub... and Charles brought his trumpet, as promised.

'I suggested he pass it over to Henry, to travel with the rest of the OSO, like I've done with my cello, but he was having none of it,' Cliff said to Aiden. 'Henry had an absolute fit when we told him what we were doing, but Uncle Charles just said he should "lighten up and loosen his fleece". His face was a picture.'

Mr Kneepatcher was looking very dapper in his check suit and walking boots, with a matching check holdall. 'I just hope I've not forgotten anything,' he said to Olaf. 'And I've only brought ten cravats, I hope that's enough.'

'Right, then, I think it's about time we made a move,' Oldfart said. 'Did you and Smid load the weapons into Ethel, Agnar?'

'We did. I've even brought the old spiked club along for good luck!'

The Companionship's path to the river was lined with cheering people and sheep. Bunting that had stayed securely indoors for the Baron's visit had been set loose, and messages of good luck constantly filled their ears as Ethel honed into view. There were also several unrepeatable messages about Baron Blacktie that questioned his parentage, and made some lascivious assumptions about his private habits.

'We should probably say something, you know,' Grundi said to Olaf, as they walked up Ethel's gangplank.

Olaf took in a deep breath and turned to face the crowd. 'Good people of Llangollen, we have been christened the *"Companionship of Wind"*, and on behalf of us all I'd like to express our gratitude for your support and good wishes. We travel now, with our loyal and brave companions, to take our music and wind to a tournament that has acquired enormous importance, and we will not let you down.'

Olaf then introduced each of the Companionship and every name was met with cheers and applause. Then someone shouted 'Hail to the Companionship of Wind', which was echoed by the crowd, followed by

'May Odin bless their wind', which was also enthusiastically belted out by the assembled throng.

Charles Corriedale had tears in his eyes as he looked over at Aiden. 'Are you alright, Charles?' Aiden asked.

'Oh, my, yes. I'm fine. It's just that ever since I was a little lamb I've longed to be part of something as important as this; something that could make a real difference to people. Bless my clacky hooves, but I feel like a hero and I don't think I should.'

'You are a hero, Charles,' Aiden said, as his eyes too began to fill with tears. 'And you're not the only one who's always wished to be part of something like this.'

And then Aiden felt compelled to speak. The words flowed true and sure from his lips and his heart beat with passion and pride. 'I am a newcomer here,' he shouted, 'but I have been made to feel as if this is my home. I look out now and I see friends everywhere.'

The crowd cheered again, with fists and hooves pumping in the air. 'But, although this is a land filled with goodness, honesty and respect, there is an evil that sits at its heart. I tell you all now, the days of this evil are numbered. These brave people, sheep and curries that I am so proud to call my friends are about to embark on a quest which could involve great danger. But they are happy to face that danger because they care more for this land, more for the people they love and more for freedom then they do for their own safety.'

The cheers were reaching deafening proportions and the atmosphere was electric. 'And, no matter what dangers they may face, no matter what sacrifices they may have to make, no matter what horrendous smells they may encounter, I will stand with them. Will you stand with us also?' And then he pulled out his pocket knife and raised it into the air.

'We'll have to do something about that, he needs a bigger weapon' Smid said to Grundi, as the crowd roared their approval.

Mara rushed towards Aiden and gave him an enormous kiss. 'That was magnificent,' she said, with a smile as beautiful as anything he had ever seen.

'I tell you what,' Olaf said to Oldfart. 'If his mixing on the night is as good as that speech then we've already won.'

And with that, Agnar blew the horn at the stern and Ethel moved gracefully up the River Dee towards Chester. The sun appeared from behind the clouds, pouring radiant beams of light over the ship and transforming the river in front into a channel of sparkling diamonds. 'How do you feel?' Oldfart said to Aiden.

'I'm not sure I can describe it,' he replied, honestly. 'But I'm struggling to think of a time when I've felt better.'

Oldfart looked up into the sky and sniffed the air. 'We could be in for some stormy tides ahead,' he observed.

He was right.

***

'You know this thing I keep saying we're missing,' Cracky said to Theo, as they lay behind one of the massive stones in the Circle of Wind, keeping a watchful eye on the entrance to the cheese mine of Hairy Growler.

'Yes,' Theo answered.

'I think we've been looking in the wrong place.'

'What do you mean, Cracky?'

'Well,' Cracky said, putting down his copy of The Prophecy, 'we've gone through this book with a fine-tooth comb, and although we've identified and correlated passages with current events, we've still no idea what Blacktie's motivation is. He's going to an awful lot of trouble to get hold of this cheese mine.'

'Yes. For some reason I was expecting the answer to leap out at us at some point, but I must admit I'm at a loss here, Cracky.'

'Maybe it's something to do with chicken?' Half-blind Ron suggested.

'Don't you ever think of anything but chicken?' Captain Marmaduke said, sighing.

'Of course I does. I'm very partial to a bit of beef as well, you know, particularly with some horseradish sauce.'

'Hang on a second, Captain,' Theo said. 'What do you mean, Ron, when you say it may have something to do with chicken?'

Half-blind Ron sat down on his haunches and began to lick his paws. 'Well, maybe he wants this cheese because he fancies a nice cheese and chicken sandwich. This Ceridwen's Cheese may taste great with chicken, or something.'

Cracky stood up as if he'd just been pricked by a particularly vengeful nettle. 'Half-blind Ron, you are a genius!'

'I am? Well I've never been called that before, Mr Cracklingfeet,'

'Crackfoot,' Captain Marmaduke corrected.

'I've been called a git, a gerroffyamangycat, and a gobshi—, er, other not so nice names,' he said, noting that Oriana was present, 'but never a genius before. Does this mean I get a bigger helping of chicken?'

'The next time you visit the Diner you can have a whole chicken to yourself,' Cracky said, tickling Half-blind Ron on the head.

Cracky rummaged in the bag he'd brought with him and took out the second old book. 'This,' he said, 'is my father's copy of the *"Cookbook of the Damned"*. I wasn't sure if there were still any other copies left, but if Blacktie has one we may have found the missing piece in the puzzle.'

'That's the book with the map of cheese mines,' Theo said.

'It is,' Cracky replied. 'And it also contains some very ancient recipes. Recipes created by Scratchy Crotch.'

Cracky scanned the table of contents with his finger, mumbling to himself as if he was looking for something very specific. Then, in a movement that made everyone jump, he shouted and stabbed his finger onto the page. 'I think I've found it!'

He rifled through the pages, turning them rapidly until he reached page 226. He read at breakneck speed, navigating the lines of text with his finger. 'By Odin's hairy backside, this is it! Your Highness would you please read the recipe aloud,' he said, placing the book on the ground in front of Theo.

'It reads, *"Cheese and Chutney Surprise. Take a thick slice of Ceridwen's Cheese and coat it with a good dollop of Mathonwy's Chutney. Allow one minute for the ingredients to mingle before eating. The crumbly texture, delicate taste and fruity aroma provide the palette with an exquisite experience, giving one a sense of peace and serenity. I cannot recommend this succulent morsel highly enough, and it also has the pleasing side-effect of providing the diner with immortality and power beyond imagining. Eat one portion daily for the rest of eternity".'*

'That was the secret of Scratchy Crotch's power,' Cracky said.

'But that would mean that the Baron must already have a jar of the chutney,' Theo said.

'I'd say that's very likely,' Cracky agreed.

'Ssh,' Captain Marmaduke said, suddenly. 'I can see movement by the mine.'

***

'Did you pack the crowbar?' Hob said to Nob, as the two of them moved through the nearby bushes, overgrown by the passage of time and lack of human presence.

'Of course, it is in the utensils bag.'

In front of them the entrance to the mine looked foreboding, and although it was only mid-afternoon the air seemed colder here. An eerie darkness seemed to emanate from behind the jumble of planks of wood nailed to the entrance, designed to keep intruders out... or perhaps something else in. Nob unzipped the utensils bag and took out the crowbar. The planks were firmly attached with large, rusty nails and Nob pulled each plank in turn, looking for weaknesses.

'They all seem very secure. This could take a while,' he said, until he reached one near the bottom. 'Wait, this one appears to be loose.'

He tugged at the plank and it gave way easily, the old iron nails falling onto the grassy earth below. 'I sense someone has been here quite recently, my good Nob,' Hob observed.

'It would seem so.'

'Well, let us tarry not. Our lithe frames should have little trouble getting through that gap.'

Five minutes later, and after much pushing, shoving and pulling, they were inside. 'I fear we may not be as lithe as we once were,' Nob said, dusting himself down.

'Sadly this may be true,' Hob agreed, rubbing his paunch. 'But our fuller figures are simply a sign of our increased experience, wisdom and pulchritude.'

'Indeed,' said Nob, as he switched on the torch.

Deep inside the mine the rumblings above had been detected and things began to stir. 'Can you smell that?' Boris said to Barry, unfurling his wings.

'Yeah, it can't be, can it?'

'Well it smells like it to me. Let's go and check it out, I can feel me fangs twitchin' already.'

The ancient mine of Hairy Growler was a myriad of passages that spiralled downwards until… well no-one knew, as no-one had ever reached the bottom. Water dribbled slowly down the walls and also dripped from the cave's roof, creating tiny splashes in the little pools on the rock-strewn floor. It was cold and dank and smelled of long-dead cheese, the pungency attacking the nostrils of its two latest inhabitants like the smell of the socks of a sailor with very stinky feet… who's been at sea for three months and hasn't changed them.

'This stench is almost unbearable,' Nob said, shining the torch in Hob's face.

'It may ease as we get deeper into the cave. If the Baron is correct, what we have here are purely the remnants of Red Cheekfizzler.'

As they continued down the narrow aisles of rock, the stench in the air lightened considerably. Eventually, after about half-an-hour, the passageway opened into a vast cavern, the ceiling disappearing high into the darkness overhead. 'Let's light the lantern,' Hob suggested.

Nob produced some matches from his pocket and placed a gas lantern on the floor. As he struck the first match he thought he heard the flapping of tiny wings. 'Can you see them yet?' Barry whistled to Boris, who was flying in front of him.

'There's some kind of bright light up ahead. And I can smell 'em now! Fresh blood, fresh human blood!'

Nob placed the lantern on the ground, and as the light filtered out into the vast cavern the walls seemed to become alive, providing a mesmerising display of magnificent greens and golds. 'I-I've never seen anything so beautiful,' he said, his mouth hanging open in awe. 'Is this all Ceridwen's Cheese?'

'I believe that it is, my good Nob,' Hob replied… just before the fangs entered his neck. 'Aaaarrghh, we're under attack!' he shouted, waving his hands in the air.

Boris had a really good grip of Hob's neck and sunk his fangs into his jugular vein. He drank deep, squeaking satisfied little squeaks of pleasure. Nob was just about to come to Hob's aid when Barry performed a similar manoeuvre, his fangs drawing blood as Nob screamed in terror. As the bats clung on, both men ran around the cavern yelping in pain and fear, before colliding head on and waving consciousness farewell in the process. Which was very fortunate, otherwise they would have heard the extremely loud roar.

'Oh, bloody hell, they've woken him up now,' said Boris.

'We'd better scarper,' Barry suggested. And the two bats withdrew their fangs and headed for the safety of the stalactites above.

There are many things that live in the caves and tunnels under the earth's surface. Some are small and harmless, happy to spend their days scurrying about searching for insects. Then there are slightly bigger things that aren't harmless and spend their days hunting the small and harmless things. Then there are big things that can get pretty nasty if there aren't enough of the slightly bigger less harmless things around to eat. Then there are Trolls, who tend to get pretty nasty with absolutely anything. And then there's Dai MacTavish.

'Can you hear singing?' Nob said, rubbing his head and trying to reinvigorate his senses.

'Yes,' Hob replied, 'and it seems to be getting closer'.

Dai MacTavish was a Welsh-Glaswegian hybrid who found it difficult to settle into a normal society. His mother was a Rhyl Trawlerwoman, known for her fierce temper, huge forearms, emerald-encrusted nose-ring and beautiful soprano voice. His father was a Glaswegian football supporter, known for his fierce temper, huge forearms, steel-plated forehead and beautiful tenor voice. Dai left home when he was four years old, after getting into a fight with the bouncers in a crèche in Rhyl and putting six of them in hospital. As he grew up, he tried various jobs that involved fighting, such as bodyguards, nightclub doormen, and, for a short time, the elected Member of Parliament for Rhos-on Sea. However, such was his propensity for violence that he would inevitably upset his employers, usually by breaking them. He did, though, have a magnificent singing voice, which endeared him to some. As a former friend once said 'Dai may break your nose with his forehead and rip out your intestines, but he'll perform a beautiful rendition of *"Men of Harlech"* while you bleed to death.'

Dai had lived in the cheese mine for the last fifteen years and Trolls scare their children by telling stories about him. His only friend is a lawnmower called Jock. And he takes Jock everywhere with him.

'It sounds like *"Green, Green Grass of Home"* by that Tam James, you know the singing dwarf,' Nob observed.

'I do believe you're right, Nob. However, irrespective of the potential friendliness of the owner of the voice, may I suggest you grab a piece of cheese of that wall?'

'Of course,' said Nob, pulling a chunk of the golden and green cheese from the wall and placing it in the utilities bag.

In the distance, they could see what appeared to be a bedraggled and very hairy figure walking towards them, pulling something behind him which made a kind of trundling noise.

'Och, then, boyos, I've dinnae seen anywoon doon here for ages. Who are ye and what are ye up tae?' Dai said, pushing his matted hair out of his eyes.

'Oh, hello, my good fellow, I am Mr Yankit and this is my good friend Mr Pullit,' Hob said. 'We are Meandering Mole Exterminators.'

'Moles, eh?' Dai said, scratching his belly. 'I've dinnae seen one o' those little beasties for a good while. Ne'er liked the taste o' them, though. Anyways, the name's Dai, Dai MacTavish.'

'Pleased to meet you, Mr MacTavish,' Mr Yankit said. 'From your words it would appear that we are thankfully succeeding in our task.'

'Aye, it would seem so,' Dai said.

'In which case, it's been charming meeting you and I hope our paths cross again soon,' Mr Yankit said, as he and Mr Pullit began to edge backwards.

So will ye not be stayin' for a bit?' Dai asked. 'I've got some Troll Stew cookin', ye know.'

'Er, sadly, no,' Mr Yankit said. 'We have pressing business up above and must away. After all, our work here would seem to be complete.'

'Och, will ye not sing a little song with me, then, afore ye go?'

Mr Pullit looked at Mr Yankit and shook his head. 'I'm afraid our voices are not quite up to your high standards, Mr MacTavish.'

Dai looked dreadfully disappointed. 'Hoots, mon, I dinnae care. Look, I'll do ye a deal. If ye have a sing I'll not run ye over with Jock. Now I cannae say fairer than that.'

'Jock?' said My Yankit.

'Aye, Jock, me lawnmower here. Didnae I introduce ye?'

Dai pulled Jock around so that he was in front of him and patted the rusted, metal handle with affection. 'This here is Jock.'

'Hello, Jock, we're pleased to make your acquaintance,' said Mr Yankit.

Jock said nothing. He was a lawnmower.

'Anyhow,' Dai continued. 'Jock's really good at strippin' flesh off things when ye push him hard enough. I'd love to let ye go on yer way, but I've got me reputation as a psychopathic, flesh-eating monster tae think o', so I cannae just let ye leave. I'm sure ye understand.'

Mr Pullit nervously sidled over to Mr Yankit and grabbed his arm. 'Are you telling us that we can either attempt to leave and be cut to ribbons by an old lawnmower, or sing a song and leave intact?'

'Aye, pretty much,' Dai said. 'But dinnae let Jock hear ye sayin' he's old. He's a cantankerous bugger at the best o' times.'

Mr Yankit and Mr Pullit exchanged a very brief and animated whispered conversation. 'We'd be delighted, please name your song and we will wholeheartedly join in,' said Mr Yankit.

'Och, that's grand!' Dai said. 'How's about one o' me own tunes. I'll start off and ye can join in on the chorus?'

'That sounds splendid,' Mr Pullit said.

Dai cleared his throat with a few coughs. 'This is about me Mammy. It's called *"Smacked Arse".'*

When I was just a little lad
Me Mammy went to sea
She used to catch the fishes
And bring them home to me
But if I had been naughty
And killed me uncle Jack
She'd grab me by the ankles
And give me arse a whack

Smacked arse
Me Mammy gave to me
Smacked arse
And raw fishes for tea
Smacked arse
Until me cheeks were red
Smacked arse
Then she'd pack me off to bed

One day when I was playing
With young Jessie Brown
I really needed to have a pee
So I pulled me troosers doon
But me Mammy saw me winkle
As I peed in the sand
So she shouted that she'd tan my hide
And me arse cheeks felt her hand

'Right,' Dai said. 'Ye can sing-along! And ye too Jock!'

Jock didn't join in. He was a lawnmower. Mr Yankit and Mr Pullit did, though.

Smacked arse
Me Mammy gave to me
Smacked arse
And raw fishes for tea
Smacked arse
Until me cheeks were red
Smacked arse
Then she'd pack me off to bed

'Well done, boyos, that was grand!' Dai shouted, clapping his hands together. 'Didnae they do well, Jock.'

Jock didn't say anything. He was a lawnmower.

'Yes, that was most salubrious,' said Mr Yankit. 'But now I fear we really must go. We do have a very pressing appointment that we are already late for.'

'Aye, fair enough,' Dai said, with sadness in his voice. 'But I'll give ye both a quick Glasgow Kiss by way o' thanks to send ye on yer way.'

'Glasgow Kiss?' asked Mr Pullit, just before Dai's forehead met with his nose.

Up above the sound of two bats laughing could be heard.

'Did he break your nose too,' Nob said, wiping it as the two of them ran through the mine back to the surface.

'Thankfully not. His aim was awry, possibly because of my height. I fear I may have several teeth missing, though,' Hob replied, dabbing his mouth with a hankie. 'But, our painful encounter should see us richly rewarded, my dear Nob. Let us make haste back to Chester.'

'Which route shall we take?'

'Let us go via Ruthin,' Hob said. 'It would be wise not to venture anywhere near the vicinity of the Queen's palace. We are undoubtedly being looked for, yet even though we are no longer in disguise it would be circumspect to take the slightly longer route at this time. We can pay a visit to the witches while we're there.'

'Good idea,' said Nob, as the light from the front entrance of the mine appeared before them.

However, as the two spies squeezed through the gap in the mine's entrance, they were unaware that they had already been found. 'Look, they're coming out,' said Oriana.

'Right, then,' said Cracky, 'let's keep on their tale, but we'll stay a good way back. If anyone asks any questions, let me do the talking.'

CHAPTER 26 – PERHAPS YOU CAN HELP ME, I'M LOOKING FOR SOMEONE

Humphrey was bored. He'd played 'fetch the stick' with Mrs Perriwinkle for the last three days, and even though she was getting very good at it now, he felt this particular amusement had run its course.

'That poor dog's been left on its own since Saturday morning,' Mrs Perriwinkle said to Mr Sparkle, the window cleaner, as he wrung out his chamois leather into his bucket. 'I'll give that Aiden a right rollicking when he gets back. I've a good mind to call the police and get them to send a Black Mary after him.'

'You mean a Black Maria, a police van?' Mr Sparkle asked.

'Yes, that's it. And some of those nice Panda cars.'

'Fat lot of good that would do,' Humphrey thought.

Humphrey had tried explaining to Mrs Perriwinkle that, in all likelihood, Aiden had shifted into another reality, due to his misunderstanding of some of the formulae he'd applied when designing the algorithms to work in the quantum computing world. 'Wuf, wuuf, wuf, woof, wowf, wow, wow, wuf,' he'd said to her. And he couldn't say it any clearer than that.

Sadly, Mrs Perriwinkle misinterpreted this completely and started to tickle his tummy, which was nice but hardly productive under the circumstances. No, it appeared that it was time for Humphrey to take matters into his own paws.

'Right, I'm just popping to the shops, Humphrey. I'll be back soon, don't worry,' Mrs Perriwinkle said, as she closed the door to Aiden's house. And that was his cue to go into action.

Humphrey had watched Aiden closely when he'd been working at home on his initial design for the quantum computing operating system. He'd try to give him a nudge from time to time when he realised that some of the calculations were incorrect, like writing the correct version in dog biscuits on the floor and hoping that Aiden would spot it, which he did once.

'Humphrey, you're the cleverest dog in the world, even if you don't know it!' Aiden had said, as the dog biscuit pattern on the floor inspired him to produce the final part of the equation he was working on.

However, not all Humphrey's attempts at guidance had been successful. The pattern of seemingly random dog food tins he placed on the kitchen floor (which if applied to one of the Navigation app's algorithms would have warned Aiden that he was about to move through dimensions) was completely misinterpreted. All Humphrey got was a scolding for being a 'naughty doggy.' So, it was now up to him to locate Aiden and help him return safely. And he already had an idea.

Humphrey was well-versed in the laws of quantum mechanics; after all he'd been reading Aiden's books for a few years and had thoroughly enjoyed them, even if they were a bit basic. He understood the principles behind quantum connections and the role of the conscious mind, working in tandem with the sub-conscious and the unconscious mind. He wasn't the cleverest dog in the world for nothing.

Humphrey trotted over to the bedside table were Aiden kept his regular phone and tapped through the directory of numbers. Eventually he found a number called 'Work Mobile QC Nova,' so he dialled it.

***

Half-blind Ron hated dogs with a passion, and to be fair they didn't care much for him. He used to tell everyone that he lost his eye after a fight with a Corwen Rottweiler called Fang. Part of this story was true, he did indeed lose his eye after a fight with a dog, but it was with a poodle called Prissy and he started the fight. When Prissy gave him a good whack with her paw he realised she wasn't quite the pushover he thought she'd be, so he turned tail and ran… straight into a rose bush. The rest, as they say, is history.

They'd been walking for a good few miles now and Half-blind Ron was getting hungry. As the sun began to set, with dusk despatching the last remnants of day so that night could arrive unhindered, he was daydreaming about chicken. The others were walking at a faster pace than him and were now a good ten yards or so in front. He could, however, still see them all quite clearly even in the low light. Well, until the English Cocker Spaniel appeared in front of him out of nowhere.

'Hello,' Humphrey said in perfect English. 'Perhaps you can help me, I'm looking for someone; a tall human with scruffy hair. Have you seen him?'

'Aaaarrrggghhhh!' Half-blind Ron cried, transmitting his thoughts in a shout. 'It's a bloody talking dog!'

He raised his hackles and hissed his loudest, hissiest hiss at Humphrey, extending his claws and scratching at the air. 'If you come any closer I'll rip ya piggin' ears off, ya freak!'

'Well, in that case I won't come any closer,' Humphrey said. 'I apologise profusely for scaring you, and please accept my assurance that this wasn't my intention. You must trust me when I attest that our encounter is undoubtedly one of profound serendipity.'

'Aaaarrrggghhhh!' Half-blind Ron shouted in his mind again, 'It's a bloody talking dictionary dog!'

By this time the rest of the group had backtracked, wondering what all the fuss was about. 'What's the problem here, Ron,' Theo said, with a wary eye on Humphrey.

'This bloody pooch appeared out of nowhere right in front of me and then he starts talking. And not only that, I can't understand half of what he's bleedin' sayin'!'

'Forgive me,' Humphrey said to Theo, 'I have travelled across realities and time to get here and I didn't mean to upset your friend. I'm looking for my human friend, you see, and I suspect that he may be in the vicinity.'

'I knew it, he's off his bloody rocker,' Half-blind Ron said to Captain Marmaduke. 'I bet he's one of those geriatric experiments that you read about.'

'Genetic experiments,' Captain Marmaduke corrected.

'Them an' all, I reckon.'

'Hello,' Cracky said, crouching down in front of Humphrey. 'I couldn't help but overhear what you said about "realities and time". Please allow me to introduce myself. I am Merlin Crackfoot, but most folks call me Cracky.'

Humphrey cocked his head to one side. 'I'm pleased to make your acquaintance, Cracky. My name is Humphrey and I'm looking for a tall human with scruffy hair.'

'Are you indeed,' Cracky said, with a glance at Theo. 'Well, I have a feeling that we may be able to help you. He wouldn't happen to drive a red automobile and carry what he tells me is a "smart phone"?'

Humphrey wagged his tail. 'It sounds like you've met him.'

'We have indeed,' Cracky said. 'He's made quite a name for himself in the short time he's been here.'

'That doesn't surprise me,' said Humphrey. 'He's a good soul and very friendly. He does have a habit of getting himself into trouble, though. Do you know where he is?'

'Well, we know where he's going,' Theo said. 'At this very moment he's with some other friends of ours, travelling by boat to Chester. They should arrive tomorrow.'

'Hmm,' Humphrey said, 'I deduce that you good people are actually heading in that general direction. Would that be correct?'

'We are,' said Theo, 'but we're taking a somewhat circuitous route.'

'In which case, would it be too much trouble if I travelled with you? I can assure you that I am quite discreet and will certainly not make your presence known to the people you are following.'

'How do you know we're following anyone?' Oriana asked.

'Just call it canine intuition,' Humphrey said. 'And I would suggest that we now continue in pursuit, else we may lose them; they are about to turn onto that main road up ahead.'

'He's right,' Cracky said. 'We'd better get a move on.'

'I'm not sure about this, Your Highness,' Captain Marmaduke said to Theo. 'He could be working for Blacktie.'

Theo concentrated slightly and probed Humphrey's mind, searching his recent memories, many of which included Aiden. 'That's quite a talent you have there,' Humphrey said.

'You can feel me in your mind?' Theo replied, astonished.

'Yes, indeed. I take no offence, though. Our meeting has been most fortuitous and if analysing my thoughts will provide corroboration of my statements then I am perfectly at ease for you to continue.'

'He's telling the truth,' Theo said to Captain Marmaduke. 'And he has quite an extraordinary mind.'

'Thank you,' said Humphrey. 'Now, we really should be continuing. From what I can see up ahead, those two individuals are about to get into a carriage.'

'Damn,' said Cracky. 'They're taking a taxi. We'd better hope we can grab one too before they get out of sight.'

Now, one of the imponderables about traversing dimensions and time is that it isn't an exact science. Once a door is opened between realities, it is possible that other doors can also open, particularly if a cross-dimensional connection already exists. So, in this particular instance, Humphrey wasn't the only one that had shifted into this reality.

CHAPTER 27 – HAVE YOU PREPARED THE ROOM FOR THE PRESS CONFERENCE?

As Ethel drifted peacefully up the River Dee, conversation between the Companionship of Wind was as light and warm as the sun on a particularly sunny day, which, of course, it was.

Aiden thought that he'd take the opportunity to have a chat with Smid. The bass player was amiable enough, but was quieter than the somewhat more extravert Grundi, which wasn't too much of a surprise to Aiden. It didn't seem to matter which universe you were in, the general personalities of musicians seemed to be consistent, and in Aiden's experience bass players were often more thoughtful and reserved. What Aiden was unaware of was Smid's background, which did come as a surprise.

'So you were a pig herder?'

'Indeed, I was. Born and bred, believe it or not,' Smid said.

'If you don't mind me saying, it's a bit of a career change. What prompted that?'

'Well,' Smid explained, 'it reached the point where I felt more like a jailer. Pigs here are nearly as clever as sheep and one day I just felt it was time to let them all go.'

'But were they not happy?' Charles asked, as he and Cliff listened nearby. 'You sound like you were very fond of them.'

'Oh, I was,' Smid said, with a faraway look in his eyes. 'I cared for each and every one of them, raised them all from little piglets. But, I woke up one day and just knew that it was time to give them their freedom. So I opened the gate of the pig pen and just left it open. They didn't all leave straight away, mind. Some thanked me and left on the same day; others felt no immediate obligation to leave but did so over the next couple of weeks. At the end of the month there was only one sow and her piglet left.'

'Why hadn't they left with the others?' Cliff asked.

'I think that Mary, the sow, would have left on the first day. It was her piglet that didn't want to leave. When I asked her why, she said that he'd never known his father and had said that he couldn't imagine anyone being as loving or as kind to him as I had been.' There were tears in his eyes, and Aiden placed a hand on his shoulder.

'Anyway,' Smid continued, 'I sat down with him one day and said that, as much as I loved him, this was a chance for him and his mum to build a new life; a life where they were free to go and do as they pleased. He loved his mum very much and he knew it was the right thing to do. I woke up the next morning and the pig pen was empty, although he'd written a little note for me.'

'What did it say?' Aiden asked.

'I don't know,' replied Smid, pulling an envelope from his inside jacket pocket, 'I've never opened it. I'm not sure that I can.'

A single tear rolled down Smid's cheek and he wiped it with his hand. 'So, I got back into my warrior's clothes, sharpened my axe, bought a bass guitar and joined the greatest Welsh Viking Flatulence Rock band there's ever been,' he said, smiling. 'It just seemed like the sensible thing do.'

'Naturally,' Aiden said, returning the smile.

'I still miss little Crusher, though. I often wonder where he ended up and whether he's alright.'

As Ethel continued her passage unabated, the sound of splashing water providing a soothing sonic accompaniment to the singing of birds, there were things lurking on the bank in the shadows.

'Don't get too close, they may catch sight of us,' Brother Vegetable Jalfrezi-Basmathi Rice hissed at his servant, who was kneeling by the bank holding him aloft*.

'Lieutenant, have your troops arrived yet?' he asked of Lieutenant Saag Bhaji.

'On the other side of the river are a company of your loyal Peshwari Naans, under my command, Brother,' the Lieutenant said. 'They are supported by a company of crack Garlic and Butter Chapattis, led by Major Mushroom Bhaji. I expect Lieutenant Shami Kebab and his Meat and Vegetable Samosas to join with us on this side of the river within the hour.'

'Excellent, Lieutenant,' said Brother Vegetable Jalfrezi-Basmathi Rice, steaming slightly. 'And are our special guests still on time to rendezvous with us at The Pig's Trotters?'

'My recent communication indicates that this is the case, but I'm still not sure it is wise to engage with foreigners, Brother.'

'Nonsense, Lieutenant,' Brother Vegetable Jalfrezi-Basmathi Rice said, splashing his carrots. 'I have assurance from General Kung Po Chicken himself that he is with us all the way. Whilst we have not always seen rice to rice with the Chinese, this is an alliance forged upon mutual interests.'

'But the General has despatched his fiercest and most uncontrollable troops, the "Wild Chinese hors d' Oeuvres". They are a mixture of Shaolin Crispy Won Tons, Ninja Vegetable Spring Rolls and, most worryingly of all, a platoon of Samurai Deep Fried Crab's Claws. If they turn on us things could get very messy, Brother.'

'They won't, Lieutenant. I understand your concern, but I can assure you that we are all together as one fighting force. And victory will be ours this night.'

It should be noted that curries do have the power to move themselves, in a sort of shuffling motion that makes crabs look graceful. They can also jump several feet in the air when the mood takes them, although this manoeuvre can often lead to spillage. However, the more affluent curries, or curries of high standing, generally employ servants to carry them from place to place.

As Charles provided some uplifting trumpeting to accompany Roisin's angelic singing, music and conversation made the time race by, and soon the large iron bridge of Alford came into view. 'It looks like news of our visit has spread fast,' Oldfart said. 'Somebody's put up a banner.'

Draped across the bridge was a huge, white banner with big, red letters that said 'Welcome Sacred Wind, and May Odin Bless Your Wind'. As Ethel moved closer to the bridge, Aiden spotted who was holding it. 'I can see pigs up there,' he said to Smid.

'Aye, well, this is pig country. They don't tend to mingle much as yet, possibly because they haven't been officially recognised in the way sheep have. They're lobbying the Welsh Parliament for formal recognition at the moment, so I'm keeping my fingers crossed.'

Ethel drew to a stop and Agnar jumped onto the bank to take care of mooring duties. A small crowd were congregated outside the pub, fronted by a well-dressed pig. 'A great welcome to you all!' he shouted, with cheers and applause ringing out as the Companionship made their way down the gangplank. 'Allow me to introduce myself; I am Archie Backrasher, the proprietor and your host this evening. If you'd all like to come this way, I'll take you to your rooms. Your ship will be quite safe; we have twenty-four hour security.'

'Much appreciated, Mr Backrasher,' Oldfart said, extending his hand to Archie. 'I'm Oldfart by the way, we spoke on the phone. Have you prepared the room for the press conference?'

'Indeed I have, Mr Olafson. I have set out tables in the Gammon Suite on the ground floor and everything is arranged in the way you requested. Given that it's just before 5:00 pm, I would be expecting the press to be arriving in the next hour.'

'Fantastic,' Oldfart said, patting him on the shoulder. 'It would appear that the legendary hospitality of pigs is well-deserved.'

Oldfart had drawn up an itinerary for the evening, which involved the press conference as 6:00 pm, followed by dinner in the pub's Snout Restaurant. The band had also agreed to play a short 'unplugged' acoustic session in the main bar in the evening, and had asked Charles to join them on trumpet. 'Bless my clacky hooves, what an honour. I'll be blowing like a crazy sheep,' Charles had said, when Oldfart had suggested it.

The Gammon Suite was very plush with a thick, red carpet covering the floor. It had a spectacular chandelier hanging from the ceiling and the walls were adorned with various paintings, some of well-known pigs. A large table, draped with a white tablecloth, had been placed at the far end of the room, facing the rows of chairs that had been set up for the journalists and guests. Oldfart had meticulously arranged everything with a professionalism that somewhat belied his happy-go-lucky persona. He'd also gone to the trouble of preparing 'character profiles' for the band, which he'd asked them all to learn, and which they were expected to relate to the assembled press.

Archie had prepared drinks and snacks for the journalists in the bar, and awaited Oldfart's signal before allowing them into the Gammon Suite. He'd also arranged for some music and sound effects, at Oldfart's request, as well as dry ice machines and lighting. So, as the journalists piled into the room they were greeted by rumblings, thunderclaps, flashing lights and a floor that was knee deep in mist.

'Okay, are you all happy with your profiles?' Oldfart asked, as the band waited in an adjoining room. Nods all round suggested this was the case, but Agnar was still reading his, frantically trying to commit it to memory.

'Are you sure you're alright, Agnar?' Oldfart said.

'Yes, yes. I'll be fine,' he responded, unconvincingly.

'Now, not a word about Ophelia or the Baron,' Oldfart said. 'If we get any questions, deflect them. We need to play this by the book, so it's simply all about the tournament, okay?'

The band nodded, although Olaf's nod was a second or so after the others.

'Right then, I'll go and introduce you.'

Archie pressed a strategically-placed button that set off two large flashbombs and Oldfart marched into the room, carrying a long wooden staff. As he stood in front of the tables and raised it in the air, the flashbulbs of the assembled press competed with the pyrotechnics and light show. Oldfart made a flamboyant gesture with his left hand and the top of the staff caught fire.

'Today, I welcome you all as friends in these dark times,' he boomed. 'Four great warriors have accepted a challenge to test their musical prowess against the best of the best. Tomorrow, at the Cestrian Music Tournament, they enter the arena with their weapons of rock and metal to take on all comers, and they will have the gods on their side!'

A giant thunderclap filled the room.

'So, ladies, gentlemen and sheep of the press, I give you SACRED WIND!!'

The band entered to cheers and more flashbulbs, joining Oldfart at the large table at the end of the room. 'I would now like to take this opportunity to introduce each of these great warriors. Firstly, please put your hands together for the lead vocalist and lead guitarist of Sacred Wind, Olaf the Berserker!' Oldfart roared, as Olaf raised his right fist in the air.

'My weapon is the broadsword and my steed is called Night Shadow,' Olaf said, in a thunderous voice. 'Together we ride into battle, hacking, slashing, growling and bottom belching until our enemies flee into the night, their weapons abandoned and their pants fragrant. I have no fear of the living, the dead, or people from Bangor. I laugh at the dark gods and urge them to attack with power, and then I unleash the force of my wind to strike them down. The skies crack with thunder, lightning illuminates the fields and the rain hammers on the ground… but my wind prevails. My cheeks of power triumph with their mighty roar. Victory for Odin! Victory for Asgard! May your sword stay sharp, may your women be comely, and may your poppadom bowl be full!'

The Companionship all stood and applauded. 'Go for it Olaf, let's give it up for the poppadoms!' shouted Vindy.

'Oh, Vindy, I do love you,' shouted Tikky, over the din, 'but be careful or you'll end up dripping on the carpet.'

As the applause died down, Oldfart continued. 'And now, please let me hear your appreciation for one of the finest drummers in the land. When he plays, the earth shakes, mountains move and the Devil does it in his pants. Put your hands together for Agnar the Hammered!'

Agnar raised his hand in the air rather meekly, his nerves clearly visible on his face. 'My weapon is the hammer and my steed is called Thunder Hoof. I pound the drums and… er…'

Sensing Agnar's failing memory, Oldfart whispered in his ear. 'You splinter your enemy's shields with the force of the storm. Mighty is your hammer as it slams down, crushing sinew, bone and steel…'

'Oh, yes,' Agnar continued with a bit more gusto, 'I splinter my enemy's shields with the force of the storm. Mighty is my axe, sorry, hammer, as it slams down, crushing sinew, bone and steel. Even the dead flee my charge, as I ravage and plunder anything in my path. I also enjoy moonlight walks, butterfly watching and candlelit dinners…'

'You fool,' Oldfart whispered, as the assembled press appeared confused. 'That last sentence is from your Viking Lonely Hearts profile.'

With a final flourish of desperation, Agnar rose to his feet and lifted his hammer into the air. 'All hail to mighty Odin! May his beard be free of badgers and may he fart in many directions. Woooarrrggghhhhh!!'

'I'm not letting him do one of these again,' Oldfart whispered to Grundi, as Agnar milked the generous applause.

Next up was Grundi, who gave an impassioned speech about the nobility of rock and metal, the joy of shredding guitar and his unrequited love for Frigg, which resulted in more tears from Mr Kneepatcher.

Smid finished off by speaking about his rumbling bass bottom-end and his fondness for leather, before twirling his axe around his head, accompanied by more pyrotechnics. 'Right,' Oldfart said, as the smoke began to clear, 'if anyone would like to ask any questions, please feel free.'

A small man with a large Fedora hat raised his hand, and Oldfart beckoned him to stand up. 'Sam Hollandaise, Chester Bugle & Gazette,' he said. 'Why do you think that Baron Blacktie has put aside his hatred of rock music and allowed Sacred Wind to enter the tournament?'

'Good question,' Oldfart said. 'The Baron told us that he feels it is time to loosen the shackles of musical bondage and allow people to judge for themselves. Next question, please.'

'Dick Swizzler, from Belting Rock magazine here,' a thin man with enormous hair and a denim jacket shouted. 'Is it true that Sacred Wind have actually sacrificed penguins on stage and ate their brains, while performing unspeakable acts with cauliflowers?'

'No, there is no truth in that,' Oldfart said.

'Oh, maybe it was a just a dream after all,' Dick said, with a glassy-eyed smile.

'Sid Scribbler, North Wales Beacon,' said a short man with a handlebar moustache and protruding forehead. 'I notice that Queen Ophelia is not with your party. I've heard a rumour that she's been kidnapped. Can you verify this, please?'

Olaf looked at Oldfart, who nodded his assent for him to answer. 'The Queen is fine and is resting at present. She will be joining us in time for the tournament tomorrow, and she will be travelling by an alternative, secret route.'

'Well done, that was excellent,' Oldfart whispered.

Questions were then fired from left, right and centre by the enthusiastic throng.

'Are the band really Vikings?'

'Yes.'

'Do they really pray to the gods by farting?'

'Yes.'

'Does Agnar have a girlfriend (asked by a sexy female journalist from the Llandudno for Ladies magazine, who received a very nasty look from

Roisin)?'

'Not at the moment, but he does have a special someone in mind,' (which saw Mara smiling at a slightly blushing Roisin).

'Have they ever thought about creating their own fashion line?'

'Not as yet, but we are giving serious consideration to "Blast from my Ass" underpants.'

'Is it true that on every full moon they have a wild party and dance naked around a campfire thrusting their weapons into the air?'

'No... at least not every full moon.'

After around half an hour, Oldfart sensed that the press conference had achieved its aim. 'Right, we have time for one more question before we dine.'

A bearded man with a long, leather coat raised his hand. 'Mike Mosher, from the Chester Musical Tribune. Does the band think they can actually win tomorrow, given the stiff competition and also the lack of familiarity that Chester has with rock music? It will sound very alien to many people in the audience.'

'That's a very good point,' Oldfart said. 'But I believe we can win. I feel the people of Chester will hear the passion and the power of Sacred Wind and that this will touch their souls and nostrils like never before.'

The Companionship roared its approval and a spontaneous round of applause spread throughout the room. 'And with that, ladies, gentlemen and sheep, we bid you farewell for the time being. We hope that we can reconvene in two days for what I'm certain will be our victory celebration.'

However, just as the members of the press began to vacate their seats, there was a small skirmish by the Gammon Suite entrance and three pigs entered the room, holding placards which read 'Equality for Pigs,' 'You Can't Stop the Chops' and 'Hug a Pig Today.'

'I'm sorry, Mr Olafson. I tried to stop them,' Archie said, rushing over to Oldfart, 'but they insisted on being allowed to speak.'

'Good people, we have a message that must be heard,' the smallest of the three pigs said. 'My name is Percy and I speak for the Porcine Order for Recognition and Kinship, more commonly known as P.O.R.K.'

The little pig placed his placard on the ground and raised his trotters aloft. 'Firstly, I would like to wish Sacred Wind well for the tournament tomorrow. You take with you the good wishes of all pigs,' he said, to a generous round of applause.

'Next week,' he continued, 'the Welsh Parliament will debate the Porcine Equality Bill, and we hope you will give us your support in finally putting a sword to the myth that all we pigs like to do is to have a good wallow in the mud.'

'But we do like a good wallow,' said the larger pig to his left.

'Er, yes,' Percy said. 'As my good friend Chopper has just stated, a good wallow is very important, and its therapeutic powers should not be underestimated. But, we pigs are also keen to be recognised for our love of literature and the fine arts, of sports, of politics and of philosophy. Indeed, as the great George Porkwell said in his acclaimed novel "Beast Ranch", we are all equal!'

Smid led the applause and it was at that point that he caught the eye of the large pig to Percy's right. He studied its face for several seconds, trying to reconcile the features with an image he had in his mind from many years ago. As the pig returned his stare, it too seemed to share the recognition, and then their eyes went wide as the memories fell into place. 'Daddy Smid?' said the pig.

'Crusher?' said Smid.

'Daddy Smid is that really you?' said Crusher.

Smid came from behind the table and headed directly for Crusher, who was nearly as tall as he was. 'You've grown so big. I never thought I would see you again,' Smid said, as tears began to well up in his eyes.

'Me too Daddy Smid,' Crusher said, as his eyes also filled with tears, 'I have missed you so much.' And then they embraced and the crowd cheered.

'I still have your letter,' Smid said. 'I've never even opened it.'

'Why, Daddy Smid?'

'Because I always hoped that one day we would meet again and that you would do me the honour of reading it for me,' Smid said, handing the letter to Crusher.

Crusher hugged Smid again and opened the letter. 'It still has stains from my tears, Daddy Smid,' he said, and then he began to read.

'*"Dear Daddy Smid, we are going away now. Mum tells me we will be living with my uncle Tim, who is very nice and kind but farts a lot. I will always think of you, Daddy Smid, and I will miss the way you cuddled me when I was sad and tickled my tummy to make me happy. I love you Daddy Smid and will miss you forever, yours sincerely, Crusher".*'

The two embraced once more and there wasn't a dry eye in the house.

'Are you crying, Oldfart,' Grundi said, as he wiped his eyes.

'No, no, of course not,' Oldfart said, defensively. 'It's just all this dry ice making my eyes smart. Anyway, let's go and have something to eat, I'm starving.'

CHAPTER 28 – FOLLOW THAT CAB!

'Look, there they are!' shouted Oriana, as Hob and Nob climbed into a horse-drawn taxi on the side of the main road to Ruthin.

'If we don't find some transport soon we're going to lose them,' Theo said.

'Quite,' agreed Cracky. 'And it could be ages before another cab comes along this early in the evening.'

'Couldn't we try and flag down another carriage?' Captain Marmaduke said.

'On this road, not a chance,' Cracky replied. 'Unfortunately folks are too wrapped up in their business to pick up hitchhikers. And anyway, who's going to stop for a man with three cats, a dog and a sheep?'

'They're nearly over the horizon!' Oriana cried.

Then, without warning, Humphrey strode into the middle of the road, just as a very large carriage hurtled towards him. At the last minute he moved away from the dashing horses and lay prone on the side of the road. The driver pulled on the reins and the carriage came to a juddering halt.

'Oh my, is your dog alright?' a very well-to-do lady said, as she looked out of the carriage window.

Cracky ran over to Humphrey and knelt down beside him. 'Just go with me, Cracky,' Humphrey whispered, before letting out a plaintive cry.

'I think he needs medical attention, my lady!' Cracky shouted.

'Please, allow me to take you to the nearest vet. It's the least I can do.'

'That would be very kind, my lady. But, believe it or not, his vet is actually in the taxi ahead of us. He is returning to Ruthin at this moment to procure special medicine that will treat my poor dog's condition.'

'That was very good,' Theo said, planting the thought into Cracky's mind.

'Well, then. Let us make haste. Please join me inside.'

'You are most kind,' Cracky replied, as they all piled into the rather luxurious carriage.

'Driver,' the lady called out, 'follow that cab!'

The carriage was extremely sumptuous and it seemed highly probable that the owner had never had to choose between kneecapping, severe ear twisting or nostril stretching as a punishment for being overdrawn.

'I'm Lady Regina Poshfrock,' Lady Regina said.

'Er, Arthur Longcloak,' Cracky said, shaking Lady Regina's hand. 'And this little chap is Humphrey.' Humphrey gave out a pitiful little yelp.

Within minutes, Lady Regina's carriage was hot on the tail of Hob and Nob's taxi. 'Shall we try and overtake him?' she suggested. 'We could signal the cab to stop.'

'Actually it would make more sense for us to follow the cab to its destination,' Cracky said, quickly. 'The surgery will be fully equipped, whereas I fear he only has a basic bag of veterinary tranklements with him, and they may not suffice.'

'But of course, you're right,' Lady Regina agreed. 'Driver, follow that cab until it reaches its destination.'

'Yus, m'lady!' shouted the driver.

When they reached Ruthin, night had completely descended and the picturesque town was illuminated by a vast array of street lamps, glowing in the mist. However, the taxi containing Hob and Nob continued onwards, heading away from the town centre.

'I thought you said his surgery was in Ruthin?' Lady Regina said to Cracky.

'Apologies, my lady, it would appear my sense of direction is not what it was. I am sure, though, that it doesn't lie much farther now.'

Fortunately, Cracky's guess was correct and in the distance they could make out a large cottage, its lanterns flickering in the windows. It was situated at the end of a short avenue of trees that arched over the road, casting long shadows that looked like they could contain more than, well, shadows.

'It looks like they are alighting at that house ahead, m'lady,' the driver said. 'Shall I continue to the door?'

'Actually, if you would be so kind as to let us out here, please,' Cracky said, before Lady Regina had a chance to speak. 'We're quite happy to go the short distance on foot. And it will save you the bother of having to turn around.'

'Are you sure?' she responded. 'Your poor dog still looks to be out of sorts.'

'Woof,' said Humphrey, jumping to his feet and licking Cracky vigorously.

'My, my,' said Cracky. 'It would appear that the very sight of the surgery has already prompted a swift recovery. Praise be to Odin!'

'Oh, I am so pleased,' Lady Regina said, patting Humphrey on the head. 'In which case I bid you all farewell, and I do pray that little Humphrey has a full and sustained recovery.'

'Well done, Humphrey,' Cracky said, smiling, as Lady Regina's carriage headed off into the distance.

'Thank you,' said Humphrey. 'It seemed like the logical course of action.'

'So, what next?' asked Captain Marmaduke. 'Do we simply sit out the night here and wait for them to leave in the morning?'

'I was thinking we may be able to monitor them from much closer quarters, and in surroundings that are perhaps warmer,' Cracky said, pointing at the 'Three Witches Bed & Breakfast' sign that swung creakily in the wind.

'That sounds risky, Cracky,' Theo said. 'We could be in danger of exposing ourselves.'

'Not if we're careful,' Cracky continued. 'Have any of you ever actually spoken to Hob and Nob before?'

The question was met with shaking heads.

'In which case, I'm the only person they may recognise, but I've never actually engaged them in conversation, and I'm pretty sure they don't know me by name. So, I'll simply say that I am Arthur Longcloak, travelling to Chester with my menagerie.'

'And I'll obviously remain taciturn and quiescent,' Humphrey said.

'Yeah, and make sure you keep your gob shut, too,' Half-blind Ron added.

The hooting of an owl wrapped-up in a gentle breeze was the only sound that accompanied their footsteps as they walked the short distance to the cottage. Although all the shutters on the windows were closed, they could see slivers of light peeping through the cracks, an indication that the occupants had yet to retire for the evening.

'Let's hope they've got a room for us,' Oriana said, as Cracky rapped the large, iron knocker against the wooden door.

At first they were simply greeted with the same silence Roisin met when knocking on Queen Ophelia's bedroom door (as silence goes this one had a pretty vigorous social life and really spread itself about). However, they soon heard activity behind the door, accompanied by the rattling of keys.

'Who is it that disturbs our peace at this late hour?' a female voice said.

'Hello. My name is Arthur Longcloak and I am seeking a room for the night, for myself and my weary animals,' Cracky said, adopting a slightly thicker welsh brogue. 'We are travelling to Chester on the morrow.'

'Who is in your company?' the female voice asked.

'I am with a sheep, a dog and three cats. They are all well-behaved, house-trained and friendly with strangers.'

'Speak for yourself,' thought Half-blind Ron, before receiving a quick slap from Captain Marmaduke's right paw.

The keys jangled as they were inserted into the lock, then it clicked and the door creaked slowly open. An old lady with matted, grey hair peeped around the door, her piercing gaze examining each of them in turn. Her eyes settled on Theo for an uncomfortable few seconds before moving back to Cracky. 'We have a room,' she said, opening the door wider and beckoning them to enter with a solitary, crooked finger.

The cottage was warm and dimly lit. A large fire crackled away on the far wall next to the bar area, casting a ghostly light on the faces of the three people sat at a table nearby. One of them had a briefcase which he held close to his side. An old radio was providing serene background music, helping to lighten an otherwise sinister ambience.

'My name is Mildred,' the old lady said, as she took a commanding position behind the reception desk. 'The room will be five pounds in advance and ten pounds when you leave. Please, sign here.'

Cracky signed as 'Arthur Longcloak', produced a five-pound note from his pocket and handed the money to Mildred. She closed the book, opened a small wooden drawer on the desk and passed him a single key, with a tag on it that said '4'.

'I am afraid we have finished serving dinner for the evening,' she said, putting the registrar book in the drawer. 'However, I can provide fresh water and some snacks for your cats and dog, but they must stay in their room.'

'That would be much appreciated,' Cracky said.

'You and your sheep —,'

'Blodwyn,' Oriana said to Mildred

'You and Blodwyn are quite welcome to join myself and Agnes, my co-manager, for a drink in the bar, although we close in thirty minutes.'

'You are most kind,' Cracky replied. And with that they made their way to room number 4.

'Did you recognise one of those guests?' Nob said, as Hob took a sip of his drink.

'Vaguely,' Hob replied. 'And you are right to be circumspect in your observations, my dear Nob. It may be nothing, but we should keep our wits about us. Do you not think so, Agnes?'

'Wull pizt macaron, seedy poopy scratch 'n sniff,' said Agnes.

'Yes, I quite agree,' replied Hob.

The room was small but functional and Mildred kept good on her promise to supply snacks and drinks for Theo, Captain Marmaduke, Half-blind Ron and Humphrey. 'Right, Oriana and I will go downstairs for a drink,' Cracky said. 'We'll join our two "friends" and see what we can find out. I can't see them giving much away, but light conversation and a few drinks could loosen their tongues.'

'May we join you, kind sirs and madam?' Cracky asked, as he and Oriana arrived in the bar. 'We have had a long day and would welcome some conversation to go with our drinks.'

'Of course,' Hob said, warily, moving his chair closer to Nob. Cracky and Oriana pulled out the two remaining chairs at the table and sat down.

'What would you like to drink?' Mildred said, from behind the bar.

'Oh, I'll have a pint of your finest ale and Blodwyn here will have —,'

'Just a glass of water, please,' Oriana said.

'And please get these two gentlemen and the lady whatever they are drinking,' Cracky said.

'Thank you, indeed,' Nob said.

'Yes, thank you,' said Hob.

'Split poo,' said Agnes.

The crackling fire's warmth provided a perfect balance to the cool drinks, and Cracky felt obliged to start the conversation proper. 'If I may be so bold as to introduce myself,' he said, 'I am Arthur Longcloak from Llangollen, and this here is Blodwyn. We are travelling to Chester, to the market.'

'I am Mr Starry and my compatriot here is Mr Twinkle,' Hob said. 'We are Peripatetic Astrologers, providing our travelling service to all those in need of a good horoscope.'

'Yes, we do love giving people a good horoscope,' said Mr Twinkle.

'And this here, is Agnes,' continued Mr Starry.

'Muckypup,' said Agnes.

'Ah, you must excuse Agnes,' Mildred said, as she pulled up a chair at the next table. 'She speaks only in Ancient Welsh Witchenese, a long forgotten language passed down from her mother, and her mother's mother, and her mother's mother's mother, and her mother's mother's mother's auntie, and her mother's, mother's mother's, auntie's mad cousin, Flappytrap, who was a high-ranking witch in Ruthin. There are few now who understand its complex tones, words and enunciations.'

'I see,' Cracky said.

'Although Mr Twinkle and I are conversant, so we will translate for you… when appropriate,' said Mr Starry.

'That would be welcomed,' said Oriana.

'Furrypots,' Agnes said, nodding.

The conversation was indeed kept light and not too intrusive. Cracky embellished the story of travelling to Chester Market by explaining his requirement for special herbs for cooking, and Mr Starry and Mr Twinkle waxed lyrical about the planets' influence on various star signs. 'For example,' Mr Starry said, 'an Aquarius should never walk naked outdoors and turn his back when Pluto is rising.'

'Indeed,' added Mr Twinkle. 'The effect can be quite a shock to the system. A fully-risen Pluto is not to be trifled with.'

Agnes said little but nodded in agreement on occasion. She was fascinated by Oriana and gazed at her intently, whilst fiddling with the warts on the end of her long nose. In the end, Oriana felt compelled to speak. 'Excuse me, Agnes, but I notice that you keep looking at me.'

'Willy widdle flumpo smackypants, Oriana Oftsheared, flutytwoot, Ossie Flopsywool Ocksi,' said Agnes.

Cracky cast a quick sideways glance at Oriana and then looked directly at Mr Starry, keenly awaiting translation. 'That's odd,' Mr Starry said. 'Agnes says you are actually Oriana Oftsheared, the flautist with the Oswestry Sheep Orchestra.'

'Ah, I see,' Oriana replied, calmly. 'That happens a lot. I'm her cousin, Blodwyn Oftsheared. We do look remarkably similar, but I'm afraid that my musical talents are not quite up to Oriana's standard.'

'Oh, that would explain it,' said Mr Starry, as he translated for Agnes, who stood up excitedly and shook Oriana's hoof.

'Apparently she's a bit of a fan,' Mr Twinkle said.

'Boodleknees, boodleknees. Iffy ticky gobbyblab,' said Agnes.

'She says that she thinks your cousin's music is beautiful and asks if you will pass on this message,' Mr Starry said.

'Of course,' replied Oriana, as Cracky let out a sigh of relief under his breath.

'Furrypots,' Agnes said, with a big toothy smile.

The clock hit eleven and Mildred rang the little bell on the bar. 'Last orders, please.'

'Not for us, thank you,' said Mr Starry. 'We are headed for an important engagement in Chester tomorrow and our client will be most upset if we do not arrive in a timely fashion.'

'Indeed,' added Mr Twinkle. 'Plus we must make sure we are both fully conscious when things start rising in the morning.'

'Quite,' added Mr Starry. 'When they both rise in conjunction, it's a truly splendid sight. In fact if you'd care to join us, Mr Longcloak, I'm sure you'd find it most uplifting.'

'Er, thank you, gentlemen, but I'll pass on this occasion,' a coughing Cracky replied.

'A pity,' said Mr Twinkle. 'Mars and Jupiter are a joy to behold when they are in conjunction, as they will be just before dawn tomorrow.'

Oriana looked at Cracky and signalled that they too should retire for the night. 'Yes, I believe we will follow your example and take to our rooms also,' Cracky said. 'Thank you once again for the excellent company and fine beverages.'

'You are most welcome,' said Mildred. 'Would you like an early morning call?'

'What time are you gentlemen leaving in the morning?' Cracky asked, as Mr Starry and Mr Twinkle headed for the stairs.

'Oh, we'll be away about 8:00 am, so we'll have breakfast at 7:00 am,' said Mr Twinkle, who received a stern look from Mr Starry.

'In which case we'll join you gentlemen for breakfast, if that's acceptable?' Cracky said.

'Of course, of course,' said Mr Starry, with a look that suggested it was anything but.

Back in the room, Cracky and Oriana were greeted by anxious faces. 'Well, what did you find out?' Theo said, once Cracky had closed the door to the bedroom behind him.

'It would appear they are headed for Chester, and we know what time they're leaving. I strongly feel they are to meet with the Baron.'

'Surely you don't think that Blacktie would be stupid enough to have Ophelia held prisoner in his palace?' Captain Marmaduke said.

'He would if he thinks that when he obtains a piece of Ceridwen's Cheese that it won't matter.'

'That is a good point,' Theo said. 'And in which case we may need to act sooner rather than later to ensure he never receives it.'

'Are you suggesting that we assail these two individuals and purloin this cheese?' Humphrey asked.

'No, stupid,' Half-blind Ron said, with annoyance. 'He's saying we should beat them up and nick it.'

'Anyway, let's get some sleep and make sure we're up early in the morning,' Cracky said, as he climbed into bed. 'We can't afford to lose track of them now.'

CHAPTER 29 – ARE THE TROOPS READY?

A hearty meal accompanied by a healthy supply of drinks was a perfect end to the day for the Companionship; freeing their minds from worries created in times past and from thoughts of potential threats in times to come.

'You know, Mr Backrasher,' Aiden said, with a mouthful of food, 'these roast potatoes are divine.'

'Why, thank you, Mr Peersey,' Archie replied, with a smile and a delighted oink. 'The secret is to soak them in pigswill for a day before roasting.'

'Really,' Aiden said, stopping in mid chew, 'well they taste delicious.'

'I couldn't agree more,' said Oldfart, who was sitting to his right on the huge banquet table, 'I've had Pigswillian Potatoes before, but never ones with such a delicate texture and sublime aroma. You are to be commended, Archie.'

As tummies began to fill and pallets became whetted, spirits began to rise and it was time for the pre-arranged 'unplugged' gig that Oldfart had promised. Olaf and Grundi sat atop two tall bar-stools, with their acoustic guitars, and Charles proudly raised his trumpet in the air, as the specially-selected guests and local dignitaries gave them a warm round of applause.

'Tonight, we'd like to play you a brand new song,' Olaf announced. 'This is a song about a loved one in danger and in need of rescuing. A valiant companionship sets sail determined to enact a rescue, but their search is stalled because there is no light to guide their way in the dark. So, they call upon the power of their wind and a cigarette lighter to illuminate their path. This is called *"Hurricane Ass"*.

She's been gone
For so long
Held in a tower far away

With a man who smells quite strong
Is she safe?
Oh, I hope that she's OK
Cause I'm missing her so very much
And I want her
I need her

Carry me on through the night
Across stormy tides
Here with my friends
By my side
And we'll save her

'And this is the chorus,' Olaf shouted. 'I want everyone to join in on the next one!'

Hurricane ass
Guide my way in the dark
With your windy light
Hurricane ass
Let your flame burn bright
Like a thousand stars
Hurricane ass
Show me the way to her heart
For in my dreams she lives
She's at my side
For all time

'Right, remember that for next time,' Olaf said, before continuing with the second verse.

I'm so scared
That she's ensnared
She's in city that's so strange
Where the people are quite weird
They won't care
If she doesn't comb her hair
She'll be locked inside a dingy cell
But I'll find her
I'll comb it

Carry me on through the night
Across stormy tides

Here with my friends
By my side
And we'll save her

As the second chorus began, the room was awash with waving arms, lit cigarette lighters and singing pigs. Crusher, Chopper and Percy locked arms and swayed gleefully together, belting out the words and the occasional oink with gusto. Archie Backrasher and his wife, Annabelle, were stood on the banquet table with their arms in the air and were soon joined by Mara and Roisin. Mr Kneepatcher was already in tears and was being comforted by Harold and Greta. 'It's so beautiful,' he cried, 'Bless you Olaf, we'll save her!'

However, outside the window, things were lurking in the night that had little concern for music, singing and dancing. 'Have the security guards been taken care of?' asked Brother Vegetable Jalfrezi-Basmathi Rice.

'Yes, Brother,' replied Lieutenant Saag Bhaji. 'They have been immobilised.'

'How so, Lieutenant?'

'Samurai Deep Fried Crab's Claws have infiltrated their underpants. If they move, or utter a word, they'll get snipped.'

'Excellent. What of our other Chinese friends?'

'They are outside the front entrance waiting for your signal,' the Lieutenant answered. 'On your command, Major Mushroom Bhaji's Garlic and Butter Chapattis will break through the window. This will be the signal for the Chinese to charge the front door. They'll be closely followed by Lieutenant Shami Kebab and his Meat and Vegetable Samosas. Finally my Peshwari Naans will storm the front window. They'll be completely surrounded and unable to escape. I predict that their death will be slow and painful, but tasty.'

'Ha!' laughed Brother Vegetable Jalfrezi-Basmathi Rice. 'I'll show Blacktie he doesn't have to rely on a bunch of pirates to rid him of his enemies. The Tan-Y-Lan Tuffies may as well slither back to their little hidden cove in Colwyn Bay, as there'll be nothing left for them to do when they get here other than clean up the blood.'

'What shall we do with the King and Queen of Wrexham, Brother?'

'Oh, I've already given instruction to our Chinese friends to give them special attention. I'm assured that the Ninja Vegetable Spring Rolls will make mopping them up a priority. Their plates will be that clean by the time they've finished with them, they'll look like they've come fresh from a dishwasher.'

Meanwhile, on the hilltop to the rear of The Pig's Trotters, two lone curries looked down at the pub in silence. 'Do we make our move now?' asked General Lamb Korma-Saffron Rice.

'No,' replied General Beef Madras-Wholegrain Rice. 'Let's wait until they commit themselves. Are the troops ready?'

'I believe they are, General,' Saffy said, as he looked out over the vast sea of curries and supporting side dishes on the hill slope behind them. 'I think Brother Vegetable Jalfrezi-Basmathi Rice is in for something of a shock.'

Inside, Charles Corriedale was blasting a soaring and emotive trumpet solo. As he reached the crescendo, rapturous applause broke out in the Snout Restaurant and he raised the trumpet in the air triumphantly... then he heard the sound of breaking glass and a vicious Garlic and Butter Chapatti appeared on his head. 'Bless my clacky hooves, what's going on!' he shouted, as Olaf grabbed the Chapatti and hurled it to the floor.

'We're under attack, draw your weapons now!' Olaf screamed, as the Chapattis continued to pour through the broken windows behind him.

The room was a scene of chaos. Pigs, people and sheep were running around with Chapattis clinging to their faces, the smell of garlic causing many to lapse into unconsciousness. Mara and Roisin were like whirling dervishes, hovering in the air and fending off any attack with a swift kick or punch. Then, as the panicking crowd opened the main door, they were met by the hordes of the Wild Chinese hors d' Oeuvres.

Archie Backrasher was quickly felled as three Shaolin Crispy Wantons sliced at his trotters. A fourth hurled itself at his throat, cursing in Crispy Wantonese, before being cut off in mid flow by Aiden's thrusting pocket knife. 'You've saved my life, Aiden,' Archie cried with relief, as Aiden kicked away the Crispy Wantons clinging to his trotters.

A Ninja Vegetable Spring Roll flung itself straight for Archie's wife, before Aiden caught it in the air and crushed it with his hand, its carrots and mushrooms splattering on the floor. Then the Meat and Vegetable Samosas arrived, bouncing through the room at great speed. 'Get back!' screamed Grundi, as he whirled the spiked ball and chain around his head, scattering the Samosas in every direction, until one caught him squarely on the nose, stunning him momentarily.

Finally, the Peshwari Naans crashed through the front window, entering the fray with bloodcurdling screams. Cliff Corriedale quickly shielded Charles, and kicked one Naan so hard it smashed through the mirror behind the bar. Charles bravely fought off a few Naans with his trumpet, but soon got out of breath. 'My, I'm not as young as I used to be,' he puffed.

'Just stay behind me, uncle. Nothing's going to happen to you while my heart is still beating,' Cliff said.

Oldfart managed to grab one of the Peshwari Naans that was heading straight for his neck. He held it tightly in a two-handed grip as it tried to attach itself to his face. 'Oldfart, hold it out, away from your face!' Olaf cried.

With one final push of his will and his muscles, Oldfart managed to push his arms out, stretching the Naan bread wide. Then Olaf's broadsword came sweeping down and cut it into two. 'Thank you, my friend,' Oldfart said, holding the two limp pieces in each hand.

Greta and Harold held Vindy and Tikky above their heads, just out of reach from the bouncing Samosas. However, a swift slash to Harold's ankle from a Samurai Deep Fried Crab's claw saw his right leg buckle. 'Harold!' Greta shouted, as a Peshwari Naan landed on her head and began to crawl onto Tikky's plate.

'So, Queen, it would appear it is I that will get to mop you up,' the Peshwari Naan said.

'Oh, I doubt that,' Tikky replied. 'I've faced far worse than you in my time. You're too doughy to get the better of me.' And then she fired a boiling hot piece of chicken straight into its middle, causing it to scream and fall to the floor. As it tried to recover, Greta ground her foot into it.

'For my Queen!' she shouted, as bits of Naan bread burst out from beneath her shoe.

'Are you alright my dear?' Vindy cried, as he sent a Meat and Vegetable Samosa packing with a well-aimed piece of boiling beef.

'I'm fine, darling. Now do be careful, those Naan breads might be doughy but they're a determined bunch.'

Crusher and Smid fought together, leaning against each other's back. Crusher's huge trotters crushed Crispy Wantons and Meat and Vegetable Samosas indiscriminately, as Smid's axe sliced through Chapattis and Naans. Mr Kneepatcher had removed his cravat and had tied it in a knot, bravely swinging it in front of him with great speed. 'Attack my friends, would you? I'll make pie-filling out of the lot of you!' he cried, as Meat and Vegetable Samosas fled his rage.

However, it was soon becoming apparent that the numbers were too great. Holding them off for a prolonged period of time, at least indoors, was not an option. 'There's too many of them.' Agnar said, as he pounded his hammer onto a Deep Fried Crab's Claw, shattering it into pieces.

'We need to get outside,' Oldfart shouted. 'We'll have more room to move.'

'Agreed,' said Olaf, 'but the Crispy Wantons have the front door blocked, and the Naan breads are bringing up their rear.'

'We've only one chance,' said Oldfart, with a panicked look on his face.

'No, that's far too dangerous to try indoors,' Olaf screamed, as he sliced through a flying Ninja Vegetable Spring Roll.

'I don't think we have a choice,' Oldfart shouted, as he ripped a crazed Garlic and Butter Chapatti off his arm.

Olaf steadied himself and looked over at Grundi, as he battled against four Deep Fried Crab's Claws who were slashing away at his boots. 'Grundi, you're going to have to let loose your wind. I have a cigarette lighter at the ready.'

Grundi nodded solemnly and with three swift strokes and a stomp despatched the Crab's Claws to seafood heaven… or hell.

'Tell everyone to get down,' Oldfart yelled to Aiden, 'and to move away from the door as fast as they can.'

Aiden had no idea what was going to happen as he saw Grundi bend forward, with his bottom pointing at the door, but he had common sense enough to suspect that it was going to be something explosive. 'Everyone move as far away from the door as possible, now!' he yelled.

'Smid, Agnar, you'll need to cover us,' Olaf shouted, as Smid and Agnar ran over to them, hacking at anything that came within reach.

'I'm ready, Olaf, light the flame,' Grundi said, his face the image of determination. Olaf clicked the cigarette lighter switch… it wouldn't light. He tried it again, but still nothing. 'Hurry up, Olaf, the wind is coming. Once it's on its way I can't do anything to stop it!' Grundi cried.

At the third click, the lighter finally ignited and Olaf quickly moved the flame in position in front of Grundi's bottom. 'Aim true, my friend,' he said, covering his eyes.

The front door was knocked outwards off its hinges as the intense jet of flame hit it, with the conflagration blasting through everything in its path. The smell of burnt Chinese Food and charred Naan bread lay heavy in the smoky air and Grundi stood up to survey the damage.

'Right, everyone outside!' Olaf shouted, as pigs, sheep and people bolted through the flaming remains of the door frame, crushing their charred foes with each step.

But, the situation outside was no better. On all three sides they were completely surrounded, and Brother Vegetable Jalfrezi-Basmathi Rice laughed like only a mad, despotic curry can.

'Bravo! Bravo!' he said, clapping his mini poppadoms together. 'I salute your resourcefulness. But now I also salute your death. On my command attack, my hordes, and leave none alive!'

'Er, actually can I make a suggestion,' Vindy said, just as the combined might of Wild Chinese hors d' Oeuvres, Meat and Vegetable Samosas, Garlic and Butter Chapattis and Peshwari Naans were about to start their charge.

'A suggestion? A suggestion?!' Brother Vegetable Jalfrezi-Basmathi Rice screamed. 'You are in no position to make any kind of suggestion, except to suggest what should decorate your plate when your ingredients are scattered to the four winds!'

'Actually, I was going to suggest you surrender,' Vindy said.

Brother Vegetable Jalfrezi-Basmathi Rice let out an insane curry cackle, and the sound of laughing in his ranks soon became an epidemic. 'Oh, my King, you surely cannot be serious. You are truly losing your mind at last. But, I will entertain you for a moment, as I have not laughed so much in a long time. So, then, give me one good reason why we should surrender?'

'Well, if you look up to the hill behind the pub, I'll give you 50,000 reasons,' Vindy said, as 50,000 curries, Naans and Chapattis marched down its slope towards The Pig's Trotters. 'And, if that's not a good enough reason,' Vindy continued, 'can I suggest that the fact you are also surrounded by 1,000 of my Elite Tandoori Naans is also something you should consider.'

The hordes of Brother Vegetable Jalfrezi-Basmathi Rice nervously turned and looked at the ranks of Elite Tandoori Naans. These were not soft and doughy like the Peshwaris; these were crispy, battle-hardened Naans, their fighting skills honed by years of intense training. Anyone who knows anything knows that you don't mess with a crispy Tandoori Naan. If you do, you'll never be the same again.

Brother Vegetable Jalfrezi-Basmathi Rice started to boil profusely, his carrots turning wildly and his incandescent rage causing his rice to puff and pop. 'Give it up, Brother,' Tikky said. 'There's been enough fighting this day.'

But it was too late; the curry madness had already taken him. A high-pitched scream shot through the night like a wolf with its tail on fire, and he gave the order to attack. As his hordes charged forward they were engulfed. Tandoori Naans are not known for their mercy in battle conditions and in only a few short minutes there wasn't a Shaolin Crispy Wanton that wasn't shredded, a Peshwari Naan that wasn't ripped, a Meat and Vegetable Samosa that wasn't squashed, a Samurai Deep Fried Crab's Claw that wasn't crushed, a Garlic and a Butter Chapatti that wasn't splattered, or a Ninja Vegetable Spring Roll that wasn't in pieces. Eventually, Brother Vegetable Jalfrezi-Basmathi Rice found himself completely isolated, apart from his servant.

'You're going to spend a long time in the cellar for this, Brother,' said General Beef Madras-Wholegrain Rice, as Saffy joined him at his side.

'I will never let you take me, you fools! Do you think I've not made preparations for an event such as this? My time may have ended but there will be others, I can promise you that!'

His servant placed him on the ground and reached into his pocket, producing a large sachet of white powder. 'Everyone back away, he's got baking soda with him!' shouted Saffy, as the servant emptied the contents onto Brother Vegetable Jalfrezi-Basmathi Rice.

The explosion was spectacular, but fortunately had little distance. The bubbling and crackling carrots, rice, mushrooms and onions shot skyward, before limply falling to earth. Once the smoke had cleared, Brother

Vegetable Jalfrezi-Basmathi Rice's plate was empty, although in need of a good wash... as was his servant.

'Has anyone received any baking soda wounds?' Vindy shouted, through the smoke, as Saffy and General Beef Madras-Wholegrain Rice surveyed their troops carefully.

'It looks like we're all clear, Your Majesty,' Saffy shouted.

'Well, that was a turn of events I don't think anyone was expecting,' Oldfart said. 'Are we all okay?'

'It would seem so,' Olaf replied, as the Companionship drew together around him. 'However, I sense there are others in need of some attention. Thankfully, though, their wounds appear mild. There are no casualties.'

'How did you know your troops were coming?' Mara said to Vindy.

'Oh, Saffy got word to us earlier in the day. I think we underestimated the enemy's numbers, but I knew there would only be one winner in this battle.'

And so 'The Battle of The Pig's Trotters' went down in folklore. Many years from now, young curries would sit listening in reverence to their grandparents as they told them the tales of bravery from that night, and how curries, men, sheep and pigs fought together.

Word of the Brother's demise quickly reached the ears of the Baron, who was less than pleased. 'The fool!' Blacktie shouted at Pimple, who cowered at his anger. 'He had strict instructions. He knew the plan and his idiocy has cost us dear.'

'Quite, my Lord,' Pimple agreed, standing up.

'This changes things somewhat,' the Baron continued, his anger hardly abating. 'Bring me Queen Ophelia, now.'

'Yes, my Lord,' Pimple said, and quickly ran out of the throne room.

Within a minute he returned with the Queen, her wings tied behind her back. 'I gather you've had some bad news?' she said, sardonically.

'Oh, I'm afraid it's bad news for both of us, my dear Queen. The time for hospitality is at an end,' the Baron snapped.

'Locking me up in your castle and denying me my comb is what you would consider hospitality, is it?'

'Quite frankly, yes,' he replied. 'Considering how you are going to spend the next twenty-four hours or so. Pimple, what do we have in the way of dingy cells available at the moment?'

'Well, my Lord, we have vacancies in all three types, the Standard dingy cell, the Superior dingy cell and, of course, the Luxury dingy cell.'

'Pray, remind me of each type,' the Baron asked.

'The Standard has a mattress, a toilet and is rat-free; the Superior has a wooden bed with straw, a hole in the floor and a part-time rat; whereas the Luxury has a wooden bed with no straw, a hole in the floor, a very limited supply of toilet paper and two full-time rats, one of which is particularly tetchy.'

'That sounds ideal.' the Baron said.

'You wouldn't dare!' Ophelia yelled.

'Oh, I think I would,' he said, with a smile. 'Pimple, please escort Her Majesty to the Luxury dingy cell.'

'Of course, my Lord,' Pimple said, leading the struggling Queen away.

'Oh, and Pimple,'

'Yes, my Lord,'

'Get word to Taffy Tuffy. Tell him to set sail immediately.'

CHAPTER 30 – IT SEEMS OUR COVER IS BLOWN

'They're gone,' a startled Oriana said, rushing back into the bedroom. It was 7:30 am.

'Are you sure?' Theo asked.

'Yes, Mildred on reception told me they left before dawn.'

'I smell a rat, here,' Cracky said. 'I don't know how exactly, but it would seem they either suspected something, or someone tipped them off. They'll be halfway to Chester now.'

'We'd better get moving straight away. I suggest we get breakfast to go,' Theo said.

'Hang on,' Half-blind Ron said, with concern, 'breakfast to go' where? I want me breakfast in me bloody tummy.'

'He means to take with us as we travel,' Humphrey said, 'You can put it in your tummy as you walk.'

'Oh, well that's alright then. I reckon we'll be fightin' afterwards and I'll need to be stocked up good and proper so I'll be at me best.'

They hurriedly gathered their belongings and made their way down the stairs, only to see their path blocked by Mildred and Agnes. The two women cackled loudly and were now dressed in black. Worryingly they were carrying broomsticks, even though there was a vacuum cleaner in the corner.

'Now, then, where are we off to so fast, my pretties?' Mildred said, with an evil, toothy grin. 'Best that you stay a while longer with us… and have breakfast, of course.'

'Er, we'd love to,' Cracky said, 'but I'm afraid we're likely to be late for the market in Chester if we do, and that really wouldn't be good.'

'Plib colliwobble wingy, glicky dongle, Oriana pub Millin Cackywacky' said a cackling Agnes.

'Oh, I don't think you'll be making it to the market today,' said Mildred.

'As Agnes just said, it's in our interests and the interests of our friends that you stay put for a bit. I'm sure you understand… Oriana Oftsheared and Merlin Crackfoot, and, I believe, Prince Theo of Corwen, too!'

'Okay,' Cracky said. 'It seems our cover is blown, but I'm afraid if you won't let us leave of our own volition then we'll have to force our way out. I am happy to pay for the room, of course.'

'Why, thank you, Merlin Crackfoot. We appreciate your custom, but I'm afraid that the Three Witches of Ruthin are not to be tangled with. You are going nowhere,' Mildred said, pointing her broom menacingly in Cracky's face.

'Fillip booglie plumpy bot,' Agnes agreed.

'May I point out a slight numerical discrepancy at this juncture,' Humphrey said. 'There appears to be only two of you.'

'Ah, a talking dog that can count. Have you ever seen the like, Agnes?'

'Numpty,' said Agnes.

'Our sister Gertrude is away on business, not that it's any concern of yours. She is raising valuable funds in Llandudno by utilising her gifts of precognition to pass on important messages of future events to the rich and powerful… or anyone with a spare £1.'

'You mean she's fortune telling on Llandudno pier?' Cracky said.

'Er, we prefer to call it Precogitive Services, but yes, she is.'

'However,' Mildred continued, 'we do not need our sister here to deal with the likes of you. It is widely known that you have no real penchant for magic, Crackfoot, so unless a member of your group happens to speak Ancient Welsh Witchenese, you will be powerless against our spells.'

'Actually, I speak Ancient Welsh Witchenese,' Humphrey said.

'Nonsense,' Mildred scoffed, as she cast a worried glance towards Agnes.

'Nobblybits,' Agnes agreed.

'How can a mere dog have learned a language that hasn't been openly taught for nearly 1,000 years, and whose words and meanings are kept a closely-guarded secret by the enlightened few? Those who speak it are sworn to secrecy upon pain of damnation to the Black Place of Our Souls for all eternity. How could you possibly have acquired knowledge such as this; from the back of a tin of dog food?'

'Actually, I read the book that was in our room last night,' Humphrey said.

'Book, what book?' Mildred said, as both she and Agnes stopped cackling abruptly.

'It was called *"Teach Yourself Ancient Welsh Witchenese"*. I found it very enlightening.'

Mildred's face started to change colour; slowly at first, starting with a subtle pink shade, before developing into full-blown scarlet. 'Agnes, what have I told you about leaving your things lying around! You see, this is what happens when you don't tidy up after yourself, you silly, old crone!'

'Viddly Sozzled', apologised Agnes.

'Anyway,' Mildred continued, pointing a bony finger at Humphrey, 'there's no way you'll be able to remember all the incantations and spells after one read. Well, not unless you've got a photographic memory.'

'Actually, I have,' Humphrey said.

'Oh, dear,' said Mildred, moving back towards the reception desk.

'Bolloxicity,' Agnes agreed.

The two witches held their broomsticks at arm's length, pointing directly at Humphrey. 'Let's see what you've got, then,' Mildred hissed.

'I suspect the rest of you should get behind me,' Humphrey said. 'This could get a trifle messy.'

Mildred and Agnes started to twirl their broomsticks in a clockwise motion, their eyes turned upwards as they entered a trance. Then they began to speak in unison. 'Icky wicky, doggfluff, button flappy wappy. Inflamus waggy bum, benotahappychappy!'

They brought their broomsticks together and a ball of fire about six-inches wide appeared in the air. It rotated wildly for a few seconds and then headed straight for Humphrey's tail. However, with dazzling speed, Humphrey raised his paw in the air and said 'Creatchen cooly pooly!' From out of nowhere, a torrent of water cascaded over the fireball sending it crashing to the floor, leaving nothing but a steaming pebble.

Chagrin made a guest appearance on the faces of Mildred and Agnes. They were not used to being thwarted at their own game, not least by an English Cocker Spaniel with an in-depth knowledge of Ancient Welsh Witchenese. 'We must combine our strength more,' Mildred whispered to Agnes. 'We must let loose the Squattybum.'

'Digglypoos,' Agnes said, looking very concerned.

'Yes, I know it's dangerous, but desperate times call for desperate measures.'

And with that, Mildred started the incantation, as both she and Agnes raised their broomsticks. 'Booduddle miffy, clocky wockle squiffy, bendy woo, fiddledy doo, icky wicky wiffy!'

Above the broomsticks the air seemed to go black as coal, swirling intensely. A menacing howl issued from the blackness, which now had the appearance of a tunnel leading to the bowels of a dark and not very nice place.

'I know this spell,' Cracky said. 'They're calling forth the Squattybum.'

'What on earth is a Squattybum?' Oriana asked.

'It's a very dangerous and very, very smelly demon. It would appear you have unnerved them a fair bit, Humphrey.'

'So it would seem. I wonder if they've read the appendix about

Squattybums,' Humphrey replied.

As the howl drew ever closer the air as filled with an awful smell. Wisps of putrid smoke began to seep out of the tunnel, tumbling to the floor and swirling like a mad, smelly, swirly thing. 'Concentrate!' Mildred screamed at Agnes.

Then, in a flash from within the acrid smoke, it appeared; a small black, hairy creature with three arms, four legs, three eyes, two noses and an awful lot of very sharp teeth. It jumped up and down, dripping green saliva, and unleashed a hellish scream at the Humphrey.

'As a matter of interest, have you ladies read the appendix on Squattybums?' Humphrey said.

'Appendix?' said Mildred.

'Appledicks?' echoed Agnes.

'Yes, the one that contains the counter-spell.'

'Counter-spell?'

'Cummyrummy-splot?

The Squattybum was poised and ready to pounce. It was waving its arms around rabidly, spitting awful-smelling sputum in every direction. 'Here, let me enlighten you,' Humphrey said, wagging his tail. 'Turny-wurney, Squattybum, pointy-wointy tickletum. Stinkygone smelloposies, nibbly-wibbly wiffy toesy-woesies!'

'No!' Mildred screamed.

'Numpty!' screamed Agnes.

The Squattybum stood stock still, as if someone had given it a really good slapping for being so smelly and rude. Then it started to gnash its teeth together involuntarily, whimpering as it did so. Its horrid smell vanished and was replaced by the tender fragrance of flowers, which really seemed to upset it. And then it started to sniff; one nose after the other, its eyes looking this way and that, as if it were trying to detect the direction of the smell that seemed to be for its nostrils only. The source of the smell was coming from Mildred and Agnes.

It dived on Mildred's feet first, nibbling wildly at her toes before jumping towards Agnes to provide an equal dose of wild nibbling. As both witches screamed and ran around the room in a vain attempt to escape, Humphrey calmly turned to Cracky. 'We should perhaps go now. I suspect our would-be kidnappers will be indisposed for several hours.'

Cracky looked at him and smiled. 'I think your friend Aiden would be very impressed, Master Humphrey.'

'Thank you.'

'Well, I hates to say it, but you're not bad for a dog,' Half-blind Ron said, as they made their way back to the main road. 'Mind you, I'll still scratch your bloody eyes out if you try and nick me breakfast, whenever that's going to be.'

When they reached the main road there was a signpost with an arrow pointing right that read 'Ruthin 2 miles'.

'Can I suggest we walk into town and get a taxi,' Cracky said. 'Hob and Nob will be virtually in Chester by now, so I think our only option is to discard any pretence of being incognito and simply head straight for the palace.'

'But how on earth will we get in?' said Captain Marmaduke. 'Once Blacktie finds out we're trailing them, there'll be guards at every entrance.'

'Well, we could have the advantage of surprise. Hob and Nob may assume that the witches have dealt with us. And we may have some assistance when we get there,' Cracky said, cryptically. 'Let's just hope fortune, and the gods, are on our side.'

CHAPTER 31 – PREPARE TO BE BOARDED

'Are you sure there's enough room in there?' Aiden said to Archie, as he and some volunteers packed a large bin with the remains of Brother Vegetable Jalfrezi-Basmathi Rice's forces.

'Oh, this lot won't be here long,' Archie replied. 'As soon as the rats get a sniff these bins will be empty quicker than you can say crispy pork bellies.'

The Companionship still felt weary after the exertions of the previous evening. Sleep didn't come easy to most, perhaps due to the adrenalin rush provided by the battle, but also perhaps because of the realisation that their journey may hold further perils. Thankfully the sun was out and the River Dee flowed peacefully by, unaware of the scene of chaos and destruction that took place on its banks only a few hours earlier.

'How long to Chester from here?' Grundi asked Oldfart, as they loaded their travelling bags into Ethel.

'Oh, I'd say about another two hours, no more than that. Assuming we don't get any interruptions.'

'It would seem that Blacktie means to stop us from entering the tournament,' Olaf said, as he sharpened his sword on a nearby rock. 'I think it's a real possibility there'll be other "interruptions" ahead.'

'Of that I have little doubt, my friend,' Smid said. 'Assuming that we make it down the river intact, there's also the small job of getting into the city.'

'Let's just cross one bridge at a time for now,' Oldfart advised. 'I'll just be praying to the gods that our path is clear.'

'Well I say, bring them on,' Agnar said, brandishing his hammer. 'If it's a fight Blacktie wants, then by Odin's bristling beard and farty backside let's give it to him.'

Charles was sitting on a small bench outside the pub, checking his trumpet for damage. Cliff was sat next to him, his body language portraying his protectiveness towards the old sheep. The events of last night had made him realise that although his uncle's spirit was still strong, he was indeed getting on in years, and Cliff's concern was palpable in his face.

'Did you too get any sleep?' Mr Kneepatcher asked, emerging from the pub with a glass of wine in his hand.

'Oh, I was far too excited for sleep… well at least for the first five minutes of lying down and then I slept like a log,' Charles said.

'Not so much, really,' said Cliff. 'I might try and get a quick sheep-nap when we're sailing.'

The rest of the Companionship had started to get all their belongings together in readiness to set sail. Although last night's experiences were still the main topic of conversation, what was going to happen next was also being hotly discussed. 'So, the troops are to advance on Chester this evening?' Mara asked Vindy, as she and Roisin accompanied the King and Queen to the quayside, along with the equally fatigued Harold and Greta.

'They are, but we need our arrival at the city gates to be as incident-free as possible. So it makes eminent sense for Saffy and General Beef Madras-Wholegrain Rice to take up positions close enough to the city to launch an attack, yet remain out of sight until such time as they are needed. Although I'm really hoping it doesn't come to that.'

'Have you asked Saffy to get word to our Russian friends?' Tikky enquired.

'I believe he contacted the Stroganoffs as soon as we left,' Vindy said. 'They've been completely briefed and have said they will give us whatever support we need. Tsar Beef Stroganoff-Sour Cream has no love for Blacktie, particularly after he made them reduce the size of their portions in restaurants and drop their prices. That was a bad move on the Baron's part; you really don't want to go upsetting the Russians.'

As Ethel was readied to sail, a small contingent of pigs stood by to wish them farewell. 'I really hope that last night's fracas hasn't put you off returning to my fine establishment,' Archie said.

'I can honestly say that when this is all over we will come back and complete the acoustic set,' Oldfart said. 'And we really should pay towards some of the damage… particularly the damage caused by Grundi's wind.'

'Nonsense!' Archie exclaimed. 'I reckon if he hadn't taken that course of action we'd have all have been goners.'

Smid and Crusher embraced warmly, and their heartening reunion had provided an emotional uplift for everyone. 'Are you sure you don't want me to come with you, Daddy Smid?'

'I'm sorry, Crusher. As much as I would be proud to have you at my side, I feel the next stage of our trip is one the Companionship must make alone. But try not to worry too much; we'll be back soon, Odin willing.'

As Ethel moved gracefully down the river and around a bend, the waving pigs disappeared from sight. Grundi had decided to take it upon himself to remain on lookout at the prow, his spiked ball and chain at his side. 'You know, where I'm from I've had a few hairy nights mixing with bands, but I can safely say that last night was on a different level,' Aiden said,

Grundi smiled and slapped Aiden's back. 'Well, it was a little unusual for us as well. We've had a couple of situations in the past, don't get me wrong. I remember one gig we played in Wrexham when we were called in as a last minute replacement for an English Folk band, at the local old people's home.'

'That must have been an interesting audience.'

'Interesting isn't a word I'd use. Vicious is more like it. They started to pelt us with vegetables as soon as we started playing. Poor old Agnar got hit with a rotten tomato, right on his nose. It just exploded all over his face. Smid had lettuce leaves between the strings and frets of his bass guitar, Olaf got a piece of broccoli in the eye, and I had a nasty altercation with a particularly large turnip. If I hadn't been holding my guitar in the right place it could have been very painful, and could have also severely affected my chances of becoming a father in the future, if you get my meaning.'

'But you managed to escape relatively unscathed?' Aiden said, smiling.

'Only when we promised that we'd stop playing!' I don't think we've ever stripped down the equipment so fast. They even chased after us on Zimmer frames as we were leaving. And don't be fooled, they can't half move those things when they've got a mind. I had this one old lady trying to stab me in the bottom with a carrot. She really seemed to be enjoying it!'

They laughed heartily together, which provided an immediate antidote for the ever-encroaching tension. 'Mind you, it's one thing having food thrown at you, but it's another thing entirely when it's trying to kill you,' Grundi added.

'Quite,' Aiden agreed.

In the distance the skies began to darken. White, billowy clouds were being bullied out of the way by grey, lumbering monsters. Flashes illuminated the sky near the horizon, and the ground was occasionally strafed by jagged forks of lightning. 'It looks like we're headed straight into that storm,' Aiden said to Grundi.

'Yes, I would say we'll hit it in about half an hour. We'd better make sure all the equipment is safely under cover.'

Olaf came and joined them on the prow. 'We're headed straight for that storm,' Aiden said to him.

'I think we're headed into more than one storm,' Olaf observed, as he squinted into the distance. 'There's a boat up ahead.'

Aiden tried to focus at the distant object in the ever-darkening light. He could just about make out the shape of a large craft, with what appeared to be black sails hanging off its tall masts. 'Any idea what kind of boat that is?' he asked Olaf.

'Difficult to tell at this range,' Olaf replied. 'I'll fetch the spyglass.'

Olaf rummaged through one of the Hessian sacks below deck and came back with a small, brass telescope. He put it to his right eye and pointed it in the direction of the boat ahead, adjusting the length of the tube until it was in focus. 'It looks like we're about to encounter an "interruption",' he said, calmly removing the small telescope from his eye. 'It's a pirate ship.'

'A pirate ship on the River Dee?' Oldfart said, overhearing the conversation. 'Do you mind if I have a look?'

'Be my guest,' Olaf said, handing the telescope to Oldfart.

As Oldfart peered through the spyglass, he realised that Olaf's identification was correct... and worse. 'Yes, it's a pirate ship alright, and unfortunately I recognise the flag it's flying. The only reason that vessel could have for being in these waters is that it's been sent here by Blacktie.'

Grundi gave a sharp intake of breath and Aiden pulled out his pocket knife. The rest of the Companionship had begun to congregate around Ethel's prow. 'Is there a problem?' Roisin asked

'It looks like we're about to encounter the Tan-Y-Lan Tuffies,' Oldfart replied. 'And unless they've had a miraculous personality change, we're in trouble.'

'Pirates! The mood I'm in, I'll take them on by myself,' Agnar snarled, moving protectively in front of Roisin.

'Agnar's right,' said Grundi. 'We're more than a match for some run-of-the-mill scurvy sea dogs.'

'These are not "run-of-the-mill" pirates, though,' Oldfart advised. 'The Tan-Y-Lan Tuffies are the most ruthless, maniacal, soulless, merciless, violent, and smelly individuals you will ever meet. Other pirates avoid them like the plague. A competition was started on the Welsh coast a few years back, called the "Nastiest, Scariest, Most Obnoxious, Least Likely to Take Home to Meet Your Mother, Pirate Gang of the Year", and that lot have won it hands down every year.'

'I would have expected them to have some stiff competition in that neck of the woods,' Agnar observed.

'Yes, you would. In the first year they were up against Captain Bedlam and his Bad-Assed Buccaneers.'

'I've heard of them,' said Smid. 'Aren't they the bunch that don't wear shoes and sharpen their toenails?'

'Well, they were,' Oldfart replied, 'but in the final event of the 1984 competition, The Tuffies challenged them to an unarmed bare-fist fight.'

'What happened?' Olaf asked.

'Well Captain Bedlam and his crew agreed and they all met at the Colwyn Bay quayside at dawn. A huge crowd had gathered to watch as

Bedlam and his Buccaneers roared their battle cry, spat tobacco indiscriminately and brandished their newly-sharpened toenails.'

'It must have been quite a fight,' Aiden said.

'Not really,' Oldfart replied, with a shrug. 'The Tuffies simply shot them all. As Taffy Tuffy said to the competition judge afterwards, "I never mentioned anything about US being unarmed".'

As the pirate ship drew nearer, the sound of maniacal laughter and howling could clearly be heard. At the prow of the ship, a man with a very big hat was waving a cutlass, shouting about blood, entrails and ears being skewered. Behind him, the rest of the Tan-Y-Lan Tuffies could be seen readying ropes, and firing the occasional shot.

'They're getting ready to board,' Olaf said. 'I suggest you grab whatever weapons you can, but stay behind us.'

'I promise I won't let anything happen to you, Roisin,' Agnar said, pushing her behind him... and then smiling as she grabbed his hand.

Mr Kneepatcher pushed through to the front and stood next to Olaf. 'I'm standing with you,' he said, brandishing his knotted battle cravat. 'I don't care how big their weapons are, if they get this baby between their legs they're going down.'

As the Tan-Y-Lan Tuffies' ship drew closer, the roaring, swearing, growling and nose-picking increased proportionately. They were ready to board Ethel and it didn't look as if it was going to be pretty.

'Prepare to be boarded and prepare for battle!' shouted Taffy Tuffy, waving his cutlass erratically, as the pirate ship came alongside.

Then, as Aiden and Oldfart shared a silent nod, Oldfart started to laugh loudly.

'I don't know what you're laughing for, you old codger,' Taffy shouted, 'Me and the boys here are going to make mincemeat out of you lot... and we've got some nice potatoes to go with it!'

'Ha!' Oldfart laughed again. 'I was led to believe that the Tan-Y-Lan Tuffies were real men.'

'What are you babbling about farty pants?!' Taffy shouted 'We are real men... well, apart from Bethan over there,' he added, pointing to a bearded pirate in a rather fetching floral dress, 'but she's having the operation soon.'

'Then surely you know that real men no longer solve their differences in battle. Why, battle is purely for children, isn't that right, lads?' Oldfart said, urging Sacred Wind to join him in more laughter. 'I'm really surprised that men of your reputation haven't heard this news before.'

'Er, no, it's the first we've heard about it,' Taffy said, scratching his head beneath his huge, black hat.

'Please, do not think we make fun of you because of your ignorance in this matter,' Oldfart continued. 'We would never wish to cast aspersions of stupidity in your direction. For is it not said that the Tan-Y-Lan Tuffies are known as the 'thinking man's pirates'?'

'Are we?' Taffy said, raising his very bushy eyebrows and turning to his men with a questioning look, only to be met with shrugs and coughs.

'Of course you are,' Oldfart continued. 'Why, only last week I read that you are renowned for your perniciousness, unscrupulousness, and imbecility. That must have been high praise indeed.'

'Oh, well, when you put it like that, I guess that'll be right. We is indeed the 'thinking man's pirates',' Taffy said, nodding, with his gesture mimicked by the rest of his men... and Bethan.

'And, as the thinking man's pirates, I would fully expect you to wish to engage us in a contest that befits your status.'

'And what contest would this be that would will allow us to settle our differences like real men?' Taffy asked.

'Charades!' Oldfart announced, lifting his arms in the air.

Taffy Tuffy scratched under his armpits and smelled his fingers. 'Charades, eh? Well, that seems fair enough. What do you think, lads... and Bethan?' he said, turning to his crew, to be greeted by initial surprise and then nods.

'I warn you now, though,' Taffy added, 'that Taffy, Taffy, Taffy, Taffy, Aled, Taffy and Ivor here won a charades competition only recently in our local night club, The Pirate's Privates. Isn't that right, boyos?'

'Aye!' proclaimed Taffy, Taffy, Taffy, Taffy, Aled, Taffy and Ivor.'

'In which case, I would foresee this forthcoming contest as one that will go down in history and be talked about with reverence by all who hear the tale!' Oldfart shouted. 'Can I suggest we moor our ships on the left bank, as we see it, and alight to that pleasant-looking pasture?'

As both the Companionship and the Tuffies moored their ships, Olaf grabbed Oldfart by the arm. 'Have you gone completely mad, you old weasel?'

'Not at all, my friend,' he replied, with a smile. 'I believe I'm buying us some time.'

'For what?' Olaf asked.

'Something unexpected.'

CHAPTER 32 – I BELIEVE I'M FEELING SLIGHTLY PECKISH

Queen Ophelia was sat in her Luxury dingy cell and was not very happy. She'd gotten used to the rats by now, and even the tetchy one proved to be not too bad if you spoke to him nicely. The wooden bed was a tad uncomfortable, but she'd slept on worse, and the raving and singing from the cell next door at least gave her something to listen to. But, the fact that she hadn't been provided her with a comb was really beginning to get on her nerves.

She heard a noise in the corridor and fluttered up to the small, barred window in the door to take a look. It was Grunt.

'Baron ask Grunt to bring Queen to him,' Grunt said, almost apologetically.

'That's okay, Grunt. It'll be nice to get out of the cell for a while,' she said, with a smile.

In his throne room, the Baron was pacing. 'When did they say they'd be here?' he said to Pimple, who was standing attentively near the throne.

'Within the hour, my Lord,'

'And they said they've got the cheese?'

'They did, my Lord.'

The Baron danced a little jig, hopping from one foot to the next and yelping, as if the floor was very hot. 'Ah, Queen Ophelia, how are you finding your new accommodation?' he said, as Grunt brought the Queen into the throne room.

'I found the rats to be better company than that which I presently find myself in,' she said with a sneer.

'Ooh, still feisty, eh?' the Baron said. 'Well, I'm expecting a couple of old friends of yours any minute now, and I thought you'd like to be here when they arrive. By all accounts they have a present for me, and I'm a little giddy about the whole thing!'

'You'll be a lot less giddy when my Olaf arrives this evening,' the Queen said, holding her head high.

'Oh, I'm afraid it's very unlikely that Sacred Wind will be able to make our little party,' the Baron said, feigning disappointment. 'Some of my other friends should be rendezvousing with them around about now, and I strongly suspect their condition at the end of this encounter will mean they'll be unable to travel. I'm so sorry.'

'I think you perhaps underestimate them, Baron,' Ophelia said.

And then the phone in the throne room rang. 'Oh, hi, it's Stacey, Baron Blacktie. Your two guests have arrived.'

'Excellent,' said the Baron, with a hiss. 'Get one of the guards to escort them to the morning room, I'll meet them there.'

As they made their way to the morning room, Grunt held the Queen's arm, albeit gently. 'Grunt will make sure that nice Queen doesn't get hurt,' he said.

'My good friends how are you both?' the Baron beamed, as Hob and Nob entered the room.

'We are well, Baron,' Hob said, with a bow. 'Although we did have some interesting escapades, including having to elude some unwelcome followers.'

'You mean you were followed?!' the Baron exclaimed.

'Oh, they've been taken care of,' Nob said, smugly. 'We left them in the capable hands of the witches, Mildred and Agnes. I doubt very much whether they'll see the light of day again.'

'Did you know who they were?' Pimple asked.

'Well, it was Agnes that spotted them. Apparently it was Merlin Crackfoot, Oriana Oftsheared, three cats and a dog,' Hob replied.

Ophelia took an audible breath at the mention of the names.

'Are you sure they were taken care of?' the Baron quizzed.

'Well, put it this way, it would have taken a genius who was conversant in Ancient Welsh Witchenese to have got the better of those two witches, and I think that rather unlikely,' Nob said.

'Indeed,' the Baron said, with a grin. 'And now, down to business, do you have the cheese?'

'We do, and do you have our fee?' Hob said.

The Baron moved over to the safe, entered the combination and opened the steel door. He took out a large envelope and the jar of Mathonwy's Chutney. 'First my cheese,' he said, holding the envelope to his chest and placing the jar on a nearby desk.

Nob put his hand in his pocket and brought out the large lump of Ceridwen's Cheese. He walked over to the Baron and held out the cheese.

The Baron held out the envelope and both men exchanged goods.

'Do you know, I believe I'm feeling slightly peckish,' the Baron said, opening the jar of chutney.

He took a small spoon from one of the desk drawers and dipped it into the jar. As he pulled out the spoon, the orange chutney glimmered and seemed to pulsate. He broke off a small piece of the green and golden cheese and carefully emptied the spoonful of chutney on top it. After only a matter of seconds, the cheese changed colour to a fiery, crimson red, glowing like a hot piece of coal. The Baron gently picked up the cheese between his middle finger and thumb. As he did the glow intensified, lighting up his face in an ethereal light. Ever so slowly he started to move the cheese and chutney towards his mouth.

'Are you ready for this, Queen Ophelia?' he said. 'For you will soon be subjugating yourself before me, as will all creatures.'

Hob and Nob moved back towards the door, Pimple retreated into a corner and Grunt moved protectively in front of the Queen. Everything appeared to have become frozen in time. The dust seemed to hang in the air waiting for the wind to move it onto better things. And a close relative of the silence we've come to know and love descended and everyone held their breath, to the supreme annoyance of the hanging dust.

The Baron's teeth were now millimetres away from gnashing down on the recipe known as 'Cheese and Chutney Surprise'. Grunt covered Queen Ophelia's eyes and Pimple's knees began knocking together.

'Actually, I'm going to save this for later on,' the Baron said, putting the cheese and chutney in a small box on the table. 'It can be the finale of the Cestrian Music Tournament… and what a finale!'

***

The road into Ruthin town centre was thankfully quiet and free of witches. It was no more than two miles' walk and the group were making good progress, even bearing in mind Half-blind Ron's protestations about not having breakfast yet. 'Look, we'll grab some chicken as soon as we get into town,' Theo said to him. 'We're all hungry, Ron.'

'Well we better. I can't be fighting and scratching on an empty tummy.'

The tranquil surroundings and the pleasant chirruping of birds provided some welcome peace of mind, and Theo knew that whatever lay ahead for the rest of the day was unlikely to offer similar opportunities for reflection. Cracky obviously had a plan as to how they were going to enter the palace, although finding the Queen whilst eluding the guards was going to be another matter entirely. Humphrey had said that the best ideas just appear in one's head, as if magically deposited by some unseen guiding force, and Theo hoped that Humphrey's undoubted genius was going to be correct.

For all Half-blind Ron's bravado about scratching and fighting, the six of them were not likely to be able to battle their way to Ophelia, rescue her and then battle their way out. No, this operation would be won with brains more than brawn, although Theo felt that it may end up being a mixture of both.

As Humphrey chatted happily with Half-blind Ron and Captain Marmaduke explained cat military tactics to Oriana, Theo remembered the conversation that had taken place between Blacktie and Cracky, outside of the Diner. Although Cracky was reluctant to talk about it then, Theo decided he would bring the subject up when the time felt right.

'Cracky, I've been meaning to ask you about the little verbal spat you had with Blacktie. You said it was a story for another time; is now perhaps that time?'

Cracky sighed and rubbed his long beard, before smiling. 'Ah, yes, I was wondering when you'd get around to asking me about that. Believe it or not, we met at school.'

'School?' Theo said, with astonishment.

'Yes, it was just before my father passed away,' Cracky continued. 'Blacktie's parents were keen that he should receive some "normal" education, so they paid for him to attend one class a week at my school. That class just happened to be History, and it just so happened to be one of the subjects I was taking. We were both sixteen at the time.'

'What was he like?' Theo asked.

'He was as arrogant and unpleasant as he is now, and he was a bully.'

'Did he bully you, then?'

'No, I was one of the taller boys; he'd always look to prey on the weak and vulnerable, so not much has changed there. Given his wealth and influence, he quickly amassed a gang of boys eager to be seen in his company. He was a typical coward, really. Physical combat wasn't his thing, so he always made sure he had a couple of chaps with him for protection. One particular day, he made the mistake of picking on one of my friends as I happened to be passing by. It was a boy called Phil Twizzlewizzle, whose father owned a sweet shop. Unbeknown to me, Blacktie and two of his henchmen had been getting poor Phil to steal sweets from his father's shop for them.'

'What did you do?'

'Well, they had him pinned up against a wall so I intervened, shall we say,' Cracky said.

'What do you mean, "intervened"?'

'Er, you have to understand I was going through some strange days back then. I was growing up fast and, ahem, odd things used to happen when I was around. I've not used magic for a long time now, mainly because I'm not very good at it, but when I was younger things would just happen. I really didn't have any control at all.'

'Go on,' Theo said.

'Well, I was very angry and wanted to turn the two ruffians with Blacktie into toads, only temporarily of course, just to teach them a lesson. The problem was that I was at that age when I used to spend a lot of time thinking about girls, if you know what I mean. So let's just say things didn't quite go to plan.'

'What did you turn them into, then?'

'I didn't turn them into anything, but they both ended up with a lovely pair of breasts.'

Theo chortled in his mind at the image. 'That's wonderful, Cracky. What did they do?'

'Oh, they ran off in terror… although I was told that after a week or so they got quite fond of them!'

'A week! How long did they stay like that for?'

'I think it was about two months in the end, I really can't recall.' Cracky said, laughing.

'So what magic did you use on Blacktie?'

'I didn't. I simply gave him a bloody nose. The snivelling little weasel cried all the way home, and he never bothered Phil again. However, he did swear he'd get his revenge… and he did, unfortunately.'

Cracky's eyes became distant, with past memories making a painful return to his mind, and Theo could sense his discomfort. 'Look, you don't have to tell me the rest if you do not wish to.'

'No, it will probably do me good to talk about it,' Cracky replied.

He composed himself and took a deep breath before continuing. 'It was the day of my father's funeral. I was distraught, but I was equally concerned for my mother, so I was trying to put on a brave face. The procession went through the entire town and the turnout of people was quite extraordinary. He was a very popular and much loved man. Anyway, as the procession reached the church on the outskirts of town, I caught sight of Blacktie and about four or five other boys. They were waiting by the church gates and I just had a feeling they were up to no good. As we got nearer, Blacktie shouted "now" and we were pelted with water bombs.'

'That's awful,' Theo said.

'Indeed. But the worst was that one hit my mother square in the face. Well, I just lost it at that point.'

'I can imagine.'

'So, I flew towards them and they scattered, but I was only interested in getting hold of Blacktie, and let's just say he wasn't the fastest. I caught up with him at the side of the church and pushed him against the wall. He was smiling. So, I looked at him and began to gather my will. The more he looked into my eyes, the less he smiled. I was about to destroy him utterly, and I knew I could have done it. I saw his smiling eyes descend into fear. He became just a scared little boy who knew he'd done something very bad and was about to get punished… more than punished. Anyway, that's when I felt the blow to the back of my head. His friends had come to his aid and ambushed me. I received several kicks and punches before they all ran off again, laughing… except for Blacktie. He looked back once, but he didn't join in the laughter.'

The two walked silently for the next minute or so, Cracky lost in his thoughts and Theo coming to terms with the story. Eventually the Prince broke the silence.

'So did you ever meet him again?'

'Only once; but by that time he was already a Baron and had a vast entourage of people with him. It was many years after the event, at a fair in Mold. Not surprisingly, he never returned to my school.'

'Did he speak to you?'

'Oh, yes. He asked how I was, but he never mentioned my mother. He was full of himself again by this time and he knew I was powerless to enact any kind of revenge. Back then, though, I think I'd have settled for a simple apology, but I don't believe it ever crossed his mind. Now it's gone beyond that.'

'So even if he apologised now, you wouldn't accept it?'

'Oh, I'd accept it alright… and then I'd set fire to his testicles.'

'Look,' Captain Marmaduke said, suddenly. 'There's a taxi coming towards us.'

CHAPTER 33 – COVER YOUR EARS, LADIES

Aiden liked charades a lot, and he was quite good at it. Mind you, he'd never played against a pack of evil, merciless, lager-fuelled, extremely stinky pirates before.

'So, what be the stakes and the rules, then, boyo?' Taffy Tuffy said, putting his huge cutlass to one side... although close enough to grab if required.

'Shall we say first team to get to three points?' Oldfart suggested. 'A correct guess counts as one point, or the other team gets a point if the charade cannot be guessed. The guessing team has three chances. If we win, you allow us to continue on our journey; if we lose, we turn round and go back from where we came. Does that sound fair?'

'I'd say so, apart from one slight change,' Taffy said. 'If we win, you have to tell everyone you ran away from us because we is so scary and obbynoxus.'

'You mean obnoxious,' said Oldfart.

'Exactly,' Taffy replied.

'And you have to say we made you lick our armpits until you cried!' shouted Ivor, as the rest of the Tuffies nodded with approval.

'And you have to tell everyone how beautiful I am and that you all wanted to sleep with me!' shouted Bethan, twiddling her beard between her thumb and index finger seductively.

'That really is stretching it a bit,' Agnar whispered to Smid.

'We agree,' Oldfart said, although he received a scowl from Olaf.

Oldfart produced a coin from his pocket and tossed it in the air. It twirled speedily upwards before gravity said 'gotcha', and then pulled it kicking and screaming downwards into his hand. 'Call', he said, covering the coin.

'Heads,' said Taffy.

Oldfart removed his hand and looked at the coin. 'Heads it is.'

'We'll go first. Who wants to play me fine shipmates?' Taffy asked of his crew. There was mumbling in the ranks and then Ivor and Aled walked forward.

'If we can't beat this lot, I swear I'll never wear a cravat again,' Mr Kneepatcher whispered to Aiden.

Aled put his two hands together and then opened them.

'Book!' the Companionship shouted as one.

He held one hand over his eye and moved his other hand as if it were turning a crank.

'Film!'

He held up one finger.

'One word!'

Then Aled waved both his arms in the air, each making a circle.

'The whole thing!' shouted the Companionship.

Then he punched Ivor really hard in the face.

'What the bloody hell —,' Ivor said, just as Aled head-butted him on his cheek.

Blood poured from the gaping gash and he collapsed unconscious. Aled calmly knelt down beside him and pointed to freshly induced wound.

'Scarface!' Aiden shouted.

Aled put the index finger of his left hand on his nose and pointed at Aiden with the index finger of his right hand. The Companionship cheered and the Tan-Y-Lan Tuffies let out a collective groan. 'One-nil to us, I believe,' Oldfart said. 'Right, I'll go next.'

Oldfart strode forward purposefully and went down on one knee, thrusting out both of his hands. 'Song!' shouted the Tan-Y-Lan Tuffies.

He stood up and held up five fingers.

'Five words!'

Oldfart then waved both his arms in the air in a circular motion.

'The whole thing!' shouted the Tuffies.

Then he held out his right hand and waved his left hand up and down in front of it, in a painting kind of motion.

The Taffies mumbled between themselves. Heads and armpits were scratched, a couple of minor scuffles broke out and Bethan began to paint her nails. After a short while and a lot of collective nodding, Taffy Tuffy turned around to face Oldfart. 'We think it's "I Wanna Grease Your Palm", by The Bertles.'

Oldfart put his finger to his nose and pointed at Taffy. The Tuffies let out a series of wild whoops and cheers, firing their pistols into the air in an explosion of hysterical joy. 'I was hoping they'd do that,' Oldfart whispered to Olaf.

'What is going on here, Oldfart? You really should tell the rest of us, you know.'

Next up was Taffy Tuffy, who also beckoned the very wary Ivor to accompany him. 'Film!' shouted the Companionship, after Taffy's opening mime.

Three fingers.

'Three words!'

Arms in circles.

'The whole thing!'

'This isn't going to be painful again, is it?' Ivor whispered to Taffy.

Taffy began by holding out his arms in front of him, stumbling this way and that and making loud groans. Ivor started to inch away from him, slowly. Then Taffy let out a roar, grabbed hold of Ivor's shoulders with both hands and bit a chunk out of his ear. Ivor screamed and Taffy turned to the Companionship and growled, his bloody teeth dripping tiny pieces of flesh onto the ground.

'Zombies Flesh Eaters!' shouted Aiden.

Taffy Tuffy let forth a few choice profanities and then pointed at Aiden to signify that the guess was correct. The Companionship cheered, Mara kissed him full on the lips, Olaf ruffled his hair, Vindy and Tikky clicked their mini poppadoms together, Mr Kneepatcher kissed his hand, and Agnar nearly squeezed the life out of him with a bear hug.

'Okay,' Oldfart said to Aiden, 'do you want to go next?' Aiden whispered in Oldfart's ear first, and Oldfart nodded.

'C'mon, me fine shipmates,' Taffy said. 'We've gotta get this right. We can't be beaten by a bunch of Vikings and some boyo with scruffy hair. We'll never hear the end of it.'

Aiden stepped forward and drew in a deep breath as the Tan-Y-Lan Tuffies scowled at him, apart from Bethan who was winking. He hoped she just had a nervous twitch. 'Song!' the Tuffies shouted, as Aiden performed the first descriptive movement.

Two fingers.

'Two words!'

Aiden threw out both of his arms.

'The whole thing!'

And so he began to jump up and down, beating his hands on his chest and roaring. 'I've got it!' screamed Bethan. 'It's "Wild Thing".'

Aiden shook his head and Bethan got a smack from Aled and a few kicks up the backside from several of the other Tuffies. 'Only two chances left,' Taffy Tuffy said. 'From now on we needs to consult with each other before shouting.'

Taffy took off his large, black hat and scratched his head, searching his brain for some semblance of thought. Then his eyes went wild, as if someone had just inserted an energy-saving light bulb up his bottom. 'Is it

"Crazy Horses"?'

There was pandemonium as Aiden ruled out the guess. Several of the Tuffies pushed their leader over and started to jump on his head. 'You said "we needs to consult" and then you just go off and open your fat, ugly mouth! I ain't being left scarred and earless for nothing, you filthy tosspot,' shouted Ivor.

'It looks like there's a bit of a mutiny going on here,' Olaf said to Oldfart. 'Is this what you were hoping for?'

'Actually, no, but it's a welcome event nonetheless,' Oldfart replied, with a chuckle.

Aiden continued his antics while the Tuffies huddled in a large group. A few punches were thrown and the air was filled with expletives, causing Mr Kneepatcher to turn his nose up in disgust. But, just as things looked as if they could get quite ugly, shouts of 'yes, yes' rang out. Taffy Tuffy was pushed forward by his crew, a beaming smile across his face and with pieces of Ivor's ear still between his teeth.

'We is pretty sure we've got it now,' he said. 'Is it "Monster Mash"?'

A hushed silence descended and all eyes turned to Aiden. 'No, it was "Monkey Man", by the Rolling Stones… and I'm also told by the Trundling Pebbles,' Aiden said.

The Companionship pumped their fists, hooves and poppadoms into the air. 'I believe we are victorious, gentlemen… and Bethan,' Oldfart said to the Tuffies.

The mayhem that followed was perhaps even more intense than could have been predicted, and even Olaf winced on several occasions at the sound of steel on bone. However, after a couple of minutes order was restored and Taffy Tuffy came forward. 'Although we be disappointed in our performance, never let it be said that the Tan-Y-Lan Tuffies are not maggynamius in defeat,' he said, as he wiped blood from a cut over his right eye. 'We congratulate you.'

And with that, the Tuffies proceeded to give the Companionship a round of applause. 'This seems to be going rather well,' Olaf observed to Oldfart.

'Thank you for the game and your sportsmanship,' Oldfart said, as the applause died down. 'But, now we must be on our way, as we have someplace we must be.'

And with that, Taffy picked up his cutlass. 'Ah, I'm afraid we can't allow that. You see, we know the place where you must be, but we can't let you be if that's where you wanna be. I mean, if there's someplace else you wanna be then we'll let you be. But we can't let you be if you try to go to the place you need to be, if you see what I be talking about.'

'Now, hold on a minute,' Agnar said, holding up his hammer. 'We won fair and square, and you agreed to let us continue on our way if we won.'

Taffy Tuffy scratched his armpits and smelled his fingers again. 'Well, I takes your point, but you really should know better than to make a deal with thieving, lying, cut-throats like us. If you tries to continue to Chester we'll be making stew out of yer innards and gloves out of yer outards.'

Aiden heard it first, a low rumbling in the distance. It was a sound he'd heard before. The birds in the trees scattered and two rabbits headed for the safety of their warren. 'Oldfart, are you sure you've got it with you?' Aiden asked.

'Yes, it's in my pocket. I just hope you're right about this.'

The ground started to shake and blood-curdling screams cut through the air like rapiers through silk. Occasional volleys of gunfire exploded between the blood-curdling screams, like the sound of gunfire interrupting rapiers cutting through silk. Several large burps were also discerned, but they just sounded exactly like several large burps, although one may have been a fart, it was difficult to tell with all the gunfire and screams.

'What in the name of Blackbeard's buttocks,' Taffy Tuffy said, as the source of the roaring, screaming, gunfire, burping and potential fart came into view.

'You're illegally parked, say your prayers you toe rags!' yelled Mr Peter Twatt/Spine-splitter, as he fired his Kalashnikov into the air… closely followed by the rest of the Wrexham Posse.

'Illegally parked? What are you going on about?' Taffy Tuffy said, as the other Tuffies drew closely around him, outnumbered by at least ten to one.

'Those boats there,' Spine-splitter said, pointing at the two boats moored on the river, 'where's their bloody parking permits?'

'Er, we have ours here,' Oldfart suddenly said, producing a piece of paper out of his jacket pocket.

'Dogsdoodahs, go and check that,' Spine-splitter said, to a man whose name badge actually identified him as Mr Phil Potty.

Dogsdoodahs slinked over to Oldfart and held his very large hunting knife just under his nose. He grabbed the piece of paper and scrutinised it. Then he sniffed it and gave it a quick lick. 'Looks genuine,' he said, somewhat disappointed.

'And what about the other boat?' Spine-splitter said, fixing Taffy Tuffy with an evil stare that would make the devil need to change his trousers.

'We've never needed a permit to moor up on the river before. You is talking nonsense,' Taffy replied.

'Now listen here, you ugly, short-arsed, little pipsqueak,' Spine-splitter spat, 'our job is to make sure people pay to park. Trying to get away without paying is a crime and the consequences are lots of pain and usually lots of death. Now, have you got a permit or are you going to force us to dish out some punishment?'

'Oh, sod off,' shouted Aled, from the back. 'We ain't scared of a greasy, farty-panted moron like you.'

'What did you call me?' Spine-splitter said, between clenched teeth.

'I said you're a greasy, farty-panted moron, you greasy, farty-panted moron!'

'Farty-panted?!' yelled Spine-splitter

'Yes, farty-panted!' shouted Aled.

'Greasy?!'

'Yes, greasy!'

'Moron?!'

'Yes, moron!'

'We should think about getting out of here just about now,' Aiden said, tugging Oldfart's arm.

'Farty-panted?!!' shouted Spine-splitter.

'Really, Oldfart, right now, right now,' Aiden exhorted.

'Yes, farty-panted with crusty underpants!!' yelled Aled.

'With crusty underpants?!!!' Spine-splitter roared into the sky.

'Run, now, back to Ethel!' Oldfart shouted, as hell broke loose around them.

As Harold and Greta ran, carrying Vindy and Tikky above their heads, they just about avoided the large club that was aimed at one of the Tuffies, wielded by a man whose name badge identified him as Mr Brian Ballache. Agnar and Aiden shielded Mara and Roisin from the chaos, with Grundi and Olaf protecting their rear. Oldfart made it to the boat first, closely followed by Mr Kneepatcher, whose battle cravat was showing signs of recent use. Smid had hold of Cliff's hoof and pushed several of the Tuffies out of the way with a single sweep of his arm.

'Where's Charles?!' Cliff shouted, as they reached Ethel.

As Aiden scoured the landscape he spotted a huge elm tree. Charles had managed to scale the trunk, avoiding the fierce fight at ground level. Without thinking, Aiden rushed towards the tree, closely followed by Olaf. At the base, two Traffic Wardens were waving machetes at Charles, imploring him to come down.

'C'mon little sheepie, we only wants to play,' said the first.

'Yes, yes,' said the second. 'We likes to play sheep choppy-uppy.'

'Not today you don't,' Olaf said, as his fist made contact with the second Traffic Warden's face, causing him to collapse in a gurgling heap.

A machete whistled passed Olaf's head just before Aiden's boot connected firmly with the other Traffic Warden's groin. He fell to his knees, screaming and clutching the wounded area.

Charles clambered back down the tree and jumped to the ground. 'Can you run, Charles?' Aiden asked.

'You bet my clacky hooves I can!'

As the Tuffies and the Wrexham Posse continued the contest of unrelenting violence, Olaf and Aiden held tightly onto Charles's hooves, as the three of them barged their way through the bloodthirsty melee. 'And you're not getting hold of my trumpet, you rotter,' Charles said, kicking one of the Wrexham Posse in the knee.

Charles huffed and puffed and ran as fast as his old legs would carry him. 'Nearly there,' he kept saying to himself, as Ethel drew ever closer. Cliff was waiting on the gangplank and he put a protective arm around Charles, guiding him on board. 'Oh, dear, I've not had to run that fast in a long time,' Charles said, breathing heavily.

As Ethel moved swiftly away from the bank, and with their escape seemingly assured, Olaf's curiosity finally got the better of him. 'So, how did you know those strange warriors were going to turn up?' he said to Oldfart.

'Well, it would appear that Aiden had encountered them several days ago, although not around here, if you know what I mean. He spotted one of them on the far bank, doing reconnaissance, and he seemed to know what they'd be after, hence the quickly constructed "parking permit". It was also why I was quite happy for the Tuffies to guess one of my charades. I figured that their celebrations would be noisy.'

Aiden overheard the conversation and felt compelled to add a point that was puzzling him. 'What I'm not sure of is how they actually got here. They seem to be from some future reality. I can only imagine that somehow an inter-dimensional portal was opened that allowed them to "travel" here, if you get my meaning.'

'Not exactly, but I'll take your word for it,' Olaf said.

Aiden looked around, checking that everyone had made it safely on board. 'Charles, are you alright?' he said, as Ethel moved away from the bank.

'Yes, yes, I'll be fine in a minute once I get my breath,' Charles replied, tottering slightly, before collapsing on the deck.

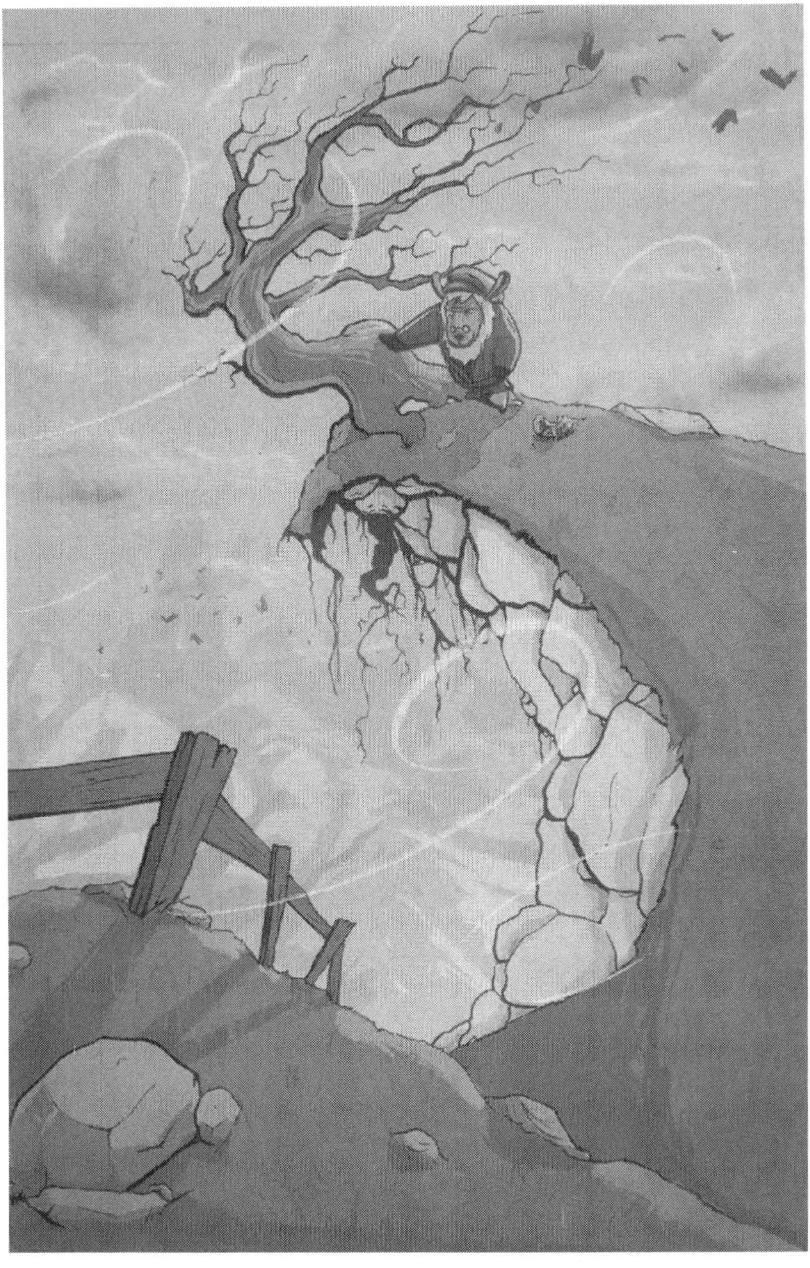

CHAPTER 34 – THE MOST NOBLE OF SHEEP

'Is there anything we can do?' Mara asked, as Cliff cradled Charles in his arms. He looked at her and shook his head.

Charles remained unconscious as Ethel continued down the river, his breathing was irregular and his pulse was very weak. Thunder growled overhead and the first large spots of rain began to explode with watery intent on the deck of the ship.

'He's known for a while now that his heart is not what it was,' Cliff said. 'He had been prescribed some pills, but I've not seen him take any since we set sail. I really should have insisted that he travelled with the rest of the OSO.'

'Don't blame yourself,' Oldfart said. 'You wouldn't have been able to dissuade him. He has the soul of an adventurer does our Charles, and he is still with us at the moment. Let's not give up hope just yet.'

As the rain began to transform from charming droplets into a less welcome torrent, Smid and Agnar quickly erected a tarpaulin to protect Cliff and Charles from the elements. Oldfart dug out some Hessian sacks to provide a pillow of sorts and placed them under Charles's head. The air was now thick with ozone and the once prevalent sunlight seemed to have decided to retire prematurely for the day.

Roisin appeared with a cup of fresh water and sat next to Cliff. 'I wish Ophy was here, she's so good at tending the sick and wounded, you know. And she does so love your uncle.'

'He's very fond of her too. He adores going to her parties, even if he does always get drunk and ends up being the centre of attention, the daft old thing,' Cliff said, a smile making a welcome return to his face.

'Did someone mention a party,' Charles said, opening his eyes.

'Oh, Uncle, I thought you were lost to us!' Cliff shouted, as the rest of the Companionship quickly made their way to the tarpaulin shelter.

'I feel so tired,' Charles said, as Roisin helped him to take a sip of water from the cup.

'You'll soon be up and about again in no time,' Grundi said, 'and no doubt entertaining us with your trumpet.'

Charles closed his eyes briefly and sighed. 'I'd so love to do that, my friend, but I think my playing days may at last over. I have so enjoyed my splendid adventure, though.'

'Hang on in there, old fellow,' Agnar said. 'You've got to be with us when we get to Chester. How can we possibly take on Blacktie without you?'

Cliff stroked Charles's head gently, and Roisin tenderly held onto his hoof. 'You must do something for me, my nephew,' Charles said, his voice becoming weaker. 'Please go and fetch my bag, there's something in it I need to give you.'

Roisin nodded to Cliff and he scurried off to fetch the small knapsack Charles had brought with him. 'Thank you, my lad,' Charles said, as Cliff returned with the bag, 'you are indeed the best nephew a sheep could have. Now, please open it and take out the large notebook.'

Cliff obediently did as Charles requested. 'There's a bookmark keeping a place, please open the notebook at that page. There are quite a few loose leaf pages as well.'

'Of course, uncle,' Cliff said, locating the bookmark and opening the notebook. He was shocked to see it was a musical score, so he quickly scanned through the pages, recognising the melodies and counterpoints.

'This is a Sacred Wind song, uncle,' he said, with astonishment. 'It's a complete arrangement for an orchestra; strings, brass, woodwind, the lot.'

'It is indeed,' Charles said, with a smile. 'I've been transcribing it for a while now.'

Olaf and the rest of the band looked at each other, genuine surprise visible on their faces. 'We're very honoured, Charles,' Olaf said, 'but why?'

'For a long time now, my fondest wish has been for the OSO and Sacred Wind to play together, just for one night. The effect would be magical. And I'm sure that, together, we'd win the tournament.'

'But Henry would never agree, uncle, you know what he thinks of rock music,' Cliff said, comprehending his uncle's wish.

'You must persuade him,' Charles said, with a wheeze. 'I know Henry comes across like an old fuddy-duddy, but I saw him tapping his foot at the band's gig at The Sheep's Stirrup. I believe it's just his silly musical snobbishness.'

'You know,' said Oldfart, scanning some of the pages, 'it could sound fantastic.'

Charles sat up, using every ounce of his strength. 'Please, my nephew, do this for me. It would mean so much. Just talk to Henry.'

'I will, uncle. You have my word.'

'And I'll add my considerable powers of persuasion to the argument as well, that's if the band are in agreement,' said Oldfart.

'Oldfart's right,' Olaf said, browsing the score. 'This would be something no-one has heard before.'

'Then I say we go for it,' Agnar said. 'Just as long as the orchestra doesn't drown out my drums.'

'I think that would be extremely unlikely,' Smid said, as Grundi nodded in agreement.

Charles lay down again and took in a deep breath. 'Thank you my friends. It has been an honour to be in your company.'

Suddenly, from the rear of the ship, the sound of creaking wood could be heard. 'Is it just me, or did everyone hear that?' Mr Kneepatcher asked.

She had stayed quiet up until now. After all, there hadn't been any good reason to say anything, and she only really spoke when there was something that needed saying. 'I think the honour has been ours, Charles Corriedale,' Ethel said, in a beautiful, timbre-laced voice.

The direction Charles was laying meant he was looking straight at Ethel as she spoke. The face of the dragon's head at the helm seemed to sparkle in the rain, illuminated by a subtle inner glow.

'You have the heart of a noble warrior and the soul of a saint, Charles Corriedale. And today you take your rightful place and walk with the gods. Odin has indeed blessed your clacky hooves and your wind.'

As the rain teemed down, the Companionship looked at Ethel in awe. Her presence was usually always in the background, perceptible yet unobtrusive. But now it seemed to pour out of the very timbers of the ship itself, touching the souls of everyone on board. It was almost as if they had a direct connection with her essence, able to feel the wisdom she had accumulated over the centuries, and all this was magnified by a force of extraordinary love. Aiden had never felt anything remotely like. His eyes welled up and he felt himself gasp as her presence seemed to meld with his own. He looked around at his companions and it was obvious they were all similarly affected.

'Well, lad, I think it's time for me to finally meet up with your Auntie Betty. I have missed her so much over these last few years, you know,' Charles said, a wan smile appearing on his face, as he coughed.

'Please, uncle, try to stay with us,' Cliff pleaded.

'Do you remember when you were little?' Charles said, 'You'd come around to my house and listen to me playing for hours. Then we'd chat and I'd make us a nice cup of tea and we'd nibble some cheese together and talk about music. And then I'd sit you on my knee and tell you stories. You used to enjoy that so much.'

'I used to get so excited at the prospect of visiting you,' Cliff said. 'Dad used to scold me and say I was spending too much time with you, but I didn't care. I don't think he really got our passion for music.'

'Oh, he did. He's so proud of you, you know. He's just not very good at saying it,' Charles said, his voice now becoming more of a whisper.

'Please don't go, Uncle Charles. You've always been a hero to me. I don't know what I'd do without you.'

'Now, now, don't be daft, lad. I love you as if you were my own son, and you've got great spirit and great strength, far more than I've ever had. You go on and achieve your dreams. And marry Oriana; she's a lovely sheep and just right for you.'

Roisin looked at Cliff, the tears rolling down her cheeks like little crystals, and she put her hand on Charles's chest. 'I love you uncle,' Cliff said, holding his hoof tightly with both hands.

And as Cliff spoke, the rain began to ease and a single sliver of sunlight, like a shimmering celestial sword, cut through the dark clouds and lit up the deck of the ship. Mara held tightly onto Aiden's hand as Charles smiled again and touched Cliff's face with his hoof.

'Bless my clacky hooves, I do believe the sun's coming out,' he said, as his eyes closed for the last time.

And so, Charles Corriedale, the most noble of sheep, passed from this world into the next. Ethel stared solemnly out at the river and, although it could have been a raindrop, a single tear seemed to roll down her wooden cheek.

***

The suggestion to provide Charles with a formal Viking funeral was made by Grundi, and he tentatively spoke to Cliff in private first. Cliff's decision was instant, as he knew it was something that Charles would have loved.

Ethel was moored at a suitable point further down the river, and Agnar and Smid had set about constructing a raft. Charles's body was laid on a small pyre on the raft and Olaf covered him with a traditional Viking cloak, only exposing his head. Grundi went below decks and reappeared with an ornately engraved short-sword.

'I'd like him to have this,' he said to Cliff. 'It belonged to my uncle.'

Cliff smiled and wiped away a tear. 'Of course, thank you, and I know that Uncle Charles would be proud.'

Grundi put the sword gently on Charles's chest and Cliff placed his beloved trumpet alongside it. Smid and Agnar carried the small raft over to the river, as Olaf lit the pyre with a crackling torch.

'It is tradition that friends and loved ones throw torches onto the pyre as it carries its passenger on the journey to the afterlife,' Olaf said, handing around small torches.

'Would you please throw these for me and Vindy?' Tikky said to Harold and Greta, who both smiled and nodded.

As the tiny raft began to wend its way down the river, the little torches rained down like falling stars, each one landing softly on the pyre and amplifying the dancing flames that began to engulf it. And, as the current carried the raft further downstream, Mara began to sing; a wonderful haunting melody that touched the hearts of all. Olaf accompanied her on acoustic guitar, the lilting strings adding to the poignancy and emotion of the moment. Then Roisin added her beautiful soprano voice in harmony. To Aiden the melodies seemed as old as time, and maybe they were. He was moved to tears, and he was not alone.

The sun was now low in the sky, making its slow, inexorable journey towards nightly slumber. Fireflies appeared from out of nearby trees, strafing and circling the flames in their own effervescent dance, their reflections on the river creating a glistening halo around the raft.

And so, as the last note of Mara's song trailed off into the fast-approaching dusk, the little raft disappeared from sight. For a while they simply stood, either with heads bowed or staring out at the river behind them. In the distance a solitary church bell rang out four times and the fireflies fluttered blissfully away, their dance complete.

CHAPTER 35 – THE PROPORTIONS LOOK SLIGHTLY UNDERSTATED

Pimple wasn't having a good day. The delivery of the celebratory edition of Nobflasher's ale hadn't arrived, and wouldn't until after the tournament. The Baron would be livid, as this was without question his favourite tipple, Plumley's Pernickety Port notwithstanding.

The specially commissioned statue of the Baron, created by the two crack sculptors Claude and Clive Chiseller, also needed altering, particularly in the trouser area. They had arrived in a fever of excitement earlier in the day, but the Baron had been less than impressed. 'The proportions look slightly understated,' he had said, after the preliminary unveiling.

'But my Lord,' Clive had protested, 'we have been meticulous in our measurements in order to ensure it is an exact representation of his Lordship.'

A swift dig in the ribs by Pimple at this point probably saved Clive from a particularly unpleasant encounter with Norman Nutcrusher, the Head Torturer, in his newly-completed torture chamber (which had the motto of 'Your Pain is Our Gain' etched in stone above the door).

'Of course,' Claude had quickly interjected, 'the error is now obvious, my Lord. That section of the statue should be at least twice the size…'

Pimple administered another swift dig in the ribs.

'… three times the size. We'll begin the corrections immediately.'

And, to top it all, the song Pimple had composed for the Knights of Flatulence to perform at the Tournament this evening hadn't been selected by General Darkblast. 'What does that idiot know about music,' Pimple muttered to himself, as he walked down the corridor leading to the throne room, with the rejection letter in his hand.

The General had selected a composition by the little-known Chester composer, Steve Screecher, entitled 'Blistered Love'. Pimple's song, 'Do the Servant's Shuffle', was considered to be 'not of the requisite melodic quality or lyrical profundity.'

However, these three unfortunate events paled into insignificance compared to the tidings he now had for the Baron's ears. 'Ah, my good Pimple, what news of our friends on the river?' the Baron asked, as Pimple entered the throne room.

'Er, it is not good, my Lord.'

The Baron took an apple from the fruit bowl next to the throne, took a bit bite and stood up. 'Define "not good", if you will,' he said, taking an even bigger bite out of the apple.

'It would appear that the Tan-Y-Lan Tuffies were waylaid by an unknown third party.'

'Define "third party", my good Pimple,' the Baron said, crushing the rest of the apple in his hand.

'From the information I've been given they were great in numbers, very fierce, and insisted on examining their parking permit.'

'Parking permit? Why would they need a parking permit?'

'I'm not sure, my Lord, but it would seem that these strangers were insisting upon payment, given the absence of any form of permit. When payment was not forthcoming, a few choice insults were traded between the two groups and—'

'Go on,' the Baron said, dropping the crushed apple onto the floor for Velvet to finish.

'— the strangers caused a great deal of damage to the Tuffies reputation as the most evil, barbaric and bloodthirsty vermin to roam either sea or land.'

'Well, I'm sure the band of odious cretins will soon recover from their reputation being usurped, Pimple. They're lucky if they've got two brain cells between them,' the Baron scoffed.

'Ah, as usual my Lord is most perceptive, and in this observation uncannily accurate.'

'Meaning?'

'Meaning that the damage to their reputation was unfortunately accompanied by even more severe damage to their personages.'

'How severe?'

'As I just mentioned, my Lord, your observation about them not having two brain cells between them would now be exceedingly accurate.'

'A pity,' the Baron sighed. 'For all their stupidity, vulgarity and questionable hygiene, I actually quite liked them. Nevertheless, it's a price worth paying under the circumstances.'

'Circumstances, my Lord?'

'Why, of course, Pimple, do I have to spell it out to you? I'm assuming this band of bloodthirsty barbarians provided Sacred Wind and their "Companionship" with a similar fate.'

'Er, not so, my Lord. It would seem they had the relevant parking permit.'

At this point the Baron's mood went very dark; the kind of dark you really don't want to venture into; the kind of dark that contains horrible things that pinch your toes in the night; the kind of dark that any self-respecting dark would steer well clear of.

'Do you mean that they escaped?' he eventually said, between teeth that were so clenched they seemed to merge into one big set of teeth.

'Y-y-yes, my Lord. They will be here within the hour.'

It began with an ear-splitting roar that seemed to shake the very foundations of the palace itself. Then the manic arm-waving started, followed by a series of expletives in what seemed to be several different languages. At this point, Velvet scurried quickly away out of sight, leaving Pimple as the sole object of the Baron's maleficent ire.

He cowered down and put his arms over his head as goblets, swords, cushions, books and candlesticks flew in every direction. Even the Baron's favourite teddy bear, Mr Buttons, received a kick so fierce that it sailed through the air, knocking over a suit of armour near the main door.

After a couple of minutes, the Baron calmed down, possibly because there was no longer anything close to hand that could be hurled. He drew in deep breaths and dusted down his sleeve. 'My good Pimple, inform General Darkblast that he must despatch his best men to the West Gate of the City. If he allows Sacred Wind to enter his life will be forfeit.'

'Of course, my Lord,' Pimple said, standing up.

'And bring me the Queen, and fetch a cage for her,' the Baron hissed. 'Even though I have every confidence in the good General, I want to ensure there is contingency in place should events somehow take yet another unexpected turn.'

CHAPTER 36 – WE'D BETTER STICK CLOSE TOGETHER

As the cab pulled into the centre of Chester, Cracky signalled for the driver to stop. 'That's fine, we'll get out here.'

The city was awash with colour and gaiety. The Cestrian Music Tournament had now become more than just a celebration of music; it was essentially the primary event in the calendar *(see appendix 4)*. Visitors and city dwellers mingled happily together, availing themselves of the wares of countless market stalls and partaking in the various amusements that also lined the city's streets.

'We'd better stick close together,' Cracky said to the group. 'This place is jam packed.'

Across the main square in front of them stood the Grand Palace of Chester, the residence of Baron Blacktie and, in all likelihood, the location of Queen Ophelia. Two heavily-armoured guards stood at the front entrance, pushing away anyone who dared to venture too close.

Humphrey was surveying the surroundings and he closely scrutinised the palace, checking for any accessible areas. 'I would suggest our best way in is probably through the servant's entrance at the rear.'

'I reckon you're right, although it's still likely to be guarded,' Cracky said. 'Can I suggest we wait for an hour or so before making our move,' he added, looking around is if expecting to see someone.

'Cracky, I get the distinct impression you know something the rest of us don't,' Oriana said.

'Let's just say I'm hoping that some, er, acquaintances will be arriving shortly. Our arm will be considerably strengthened if they manage to get here on time.'

'Why are you being so cryptic, Cracky?' Theo said. 'Do you not think it would be beneficial just to tell us?'

Cracky sighed. 'Look, I don't know for certain that these acquaintances will arrive, so I can't see the point of building anyone's hopes up. The chances are we're in this by ourselves and if we accept that we're far more likely to positively adapt to the situation. But, just in case fate tips us a kind wink, let's please hang fire for an hour or so. Agreed?'

'Okay,' Theo said, smiling, 'and I promise that I won't read your mind to find out.'

'Thanks,' Cracky said, returning the smile. 'Shall we have a wander down to the theatre? I'm actually curious to see who the band will be up against this evening.'

The Grand Gateway Theatre was situated only a short distance from the palace and had recently been refurbished. It had been one of the Baron's pet projects and he had spared no expense, and he insisted that the Blacktie crest be fixed to the royal box. The letters on the large electric sign above the main door chased each other constantly across the display, flashing in anticipation. *Tonight! The Music Event of the Year! The 1987 Cestrian Music Tournament! Doors Open – 6:30 pm (Farting Not Permitted)*.

The rear of the palace was adjacent to the theatre and the servant's entrance was clearly visible. There was only one guard; a short man with an oversized metal helmet. 'That's a bit odd, you know,' Theo remarked. 'I'd have expected to see at least one of the Baron's elite guards on that door. That fellow looks more like a reservist or a volunteer.'

'Yes, I agree,' Cracky said. 'That may suggest the elite guards have been positioned elsewhere in the city, or that Blacktie feels that palace security is unlikely to be tested today. Either way it's good news for us.'

There was already a queue building up at the theatre, even though the doors weren't due to open for another two hours. Street vendors were ambling along selling programmes and t-shirts, and the buzz of excitement above the crowd buzzed about in an excited manner.

'Look, there's a poster advertising the contestants,' Oriana said, rushing over to the theatre door.

'So, there are seven entrants in the final,' Cracky said, looking at the poster, 'and Sacred Wind are last to play. That's a good omen.'

1. *Willie Barebum – Country & Western Singer Supreme!*
2. *Rip Cotton and the Holy Socks – Rock 'n' Roll with God!*
3. *Kyleene Mingin – Ridiculously, Bouncy, Happy Pop!*
4. *Cestrian Baroque Ensemble – Progressive Jazz Chamber Music!*
5. *The Knights of Flatulence – New Romantic Evangelists!*
6. *The Oswestry Sheep Orchestra – The Best Classical Music, Baa None!*
7. *Sacred Wind – The Finest Welsh Flatulence Rock Band Around!*

...and opening the show, our special guests – The Harmonic Monks!

'I see that the Cestrian Baroque Ensemble made it to the final,' Cracky said to Humphrey, with a smile. 'Well, they'll not be a threat.'

'Is that because you feel the Baroque tendency to use diatonic scales and complex counterpoints will not be to the audience's taste?' remarked Humphrey.

'No', Cracky replied, 'it's because they're crap.'

'Ah, there you are, my dear. I was getting worried you weren't going to make it,' a voice from the theatre door said.

Oriana turned to see Henry Fluffywool waving at her. He already had his baton in his hand and looked very excited. 'Oh, hello Henry, yes, I'm fine now.'

'Have you seen anything of Cliff or Charles?'

'No, I'm afraid not. We've only just arrived ourselves.'

'No matter, I'm sure they'll be along soon. Now, I'm going to have a preliminary run through tonight's arrangement with the others,' he said, handing her a lanyard with an 'Access All Areas' pass attached. 'I could really benefit from you being present,'

Oriana looked over at Cracky, almost as if she were asking permission. 'You should go now,' he said. 'It's been wonderful having you with us, but I sense the next stage of our journey could be quite hazardous. I'd hate to see anything untoward happen to you. And Cliff would never forgive me.'

'Cracky's right, Oriana,' Theo added. 'If everything goes to plan we'll all back in time to hear you play, but you should go with Henry.'

Oriana sighed and nodded. She hugged each of them in turn, her eyes battling against the tears that fought hard to be set free. 'You must promise me that you'll all take care,' she almost scolded. 'And please, please find Ophelia and bring her back safely.'

'You can rest assured we'll be doing our best on both counts,' Cracky said, as she went through the theatre entrance with Henry.

'Right, now I must get changed,' Cracky said, rooting in his backpack and producing his ceremonial cooking cloak.

'I was wondering why you'd brought that along,' Theo said.

'Well, you never know when you'll need these things,' Cracky said, as he put the cloak on over his clothes.

'Okay, let's approach the guard on the pretext that I'm here to cook the Baron a specially-commissioned dish in honour of the tournament,' he continued. 'If he is indeed a reservist, my hoodwinking plot may have a good chance of succeeding.'

'And if it doesn't?' Theo said.

'We may have to go for a more direct route.'

***

Eddie was enjoying himself being a guard. He liked the costume, he liked the hours, he particularly liked the sword, and he liked the fact he didn't have to ask anyone if they wanted salt and vinegar on their fish and chips anymore. When General Darkblast offered the people of Scouseland the chance of an 'exchange deal' for 'cultural enlightenment', Eddie was the first to put his hand in the air.

Eddie had ambitions. True, he had no idea what they were, but he knew he had them somewhere and wasn't likely to achieve them working in his Dad's chip shop. He'd learned everything there was to know about battering fish, everything there was to know about pie fillings, and he knew how to make really lumpy gravy. But that wasn't enough for him. His father may have been happy wallowing in mushy peas and extolling the virtues of crispy fish cakes, but Eddie? No, Eddie had an adventurer's soul. He wanted to see the world, and he wanted to see it without chips.

'Excuse me, my good man,' Cracky said, sweeping his cloak in an ostentatious display of bowing. 'I believe I am expected by the Baron.'

Eddie looked him up and down, hardly noticing the three cats and the dog that accompanied him. 'Oo are yer, den, mate,' he replied, in his distinctive scouse twang.

'Who am I? Who am I?!' Cracky said, with mock disbelief. 'I am none other than Horatio Hustlebustle VIII. And I am, sir, the finest exponent of esoteric cuisine in the land. I have been especially commissioned by the Baron to produce a meal so delectable, so delightful in taste, so scrumptious, and so floopypoofyous that his taste buds will be in a state of ecstasy for weeks.'

'Oh,' Eddie said, quite taken aback. 'I've not been told about dis. I'll 'ave ta check, yer know. An' what's wit' all deh fancy werds?'

'Ah, 'Cracky said, 'my dishes are of such quality, texture and piquancy that I have been forced to invent words to describe them. They are indeed tonguetastic and tummynicelyful.'

Eddie had a clipboard as well as a sword. He picked it up from the side of the narrow door and started to read the list of names. 'I can't see yer name on 'ere, pal, an' I've been told dat if yer name's not on deh list, den yer don't get in.'

'There must surely be some kind of dreadful error,' Cracky said, looking at the list over the top of the clipboard. 'Why, I'm preparing the most marvellous strawberry lamb soufflé. Perhaps if you'd just let me through and I can confirm with the head chef?'

Cracky made an attempt to sidestep Eddie, but Eddie was having none of it. He'd thrown enough drunks out of chip shops in the past and he knew how to handle himself. 'Ay, ay, you get back now,' he said drawing his sword.

'It would appear this particular ruse is not quite living up to initial expectations,' Humphrey said. 'Perhaps it's time for a more direct approach.'

'Ay, did dat dog jus' talk?' Eddie said.

And these were the last words Eddie said today, just before he fell asleep… after the giant hilt of the giant sword being wielded by the giant blonde man crashed down on his head.

'Looks like I got here just in time, laddie,' the giant blonde man said to Cracky.

'Yes, quite. I've never been that good at acting, I'm afraid,' Cracky replied, with a grin. 'You obviously got my message.'

'Aye, and I figured it was one message that needed to be answered personally. I've brought a few friends too, just in case things get a bit tasty.'

'Right, thanks for the intervention but we'd better be getting inside,' Cracky said. 'We've a queen to find, and to free. Are you coming along?'

'If it's all the same to you, I'll hang around here,' the giant blonde man said, lifting up the unconscious Eddie and placing him under his arm. 'But I'll lay low for a while. I've got a nose for battle and there's a strong smell coming from that direction,' he added, pointing towards the Grand Gateway Theatre.

And off he went, carrying Eddie like a child carries a doll.

'Who on earth was that?' Captain Marmaduke asked, as they walked through the palace kitchens. 'I had no idea humans could grow to be that big.'

'Let's just say that if there's any trouble later I wouldn't want to be on the other side,' Cracky replied, with a renewed spring in his step.

The palace seemed quiet and Cracky simply bowed politely to any staff they happened to encounter, as they walked through the labyrinth of corridors. 'Is it worthwhile utilising the powers of his highness at this juncture?' Humphrey enquired, as they came to what appeared to be the main hallway.

'You must have read my mind this time,' Theo said. 'Stop here and give me a minute.'

Theo closed his eyes and concentrated. Although many of the palace servants and officials had left for the day, their thoughts and memories were cluttered about the building like an emotional fog. He concentrated harder, using his memories of Ophelia to harness the connection. After about a minute he opened his eyes and purred. 'She's here,' he said. 'And she's safe. But she's extremely unhappy with the state of her hair.'

'Can you get any kind of fix on her location?' Captain Marmaduke asked.

Theo concentrated again, sniffing the air as he did so. 'She's actually very close. Has anyone any idea where this corridor leads?'

'Absolutely none,' Cracky said. 'But let's continue walking.'

The corridor was very wide and grand, and seemed to run right the way through the ground floor of the palace. It was festooned with pictures of previous rulers and other dignitaries, separated by the odd suit of armour. A deep-ply, blue carpet stretched off into the distance and servants occasionally scurried up and down its expanse.

What appeared to be a group of people on a sight-seeing tour could be seen about half way down the corridor. They were gazing intently at a large portrait, while a small man with a very squeaky voice and a large ruff seemed to be providing them with an animated description.

'Would you believe it,' Cracky said, shaking his head. 'We went to all that trouble to sneak in and they're running tours of the palace.'

'That sounds like an ideal cover, then,' Humphrey said. 'Why don't we simply tag along with the crowd?'

'And so,' said the small man with the squeaky voice and large ruff, whose name badge identified him as Timothy, 'what you have here is a portrait of our esteemed Baron Blacktie. It was commissioned not long after he came to power, and was painted by the celebrated artist Piccolo Von Gout. As you can see, the portrait also contains the Baron's pet ferret, Velvet, his loyal and noble companion to this day.'

As Timothy led them along the corridor, delighting in relating his acquired knowledge of palace life and its history, Theo's ears pricked up as they approach a set of huge, wooden doors. 'She's in there,' he said, sending out his thoughts to his companions.

'And this,' said Timothy, with an ostentatious wave of his arm, 'is the throne room, where the Baron holds court, and indeed spends time being wise, musing and reading.'

'Can we not take a look?' a large woman in a floral hat said.

'Ah, I'm afraid not, dear lady. It is strictly out of bounds during this visit, as can be seen by the *Do Not Disturb* sign.'

'Hmmph, we pay two pounds each and we don't even get to see the throne room. It doesn't seem right, does it Sidney?' she snorted, jabbing her short husband with her finger.

'But,' Timothy exclaimed, with another ostentatious swing of the arm, 'you will get to go upstairs and see the Baron's sleeping quarters.'

'Oh, I say, that sounds good, doesn't it dear?' Sidney said, hopefully.

'I suppose it will have to do,' the large woman in the floral hat huffed, as the tour party disappeared around the far corner of the corridor.

'Right, they're out of sight,' Captain Marmaduke said.

Cracky tried the handle of the door. Remarkably it was unlocked.

As they stepped inside the huge room, they could see a cage against the far wall, behind the gold and marble throne. It contained the Queen. She frantically struggled to break free of her bonds, mumbling through the gag around her mouth.

'Your Majesty, you're a sight for sore eyes. Let's get you out of that cage shall we,' Cracky said, as he reached through the bars and untied the gag covering her mouth.

'Oh, Cracky, run. It's a trap!' she shouted

'It is indeed,' said Baron Blacktie, as he entered through the side door with six of his elite guards. 'Did you really think that anyone can enter my palace without me knowing, Cracky? Dear me, old age is definitely catching up with you. I've been aware of your presence in the city ever since you arrived, isn't that right gentlemen?'

Hob and Nob appeared at the throne room door, with Pimple one step behind them. 'You see, I have eyes everywhere,' the Baron said. 'So, as you seem so keen to sample the delights of the palace, the least I can do is be hospitable and find some appropriate accommodation for you, Prince Theo, Captain Marmaduke and, oh, whatever that scruffy one is called.'

'Scruffy?!' Half-blind Ron shouted with his mind. 'I'll show you scruffy,' and he hurtled towards the Baron, claws extended… only to be downed by a rasping blow from Velvet, who had been hiding behind the throne.

'Ron!' Theo shouted, rushing over to the injured cat.

Velvet looked on, smiling, and then jumped onto the Baron's shoulder, as Theo licked the bleeding wound on Ron's head.

'My Lord, they had a dog with them as well, although we could not identify him,' Nob said.

'Oh, he was simply a stray that followed us,' Cracky said, quickly. 'He must have run off.'

'Thank you for the astute observation, my good Nob, but a stray dog is not really a concern,' the Baron said. 'However, let us now house our guests in a manner in which they will have to become very accustomed. Pimple, do we have a spare Luxury dingy cell?'

'We do indeed, my Lord.'

As the guards led them away, with Cracky protectively cradling the injured Half-blind Ron, Theo sent out his thoughts. 'What happened to Humphrey?'

'I've no idea,' Cracky thought back. 'But if that dog's half as smart as he seems, I'd be very surprised if we don't see him again shortly.'

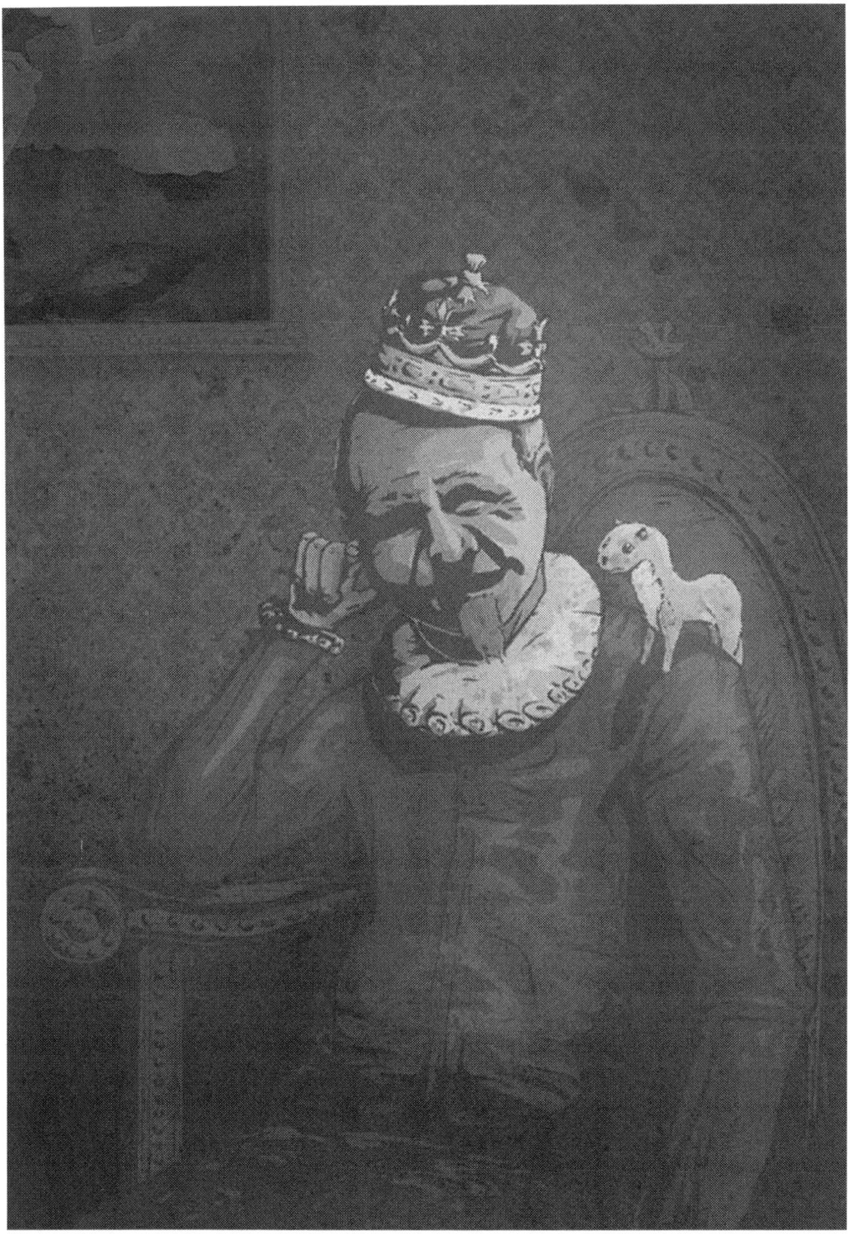

CHAPTER 37 – HOPE ALWAYS FINDS A WAY

Tikky was in contemplative mood as Ethel glided smoothly towards Chester. Given the Baron's attempts to derail them thus far, she'd be very surprised if there wasn't something waiting for them when they arrived at the quay to the West Gate, and she doubted very much it would be bunting and waving crowds. After all, word must have reached the Baron by now that they had successfully thwarted his dastardly schemes.

'Penny for them, my Queen?' Vindy asked.

'I was just wondering what surprises the Baron will have in store for us when we arrive.'

'Well, I think we should look on the positive side,' Vindy said, puffing his rice. 'For all we know the Baron may think we perished at the hands of those ridiculous pirates.'

'Somehow I doubt that. He has eyes and ears everywhere.'

'I'm not looking at it like that, my Queen. As far as I'm concerned we've got fate on our side. Remember what Cracky said about the Prophecy? I think our mission is being influenced by other forces more powerful than the Baron can imagine.'

'Well, whatever happens, my King, I want you to know I'm very proud of you,' Tikky said.

'Not as proud as I am of being at your side.'

'Oh, stop it now, Vindy,' she scolded, affectionately. 'You'll be making me all mushy, and you know what that does to the texture of my rice.'

Aiden was also deep in thought, standing at Ethel's prow watching seagulls swooping for fish. Mara was at his side, her tiny frame snuggling into him as he wrapped his arm around her shoulders.

'You know, I've actually got a feeling that everything's going to work out fine,' he said to her. 'I've no idea why, given that we're heading straight to a city ruled by a merciless despot who's been doing his utmost to get rid of us… permanently.'

Mara snuggled into him even more. 'Hope always finds a way, if you truly believe, you know. My Granny used to say that to me when I was a tot. She was very wise, although she did have quite smelly feet.'

Aiden let out a chuckle. Mara could always make him laugh. 'Well, I think your smelly-footed Granny was right,' he said. 'And I think it's time to make a call to someone who may also be able to provide some hope.'

He kissed Mara's head and wandered down towards Ethel's stern, passing the ever-watchful wooden dragon on the way. He pulled out his phone and dialled the last number in the phone's log. 'Hello,' said a booming voice.

'Hi, am I speaking to Lord Odin?' Aiden asked politely.

'You are,' Odin replied, 'but I'd just like to say whatever it is you're selling I'm not interested. Only last week my poor wife, Frigg, was taken in by one of you lot. What in Hades name am I supposed to do with a "Super-Deluxe All-Inclusive Life Assurance Policy", I'm bloody immortal! And the complimentary pens we received as a free gift were rubbish. One of them doesn't even write properly and the other fell to bits when I stuck it in my ear, trying to get a bit of wax out.'

'I'm not trying to sell you anything, Lord Odin,'

'Good, I should bloody well hope not. And how did you get this number? I'm supposed to be ex-directory.'

'Er, I simply pressed dial on the last number that called me, Lord Odin. It's Aiden Peersey, we spoke a few days ago. You gave me a message from Tom.'

'Oh, yes, I remember. Hey, thanks for the tip about the radio show, I've got twenty billion listeners already. Have you heard it yet?'

'Not yet, I'm afraid, but I promise I'll listen out for it.'

'Excellent! It's called *Rock Your Deity*. I've got the mid-morning slot, from ten 'til twelve on Mondays, Wednesdays and Fridays. Top quality guests and top quality music. I've got Beelzebub on next week, you know. That could get a bit fiery.'

'I'll definitely listen in.'

'Super! So, what can I do for you, young man?'

'I'd like to ask you a favour. It's not for me exactly, it's for my friends. They're a rock band called Sacred Wind.'

'Hey, I've heard of those lads and by all accounts they're very good. Perhaps I should get them on the show, as long as they don't fart too much.'

'I think they'd be very honoured if you did that.'

'So, what's this favour then?' Odin asked.

'Well, in all likelihood, we're probably about to go into battle with the evil forces of the despicable Baron Blacktie, in an attempt to play at tonight's Cestrian Music Tournament; to win back a cheese mine, to win freedom for the land, to be able to fart freely, oh and to rescue Ophelia, the Faerie Queen.'

'No kidding; good luck to you then. That Blacktie's a nasty piece of work. His farts stink and there's no goodness in them, if you know what I mean.'

'I was sort of hoping you could perhaps lend a hand?' Aiden said.

'Ah, I'd love to, but if you remember I'm bound by the universal laws relating to freewill. I agree that they're a pain, but you'll have to find your own way, I'm afraid.'

'Okay, I accept that,' Aiden said. 'What I was after wasn't so much interference as an "appearance", to provide a bit of motivation.'

'An appearance?'

'Yes, like maybe a bit of a vision.'

'Hmm, well I don't tend to do just a bit of a vision; it's the full on thunder, lightning, singing angels and special-effects job or nothing. Anyway, what would you want me to say? Remember, I can't be seen to be interfering.'

'Well, you could just bless their wind. That can't be construed as interfering at all; you're simply thanking them for farting and bestowing your good will upon them.'

'I suppose that would be okay, but I'll have to think about it. I normally only do the vision thing on really special occasions, like global catastrophes, inter-planetary wars, heralding in a golden age, those sorts of things.'

There was a pause for a few seconds as Odin mulled over his request. In the background Aiden could make out a female voice. 'Odin, dear, the window cleaner's at the door, can you pay him, please'.

'Be right there, my lovely,' Odin shouted, away from the phone.

'Look, I've got to go but, okay, you're on,' he said to Aiden, who could hear the muffled sound of jingling coins. 'I'll appear when I think it's most appropriate. I can't say fairer than that now, can I?'

'Thanks very much, Odin. I really appreciate this.'

'You're welcome. And don't forget to listen to the show.'

'I won't.'

The city lights were now visible and the Dee widened appreciably, as they passed many large and seemingly luxurious dwellings that looked out imposingly on the river. Little boats bobbed gently in the water until they were caught in Ethel's wake, the amplified undulations threatening to free them from their moorings.

'It's too quiet, Oldfart, I don't like it,' Olaf said, as they looked out at the silent wharfs.

'Don't forget, everyone's likely to be in the city,' Oldfart reminded him. 'Anyway, look, there's our transport.'

Olaf smiled and shook his head. The transport was a large, covered wagon with the Sacred Wind logo on the side, drawn by six sturdy horses. 'You old fool; do you not think we will draw attention to ourselves travelling through the city in that thing?'

'That's the whole point,' Oldfart replied. 'Look, Blacktie's advertised this event all over the region and we've been splattered all over the local press. He won't want to do anything that makes the populace suspicious once we're in the city. Now, granted, we may have a problem actually getting through the gates, but once we're in I want as many people to see us as possible.'

'I think it looks rather splendid,' Mr Kneepatcher said, waving at the driver. 'I love the colour, it matches my cravat.'

The West Gate could now be seen in the distance. On the ramparts were scores of heavily-armed guards, members of the notorious Knights of Flatulence. Ethel moved closer to the bank so she remained out of sight, and drew to a stop by a small quay around two hundred yards from the gate.

'Whatever happens, I'll protect you,' Agnar said to Roisin, placing his hand on her shoulder.

'I know,' she replied, touching his hand. 'You always do.'

'And if anyone tries anything, they'll have these to answer to,' he added, brandishing his drumsticks with menace.

Oldfart was deep in conversation with Vindy and Tikky as the Companionship helped Sacred Wind load their equipment into the waiting wagon. 'Are you two absolutely sure you want to go through with this?' he said. 'It sounds very risky.'

'We do,' Vindy said. 'Tikky and I talked about it earlier and we believe it's the best solution to get everybody through that gate without having to battle past the guards. We're not entirely sure what will happen afterwards, so, yes, it's a bit of a risk'

Although the West Gate was well-fortified and the ramparts stocked with troops, two solitary guards flanked the actual gate itself. 'D'ya tink we'll get ta keep dees 'elmets when we go 'ome?' Tommy said to Jimmy.

'Oh, god, dat'd be great,' Jimmy replied. 'We'd be sure to cop off with dees on. We'd be proper babe magnets.'

'Oy!' Sergeant Savagebreath shouted down to them. 'Concentrate on the job in hand and less talk!'

'Alright, Sarge!' Tommy shouted, looking up at the ramparts and saluting. 'We was just talking about women an' our 'elmets.'

Sergeant Savagebreath shook his head. 'Typical scousers,' he said, under his breath.

'Ay, Sarge, isn't it time for our break? Me tummy tinks me throat's been cut!' Jimmy shouted.

Sergeant Savagebreath sighed and looked at his watch. 'Go on, then. But only ten minutes. I'll keep watch. If you're late back, you'll both be clapped in irons, though.'

'Aw, tanks, Sarge!' Tommy shouted.

Oldfart was looking through the small telescope as Tommy and Jimmy walked away from the gate. 'This could be easier than we thought,' he said to Vindy. 'The two guards outside the gate seem to taking a break, and by the looks of things they're headed this way.'

'Right, we need to intercept them before they reach one of the food outlets,' Vindy said.

There were several food stalls randomly scattered outside the city gates and all were open for business. Harold and Greta carefully held Vindy and Tikky aloft and walked straight towards the two guards, who were racing eagerly to a burger outlet at the side of the road.

'Quickly, Harold,' Vindy said, 'I'm not going to be outdone by some lowlife burger.'

The rest of the Companionship gathered around Oldfart, who was watching through the telescope, as the two curries and their loyal servants drew closer to Tommy and Jimmy. 'What in Asgard's name is this all about?' Grundi said.

'It was the King and Queen's idea,' Oldfart replied. 'There's no way we could simply charge the gate, we'd never make it through. So we need a distraction.'

'What kind of distraction?' Smid said.

Oldfart took a deep breath. 'Well, Vindy and Tikky are going to allow the two guards to eat them.'

'What!' Olaf shouted, with his shout echoed by gasps of disbelief from the rest of the Companionship.

'It's okay, they won't eat all of them,' Oldfart said. 'Once they've had a few mouthfuls, the essence of Vindy and Tikky will replace their consciousness, from what they told me. Then, Vindy and Tikky will be able to get them to do as they wish.'

'You mean the two guards will be possessed by curry?' Aiden said.

'That's about the top and bottom of it, yes,' Oldfart replied.

'That happened to me once,' Agnar said. 'I had this really hot curry after a gig and it made me drink ten pints of ale. I swear I had no control whatsoever.'

'But you always drink ten pints of ale after a gig,' Grundi said, with a sideways glance at Agnar.

'You see, it's still got control over me to this day,' Agnar said, with a smile.

'Get your free curry here; free curry for scousers!' Harold yelled, at the top of his voice.

Tommy and Jimmy were just about to order a 'Blacktie Bumper Burger' each when they stopped dead in their tracks. They sniffed the air and turned towards Harold and Greta, like ships drawn to a rocky coast by the Siren's cry.

'Er, did you say "free curry"?' Jimmy said to Harold.

'Yes,' he replied, 'it's a special offer, today only. And exclusively for scousers.'

'Ay, we're both scousers, aren't we Jimmy,' Tommy said.

'Yeah!' Jimmy answered, enthusiastically. 'Me Mam even went to school wit Gringo from The Bertles.'

'Well, in which case, you qualify for a free curry,' Greta said. 'I have a Chicken Tikka Masala and my partner has a Beef Vindaloo.'

'Dat's ace!' Tommy shouted, grabbing Tikky off Greta, and producing a spoon from his pocket.

'Would sir like the Vindaloo?' Harold enquired of Jimmy.

'Bloody right!' Jimmy said, as he snatched Vindy from Harold's grasp.

'Enjoy, then, gentlemen,' Greta said.

'We will, and tanks very much,' Tommy said, as he and Jimmy headed off to a nearby bench.

Oldfart pulled the telescope away from his eye. 'Well, they've taken the bait. Let's wait for a sign before we move.'

'Can ya believe dis? Free curry,' Jimmy said, as he sat on the bench next to Tommy. 'An' I'm starvin'. It won't take me long to polish dis off.'

'Good luck, Vindy.' Tikky whispered.

'Ay, did your curry just say summat'?' Jimmy said.

'Don't be daft. It's deh hunger playin' wit yer mind,' said Tommy, as he proceeded to tuck into Tikky.

Vindy and Tikky's plan was a sound one, but with one fatal drawback. They had both underestimated the voracious appetite of hungry scousers when it comes to curry. In less than a minute both plates were virtually cleaned.

'I'm startin' to feel a bit woozy, yer know,' Jimmy said.

'Ay, me too,' said Tommy. 'I feel like I jus' wanna go asleep...'

And so Tommy and Jimmy's consciousness ebbed away to a place where they would dream of curry, poppadoms, strong ale, buxom women and shiny helmets.

'Oh, my,' Tikky/Tommy said. 'They've eaten all of us.'

'Yes,' Vindy/Jimmy said. 'That was a bit unexpected, my dear. But I think we need to deal with the matter in hand, firstly.'

Tikky/Tommy and Vindy/Jimmy were met by many wary eyes as they re-joined the Companionship. 'Right, I know this probably seems a bit odd,' Vindy/Jimmy said, with a scouse accent, 'but it really is us.'

'How do we know it's not another Blacktie trick?' Agnar snorted.

'Well, do you think his guards smell as divine as me?' Tikky/Tommy said, as she/he held out her/his hand.

Agnar lifted it to his nose and the smell of warm tomato, onions and coconut wafted up his nostrils. 'Well, may Odin cause my buttocks to sag; it really is you, Tikky!'

'Look, we really are going to have to get a move on here,' Vindy said. 'Now, Tikky and I will return to the West Gate and say that Sacred Wind have been spotted at the East Gate with an army of curries and Trolls. You wait here for our signal.'

Sergeant Savagebreath was certainly a man to be feared. He stood well over six feet tall, with his width virtually commensurate to his height. His bushy, black beard was now flecked with grey and was rumoured to contain living things; an assertion with some foundation as a family of starlings once nested there for a short time, before eventually succumbing to his raging halitosis. He may have seen better years as a soldier and leaner days when it came to his physique, but he prided himself on his sharp mind and soldier's instinct.

'Sarge! Sarge!' Vindy/Jimmy shouted up from the bottom of the gate.

'What is it, you irritating scouse git?!' Sergeant Savagebreath yelled back.

'It's Sacred Wind. Dey've been spotted at deh East Gate wit ugly Trolls and an army of curries! It's pandemonium, Sarge, der's Naan bread everywhere and deh Onion Bhajis are on the rampage.'

'What!' he bellowed. 'Rampaging Onion Bhajis in Chester?!'

'It's true Sarge,' Tikky/Tommy said. 'We met a witness. She said she was lucky to escape wit her taste buds intact. Dey're not taking any prisoners.'

'Is that right?' Sergeant Savagebreath said, unsheathing his sword. 'Well, it looks like chopping time's arrived.'

An evil smile crept slowly over his face and his eyes shone with a particular nasty malevolence; the type of malevolence that everyday malevolence hero-worships and aspires to be. 'Corporal Bluster,' he bellowed, 'gather the men, we head for the East Gate!'

'Yes, sir,' Corporal Bluster replied, with a salute.

'Now, you two,' the Sergeant shouted at Vindy/Jimmy and Tikky/Tommy, 'stay put and don't let anyone through that gate!'

'Yes, Sarge!'

As the hordes of the Knights of Flatulence raced towards the East Gate, Vindy/Jimmy gave the all-clear. 'Quickly, you've probably got about ten minutes before they return,' Tikky/Tommy said as she/he pulled open the gate to let the wagon through.

'But what's going to happen to you?' Aiden said.

'We'll be back... at some point. Look both Tikky and I are firm believers in Curryincarnation, you know.'

Harold and Greta got out of the cart and warmly embraced the King and Queen. 'How will we now serve your Majesties,' Greta said, as little tears rolled down her porcelain cheeks.

'Now, now, be strong,' Tikky/Tommy said. 'Go now and get word to Saffy. Tell him our forces must be readied. I think we're in for quite an eventful evening.'

'I don't know how we can thank you both,' Oldfart said.

'Just win the tournament and get rid of Blacktie; we'll consider that thanks enough,' Vindy/Jimmy said.

'Oh, you can rest assured we've got even more incentive now,' Olaf growled. 'May Odin bless your wind, and I pray you find a path back to us.'

And so, as Harold and Greta went in search of the troops of Wrexham and Mold, and as the Companionship finally rolled into the city of Chester, Vindy/Jimmy and Tikky/Tommy simply sat in front of the open gate, staring at the last rays of the sun as it dipped below the horizon.

'What do you think will become of us, my King,' Tikky/Tommy said.

'I'm really not sure, my dear. But I honestly don't think this is the end. Life is full of surprises. Hope always finds a way.'

'Darling,' Tikky/Tommy said, 'there is something I need to ask you now.'

'Go on, my Queen.'

'I can hardly bear to say it.'

'Please, ask away.'

'Well, will you still love me when… oh, it pains me to think about.'

'You know I will always love you, Tikky.'

'No, please let me finish.'

'Very well, my darling.'

'Will you still love me, when… when… when I'm poo-poo?'

Vindy/Jimmy reached over and took hold of Tikky/Tommy's hand. 'Of course, my dear. I'm sure you'll make a lovely turd.'

And with that, the essence of Vindy and Tikky began to ebb away. They smiled at each other one last time, in this life, and tenderly held on to each other's hands.

Sergeant Savagebreath ran through the open gate and looked at the two guards, as they sat gazing into each other's eyes. 'Now, why am I not really that surprised,' he said, shaking his head.

CHAPTER 38 – THERE HAS BEEN A MASSACRE!

Word of the demise of King Beef Vindaloo-Boiled Rice III and Queen Chicken Tikka Masala-Coconut Rice spread through the ranks of Mold and Wrexham curries like coriander dressing. Saffy was almost inconsolable and his mini poppadoms sagged as a mark of respect. General Beef Madras-Wholegrain Rice ordered a one-minute silence, followed by a twenty-one poppadom snapping salute.

'Has there ever been a more noble sacrifice made by two curries,' he said to the assembled troops. 'The King and Queen have given their lives for the greater good, so the Companionship of Wind may have a better chance of prevailing against the evil that has blighted our land and that blights the fair city in front of us. Will we let that sacrifice be in vain? I think not. For in this war curries, men and sheep will fight as one; for our friends; for our allies, and for the memory of the Great King Beef Vindaloo-Boiled Rice III and the Great Queen Chicken Tikka Masala-Coconut Rice. Are you with me?!'

'Aye!' was the resounding response.

'General,' a reconnaissance curry shouted. 'I bring news from the Chester Stroganoffs.'

'Speak up, then, soldier. What do they say?'

'Tsar Beef Stroganoff-Sour Cream sends his deepest condolences for the loss of the King and Queen. He said his troops have infiltrated key points in the city and are prepared to unleash Stroganoff hell, on your command.'

'And so it begins,' the General said, his rice popping in anticipation of the battle to come.

***

'What ails you so?' Archie Backrasher said to Crusher, as he sat disconsolately on the bank of the river, his trotters dangling into the water.

'I'm worried about Daddy Smid,' Crusher replied, looking up at Archie. 'I have a feeling he's in danger and I want to help him.'

'Now, now, Crusher, I'm sure Smid will be alright,' Archie said. 'He's a mighty warrior, you know.'

'I know,' Crusher said, with a sigh, 'and a very good bass player, but now I've found him again I couldn't bear it if something nasty happened to him.'

Behind them the repairs to The Pig's Trotters were already in full swing. 'Come on,' Archie said, patting Crusher on the shoulder, 'I'll get you a nice cold drink of Muckyade, that'll cheer you up.'

'News, news, terrible news!' Percy from P.O.R.K shouted, running down the path towards the pub, closely followed by his compatriot, Chopper.

'What is it, Percy?' Archie shouted.

'There has been a massacre. It's awful!'

'Now, calm down, Percy. What's all this about a massacre?' Archie said.

'It's true, Archie, about half a mile down the river, towards Chester. I fear our friends Sacred Wind may have been killed.'

'No!' Crusher shouted, and ran off as fast as his large trotters would carry him.

'C'mon,' said Archie, 'we better go and check this out. Chopper, go and fetch as many pigs as you can and follow us.'

The scene was indeed as awful as Percy described, with bodies… and body parts… strewn everywhere. In the river, the ship of the Tan-Y-Lan Tuffies had keeled over, its mast snapped into many pieces. The hull of the ship was covered with parking tickets, as were most of the bodies… and the body parts.

'What in the Great Porker's name has happened here?' Archie said, as they viewed the scene of carnage in front of them.

'They were strange beings in yellow and black, the likes of which I have never seen before,' Percy said, trembling. 'When I arrived there were only two left and they seemed to be finishing off anyone who was still alive. I shudder now just thinking about it. I could see many more of them heading off into the distance, so I hid in the bushes.'

'Did they say anything?' Archie asked.

'I did hear one of them say "that'll bloody teach them to illegally park" as they ran off laughing,' Percy replied.

Chopper searched frantically through the mass of bodies… and body parts. 'Daddy Smid, Daddy Smid!' he kept shouting, but there was no reply.

'I don't recognise anyone here,' Archie said, turning over another body with one of his hind trotters. 'They seem to be pirates of some description, although there's a very weird-looking one in a dress by the riverbank.'

Chopper and a large group of pigs arrived, aghast at the devastation that met their eyes. 'What monsters could do this?' one of them said.

'Look, I've found something,' Percy shouted. 'It looks like some kind of name badge, and it's got a photograph on it.'

Archie ran over and took the badge from Percy's hand. It said 'Phil Potty – Wrexham County Council Traffic Warden'. Written in rough, black lettering at the bottom was 'Dogsdoodahs'.

'What kind of creature is this?' Chopper said, looking at the badge. 'A creature so evil, so malicious, so lacking in a soul that it surely must be akin to the Devil himself.'

'They would appear to be called "Traffic Wardens",' Archie said. 'And I pray that I never meet one.'

It was now apparent that none of Sacred Wind or the Companionship had suffered the fate of the pirates, so Crusher started to calm down. He sat on his haunches, breathing heavily. 'I must go to Daddy Smid,' he said. 'If there is further danger, I cannot let him face this without me by his side.'

'Well, young Crusher, I reckon you won't be alone there,' Archie said, sitting down beside him. 'Chopper, tell the rest of the herd that if they're with us we trot to Chester.'

'With pleasure,' Chopper said, rapping his front trotters together.

***

Humphrey padded quietly along the corridor towards the kitchen. He suspected a trap early on and figured that the best way to assist his friends was by not getting caught, so as soon as he spotted the Baron he made good his escape. He also figured that his friends would likely be taken to a dungeon of some description, so he sought out a set of stairs that went downwards.

The lower level of the palace was a dark and dismal place, almost as if this were the real residence of the soul of Baron Blacktie. There were many locked doors to rooms or cells that were obviously occupied. Some of the residents moaned, some screamed; some moaned and screamed; some gurgled; some cackled, some gurgled and cackled; some moaned, screamed, gurgled and cackled. Someone was even reciting Shakespeare. However, one sound rose above the cacophony of woe; one resident was singing.

Humphrey noticed that the only unlocked door on this level was right at the end of the corridor, so he tentatively padded along and peeped around the door frame. Inside was a huge man, or at least it was man-like, sitting on a large wooden bed. The room was virtually empty, apart from a pile of books in the far left corner.

'Grunt can see you doggy, please come in,' Grunt said, holding out his enormous hand in a welcoming fashion.

Humphrey warily stepped into the door frame and slowly walked over to Grunt, who affectionately patted his head. 'Good doggy.'

'You have a very pleasant singing voice,' Humphrey said.

'Doggy can speak!' Grunt said, with wide eyes. 'Grunt never met a talking doggy before.'

'My name is Humphrey,' Humphrey said, extending his paw.

'My name is Grunt,' Grunt replied, as he gently shook Humphrey's paw.

'You don't appear to be locked up like the others, Grunt.'

'No, Grunt work for Baron. This where Grunt lives.'

'Do you like working for the Baron?'

'Sometimes, when he not shout at Grunt. Baron gives Grunt food and let Grunt beat up nasty men.'

'Yet you seem sad,' Humphrey said. 'Your singing was full of longing and sorrow.'

Grunt stood up and walked towards the door, checking there was no-one within earshot. 'Yes, it is true Grunt is sad. Grunt not feel like he has purpose in life, and Grunt feels alone.'

'But there must be others of your kind?'

'Grunt don't know. Grunt don't know what Grunt is. Maybe Grunt is Troll. Grunt feel like Troll. Baron promise Grunt home in mine, lick water off walls and sing about how great it is to be Troll. But Grunt don't think Baron will keep that promise.'

'Then why don't you simply leave and find your purpose, and your own kind?'

Grunt sighed and sat back down on the bed. Humphrey jumped up and sat next to him. 'Grunt think hard about this, but something deep inside stop Grunt from leaving. Grunt don't know what it is. Grunt learn to read books,' he said, pointing to the corner, 'and Grunt study… but Grunt not find answer yet.'

Humphrey jumped off the bed and went to look at some of the books. They were mainly about philosophy, apart from a storybook about Trolls. 'These books are quite difficult to understand, Grunt, I've read some of them myself.'

'Grunt know. Grunt spend many hours trying to grasp core of philosophic idealism. Grunt come to conclusion that there are many branches and each branch contain a different outcome, or destiny. Grunt yet to decide which branch to take.'

'My, you are a bit of a surprise,' Humphrey said, skimming through one of the books. 'I like metaphysics myself, you know.'

'Grunt has read about this. Grunt read Plato, Aristotle and more recently Kant. Grunt cogitate hard over interpretation and meanings, allegorising these with aspects of Grunt's life. For example, Grunt understand principle that for every action there is a reaction, cause when Grunt hit something hard it normally breaks.'

'And,' he continued, 'Grunt also believe existentialism is perfectly correct when it say *"be true to one's self"* and that authenticity is paramount.'

'I think you and I have a lot in common, Grunt,' Humphrey said, jumping back on the bed and licking Grunt's face, which made him giggle. 'You need to choose whether to continue your life of mundane servitude to the Baron, or to finally be true to yourself and break free of the mental shackles that bind you here.'

'Humphrey is smart,' Grunt said. 'This is indeed the dichotomy Grunt is faced with.'

Humphrey patted Grunt's giant hand with his paw and jumped off the bed. 'I've really enjoyed chatting with you, Grunt. But I'm afraid I must leave now.'

'Where Humphrey go?' Grunt said, with sad eyes.

'Well, my friends have unfortunately been captured and I must find a way to free them. We have to rescue the Faerie Queen.'

'Grunt has seen Queen. Grunt likes Queen.'

Grunt stood up and flexed his huge muscles. 'Grunt want to help.'

'I'd be very grateful, Grunt, but you would jeopardise your good standing with the Baron.'

'Maybe it time for Grunt to choose path. Inner voice telling Grunt this is right thing to do.'

'Let us make haste, then,' Humphrey said. 'They can't be far away.'

'Okay, but Grunt better have plop first, just in case.'

CHAPTER 39 – JUST THINK OF THE MERCHANDISING SALES LATER!

'Well I never expected a reaction like this!' Olaf shouted above the cheering crowds, as the Sacred Wind wagon carried them through the streets of Chester.

'Don't forget, that press conference made all the local papers and it will have been broadcast on television,' Oldfart said with a beaming smile. 'You've obviously struck a chord with the populace.'

'It's fantastic, Oldfart,' Aiden shouted, as he waved.

'I know,' Oldfart said. 'Just think of the merchandising sales later!'

'Ooh, hello love!' Mr Kneepatcher yelled, at a waving fan. 'What? You want my autograph? Are you sure? Here you go then,' he said, scribbling excitedly on a poster.

'Is this the welcome you were hoping for?' Cliff said to Oldfart, moving to the front of the wagon.

'Let's just say I felt that once we were in the city we'd be recognised, and that this would perhaps provide us with safe passage to the tournament. But, if I'm honest, this has exceeded my expectations by a fair degree. Blacktie must be gritting his teeth.'

Inside the palace, Pimple was doing his utmost to placate the Baron. 'Please, my Lord, if you grit your teeth any harder I fear your head will explode.'

'Well maybe that would be for the best!' screamed the Baron. 'Have you summoned General Darkblast?'

'Yes, my Lord.'

'Good. Then perhaps he can explain how a simple instruction such as "if you allow Sacred Wind to enter your life will be forfeit" could possibly be misconstrued!'

On cue, the General arrived in the throne room, flanked by two quaking guards. He quickly dropped to one knee and bowed his head. 'My Lord, I cannot begin to tell you how sorry I am that this error has occurred.'

'You can, and I believe that you have,' the Baron replied with a sneer. 'What in the name of the great Scratchy Crotch happened? I have Sacred Wind riding through my city being cheered like conquering heroes.'

'It appears the gate guards were drugged, or possessed, my Lord,' the General explained. 'One of my sergeants informed me that the guards alerted him to information that Sacred Wind had been sighted at the East Gate, accompanied by an army of Trolls and curries. As the two guards had proven to be reliable and loyal to this point, he saw no reason to doubt their words, so he took his knights and made haste to the East Gate. Upon finding it quiet, he returned to the West Gate to find it wide open. Both the guards were incoherent and claimed they had no recollection of events after they had both eaten a free curry, provided by some unknown vendors. The two guards have now been placed in irons, my Lord.'

The Baron shook his head and flung a handily placed apple at the general, hitting him on the top of his plumed helmet. 'This incident does indeed bear the mark of curry infiltration, General; I can smell it a mile off. It would appear that my many detractors and enemies are positioning themselves behind the Sacred Wind banner. But I tell you now, by the end of this evening they will wish they had never been born... or cooked.'

'Should I take my men and arrest Sacred Wind and their companions?' the General asked, standing upright and brushing pieces of apple from his helmet.

'No, don't be a fool! If we try to intervene at this point it could start a revolution,' the Baron yelled. 'We must be more subtle, at least for now. I need the people to see I am continuing to be equitable in this matter. Let Sacred Wind carry on unopposed for the time being. However, whatever happens they must not play in the tournament. Are we clear about that?'

'Yes, my Lord,' the General said, bowing as he left the room.

'Pimple,' the Baron sighed, as the soldiers closed the door. 'I'd really like a glass of my celebratory edition of Nobflasher's ale. I'm assuming it's arrived?'

Pimple steeled himself for the torrent of abuse and fruit that was to likely come his way.

Outside in the city, the Sacred Wind wagon drew to a halt at the stage doors of the Grand Gateway Theatre. Oldfart jumped out and waved at the cheering crowd. 'Tonight we bring rock and metal to Chester!' he shouted, to more cheers.

'I think he's a frustrated showman, you know,' Smid said to Aiden. 'He just loves playing to the crowd.'

'Maybe you should let him get on stage with you at some point?' Aiden said.

'C'mon, sing with me Chester, "My Sword is my Sword, My Shield is my Shield",' Oldfart screeched, his voice wavering and quivering.

Smid gave Aiden a sideways glance and slowly shook his head 'Okay, maybe not, then,' said Aiden.

'Oldfart?' a tubby man with a pock-marked face shouted, running up to the wagon. 'Oldfart Olafson?'

'I am Oldfart,' Oldfart replied, shaking the man's hand.

'Freddie Fiddler, merchandising,' the tubby man said.

'Pleased to meet you Mr Fiddler. I assume everything is in order?'

'Absolutely!' Freddie replied, enthusiastically. 'We've got t-shirts, badges, plastic Viking helmets, plastic weapons, commemorative mugs, posters, battery-powered imitation flaming torches, stickers, coasters, key rings, patches and a collection of fake beards.'

'What about the consignment of "Blast from my Ass" underpants?'

'Didn't make it, I'm afraid. The supplier had a problem with his printing press.'

'Damn, I was really hoping that we'd have a run on those,' Oldfart said.

'Sacred Wind?' an officious-looking man with a clipboard and a large bag said.

'That's us,' Olaf answered, crossing his huge arms.

'Good,' the officious-looking man replied, pulling a bunch of lanyards out of his bag. 'Here are your "Access All Area" passes. Ensure you wear these at all times. Now, if you would please unload your equipment and transport it through the stage door, there's a designated area of the stage prepared for you. We'll be looking to start sound checking in about half an hour.'

'Cliff! Cliff!' Oriana shouted, emerging from the stage door as Cliff stepped out of the wagon.

'Oriana, you made it!' Cliff cried back, as the two sheep embraced warmly. 'Where are the others?'

'As far as I know they're headed for the palace,' Oriana said, as the rest of the Companionship gathered around. 'We're pretty sure that's where Ophelia is being held.'

'So it is Blacktie's doing, as we suspected,' Olaf said, unsheathing his sword. 'I say we go and provide them with some assistance.'

'No,' Oriana said, placing her hoof on the hilt of Olaf's sword. 'Cracky has devised a plan and we should give that a chance to work first. I know how you feel, Olaf, but let's give Cracky, Theo, Captain Marmaduke, Half-blind Ron and Humphrey some time.'

'Pardon me,' Aiden said, 'did you say "Humphrey"?'

'Yes,' Oriana replied. 'He joined us not long after we left Llangollen. He's a lovely dog, and so intelligent. You should be very proud of him'

'I should?'

'Of course, he's your friend, isn't he?'

'Hang on,' Aiden said. 'Where I'm from, I have an English Cocker Spaniel called Humphrey. But that happens to be in an entirely different reality.'

'I know, Humphrey explained that to me. He travelled here to find you. He was worried you might get into trouble without him.'

'How on earth do you know that?' Aiden asked.

'Because he told me. He's ever so eloquent, although he does use some big words that I don't always understand.'

'Are you telling me my little dog worked out how to cross space and time to find me, and has acquired the power of speech… and has a reasonably large vocabulary?'

'Yes,' Oriana replied, without any hint of surprise. 'He's a bit of a genius, actually. And a hero; he saved us from some nasty witches by battling them with their own magic.'

'Humphrey learned magic?'

'Yes, he has a photographic memory and he read a book on Ancient Welsh Witchenese.'

'This is incredible,' Aiden said. 'And now he's in the palace helping to free Ophelia?'

'Yes, and we must give him and the others time. We may risk exposing them if we simply blunder in.'

'Oriana's right,' Grundi said, lifting his guitar amplifier out of the wagon. 'Let's deal with the tournament first and Blacktie later.'

'Yes, you must do that,' Oriana said. 'Because we also believe we have found out why Blacktie wants the cheese mine.'

As Oriana explained Cracky's discovery, the Companionship listened with wide-eyed amazement. 'So, my cheese mine contains the most magic cheese that has ever been?' Agnar said.

'We believe so,' she replied, 'But only when it's eaten with Mathonwy's Chutney. Cracky reckons the Baron must have a jar. We also believe Hob and Nob succeeded in obtaining a sample of Ceridwen's Cheese from the mine, and that they've already given this to the Baron.'

'Well, things are certainly falling into place now,' Oldfart said. 'And if we don't win the tournament, that mine will legally be Blacktie's.'

'In which case we better go and win,' said Smid, grabbing his bass guitar.

'And we better hope Cracky and the others can stop the Baron having supper,' Mr Kneepatcher said, with a worried look.

As the Companionship continued to unload their equipment from the wagon, Oriana noticed that several of the group were missing. 'Where's Charles?' she asked Cliff.

Cliff drew in a deep breath, in readiness for a fresh flow of his own tears and in preparation for them to be joined by Oriana's.

'We must tell Henry and the others. Poor Charles,' she said, wiping her eyes with her hoof after Cliff told her the sad news.

'There's also something else I need to discuss with Henry,' Cliff added, producing the book containing the score that Charles had completed. 'And I've got a feeling it could be very important.'

Inside the theatre, the atmosphere of excitement was tangible. The Grand Gateway was an imposing venue, much larger than the equivalent building in Aiden's reality. The huge stage was already full of equipment and the first act had begun sound checking.

The mixing console was situated towards the rear of the lower tier of seats, and engineers were busy twiddling knobs and adjusting slider controls. Two further tiers of seats arched upwards and were flanked by galleries of executive and royal boxes. A gigantic chandelier hung from the ornately-crafted ceiling, providing a spectacular illuminated centrepiece for the venue.

Aiden wandered over to the huge mixing desk as an engineer was plugging in various coloured cables. 'Oh, excuse me, I'm the mixing engineer for Sacred Wind,' he said. 'Is it okay for me to have a look around the desk?'

'Help yourself, mate,' an engineer with a large spot on his nose said. 'Have you used anything like this before?'

'Once or twice. It's a bit of a beast isn't it?'

'And temperamental,' the engineer replied. 'Over the last couple of days there are times I'd swear it's either got a mind of its own or it's haunted. But that's just silly, isn't it. I mean, electrical appliances being possessed, ridiculous.'

'Quite,' Aiden replied, raising an eyebrow. 'What do I need to watch out for?'

'Well, the slider on channel 12 often moves up and down by itself. And it has a nasty habit of whacking up the gain knob on channel 16, but only when we put bass guitar through it. That's pretty odd. And something really bizarre happened yesterday. We were at an event in a community centre and this old lady was cleaning around the place with a vacuum cleaner, after the gig had finished. Anyway, as soon as she got close to the desk all the lights started flashing, sliders moved up and down and some of the cables disconnected themselves. If I didn't know better, I'd swear it was excited.'

'Really?'

The engineer wandered off to the stage, leaving Aiden alone by the mixing desk. 'Have we met before by any chance?' he said, under his breath.

'Might have done,' the mixing desk said, nonchalantly.

'And would I be right in thinking the last time we met you had taken up residence in a vacuum cleaner?'

'Maybe,' said the mixing desk. 'I'm a free spirit and I do get around a bit.'

'Well, my friends have a very important night ahead of them and I'd really rather not have any trouble with the mixing desk.'

'I see,' the mixing desk said, smugly. 'So, I guess you'd better be nice to me.'

'Or I could simply exorcise you again.'

'Hey, no fair! I was floating between bloody dimensions for what seemed like an eternity last time. That kind of thing can really stress you out.'

'But you were causing havoc and scaring people half to death. That vacuum cleaner was levitating and speaking in tongues,' Aiden almost shouted, as he waved at another engineer who was giving him odd looks.

'I'm just very misunderstood,' the mixing desk said. 'I've got issues.'

'Oh, so now you're after sympathy?'

'Not really sympathy, just acknowledgement that even evil, discarnate entities need love and understanding. Maybe I just need a hug.'

'You're winding me up now, aren't you?'

'Not at all. Maybe that's why I'm so mischievous and ill-behaved. I'm starved of affection.'

'Well I'm not surprised when you go around possessing people's electrical appliances,' Aiden said. 'If it's affection you're after I suggest you rethink your social strategy.'

'But it's all I know. Maybe I just need a bit of stimulus to help me change my ways. It's got to be worth a try.'

'So you want me to hug you?'

'Please, it would mean so much,' the mixing desk said, its little lights blinking in anticipation.

Aiden bent down and laid his head on the console, spreading his arms out as far as they would go. 'Are you alright, mate?' one of the engineers shouted to him.

'Oh, yes, just fine. I'm just having a closer look at the controls. I'm a bit short-sighted,' he replied.

'Could you say you love me?' the mixing desk said.

'What?'

'Say you love me. Look, I can feel goodness stirring in my essence. Please give it a go.'

'Okay,' Aiden said. 'I love you,'

'Oh, say it again, please. That felt so nice. A little bit louder.'

'I love you, I love you,' Aiden said, stroking the console affectionately.

'Ay, mate, are you sure you're alright?' said the engineer, who was now standing next to the desk.

'Er, of course,' Aiden said, standing up sharply. 'I was just trying to get a bond with the mixing desk. I've found it helps the performance, you know.'

'It's a bleedin' mixing desk, mate, not a horse,' the engineer said, shaking his head and mouthing the word 'prat' as he walked back to the stage.

'Right, did that make a difference?' Aiden whispered to the mixing desk, when the engineer was out of earshot.

'Oh, not at all, but you looked absolutely hilarious. That's the best laugh I've had in millennia!'

'Why you devious, conniving, little sod!' Aiden screamed, his right hand forming a first.

'Hey, easy now, big fella,' the mixing desk said. 'Don't do anything you might regret.'

'Had a fall out, have you?' the engineer shouted from the stage, before turning to his friend. 'That guy's a bit of a nutter; we'll have to keep an eye on him.'

'No, no. All fine here!' Aiden shouted, waving. 'Just stubbed my toe.'

Aiden did his best to regain his composure. He wasn't used to being made a fool of by a mixing desk. 'So that whole thing about affection was just a put on?'

'Yeah, I'm afraid so. Hey, you have to admit I'm a pretty good actor, though.'

'Oh, absolutely. If they ever have awards for the "Best Lying Bastard Mixing Desk" you'll be a cert to win it.'

'Now look, I had to get you back for that exorcism malarkey. Why don't we call it quits? I actually quite like you,' the mixing desk said, with apparent sincerity.

'Or I can just exorcise you again. That seems eminently appropriate to me.'

'You could, but those engineers already think you're a couple of sandwiches short of a picnic. My bet is you'd be escorted out the door by security faster than a cheese-sniffer.'

'Okay, you have a point.,' Aiden said. 'We appear to be at an impasse.'

'Or... we could strike a deal.'

'What kind of deal?'

'Well, if truth be told, being a mixing desk isn't anywhere near as much fun as being a vacuum cleaner. There's the mobility issue for a start. This thing's an absolute bugger to levitate. It really zaps the old energy, I'm sure you can imagine.'

'Of course,' Aiden replied.

'So, I promise to behave impeccably for the evening if you get me a nice vacuum cleaner later on.'

'How can I trust you after the stunt you've just pulled?'

'Demon's honour,' the mixing desk said.

As Aiden mulled over the offer, Olaf and Oldfart ran over from the stage. 'Right, we're all set up. Are you ready to start sound checking?' Olaf said.

'Oh, right. Of course,' Aiden replied, giving the thumbs up.

'We're going to have an amazing sound with this set up,' Oldfart enthused, as he and Olaf made their way back to the stage.

'Demon's honour?' Aiden said, looking at the desk.

'Demon's honour,' the mixing desk replied, with a flash of blinking lights.

'Okay, you're on.'

CHAPTER 40 – IT'S A FULL HOUSE, MY LORD

'How do I look, Pimple?' the Baron said, as he twirled in the throne room, his ceremonial red, velvet cloak twirling obediently with him.

'Simply stunning, my Lord. You have reached new levels of imperiousness.'

'Thank you, Pimple. I do so enjoy looking my best at the opening ceremony. My people deserve nothing less.'

'Absolutely, my Lord.'

'And what do you think, dear Queen Ophelia?' he said to the Queen, who was still locked in the cage at the rear of the room.

'Oh, you look divine, dear Baron,' she replied.

'Really?'

'No, of course not. You look like an overdressed, jumped up, little despot with bad wind who's going to get his just desserts later on!'

'Ha! I see you've not lost your spirit yet, dear Queen. However, it's not "just desserts" I'll be getting afterwards,' the Baron said, lifting a silver platter to reveal the glistening mixture of Ceridwen's Cheese and Mathonwy's Chutney, 'it's going to be a charming little snack for supper.'

A guard entered the throne room and stamped his spear on the floor. 'My Lord, I have been sent to inform you that The Cestrian Music Tournament awaits your esteemed presence.'

'Excellent,' the Baron said. 'How is the crowd?'

'It is a full house, my Lord, and they are most joyful.'

'Good, good. Now, Pimple, have the guards been informed not to let anyone enter the throne room until we return?'

'Yes, my Lord,' Pimple replied, as he grabbed the back of the Baron's cloak and lifted it off the ground. 'We have two of our most sadistic guards on the door. They are qualified in flaying, knuckle crushing and extreme tortures, such as basket weave flesh-knitting. If anyone attempts to enter they are likely to lose several limbs… or worse.'

***

Captain Marmaduke stroked Half-Blind Ron's head with his paw, as the old cat slept. The dingy cell was very damp, with constant drips of water running down the cold walls. Fortunately, they had found some dry straw and had made a small bed for Ron to rest on while he recuperated.

'That wound does look to be settling down now, and the bleeding has stopped,' the Captain said to Theo. 'I really hope the old fellow pulls through.'

'I thought you found him irritating?' Theo said, somewhat surprised at the affection displayed by the Captain.

'Well, he can get my hackles up on occasion, I admit. But he really is a quite a character. And he's got some spirit for an old moggy.'

Captain Marmaduke had been in the service of the Prince since Theo was a kitten. He had always prided himself on his loyalty to the royal family and considered it an honour to be Theo's personal guard, and one of his closest friends. He enlisted in the Feline Military when he was barely out of kittenhood and quickly rose through the ranks. Due to his great size, fierce fighting ability, tactical nous and colour he soon joined the crack army division the Special Cat Service (SCS), or 'The Fighting Ginger Toms', as they were generally known. He took part in many covert campaigns, including the infamous 'Bulldog Gorge', where he and only four other cats fought valiantly against a wild horde of Bull Mastiffs from Cynwyd Forest. Following a raid on Mr Pooch's Pet Store, the pack was high on dog treats and specially-formulated dog food, and was threatening to overrun the city. Captain Marmaduke and his troops heroically clung onto their necks and scratched them severely, sending them howling into the night. This campaign earned him the prestigious 'Pussy Cross' medal, the highest military honour any feline can receive.

Half-blind Ron stretched out his front legs and opened his eyes, for the first time since Velvet had dealt him a potentially life-threatening blow. 'Ow, me head. What happened?'

'Easy now, old chap, you've been badly injured,' the Captain said.

'Oh, now I remember,' Ron said, stretching again. 'Where did that bloody ferret come from? I'll give her such a pasting when I see her again.'

'You should rest,' Theo said. 'We'll deal with the ferret as soon as we manage to get out of this cell.'

'Fair enough,' Ron said, as his eyes began to close once more. 'Has anyone got any chicken on them, though?'

Cracky was peering through the bars on the tiny cell door window. Surprisingly there were no guards visible and, apart from the occasional moan or scream, the corridor was quiet. 'You know, I'm actually considering doing something I've not tried for a long time to get us out of this predicament,' he said.

'Meaning?' Theo said.

'Magic.'

'Do you really think you could?'

'Potentially, although I'll be the first to admit there would be a bit of a risk.'

'How much of a risk?' Theo said, with concern.

'Well, I've never tried to break a door down before. I'm not even sure I'd know the right words.'

'You may as well give it a go. I mean, we won't achieve anything while we're stuck in here, and what's the worst that can happen?'

'I could bring the entire cell down on top of us.'

'Ah, now that wouldn't be good.'

'No, it wouldn't,' Cracky said, turning to look at the three cats. 'Now, look, I'm willing to give this a try if you'll forgive me if we all get crushed by rocks.'

'I'll forgive you if you cook me a very special whole chicken to myself,' Half-blind Ron said, narrowly opening his eyes. Theo and Captain Marmaduke simply nodded.

Cracky drew in a deep breath and raised his arms into the air. Closing his eyes, he pointed the palms of his hands at the door... and it flew off its hinges, hitting the wall opposite.

'Well done, Cracky,' Theo said. 'That was astounding.'

'But I didn't even say any words,' Cracky said, in disbelief.

'In this instance no words were necessary,' said Humphrey, popping his head around the remains of the door frame. 'It's so nice to see you all again, and may I introduce my friend, Grunt, who's kindly removed the door for us.'

Grunt sheepishly peeped into the cell, waving his huge hand. 'Grunt pleased to meet you,' he said.

'I thought it was too good to be true,' Cracky smiled, patting Humphrey on the head and giving Grunt the thumbs up.

'Well done, Humphrey,' Theo said, licking Humphrey's ear. 'We should get out of here quickly now, that noise may have alerted someone.'

'Agreed,' said Cracky. 'But there's no way Half-blind Ron can travel. He's far too weak and that wound could open up again.'

'You're right,' Theo agreed. 'And more to the point we shouldn't really leave him here alone.'

'That's absolutely correct, Your Highness,' Captain Marmaduke said. 'And you're probably not going to like what I have to say next.'

Theo put his head on one side, pensively looking at the Captain. 'Go on.'

'Well, Your Highness, we are reaching the point in our endeavours when fighting prowess is going to come to the fore, would you not agree?'

'I'll admit that it's a likelihood,' Theo said. 'And I'm perfectly capable of defending myself, Captain.'

'Agreed, Your Highness, but I fear that you would be no match for a nasty, devious ferret. As your appointed guard, I politely request that you stay here, for your own safety and to protect Half-blind Ron.'

'But you're not actually making a request, are you?' Theo said.

'No, Your Highness. In this instance I think I'm insisting.'

'Captain Marmaduke's logic is impeccable,' Humphrey said. 'Meaning no disrespect, Prince Theo, you are better equipped to take care of Half-blind Ron and the Captain is better equipped for any battles we may encounter.'

Theo looked down at the floor, resigned that his friend's conclusions were indeed the correct course of action. 'Very well,' he said, raising his head. 'You go now with my fondest wishes for victory.'

'Thank you, Your Highness,' Captain Marmaduke said, saluting. 'It's time this Fighting Ginger Tom exercised a bit of good old-fashioned retribution. I just hope that ferret's up for a fight when I'm looking into the yellow of her eyes.'

'Good luck,' Half-blind Ron said weakly, as they moved towards the door. 'Don't forget my Chicken, Cracky.'

'Take care, old friend,' Theo said, warmly embracing the Captain and licking the top of his head. 'And make sure you return in one piece.'

'Come this way,' Grunt said, pointing down the corridor. 'Grunt knows secret ways around the palace.'

***

News of the death of Charles Corriedale was greeted with an outpouring of grief by the members of the OSO. Charles had not only been a founder member but had always been a mentor to all of the musicians. His kindly ways and knowledge of music had provided inspiration to several generations of sheep.

'He should get his own statue,' Edna Curlyback (violin) said.

'Absolutely,' agreed Wyn Downeyfleece (cello). 'And we should write a concerto for him.'

'But what do we do about tonight's performance?' Cecil Curlyback (French horn and husband of Edna) said. 'How can we continue without him?'

'I think we all know the answer to that,' Cliff said. 'My uncle would always want the show to go on. In fact we can dedicate tonight's performance to him… well, one of our performances.'

'One of our performances? What do you mean, Cliff?' Henry Fluffywool said. 'We are only allowed to perform one piece of music.'

'Yes, I know,' Cliff replied. 'Henry, many things have happened on our journey here. Oriana and I have learned that there are grander plans being played out. I think it's about time we told you what we've discovered.'

Henry and the rest of the OSO sat in silence while Cliff and then Oriana related their respective tales of the journey, and of the Baron's dastardly scheme. Eyes were wide and many of the sheep were visibly shaken as the stories were told.

'That's quite incredible,' Henry said, shaking his fleece. 'If what you say is true then we should not play tonight. After all, there is no way that Sacred Wind can win this competition if we play as we can.'

'Well, for a start, I wouldn't say that's an absolute certainty,' Cliff said, as Henry turned up his nose at the reply. 'Sacred Wind are much better than you give them credit for, but I think you already know that; certainly, Charles did.'

'Dear Charles did have some unusual musical tastes,' Henry replied, his tone softening.

'And he also had some inspired ideas,' Cliff said, pulling out the book containing the transcription Charles had given him and handing it to Henry.

Henry flicked through the musical score, deftly scanning the pages, the look of incredulity on his face increasing as he did so. 'You cannot be serious.'

'It was Charles's dying wish, Henry. It's something he'd dreamed of for a long time. You've only got to look at the painstaking detail he's gone to with the arrangement.'

'No, I cannot countenance this, Cliff. And anyway, I doubt the rules would allow it.'

'I've already checked,' Cliff said. 'The rules make no mention of band members; it is purely the name of the entrants.'

'But we've never even rehearsed it, and anyway how do we know that Sacred Wind would agree to a joint venture such as this?'

'They already have,' Cliff replied. 'The decision lies very much with us.'

CHAPTER 41 – MAY THE BEST CONTESTANT WIN!

'Ladies, gentlemen and sheep, are you ready to be entertained?!' the short announcer standing in the middle of the stage screeched, to deafening cheers.

'Tonight,' he continued, lowering his voice, 'we bring you seven glorious musical acts, each of whom wishes to be crowned the Cestrian Music Tournament Champions of 1987. So, please welcome to the stage our contestants; I give you Willie Barebum... Rip Cotton and the Holy Socks... Kyleene Mingin... the Cestrian Baroque Ensemble... The Knights of Flatulence... the Oswestry Sheep Orchestra... and, for the first time, tonight's extravaganza will have a touch of rock... I give you Sacred Wind!'

The audience went wild as the contestants walked onto the stage. Many in the crowd were waving imitation swords, axes and torches, and quite a few had purchased the plastic Viking helmets. Somewhat surprisingly fake beard sales had also been high, even with the ladies.

'Oldfart doesn't miss a trick when it comes to merchandising,' Smid observed to Grundi.

'And, to judge tonight's tournament,' the announcer continued, 'will you please put your hands together for our three judges. I give you, from Clover Music Management, Paddy McLeprechaun; local singer-made-good, Shirley Divastropalot; and the Head of Dee Records himself, Mr Colin Mowsell!'

A large spotlight zoomed in on one of the theatre boxes to the left of the stage, as the judge's waves were met by resounding applause and several wolf whistles.

'But, before proceedings get underway, I'd like to hand you over to our imperious leader,' the announcer said. 'This is the man who makes Chester tick; the man to whom we owe so much; a man of supreme intelligence, supreme modesty, supreme virility, and supreme wind; a man who has the needs of his people at the forefront of his mind at all times; a man who would shed blood to keep our city free from undesirables, and from people who cannot control their own bodily gasses or resist sniffing another's cheese. Yes, this is a man who needs no introduction. Please show your appreciation for the one, the only, BARON BLACKTIE!!'

As a man, woman and sheep the audience stood to applaud, turning in reverence towards the Royal Box. There were a few cheers, Aiden noticed, but it did appear the applause was a tad forced. However, there was not one person in the venue who failed to join in.

'My wonderful citizens,' the Baron said, rising to his feet and raising his hands aloft. 'I cannot tell you what an honour it is to be here tonight. Whenever I am in your presence my heart is filled with delight, my head is giddy with love and my bowels long to bless you all!'

More applause and increased cheering, including a couple of whoops from a fat man with a large nose and a flagon of ale.

'And I'd like to wish a warm welcome to all of the contestants,' the Baron continued. 'And in particular to our friends from Llangollen, Sacred Wind.'

Tremendous applause and weapon waving from the audience.

'The inclusion of a rock band this year aptly demonstrates our appreciation of diverse musical forms. So, let the tournament begin and may the best contestant win!'

The Baron sat down to more applause from the audience and scowls from Sacred Wind. 'I'll stay and watch the opening act, Pimple, but then I think I'll return to the palace. Although I'm sure General Darkblast will see to it that those Vikings don't get anywhere near their instruments later, I feel that the little snack waiting for me should be consumed as a contingency. And then the fun can really begin.'

'Of course, my Lord.'

'But,' the announcer roared, 'before our seven contestants fling themselves into musical battle for the first prize, which includes a one-album record deal with Dee Records, it gives me great pleasure to introduce our special guests for the evening. Bringing their own unique musical style of *"Chanting Ska"*, and performing their new single, *"Bad Habits"*, will you please show your appreciation for The Harmonic Monks!'

***

Sergeant Savagebreath looked out from the ramparts of the West Gate to a tranquil scene. Spotlights scoured the area, but everything seemed to be as quiet as a mouse who had taken a vow of silence.

'Sergeant, how looks it?' General Darkblast said, as he arrived with four of the larger members of the Knights of Flatulence.

'General,' Sergeant Savagebreath said, saluting, 'I would have thought you'd have been cheering on our musicians in the tournament.'

'Oh, I'll wander back to see the lads perform later,' the General replied. 'They're fifth in the running order and I can't say I'm a fan of any of the first four acts. Besides, I want to check that nothing unexpected happens. The East Gate appears calm, it's unlikely that the North Gate will be threatened due to the security cameras and the South Gate is completely closed.'

'Well, it's all quiet here, sir' the Sergeant said. 'Did you manage to apprehend Sacred Wind?'

'No, the Baron gave orders that we should allow them safe passage to the tournament. However, you can rest assured they'll not actually get to play... and I think it's most unlikely that they'll leave.'

'I had heard they are great warriors, General. Are you not concerned there could be some trouble later?'

'I think that's highly unlikely, Sergeant. You see they're not really into violence, as it happens. They may have very large weapons, but they're just a right bunch of posers.'

'It sounds like you're speaking from some experience there, sir,' said the Sergeant.

'Well, I had a run in with their lead singer, Olaf the Berserker, a few years ago. He entered a swordsmanship competition and we met in the semi-final.'

'Where I assume you gave him a damn good thrashing, sir?'

'Actually, it was closer than you may imagine, Sergeant. In fact there are some who said he should have got the decision.'

'May I ask what happened, sir?'

The General looked out over the ramparts into the still night, compiling his recollections. 'It was a fierce contest, and I'll admit he is a first-class swordsman. Anyway, we were level on the scorecard when, after a particularly long and draining exchange, he felled me with one of the mightiest blows I have ever felt. It nearly broke my sword in two. However, he refused to strike while I was on the floor and twirled his sword in an act of showmanship waiting for me to rise. While he was off his guard, I struck a blow which knocked the sword out of his hand. I rose quickly to my feet and, with the point of my sword at his chest, he had no option but to yield.'

'So it was a noble act that saw him suffer defeat?' said the Sergeant.

'Well, that's one way of looking at it,' the General said, sniffing the air in disdain. 'But I feel he paid the price for not having a killer instinct... or just being a poser.'

'Quite obviously, sir.'

'So, as everything seems to be in order here I'll head back into the city, Sergeant', the General said, saluting. 'Keep up the good work.'

'Right you are, sir,' the saluting Sergeant replied.

As the General disappeared from sight, a puffing Corporal Bluster appeared at the front gate. 'Let me in quickly, I beg you!' he screamed.

'What's the matter man? You look like you've seen a herd of ogres!' the Sergeant yelled.

'Worse, sir. There's an army of pigs coming this way.'

'By my scruffy beard, open the gates and let him in!' the Sergeant bellowed.

'And it gets worse still, sir.'

'Worse?' the Sergeant said.

'Yes, sir, they're carrying placards.'

'Private,' the Sergeant shouted, at a small man with an oversize spear, 'get word to the General immediately. Inform him we are about to encounter demonstrating pigs.'

'Yes, Sergeant.'

***

'So, a massive round of applause for the unique sound of The Harmonic Monks!' the announcer in the theatre roared. 'But if you were confused, don't worry, so was I.'

'And now it's time for the moment you've all been waiting for,' he continued. 'Yes, our first act tonight has been ploughing his trade on the Wirral Country & Western circuit for nearly fifty years. His life has been a series of disasters, which has fortunately provided him with a wealth of lyrical material for his mournful, and some would say downright depressing, compositions. And I should point out that we do have attendant members of the Samaritans at the end of each aisle if anyone is particularly badly affected by his music. But now, singing *"My Dog is Sick"* put your hands together for the one and, thankfully, the only Willie Barebum!'

As Willie shuffled onto the stage, acoustic guitar in hand, the crowd clapped warmly, and indeed several tears were already being shed when he sat down on the specially prepared tall stool. 'Howdy, y'all,' Willie said, doffing his Stetson. 'This is based on a true story.'

And then he started to play.

Mah dog is sick, and he's real small
He's got sore ears, and he's got sore balls
It makes me sad watching him die
As he tries to eat some blueberry pie

Mah dog is sick, he's on the wane
His mind has gone, and he's got no name
His bladder's weak, it's a disgrace

Andy Coffey

When I'm in bed, he pees on my face

So here's to mah sick doggy
He's in so much pain
And sometimes I feel
That it's me to blame
His teeth fall out
When he gnaws on bones
But mah sick doggy
I still love him so

Mah dog is sick, in fact he's dead
So now I'm crying, as I hold his head
But I've still got fond memories
And now I've also got all his fleas

More warm applause and tears followed Willie's performance, and even the judges appeared to be moved as the announcer asked them for their opinion. 'Well, I liked it,' said Paddy McLeprechaun, blowing his nose, 'but if I have one criticism I think it could have been emotive.'

'Are you serious, Paddy?' Colin Mowsel said, wiping his eyes with a silk handkerchief. 'The poor man's dog has died and he's telling us the story. How much more emotive can it be?'

'He could have mentioned some more of the dog's maladies in the lyrics, that's all I'm saying,' Paddy said.

'Oh, please,' Colin Mowsel replied, turning his eyes upwards.

'Well,' Paddy said to Willie, 'did the dog have any other problems?'

'He did indeed, sir,' Willie replied. 'He was deaf, he had an in-growing toenail, he only had three legs, and he could only bark in Welsh.'

'Oh, was your dog from Wales?' Shirley Divastropalot asked.

'No, ma'am, he was from the Wirral. That's what made it so darned sad; none of the other dogs could understand him.'

'Anyway,' the announcer interrupted, 'thanks to our judges for their comments. And remember, the judges' scoring is kept a strict secret until all the contestants have performed. So, without further ado, please give a rapturous Grand Gateway Theatre welcome to our second act. Bringing their own brand of religious rock and roll for our pleasure, and singing what they hope will be their debut single, *"Rock Around The Font"*, it's Rip Cotton and the Holy Socks!'

***

'Now, now, go about your business if you please,' Sergeant Savagebreath shouted, to the several hundred pigs standing outside the West Gate. 'There's a special event on in the city, so you may as well come back and protest at another time.'

'We know full well what event is taking place in the city and we've come to assist our friends if they get in trouble,' Archie Backrasher yelled.

'And which friends are these?' the Sergeant asked.

'The Companionship of Wind and my Daddy Smid!' Crusher shouted. 'And if you don't let us in, why we'll huff and we'll puff and we'll flatten your bloody gate!'

The troops on the ramparts looked very ill at ease and shuffled about nervously, listening and watching the scene below. Sergeant Savagebreath knew there are times when diplomacy is called for. He knew that brute force isn't always the answer to resolving disagreements. He knew that tact and placatory words could calm an otherwise dangerous scenario, and could be powerful tools for peace. He knew all this but, unfortunately, it very rarely crossed his mind to put any of it into practice. 'I'd like to see you try, you mud-wallowing porkers!' he bawled.

So they did.

Several hundred rampaging pigs can pack a fair punch, and they were more than a match for the West Gate. 'Oh, bugger,' Sergeant Savagebreath said, as the West Gate lay in pieces and the pigs stampeded into the city.

'Sergeant, what do we do?!' Corporal Bluster shouted. 'We're no match for their trotters and placards.'

'Tell the General it's bad news,' the Sergeant said. 'Chops are off the menu. And get reinforcements to the theatre, immediately.'

Meanwhile, on a nearby hillock, one of General Beef Madras-Wholegrain Rice's reconnaissance Naan breads watched the scene, with specially adapted field glasses.

'Inform command that the West Gate has fallen and that the pigs are in the city,' he said into his walkie-talkie. 'If we move now we will face only minimal resistance.'

CHAPTER 42 – DO WE TURN LEFT OR RIGHT AT THE CITY GATES?

'Damn it, there are two guards on the door,' Cracky said, as he peeped around the corner of the corridor leading to the throne room. 'And they look pretty nasty.'

'Grunt go and speak to guards,' Grunt said. 'Grunt often find people can be reasonable if you talk to them nicely.'

'And if they're not reasonable?' Captain Marmaduke said.

'Grunt will explain that reasonableness and understanding make world a better place. Grunt will also say time for pain is over and that it much better to live in peace and harmony.'

'And if they still won't listen?' the Captain said.

'Then Grunt will crush, break and rip,' Grunt said, with a sigh.

The corridor was quiet, the only noise being the occasional shouts from Queen Ophelia for help. The two guards ignored her cries and looked menacingly from side to side, their hands twitching.

'I'm bored with all of this,' said Guard number 1, who had a very large, studded ring in his nose. 'I wanna go and hurt something.'

'Yeah, I know what you mean,' said Guard number 2, who had a very large cross hanging from his ear and a tattoo that said 'Mum' on his arm. 'I've just finished reading about a new knitting pattern and I'm dying to get hold of someone to try it out on. I've not had blood on me knitting needles for over a week.'

Grunt ambled slowly up the corridor and was quickly spotted by the two guards. 'Ay, big fella, how's it going?' Guard 1 said, waving.

Grunt said nothing until he was stood in front of them. Then he smiled his biggest toothiest smile. 'Grunt here to do favour for friends.'

'What's that then?' Guard 2 said.

'Grunt need guards to go away so friends can rescue nice Queen from cage in throne room.'

The two guards exchanged bemused glances and tightened the grip on their very large axes. 'Are you having a joke with us, big fella? Is this Grunt humour we're seeing?' Guard 1 said, laughing.

'No, Grunt is deadly serious.' Grunt said, bowing his head slightly. 'Baron is being nasty to Grunt's new friends, so Grunt need to intervene.'

'Intervene, eh?' Guard 1 said, laughing again. 'That's a big word for you. I'm willing to bet you don't know what it means.'

'Actually, Grunt is picking his vocabulary very carefully so guards will understand. If Grunt had said that the Baron's pernicious and rapacious doctrine of megalomaniacal domination needs to be curtailed before our freedoms are perpetually nullified and we are plunged into an ever-increasing spiral of despair and desolation, finally leaving us in an interminable morass of negated morals and obligatory subservience, Grunt not sure guards would know what Grunt means.'

'Now that was impressive,' Humphrey whispered to Cracky, as they hid at the end of the corridor.

'Er, yeah, you've got a point there,' Guard 2 said.

'So will guards leave door now, please? Grunt think it would be much better if guards live harmoniously in state of Nirvana.'

'We'll have to think about that,' Guard 1 said. 'I mean are we allowed to torture people in this Nirvana place?'

'No,' Grunt said.

'What about a bit of maiming?' said Guard 2, looking concerned.

'No.'

'Eye-poking?'

'No.'

'Nipple-twisting?'

'No.'

'Not even Chinese Burns?'

'No,' Grunt said again, shaking his head.

'Well, I'm not sure we want to live harmoniously in Nirvana if we can't hurt anything,' Guard 1 said.

'Guards will have to learn,' Grunt said. 'Make for a better, kinder world. Hurting things not good.'

'And what if we refuse, then?' Guard 2 said, defiantly.

'Then Grunt will have to rip off guard's legs and arms, and smash guard's skulls,' Grunt said, apologetically.

'Er, that doesn't sound very harmonious,' Guard 1 said.

'No, Grunt agrees. But sometimes search for peace and everlasting harmony in world mean going through pain first.'

The two guards exchanged animated whispers for several seconds and then nodded to each other. 'We've decided we want to keep our arms and legs,' Guard 1 said. 'And keep our skulls intact,' added Guard 2. 'So we'll take your advice and seek harmony in Nirvana.'

'Grunt pleased. Guards make right choice.'

'Oh, one last thing,' Guard 1 said, as they walked off down the corridor, 'do we turn left or right at the city gates?'

'Grunt not know what guards mean.' Grunt said.

'To get to Nirvana. Do we turn left or right?'

'Grunt suggest guards just keep walking. Guards will know when they find it.'

***

Rip Cotton and the Holy Socks left the stage to rapturous applause, with the audience won over by their blend of energetic rock and roll and some great special effects, including the lowering onto the stage of a giant font for the band to rock around. 'What about that then!' the announcer cried. 'A real rock and roll baptism if ever I saw one. Judges, over to you.'

'Well, it was all a bit cheesy, wasn't it? Colin Mowsel said. 'And I don't know what that font was all about.'

'The song was called *"Rock Around The Font"*, Colin. And that's what they were doing,' the announcer retorted.

'I didn't like it,' Paddy McLeprechaun said, as the audience booed. 'It was all a bit too mad for me.'

'Are you boys serious? I loved them!' Shirley Divastropalot said, to roars from the crowd. 'They can come and rock around my font anytime!'

'Oh, and have you got a font, then, Shirley?' Paddy asked, with more than a hint of sarcasm.

'No, but I've got my super-duper-mega-ultra-celeb birthday party coming up soon, and I'm going to get one… in pink!'

General Darkblast was at the back of the hall, looking around the theatre with eagle eyes. 'Any sign of those pigs yet?' he asked one of the guards.

'No, sir. But we've got reinforcements at the end of the road. It's cordoned off, they'll never make it through.'

'Good,' the General said. 'I've a feeling in my bones that we've not seen the last of the troubles for tonight. We all need to keep vigilant.'

'Right then, next up we've got the Queen of Pop herself,' the announcer shouted. 'She told me beforehand that if she gets any happier she's likely to explode, and I'm sure many of us would agree this would be an excellent addition to her stage show. So, I hope you're all ready to get off your seats and get those feet dancing, as I introduce to you, singing *"Bouncin' for your Love"*, the little ball of energy that is Kyleene Mingin!'

'Hello, Chester!' a small blond lady in a bikini shouted, as she ran on stage. 'Are you ready to have some fun?!'

Bouncin', bouncin', bouncin' for your love
I'm jumping up and down and I'm really quite excited
Bouncin', bouncin', bouncin' for your love
I wanna bounce around with you

I look into your eyes and I get kind of dreamy
I get a funny feeling all over my bikini
I wanna be your girl and take you back to my place
We can dance all night, and I can bounce on your face

You're just a boy and I'm just a girl
So let's get together now and twirl till we hurl
Cause I'm...

Bouncin', bouncin', bouncin' for your love
I'm jumping up and down and I'm really quite excited
Bouncin', bouncin', bouncin' for your love
I wanna bounce around with you

I think you're so cool; you've got a lovely hairdo
So let's get out of here, oh go on I dare you
I wanna make you mine and lock you up forever
You're so very sweet, so I'm gonna call you Trevor

I'm just a girl and you're just a boy
So stay with me tonight and be my cuddly toy
Cause I'm...

Bouncin', bouncin', bouncin' for your love
I'm jumping up and down and I'm really quite excited
Bouncin', bouncin', bouncin' for your love
I'll cook you cheese on toast and I promise to use white bread
Bouncin', bouncin', bouncin' for your love
Please don't run away, there's no reason to be frightened
Bouncin', bouncin', bouncin' for your love
Yes, I wanna bounce around with you
Cause it's the only thing that I can do
Yes I haven't really got a clue
What I'll do if I can't bounce with you
Tonight!!!

'Well, well, well,' the announcer said, as the audience went wild. 'I don't think she'll have any problem getting a date after that performance, will she judges?'

'Can I just say I thought that was genius, sheer genius,' Colin Mowsel said, to great applause. 'Did you write the lyrics, my love?'

'I did! I did!' Kyleene said, jumping up and down, clapping her hands.

'Wonderful, you should be a poet.'

'Kyleene!' an excited Paddy McLeprechaun shouted. 'I think you're the one to watch in this tournament. That was fantastic!'

'Ooh, thank you Paddy!' Kyleene yelled, bouncing around the stage. 'Can I come up there and kiss you?'

'No.'

'Well, there were some tuning issues, my dear,' said a more subdued Shirley Divastropalot. 'Particularly in the chorus,' she added, to boos from the crowd. 'And you really should get a bigger bikini.'

***

'Guards gone now,' Grunt said. 'Friends can come out.'

'That was excellent work, Grunt,' Cracky said, as they rushed down the corridor to the throne room door. 'But do you think the guards will say anything?'

'Grunt not sure. But Grunt think guards now learning wisdom, and wisdom help guards keep their arms and legs.'

'Damn, the door's locked,' Cracky said, as he turned the handle.

Grunt pulled his huge arms back and slammed both fists into the door. It fell inwards with a mighty crash. 'Grunt have spare key,' he said, smiling.

Ophelia screamed with joy as she saw them enter the room. Grunt stayed by the door to keep watch. 'Right, then, my Queen, let's get you out of that cage,' Cracky said, fiddling with the lock.

'Oh, Cracky, it's wonderful to see you all,' Ophelia said. 'Have you got my comb?'

'Er, no, Your Majesty. We haven't got it with us but I believe it's not too far away.'

'And who is this lovely doggy?' the Queen said, as she came out of the cage and hugged Cracky.

'My name is Humphrey, Your Majesty, and I'm delighted to make your acquaintance.'

'You can talk?!'

'Oh, he can do much more than that, Your Majesty,' Cracky said, with a wink. 'Now, let's make our escape before we're spotted.'

'Wait, we must take this with us,' Ophelia said, as she went over to the small table near the throne and picked up the platter containing the pieces of Ceridwen's Cheese and Mathonwy's Chutney.

'Is that what I think it is?' Cracky asked.

'You mean you know about the *"Cheese and Chutney Surprise"*?'

'Fortunately, yes,' Cracky replied. 'It's the only reason the Baron wanted Sacred Wind in the tournament. He just wants to get his hands on their cheese.'

'Wait,' Grunt said, as they headed for the door. 'Baron coming with guards.'

'What do we do now?' Captain Marmaduke said.

'Can I suggest that we adopt a creative approach,' Humphrey said, speaking quickly. 'Grunt will you stay on the door. You can say that the guards asked you to fill in while they went on a break... and then perhaps you can have a chat with them, if you get my meaning.'

'Grunt can do that,' said Grunt.

'Queen Ophelia, I'm sorry, but you're going to have to get back in your cage for the moment.'

'What?!' she yelled.

'Please, Your Majesty, it's for the best,' Humphrey said. 'And I'm afraid that you must put that platter back on the table.'

Ophelia looked particularly ill at ease, but did as she was asked.

'Cracky, you should hide behind the large curtain next to bookcase, and the Captain can join you.'

'What about you?' Captain Marmaduke said to Humphrey.

'Oh, I'm just going to stay here and have a chat with the Baron.'

CHAPTER 43 – STAND FIRM! STAND FIRM!

'Tonight, we are going to make history!' General Beef Madras-Wholegrain Rice bellowed.

The assembled ranks of Mold and Wrexham curries and side dishes roared their approval, and there was much poppadom clapping and snapping.

'Before us is the great city of Chester,' the General continued. 'Once a proud place for a curry to be seen; yet now, unfair legislation and uncompetitive pricing has driven us away. This "Foodist" dogma has been perpetuated by a vile dictator, under the guise of a puppet democracy. But I say his time is short, what say you?!'

More roars, poppadom cracking and snapping, accompanied by the sound of boiling curry sauce.

'As I speak, a group of brave warriors are putting their lives and their musical reputation on the line to try and win our freedom. Hordes of equally brave pigs have entered the city with placards; a sight to scare even the hardiest of Blacktie's lackeys. Even now, the troops of Tsar Beef Stroganoff-Sour Cream are poised and ready to rally to our cause. For this is no idle adventure; this is no trek of folly. This, my friends, is a pivotal moment in time. It is a time for heroes, a time for honour, a time to rid the land of this insidious regime once and for all. This is our time! Carpe Diem! Seize the day!'

The roars reached deafening proportions. Beef, chicken and lamb was firm and succulent; rice was fluffy and ready for action, and sauce bubbled with pride and passion. Naan breads honed their crispy bits and Samosas softened their fillings.

'This is no night for faint hearts,' the General continued. 'This is no night for inferior foodstuffs. Yes, this is a night when we take back our freedom. For I say to you now, are we ravioli or are we curries?!'

The poppadom snapping reached fever pitch and bits of meat popped and crackled in the cool evening air. 'Then follow me now on our day of destiny,' the General exhorted. 'For the King and Queen, for everything you hold dear, for our right to be served at a reasonable price, onwards my friends, onwards!'

At the remains of the West Gate a line of soldiers stood firm, their eyes emotionless and their weapons at the ready. These were battle-hardened veterans not prone to weakness of heart or arm. They had seen many fearful sights in their time of service; monsters from the mountains of Snowdon; dragons from the darkest pits of Denbigh; and even Saturday night in Rhyl. But, despite all their experience, despite all their steadfastness and resolve, nothing could prepare them for the sight of over a hundred thousand curries charging towards them with passion and fire in their sauce.

'By all the gods,' Corporal Bluster said. 'Stand firm! Stand firm!'

A Vegetable Samosa caught him square in the face and he dropped to his knees. An Onion Bhaji smacked into his right eye and he fell to the floor, unconscious. The combined troops of General Beef Madras-Wholegrain Rice and General Lamb Korma-Saffron Rice poured over the guards and into the city, leaving only pain and stained clothing in their wake.

***

'Let us through!' cried Crusher, as the ranks of pigs pressed hard against the hastily erected barriers in front of the Grand Gateway Theatre.

'If you haven't got tickets, you can't enter the theatre,' a soldier with a large halberd shouted.

'But we're here to support our friends,' yelled Percy, brandishing a large placard which read 'P.O.R.K – Freedom for Pigs, Let us trot in peace together'.

'Well, you'll have to support them from here, because you're not getting in the bloody theatre!' the soldier shouted. 'Now get back and stay behind the barrier. If you want to watch the tournament there's a big screen in the park.'

'This is oppression, this is!' Chopper yelled, waving his placard, which read 'Hug a Pig Today, Feel the Love'.

The soldier with the halberd lost his temper at this point and poked Chopper hard in the stomach, causing him to double over in pain. 'Now, let that be a lesson to you pigs. We want no trouble here, but if you persist we will be forced to use reasonable force; and probably some unreasonable force as well.'

As the ranks of pigs moved back from the barrier, Crusher helped Chopper back to his feet... then they were pushed aside gently by a huge hand. 'Now, laddie,' the giant blonde man said to the soldier, 'that's no way to treat animals who are just exercising their right to free speech, is it?'

'Er, you j-just s-stay back,' the soldier said in a quivering voice, his halberd shaking in his hand.

'Oh, I'll stay back for now, laddie. But I warn ye, if I hear anything from that theatre that indicates my friends and kin folk are in trouble, I'd advise ye get out of mah way, is that understood?'

'O-oh, I-I'm sure if won't come to that,' the soldier said.

'It better not, laddie. It better not.'

***

'And now it's time for us to have our cultural taste buds whetted as we delve into the wonderful world of baroque,' the announcer in the theatre said. 'And I think it's safe to say that our next act is perhaps one of the more unusual listening experiences we'll have on this fine evening. Playing what they describe as *"progressive jazz chamber music"*, although I can think of some other things it could be called, with a piece called *"Overture for Chester in A, B#, C and E#"*, please welcome onto the stage the Cestrian Baroque Ensemble!'

'What in Odin's beard is this racket,' Agnar said, watching from the side of the stage.

'Ah, I believe they consider themselves progressive,' Smid said.

'Will I wish they would progress,' Agnar snorted. 'And progress off the flippin' stage. It sounds awful.'

'I can see your point,' Grundi chipped in. 'They're actually playing the same melody and counterpoints, but they each play them in a different key. In a bizarre way it's actually quite clever, it just sounds atrocious.'

The audience started booing within the first thirty seconds, apart from a very hairy man in the front row with a pipe who really seemed to be getting into it. A slow handclap started and this was the prelude to the throwing of rotten fruit. As the music reached its discordant climax, boos and catcalls echoed in the rafters of the theatre.

'You've all got no taste, whatsoever. You're just a bunch of philistines!' the lead violinist shouted.

'And you've got no talent, mate!' someone shouted back.

'Can I start this off?' Colin Mowsel asked, holding his hand up to try and get some silence.

'Please feel free, Colin,' the announcer replied.

'That was truly painful,' he said. 'It sounded like you were all playing in a different key.'

'We were,' the lead violinist said.

'But, why?' Colin asked. 'It sounded like a group of cats who've been told that they can't hang around with the other cats because their singing is so bad.'

'I actually thought it had a certain charm,' Paddy McLeprechaun said.

'Paddy, have you got your hearing aid in?' asked Colin.

'Yes,' Paddy replied.

'Has the battery gone?'

Paddy checked his hearing aid. 'Oh, yes, it looks like it has.'

'Well, I think you should consider whether music is really for you,' Shirley Divastropalot said.

'But madam, we have all qualified from the Cestrian Music Academy with "A" grades,' the lead violinist responded. 'We have juxtaposed counterpoints, interspersed harmonics, introduced hidden homophonies, and incorporated obtuse cadenzas.'

'Exactly,' Shirley Divastropalot replied.

Backstage, General Darkblast was giving a briefing to the Knights of Flatulence. However, he was providing more than musical direction.

'We are going to have to delay the performance somehow.'

'Why, General?' the lead guitarist replied, replete in his stage helmet. 'All our instruments are primed and ready for battle. We desire to take this tournament by the horns and wangle it around until it moos quite severely.'

'I'm sure you do,' the General replied. 'But we need to create a delay so only six acts can perform before the strict 10:30 pm curfew. We cannot allow Sacred Wind to play this evening.'

'But sir, surely you are not concerned that they may beat us?' the extremely tall and thin keyboard player said, pushing back his stage cape over his shoulder. 'They are but noisome amateurs, a musical irritant to be swept aside as one swats a fly.'

'Perhaps,' the General replied, 'but I see no reason to take a risk. And it is the will of the Baron. We will tell the announcer and the judges that we have a technical problem and that they must provide us with a short time to resolve this.'

'What's going on, Oldfart said to Aiden, as he walked up to the mixing desk. 'It's been nearly ten minutes and the next act hasn't taken to the stage.'

'Apparently there's a technical problem with one of the band's instruments,' Aiden replied. 'The announcer said it should be fixed shortly.'

'Well I better go and check with the officials. You do know there's a strict curfew here. All the music has to be finished by 10:30 pm sharp.'

As the delay continued the crowd became restless. Whistles and jeers rang out and the announcer was forced to return to the stage. 'Now, now, if everyone can stay calm, please,' he said, raising his hands in a placatory manner. 'I'm told that our next act, the extraordinary Knights of Flatulence, will be on stage any minute now.'

'So you're sure there won't be a problem?' Oldfart said, to one of the officials backstage.

'Absolutely,' he replied. 'I believe they're just about ready to go on. It's cutting it a bit fine, but providing their song doesn't last for more than ten minutes we should be okay for time.'

'And so, my friends,' the announcer said, as he returned to the stage and did his obligatory twirl, 'without further ado, please put your hands together for the band that has been selected from the very people who keep our city safe. They have been called the finest exponents of New Romantic music in the land, and tonight they're to perform a brand new song, written by the acclaimed local songwriter, Steve Screecher. So, singing *"Blistered Love"*, I give you the Knights of Flatulence!'

As the band took to the stage to thunderous applause, General Darkblast stood nearby. 'Don't forget,' he whispered to the lead vocalist, 'play the extended version.'

My love it is in pain (pain, pain)
My heart is all aflame (flame, flame)
For you I'll give it all (all, all)
Yes, I'll take you to all the balls (balls, balls)

But now I need you here
For my love is feeling queer
Without you I'm kinda lost
My hands are clammy, my knees are crossed

Blistered love is all I have
Blistered love driving me mad
Blistered love there's so much pain
Blistered love and you're to blame

You think that you're so smart (smart, smart)
You're playing with my heart (heart, heart)
And so this song I'll hum (hum, hum)
It goes bum, bum, bum, bum (bum, bum)

You're toying with my feelings
And now you've got me kneeling
You know my shorts are tight
But I'll make sure I keep them on tonight

Blistered love is all I have
Blistered love driving me mad

> *Blistered love there's so much pain*
> *Blistered love and you're to blame*

At this point the band launched into a lively middle-eight… which became a middle-sixteen… which became a middle-thirty two… and then had an audience participation section. 'Sing with me Chester!' the lead vocalist shouted, pointing his microphone to the crowd.

> *Blistered love is all I have*
> *Blistered love driving me mad*
> *Blistered love there's so much pain*
> *Blistered love and you're to blame*

As the crowd sang along enthusiastically, Oldfart remonstrated with the official. 'They've been on stage for nearly ten minutes!'

'I'm well aware of that, Mr Olafson, but the audience seem to be enjoying it. We can't just pull the plug you know.'

In the wings General Darkblast smiled a knowing smile and winked at the official. A minute later, the Knights of Flatulence left the stage and the audience were delirious. 'Talk about a potential winning performance!' the announcer shouted. 'What did you make of that, judges?'

'Ooh, those boys can give me their blistered love all night,' an excited Shirley Divastropalot gushed. 'Original, quirky and brilliant!'

'I couldn't agree with Shirley more,' said Colin Mowsel, to more cheers from the crowd. 'That was world class. A bit on the long side, but pure quality, and I loved the keyboard player's cape.'

'Well thank the gods I put a new battery in my hearing aid,' Paddy McLeprechaun said. 'I think you lads are just fantastic.'

Oldfart's rage was incandescent as he spoke to the official. 'So what happens now?'

'Let me look at the itinerary for the rest of the evening. I'll need to work out approximate timings.'

The official went off and joined his compatriots. After a minute or so, they were joined by the announcer. The exchanges were animated but eventually they seemed to come to an agreement, just as the rest of Sacred Wind emerged from their dressing room. 'What's going on?' Olaf asked.

'Trouble,' said Oldfart.

The announcer rushed back onto the stage and did another twirl. 'Okay. Is everyone having a good time?' he shouted, to a noisy tidal wave of cheers.

'Super, super,' he continued. 'Now, I'm afraid there's going to be a slight change to tonight's programme.'

Oldfart gave Olaf a stare that indicated he already knew what was likely to come next. 'Due to time constraints, because we have a strict 10:30 pm curfew, I'm afraid the tournament will have to be restricted to six contestants this evening.'

The audience gasped to a man, woman and sheep.

'So, as the running order was set in advance, drawn by Baron Blacktie under minimal supervision, the last act of the evening will be the Oswestry Sheep Orchestra. I'm afraid Sacred Wind will have to come back next year, and it's been agreed by the organisers that they can have automatic entry into the final.'

The theatre was in uproar. Boos rang out and the stage was soon awash with fake beards and weapons thrown by the crowd. Scuffles broke out at the back of the hall and scores of General Darkblast's guards entered the theatre, using a heavy-handed approach to quell any disorder. Oldfart and Sacred Wind were protesting angrily with the nervous official, who was being protected by several of Darkblast's soldiers

'Do we have a problem here?' General Darkblast said, joining the official.

'Yes, we do have a problem, Darkblast, and you know full well what it is!' Olaf screamed. 'We've been cheated out of being able to perform. And I know for certain that it's all down to you and Blacktie. You know exactly what he's after.'

'I think you should calm down, Olaf,' the General said. 'Why, these things can happen in tournaments of this nature. And, anyway, you've been given automatic entry into next year's tournament. I think that's very fair.'

'You know the agreement we have with Blacktie,' Olaf growled, 'and you know what happens if we don't win. Well, there's no way we're going to let that happen.'

Olaf drew his sword and quickly found the points of four spears at his throat. 'Now, now,' the General said, smiling. 'I suggest you put that thing away. I'm afraid now is not the time for combat, although I can assure you that if the time does arrive you'll not have to look far to find me.'

Olaf sheathed his sword, the look of anger on his face telling its own story. 'So, I suggest that you either go back to your dressing room,' the General grinned, 'or join me and this lovely audience in listening to the pleasant sounds of the sheep… the last act of the night.'

CHAPTER 44 – IT LOOKS LIKE YOU'VE BEEN USURPED

'Grunt, what are you doing here? Where are the guards?' the Baron asked, as Grunt stood in front of the throne room door.

'Guards said they go for break. Ask Grunt to stand here. Let no one in room.'

'Well that's highly irregular, and I can see some chastisement coming their way when they return,' the Baron said. 'In the meantime, Grunt, you are relieved. These guards will wait for me while I have my snack, before returning to the tournament for what promises to be an interesting conclusion.'

Grunt opened the door for the Baron and Pimple to enter. Velvet appeared from an adjacent room and ran in after them. 'So, Grunt, have you learned anything interesting today?' one of the guards said, smiling. 'I believe you've taken up reading.'

Grunt simply looked at the sniggering guards and sighed as he closed the door to the throne room. 'Grunt need to explain to guards about Nirvana.'

'My Lord, there appears to be a dog sitting on the throne!' Pimple exclaimed.

'It looks like you've been usurped,' Ophelia laughed, from within her cage.

'Most amusing, my dear Queen, but I think not,' the Baron replied. 'Pimple, remove that animal immediately.'

'Yes, my Lord.'

'Actually, I'm feeling quite comfortable. Would you mind awfully if I just stayed here for a while?' Humphrey said.

'It talks, my Lord,' Pimple said, backing away from Humphrey.

The Baron eyed Humphrey warily and looked around the throne room. Velvet sniffed the air and her eyes gazed at the curtains against the far wall. 'How did you get in this room, my little canine friend?' the Baron said, moving closer to the table containing the platter of cheese and chutney.

'Firstly, I would prefer that you do not refer to me as your friend,' Humphrey said. 'I pick my friends very carefully and I deduce by your general despotic demeanour and unseemly aroma that it is highly unlikely you will ever be elevated to that status.'

'I see,' the Baron replied. 'A dog who speaks with perception and, I detect, a good deal of intelligence. However, you've still not answered my question.'

'How I entered the room is of little importance,' Humphrey said. 'Baron, you must realise that this ridiculous scheme of yours is destined to fail. As we speak there are forces from far and wide converging to ensure you do not succeed.'

'Oh, I'm well aware of the opposition,' the Baron said, smugly. 'But I think you fail to take into account exactly what I'll be capable of when I partake of some of this charming recipe.'

The Baron uncovered the Cheese and Chutney Surprise, which still glowed with an eerie crimson light. 'Actually, we are well aware of the likely outcome of you consuming the mixture of Ceridwen's Cheese and Mathonwy's Chutney. And I'm afraid we cannot allow that to happen.'

With lightning speed Humphrey jumped off the throne and whacked the platter with his paw, breaking the Cheese and Chutney Surprise into little pieces. Velvet dived headlong towards him, her eyes glowing with anger and her claws extended… only to be flattened by the powerful right paw of Captain Marmaduke. 'That was for Half-blind Ron,' he said, as Velvet writhed on the throne room floor.

Cracky pulled back the curtains and made straight for the Baron. 'Ah, It seems I've underestimated your resourcefulness,' the Baron said, drawing a short-sword from his belt. 'And I sense you're still a little upset regarding our altercation of many years ago.'

'It's gone beyond that, Blacktie,' Cracky said. 'It's time to stop you once and for all.'

'Well, as much as I appreciate your sentiments and motive, I'm afraid I've no intention of being thwarted,' the Baron said, pointing the sword towards Cracky. 'Guards, we have intruders!' he shouted.

The door opened slowly and Grunt walked in. 'Where are the guards, Grunt?' the Baron said, with a confused look.

'Guards gone to look for Nirvana,' Grunt replied.

'What? Oh, no matter. Now, Grunt, you have my permission to rip, crush, break and perform whatever other damage you desire on these creatures who seek to perpetrate harm to my royal personage.'

The Baron backed away from Cracky and smiled. 'It's been nice knowing you, but all good things must come to an end, and I'm afraid that your end is probably only seconds away.'

'Actually, Grunt need plop,' Grunt said.

'What?!' the Baron screamed.

'Grunt said Grunt need go plop.'

'You can't go plop now Grunt, my life is being threatened. You're my personal bodyguard and I need protecting!'

'But Baron said when Grunt need plop, Grunt should just go plop.'

'Look, I know what I said, but there's a time and place for everything and the time for plop is not now!'

'Baron want Grunt go plop here?' Grunt asked.

'No!' was the cry from everyone in the room.

'Well, Grunt need plop, so Grunt go plop,' Grunt said, as he turned and walked towards the door.

'Stop, you Neanderthal!' the Baron cried. 'If you take one more step I'll have you executed.'

Grunt stopped just by the door and turned around. 'Baron really need to look at himself in mirror. Baron not a nice person. Baron shout at Grunt. Baron belittle Grunt and make Grunt sleep in cell. Baron too engrossed in egotistical plan for world domination to recognise Baron's innate emotional shortcomings. Constant yearning for omnipotence and manipulation just show that Baron is actually masking Baron's inner diffidence and lack of self-esteem… and Baron's frustration at size of his manhood.'

'Well, that's told him,' Humphrey said to Captain Marmaduke.

'Oh, and for Baron's information,' Grunt continued. 'Neanderthal's are extinct species or subspecies within the genus Homo, and were closely related to modern humans. Grunt is Troll, and Grunt is proud to be Troll.'

And with that Grunt marched proudly out the door.

'It looks like it's just you and me after all,' Cracky said, rolling up his sleeves and grabbing a nearby candlestick.

'No matter, the outcome will be the same,' the Baron replied. 'Now, en garde.'

He lunged at Cracky with the short-sword but Cracky deftly parried it with the candlestick, and then struck a blow to the Baron's leg. 'Ow, that hurt!' the Baron cried.

Pimple went to go to the Baron's aid, only to find Humphrey standing in his path with his teeth barred. 'Now, now, good doggy,' Pimple said. 'You'll only end up getting yourself injured if you continue to block my path. I must warn you I am a master of martial arts.'

Pimple spread his arms and legs, adopting what seemed to be a variation on a classic martial arts defence pose. 'I'm glad you told me that,' Humphrey said, sitting down. 'That changes things completely.'

'I had a feeling it might,' Pimple said, moving his arms around.

'Yes, you see I'm a fifth-Dan black belt in Jeet Kune Dog,' Humphrey said. 'I've been studying for years, when my owner was at work. I thought I was going to have to hold back on you, but as we seem to be equally qualified it looks like I can "turn the beast loose", so to speak.'

Pimple moved back several steps and gulped loudly. Humphrey jumped up onto two legs and adopted an aggressive fighting pose. 'Well, I'm waiting,' he said, beckoning Pimple forward, who gulped again, turned and ran away quite fast.

'Looks like I'll have to go down a more traditional route,' Humphrey sighed, as he chased after Pimple and sunk his teeth into his bottom.

Velvet and Captain Marmaduke were actually very evenly matched. Thrust of paw and jaw were applied in equal measure by both combatants, with Velvet already bearing a scar on her left cheek and Captain Marmaduke a cut on his front left leg.

'You do realise this is only going to go one way, don't you?' Velvet said, as she dived at the Captains neck, only for him to parry her away with his right paw.

'I do,' the Captain replied, as he swung his left paw into Velvet's head. 'And I doubt very much it's the way you expect.'

As Velvet and Captain Marmaduke wrestled on the floor, and Pimple continued to run around the room with Humphrey's teeth sunk firmly into his behind, Cracky and the Baron duelled around the throne. 'Give it up, Crackfoot, your candlestick is hardly a match for my sword,' the Baron said.

Cracky fell to his knees, holding the candlestick with two hands above his head as the Baron rained down blow after blow. However, he quickly got back to his feet and pushed the Baron back against the table containing the remnants of the Cheese and Chutney Surprise. In a flash, the Baron turned and grabbed a sizeable piece in his left hand while keeping his sword pointing firmly towards Cracky.

'And now I think it's time to see just what kind of surprise this delicate little morsel will provide,' he said, moving the piece of cheese and chutney towards his mouth.

With Cracky held at bay, Captain Marmaduke moved into action. With a deft swing of his left paw he knocked Velvet to one side and sprung at the Baron. Both his front paws smashed into Blacktie's face and the cheese and chutney flew across the room, landing by the far wall… just next to the little mouse-hole.

'Blast you, you infernal cat!' the Baron roared.

Captain Marmaduke landed awkwardly and Velvet was on him in a second. She sunk her teeth deep into his back right leg and he cried in pain. He struggled to get to his feet but his right leg gave way almost immediately. Sensing her opportunity, Velvet hurled herself onto him, grabbing his neck in a vice-like grip with her teeth. As the Captain desperately clawed at her she yanked her head back, tearing the flesh in his neck. He collapsed to the ground, with blood pouring from the open wound.

Velvet sat upright and lifted her head, loftily. She knew he was now at her mercy and she readied herself mentally for the kill. Captain Marmaduke was breathing heavily but he was still conscious, still aware of the threat of the rasping jaws that could end his life.

'So, my good Captain, it appears the outcome is perhaps what I expected after all,' Velvet said, with a sneer.

'Do your worst, ferret!' the Captain said, spitting out the words.

'Oh, I intend to,' she replied, readying herself to pounce.

'But if you think that simply ridding yourself of me will make any difference in the grand scheme, you are sadly mistaken,' the Captain said, defiantly lifting his paw. 'The forces of good will overcome.'

And it was at this point that Velvet felt the tap on her shoulder. 'Excuse me,' said the mouse, 'but I feel I must ask you to stop what you're doing right now. Killing this brave cat is dishonourable and I won't allow it.'

'Oh, leave it out,' Velvet said, without turning around. 'I'll deal with you later.'

'Perhaps you should deal with me now,' the mouse said.

'Right, you annoying little pipsqueak,' Velvet said, as she turned around, 'I'm going to bite your soft head off and throw it out of a window, so please pick one in advance.'

Velvet looked down at where the little mouse should have been, but saw only two huge paws. She had to lift her head up quite a way before she made eye contact. 'Ah, there seems to have been some kind of mistake,' Velvet said, cowering from the enormous mouse. 'You see, I thought you were a little mouse that I've been, er, playing with. Obviously I apologise for this error, and I'm sure that if we talk we can come to some kind of compromise.'

'Hmm,' the mouse said. 'Actually, I was just deciding whether to kill you now or later.'

Velvet's little eyes went wide as the reality of the situation began to bite. She cowered down even more and put her front paws over her face. 'However,' the mouse added, 'I am not like you and I do not get pleasure out of inflicting pain upon small animals.'

'You are wise and just, oh big mouse,' Velvet said.

'Thank you,' the mouse replied. 'But I'm afraid it is time for you to leave now, so please pick a window.'

'Er, can't I just sort of shuffle away quietly?'

'No, please pick a window.'

'Well, perhaps if I just backed away towards the door and…'

Velvet left through the top window on the far wall, propelled by an extremely hard kick. 'Oh boy did that feel good!' the mouse said, as it promptly reverted back to its normal size and scurried off into the little mouse-hole.

The Baron and Cracky were stood either side of the table containing the remains of the Cheese and Chutney Surprise. Every time the Baron went to pick up a piece, Cracky brought the candlestick crashing down onto the table, forcing the Baron to withdraw his hand. 'This can't go on forever, Crackfoot,' the Baron said. 'Sooner or later I'll win.'

'Well you'll win with broken fingers then!' Cracky shouted, bringing the candlestick down only inches from the Baron's hand.

Pimple was still screaming in agony as Humphrey clung onto his behind with his teeth. 'Get off me, you horrible little dog!' he cried, as he bumped into the throne... and that was all it took to loosen Humphrey's grip slightly. Pimple pushed Humphrey away with his feet, sending him sprawling on the floor and crashing into Ophelia's cage.

'Humphrey!' she shouted, as the little dog tried to regain his senses.

Pimple got to his feet and jumped straight at Cracky, knocking the candlestick out of his hand. As Cracky turned to face him, Pimple adopted his variation on a martial arts defence pose once more.

'I'm not scared of you, Crackfoot!' he yelled. 'You're just a middle-aged man with a good imagination in recipes. Why, my martial arts skills can easily render you helpless and infirm. I'll hit you in all those nasty places that cause real pain. I'll make your eyes judder in their sockets. I'll…'

Cracky's fist connected squarely with Pimple's nose and he collapsed to the floor in an unconscious heap. 'That particular recipe is called the Fist of Sleep and it does exactly what it says on the tin.'

However, Pimple's ill-advised momentary interruption had played right into the Baron's hands. He grabbed one of the larger pieces of the shimmering cheese and chutney and shoved the tip of the sword into Cracky's neck.

'You know, the only reason I'm not going to kill you now is that I want you to bear witness to this moment,' the Baron said. 'For this will be the start of a momentous time, and not just for these lands but for the whole world. Once I have legitimately claimed Hairy Growler's cheese mine as my own, I will have an endless supply of Cheese and Chutney Surprise. I will be a legend! I will be a God! I will have power! Women will find me attractive!'

'Oh, I think you may struggle with the last one,' Cracky scoffed.

The Baron slowly raised the piece of cheese and chutney to his lips. His eyes shone with excitement as he inserted the magical little morsel into his mouth, closing it quickly with aplomb. Ophelia gasped and Cracky's face had the look of defeat etched upon it. Humphrey also looked on with horror, his mind working overtime on potential solutions. In the end he decided to go down the traditional route once again, and sunk his teeth deep into the Baron's rear.

Blacktie's mouth opened immediately and he let out a scream, spitting out the piece of cheese and chutney in the process. The little morsel of food left his mouth like a missile, taking the only trajectory it could; it headed straight at Cracky... and into his mouth... and down his throat.

The first sensation was that of warmth; a pleasant, comforting feeling spread over his body and he felt incredibly relaxed. Then he farted loudly, which was perhaps a touch incongruous. However, the odour that emanated from his rear end was a delicate perfume, reminiscent of the smell of flowers on a rain-soaked afternoon. He lifted his hand to his face and noticed his skin was changing colour to a fiery red. Small flames of energy flickered between his fingers, yet there was no pain. Then, all of a sudden, his mind exploded with knowledge; he felt at one with everything and understood the deep mysteries of the universe and the wonderful simplicity of nature. He even understood quadratic equations.

Cracky looked around the throne room and saw the injured figure of Captain Marmaduke. The Captain was beginning to lose consciousness, as the loss of blood was taking its toll. Cracky held out his hand and said one word. 'Heal.'

A bright yellow beam of light radiated from his hand and flew across the room, engulfing the Captain. The wound on his neck closed instantly, followed by the healing of the ripped tendons in his hind leg. The light then vanished and the Captain got to his feet. He walked over to Cracky and rubbed himself against his legs, purring loudly.

Ophelia clapped and cheered as Cracky said 'open', and the door of her cage duly obeyed. She ran over and planted a massive kiss on his cheek. He smiled warmly at her and the red pigmentation of his skin grew brighter.

Sensing it was time to get out of the way, Humphrey removed his teeth from the Baron's bottom and trotted over to Cracky, who bent down and stroked his head. 'Well done,' he said to Humphrey.

'Likewise,' Humphrey responded, licking Cracky's hand.

Cracky fixed his gaze firmly on the Baron, whose eyes bore the same look of fear that they had so many years before. His face drained of colour completely and he began to edge towards the door. Cracky raised his hand and simply said 'still'. Blacktie stopped dead in his tracks.

'I see you've become fond of using only monosyllabic words now,' the Baron said, his trembling body belying his apparent defiance.

'Actually, I've got two words to say to you,' Cracky replied. 'And one of those has three syllables.'

'Really,' the Baron snorted.

'Inflamus rocks,' Cracky said, in a low voice.

At first nothing seemed to happen. The Baron looked around in surprise and a smile returned to his lips. But then he smelled smoke. 'Where's that coming from?' he said, continuing to sniff the air.

Ophelia pointed to the Baron's trousers, and it was at that point he began to feel the heat between his legs. 'What have you done?!' he shouted, as tiny wisps of smoke started to creep out of the groin area.

'Let's just say it's something I've thought about for years,' Cracky said, with a mischievous grin. 'It's a bit of a slow burner, so if you can make it to the canal in, say, two minutes you might be okay.'

Blacktie put his hands on his crotch and pulled them away quickly as the first small flames began to appear. 'I'd really get a move on if I were you,' Cracky suggested.

The Baron let out a manic scream and bolted for the door, sprinting down the hall and out of the palace. 'Now, I really think it's time we left,' Cracky said. 'We've got a tournament to attend.'

CHAPTER 45 – SHOW NO MERCY!

'Where are the others?' Cliff asked, as he ran into the OSO's dressing room.

'I told them to go outside and take in the atmosphere. They're all a bit nervous, I suspect,' Henry Fluffywool said, not even lifting his head as he poured over the score the orchestra was due to perform.

'Have you not heard what's happened?' Cliff asked.

'No, I've not even been outside to watch any of the other acts, although I've been able to hear them clearly enough from here. Dreadful.'

'Sacred Wind have been pulled from the tournament, apparently because of time constraints.'

'That's terrible.'

'It's more than that, Henry. You know the consequences. We have to act. We have to do something.'

Henry sighed and put the score down on the table in front of him, before looking earnestly at Cliff. 'But what can we possibly do that will make a difference? We are simply sheep, Cliff. Blacktie is too powerful, his web far too wide and his cohorts too high in numbers; the place is crawling with soldiers.'

'Then we should do what we do best,' Cliff said. 'We should play music with passion and sincerity; we should support our friends in their hour of need; we should do what Charles wanted. We should withdraw from the tournament and let Sacred Wind take our place, and we should play with them.'

Henry rose from his chair and placed his hand on Cliff's shoulder. 'Now you do sound like your uncle. He'd have been very proud. But think logically; do you really believe we'll be able to do that? I'm not even sure the rules allow it; and even if they did, if Blacktie is determined to stop the band playing then that's what he'll accomplish.'

Cliff shook his head and turned towards the door. 'You know, Henry, the reason why Blacktie wins is purely because people don't believe he can be beaten. All it takes is the courage to make the decision to stand up to him; and you've got it within you to make that decision, I only wish you could see that.'

The dressing room door opened and the rest of the OSO filed in. They stood in a line and picked up their instruments. Cliff's eyes widened and he looked straight at Henry. 'It looks like the decision may have been made for you,' he said.

***

'Show no mercy!' General Beef Madras-Wholegrain Rice shouted, as the army of curries blitzed through everything in their path, the ragtag remains of the guards of the West Gate fleeing before them. But, as they turned and charged down the street towards the palace they found their way blocked… by over two hundred of General Darkblast's elite troops, wearing protective body armour and specially adapted 'spice resistant' helmets.

'The theatre is just around the corner, my friends, so let's serve up a menu that Blacktie's forces will never forget!' the General shouted, hurling particularly hot onion slices in all directions.'

In a nearby building, General Darkblast stood on a balcony observing the scene of devastation below. 'Is it ready?' he asked.

'It is sir,' a soldier replied. 'Shall I give the order to proceed?'

'Let them get just a little bit closer… that's it,' the General said, as the army of curries advanced on his soldiers. 'Now, give the order now!'

As the solider lit a flare on the balcony, the front rank of troops separated and a single cart was pushed forward. 'Fire!' the soldier barked into his walkie-talkie, and the water cannon sent a powerful jet of liquid right into the oncoming curries. Moving from side to side, it splattered plates, soaked Naan breads, sent Onion Bhajis flying, and split Chapattis into pieces. General Darkblast's forces cheered and started to advance. Instead of swords and spears, they drove forward with mops and buckets, gleefully wiping the plates of the fallen.

'We've got to pull back, sir,' a half-soaked Elite Tandoori Naan said, to General Beef Madras-Wholegrain Rice. 'We're getting rinsed out there.'

The General puffed his rice and cracked one of his mini poppadoms in the process. 'You're right. Pull back, pull back!' he commanded.

'Onwards!' General Darkblast yelled, joining his troops at the front line. 'Chase them out of the city, let no plate remain unwashed, let no Naan remain crispy!'

As the water cannon moved forward, drenching the fire of the retreating curries, Darkblast smiled. 'I'm returning to the theatre now,' he told one of his Captains. 'It's time to deal with Sacred Wind once and for all.'

Meanwhile, in a side street, whispering was taking place in dark alcoves and recessed doorways. A couple of adventurous rats sniffed around but were soon expelled by a blast of asparagus.

'Do we make our move now, your Imperial Majesty?'

'Da. It is time we show Blacktie the price for placing pricing restrictions on the Russians.'

As the cart carrying the water cannon passed by the side street, the troops of Tsar Beef Stroganoff-Sour Cream burst into action. Two platoons of Steamed Asparagus Infantry, backed up by a crack squad of Braised Cabbage Marines hurled themselves into the fray. 'What in the devil's name is that smell?' Corporal Bluster said, as a Braised Cabbage Marine smashed into his nose.

Then it was the turn of the armoured paratroopers, as Stroganoffs on steel plates hurled themselves from the upper windows of the buildings on each side of the main street, landing heavily on the bemused soldiers below.

In the water cannon cart, the gunner was facing a losing battle with a Steamed Broccoli Commando, as it stuffed itself in his ear. The driver pulled to a stop and grabbed the walkie-talkie on the front seat, just as a Steamed Asparagus Infantryman darted up his trouser leg. 'Tell the General we've been caught by the Stroganoffs. They're everywhere. I've got Steamed Asparagus in my underpants and it's not looking good.'

'Da, you can say that again,' said the Steamed Asparagus.

***

'This is highly irregular,' one of the organisers said to Henry, as he thumbed through the competition rules. 'But I've not seen anything that prohibits it. Are you absolutely sure?'

'Yes, completely,' said Henry.

'Well, in which case, I'll inform the announcer. I would advise you to speak to Sacred Wind immediately; you'll need to be on stage within the next five minutes.'

In Sacred Wind's dressing room, a sombre mood had been joined by dejection and despondency and the three were getting along famously. Mara sat on Aiden's knee and Roisin was sitting supportively next to Agnar, her hand resting on his.

'So now what?' Olaf said.

'Don't give up hope yet,' said Mr Kneepatcher, with a flamboyant twirl of his cravat, 'you never know what's around the corner. We've been through a lifetime's worth of trauma to get here and I, for one, am not going to be dithered until I feel like being dithered.'

There was a knock on the door and Cliff walked in, carrying his cello. 'I think there's something you need to see,' he said.

As the members of the OSO walked into the dressing room a sombre mood, dejection and despondency decided to leave and have a party elsewhere. Oldfart smiled an infectious smile as he stared at the orchestra of sheep… all wearing Sacred Wind t-shirts. 'Well, that's a sight I never thought I'd see, and a very welcome one,' he said.

'Actually it's more than just a show of support,' Henry said as he came in the room. 'We've decided to retire from the competition.'

'Pardon me, you've what?' Olaf said.

'We've decided not to compete, at least not by ourselves. I've spoken to the organisers and it would appear you're now reinstated.'

'That's incredible,' said Oldfart, hugging Henry. 'How can we ever thank you?'

'You can let us accompany you on stage,' Cliff said, holding the manuscript containing Charles's score. 'It's what uncle wanted, so I think we should fulfil his fondest wish.'

'By Odin's farty backside, what are we waiting for?!' Agnar cried, jumping up and grabbing his drumsticks.

'One more thing,' Henry said. 'We sheep have traditionally never been particularly fond of cheese; however there is one variety we occasionally partake of. It's called White Fleecetickler and we find that it heartens the soul and gives courage when courage is needed most. We would be very honoured if you would join us.'

'We'd be delighted,' Oldfart said, as Henry handed out the little pieces of white cheese.

***

The announcer took to the stage with a piece of paper in his hand and did his twirl. 'Well, it looks like there's going to be another slight change to the evening's programme, as the Oswestry Sheep Orchestra have decided not to compete in tonight's event.'

The audience were shocked, and mumblings bumbled and rumbled around the theatre.

'This means our night will not be starved of rock after all, as Sacred Wind are ready to compete,' he added, as cheers and applause from the audience chased away the rumbling, bumbling mumblings.

'And, to add a further twist to the story,' the announcer continued, 'Sacred Wind will be supported by… the Oswestry Sheep Orchestra, for what promises to be an eclectic musical experience. They'll be on stage in a couple of minutes, so don't go away.'

'General, I bear grave news,' a soldier said, as General Darkblast pushed his way through the ranks of pigs, held back by the hastily erected barriers.

'Well, spit it out, man.'

'Actually, there are two bits of news, sir. Firstly, our troops outside of the palace have been accosted by the Stroganoffs. They are in retreat as we speak. It is only a matter of minutes before the combined forces of Wrexham, Mold and Cestrian-Russians get here.'

'Good lord, man, call for back up immediately. We must not let them enter the theatre,' the General ordered. 'What's the other news?'

'The Oswestry Sheep Orchestra have pulled out of the tournament, sir. Sacred Wind will be on stage in a few minutes.'

'Over my dead body,' the General said, rushing towards the theatre entrance.

'Let me through, you imbeciles,' a voice from within the crowd of pigs shouted. 'General Darkblast, I am in need of assistance.'

Baron Blacktie pushed his way through the throng, keeping tight hold of the towel wrapped around his lower body. 'My Lord, what has happened to you?' the General said.

'It would appear that stage one of my plan will have to be put on hold for the present,' the Baron said, tightening the towel and wincing slightly. 'I am also somewhat tender at the moment and would appreciate some light bandages and a pair of fresh trousers.'

'See to it immediately,' the General said, to a nearby guard.

'My Lord, Sacred Wind are due on stage at any minute,' a soldier cried, from the door to the theatre.

'What?!' screamed the Baron. 'I seem to remember tasking you to ensure that this particular situation did not arise.'

'Rest assured it won't, my Lord,' the General replied, his words tinged with steel.

Inside the theatre, the audience bristled with excitement. 'And so,' the announcer said, 'we come to our final act of the evening, and what an evening it's been, I'm sure you'll agree.'

Aiden arrived at the mixing desk and quickly began resetting the sliders and knobs in preparation. There hadn't been any time to think about how he was going to mix the orchestra in. 'Now, are you sure you're going to behave yourself,' he said to the mixing desk.

'Demon's honour,' the mixing desk replied. 'But don't forget our deal.'

'So,' the announcer continued, 'please put your hands together for some Vikings that you'll be liking, who'll be playing with some sheep that'll make you weep. Yes, it's the fantastic, the wonderful, the very hairy Sacred Wind, supported by the Oswestry Sheep Orchestra!'

The audience were ecstatic as Sacred Wind and the OSO made their way onto the stage. Plastic weapons were waved with gay abandon and many people had already switched on their battery-operated torches. Olaf stood in front of the microphone stand in centre stage. 'Good evening, Chester! Are you ready to rock?'

'No, they're not!' General Darkblast bellowed from the back of the theatre, as scores of fresh guards ran down each aisle. 'There'll be no rock music in here tonight.'

The audience gasped and shuffled nervously in their seats.

'Indeed,' said Baron Blacktie, as he entered the theatre and walked over to the mixing desk. 'We are going to have to cut the tournament short, for safety reasons.'

'That's nonsense, Blacktie!' Olaf shouted. 'What safety reasons?'

'Oh, I'll think of something,' the Baron said.

'Right, put those instruments down and get off the stage,' said the General.

'Why don't you come and make me, Darkblast?' Olaf snarled, drawing his sword.

'I was really hoping you'd say that,' the General said, unsheathing his sword.

'And about time too,' said Agnar, picking up his hammer and running at the guards. 'Diplomacy's a word I've never been fond of, let alone one I can say very well.'

The Baron drew his sword and moved threateningly towards Aiden. 'So, Aiden Peersey, isn't it? I need you to step away from the mixing desk.'

'No chance,' Aiden said, drawing his pocket knife. 'It's one for all and all for one.'

'How charming,' said the Baron, as he thrust his sword towards him.

CHAPTER 46 – IS THIS PART OF THE ACT?

'What's all the commotion inside, I can hear shouting?' Crusher said, to one of the soldiers behind the barrier.

'The tournament's closing early. It would appear there are a few objections. Now, get back before I feel the need to start using unnecessary violence.'

As Crusher seethed inside, the ranks of pigs at his rear began to part like water in front of a ship. A new voice joined the discussion, and this voice spoke with the confidence of someone who wasn't concerned about the point of a halberd being poked at him.

'Actually, I would strongly advise you to let us all through,' Cracky said, standing alongside Crusher. 'Otherwise things may get a little hot.'

'I don't take kindly to threats,' the soldier said, pointing the tip of his weapon at Cracky.

'And I don't take kindly to not being able to help my friends in their hour of need,' Cracky said, lifting his arms skyward. 'Inflamus rocks!'

The soldier simply stood looking at him. Nothing happened.

'Inflamus rocks!' Cracky roared, again.

'Is that supposed to mean something?' the soldier asked.

'Cracky, your colour, it's returned to normal,' Humphrey said.

'Wow, a talking dog,' the soldier said. 'I thought I'd seen it all. You should put him on the telly, mate.'

'Oh, my, so it has,' Cracky replied, looking at his hands. 'The effects are wearing off. That's because I only ate a tiny piece.'

'Actually, I thought I'd seen everything,' the soldier said, noticing a commotion in the distance, 'but I've just spotted a cat with its arse on fire heading for the canal.'

'Damn,' said Cracky. 'This really has put the cat among the pigeons.'

'Or in the canal, as it happens,' the soldier said.

'Did you bring any more with you, Cracky?' Ophelia asked.

'No. Oh, blast, I knew I should have picked up a few pieces.'

The shouting from inside the theatre became more raucous and the sound of steel on steel could be heard. Cracky looked around desperately, searching for something, or someone.

'Who are you looking for?' Chopper said. 'It's not a big giant blonde man, is it?'

'Yes,' Cracky said, 'have you seen him?'

'Are you talking about me, mah little porky friend?' the giant blonde man said, tapping Chopper affectionately on the head.

'Oh, heavens, am I glad to see you, again,' Cracky said. 'Have you brought any others with you?'

'Aye, the boys and some lads from mah Yoga class insisted they come with me,' the giant blonde man said, pointing over his shoulder, as twenty or so equally large men moved to the front of the crowd of pigs. 'They think I'm getting too old for this kind of thing. Bloody cheek'

The guard nearest to the barrier moved back several feet and readied himself and his weapon. The other soldiers followed suit, and a line of trembling spears and shaky halberds added some extra space between them and the barrier.

'Now then, it seems there's some kind of skirmish going on inside, would that be the case?' the giant blonde man said.

'Nothing to concern yourself with,' the soldier replied in a quivering voice.

'I think I'll be the judge of that, laddie.'

'I must warn you that there are at least two hundred soldiers in that theatre,' the soldier said. 'And they're all nasty buggers with a tendency to use unnecessary violence at any opportunity.'

'Only two hundred!' a shout came from behind the giant blonde man. 'Ah, for pity's sake, Angus, ye may as well not have brought us.'

Another loud crash emanated from within the theatre, followed by a high pitched scream. 'It's time for ye and yer friends to step aside now laddie, if ye don't want to get hurt,' the giant blonde man said, removing his huge sword from its sheath.

'Now, now, get back. We're not going to be intimidated by you,' the soldier said, his right leg shaking.

'Well, perhaps if I introduce us ye may think about changing yer mind. I'm Angus McSvensson of the clan McSvensson. These here are my sons, Robert, Alec, Brian, Fraser, Todd, Gordon, Donald, Connell, Duncan and Mungo. Oh, and the others are some lads who just like a good scrap… and a bit of Yoga.'

The guards ran away very fast, towards the palace… and straight into the oncoming curry and stroganoff armies of Mold, Wrexham and Chester.

Things quickly got very spicy.

'I think it'll be best if ye all stay here,' Angus McSvensson said, to the crowd behind the barrier. 'Ye and yer friends too, Cracky. There's no reason to be putting yerself in harm's way. Me and the boys'll get this sorted out in nay time.'

The scene in the theatre was pure mayhem. Olaf and Darkblast were going head-to-head with each other, the clash of their swords reverberating heavily around the auditorium; the rest of Sacred Wind were locked in battle with the Knights of Flatulence.

Mr Kneepatcher had jumped onto the back of one of the soldiers and was beating him over the head with his battle cravat, while various members of the OSO jostled, kicked and threw anything to hand at the General's troops.

Roisin and Mara were hiding behind Agnar's huge drum kit, hurling drumstick after drumstick into the fray. And Oldfart had produced his long staff and was taking great delight in whacking any soldier who came within five feet of him in the shins.

'Is this part of act?' Paddy McLeprechaun said to Colin Mowsel, who simply shrugged.

The audience were totally engrossed in the action to the point of participation, cheering on every successful blow from Sacred Wind and their allies. Boos were aimed at the Knights of Flatulence and pieces of rotten fruit were regular visitors to the maelstrom taking place on the stage. And by the mixing desk, Aiden and the Baron circled each other.

'I've no idea why you've allied yourself with this motley selection of no-hopers,' the Baron said. 'It seems to me you're better than that.'

'Oh, I pick my friends very carefully, Baron,' Aiden replied. 'And I doubt whether I'll ever include you in the list.'

'Pity, you've got potential I feel,' the Baron said, missing Aiden with a swipe of his sword and catching the corner of the mixing desk.

'Ay, be careful, mate,' the mixing desk said, 'you nearly took out my master volume sliders then.'

The Baron was momentarily nonplussed and backed away from the desk. 'How fascinating, you obviously really do have talent. I could definitely use a man of your resources. I'm sure we could agree a position for you in my employ that would be significantly better than the position you have now.'

Aiden stuck out his pocket knife and shook his head. 'I'm a mixing engineer,' he said. 'And that's good enough for me.'

The battle on the stage was slowly turning the way of the Knights of Flatulence. Although supported by their friends, and with their will strengthened by White Fleecetickler, the overwhelming odds were beginning to take their toll. As Olaf struggled to keep General Darkblast at bay, Agnar, Grundi and Smid were surrounded by about twenty soldiers. They fought back to back, defending each other against the onslaught of blows that came at them like an angry swarm of birds whose favourite tree has been chopped down.

Mr Kneepatcher's battle cravat had been cut in two by a scything swing of a sword and he was pinned down by two soldiers. 'Ooh, get off me you rotters!' he shouted. 'You're crumpling my shirt.'

Mara and Roisin were hovering behind Agnar's drum kit, but every way of escape was blocked by grinning soldiers. 'Will you stop looking up my skirt, please,' Roisin said. 'I'm not that kind of faerie!'

'I am,' Mara said, with a wink, 'but never with the likes of any of you.'

The members of the OSO had been herded to the other side of the stage, with Cliff the last to be rounded up. He had fought and with great heroism, protecting Oriana from any soldier who dared go near her; but the sheer number was too great and even he was forced to capitulate.

'So, it's left to me to finish the tidying up,' a smiling General Darkblast said, as he delivered another mighty blow against Olaf's sword.

Olaf toppled backwards and fell off the stage. The General jumped down after him but Olaf stuck out a leg, putting the General flat on his back. He leapt to his feet, twirled his sword and pointed it directly into the prone General's chest. 'I'll not make the same mistake again, Darkblast. Yield, or feel my steel.'

'Oh, I'll do neither,' the General said, rising to his feet, as two spears were pointed at Olaf's back and two at his chest. 'You see it's you who'll be feeling my steel, Olaf the Berserker. You've caused me and the Baron enough grief with your quest for free farting and that awful noise you call music. I think it's time you prepared to meet your maker.'

Olaf stared straight into Darkblast's eyes, as the General raised his sword in preparation to deliver a fatal blow. 'Oh, one last thing,' Olaf said.

'Yes.'

'Your Knights of Flatulence band was the biggest pile of crap I've heard for ages. Agnar's got more talent in his big toe.'

The General growled and lifted his sword higher. 'Force him to his knees,' he said between clenched teeth.'

'Now, that's enough of that!' a bellowing voice said, from the back of the theatre. General Darkblast looked up and his mouth dropped open.

'Laddie, I think this would be a good time for ye to reconsider yer strategy here,' Angus McSvensson said to the General, as he strode purposefully towards the stage.

The General's sword arm went limp as he looked at the mass of tartan and hair walking down the aisles towards them. The soldiers rapidly backed away from Olaf, like scuttering mice who've just eyed a hungry cat.

'McSvenssons!' Angus shouted; a cry that was echoed by the rest of his clan. 'Now then,' he continued. 'Where's my little cousin Agnar?'

'I'm over here, Angus!' Agnar yelled.

Two of the McSvensson clan stepped onto the stage and pushed the soldiers aside, creating a clear path. One soldier went to draw his sword, only to be met by a frosty narrowed-eyed McSvensson stare and a slow shaking of the head. Agnar, Grundi and Smid looked at each other and grinned, slowly walking through the ranks of Darkblast's wary knights.

'It looks like ye've got yerself into a wee bit of bother, cousin,' said Angus.

'You could say that,' replied Agnar.

'And so, where's that swindling Sassenach, Blacktie? I'm led to believe that he's responsible for all this,' Angus said.

'Oh, I'm up here,' shouted the Baron, from behind the mixing desk, 'but I'd strongly advise you to stay where you are. That's if you want to spare the life of this fellow.'

Like a mob of particularly nosey Meerkats, the audience looked up and turned towards the direction of the voice, their heads bobbing up and down as they tried to pinpoint the location of the Baron, who had the tip of his sword pressed into Aiden's neck.

'C'mon Blacktie, let the boy go,' Angus McSvensson said, 'it'll do ye nay good in the end.'

'You cannot be serious,' the Baron scoffed. 'I'm hardly likely to dispense with my primary form of leverage at this current time. What do you take me for?'

'Don't worry about me, I'll be fine,' Aiden shouted, as he leaned back against the mixing desk.

Ensuring that the point of his sword didn't stray by an inch, the Baron grabbed the collar of Aiden's jacket. 'I think it best if you come with me, at least for the time being. It appears I will need to make my escape and I'm afraid that you are ideal hostage material.'

At the end of the aisle to the right of the mixing desk was a door with a red 'Exit' sign above it. Slowly, the Baron and Aiden walked towards it, the point of the Baron's sword pushing Aiden along.

'Of course I'll have to kill you when we get outside,' the Baron whispered. 'Which is a pity, but that's life… or death, in your case.'

The mixing desk's lights suddenly brightened angrily, its sliders moving up and down. 'You'll do no such bloody thing, that lad's got to get me a vacuum cleaner later!'

Visible bolts of blue electricity shot up the Baron's arm; he screamed, dropped his sword and fell to his knees. Aiden was on him in a flash, knocking him on his back and pinning him to the ground. He put the blade of the pocket knife against the Baron's throat and grabbed his hair with his other hand.

'Ah, now this is an unfortunate turn of events,' Blacktie said, wriggling, until Aiden pressed the blade more firmly into his skin.

'You've got some explaining to do,' Aiden said, 'and perhaps you'd be kind enough to tell the good people here exactly what it is you've been up to.'

'I don't believe I've the faintest idea of what you're talking about.'

Aiden took an even tighter hold of the Baron's hair, causing him to yell in pain. General Darkblast ran towards the mixing desk, but found his way blocked by the imposing figure of Angus McSvensson. 'I'd advise ye to stand yer ground, Darkblast, unless ye've a liking for pain.'

The General eyed Angus nervously and backed away.

'So,' Aiden said to the Baron, 'Did you or did you not hatch a plan to obtain the ancient cheese mine owned by Agnar the Hammered by duping Sacred Wind into thinking they would be able to play at the Cestrian Music Tournament?'

'Oh, very well, yes,' the Baron said, to gasps from the audience.

'But you never intended for them to get to the tournament did you? That's why you despatched forces to try and kill them, isn't that the case?'

'I might have done,' the Baron said, until Aiden pressed the blade into his skin even harder, and the first specks of blood appeared. 'Oh, very well, yes. They should all be dead by now.'

The audience gasped again and the rumbling, bumbling mumblings returned with a vengeance. 'And why did you want this cheese mine?'

'Because it contained a magic cheese like no other,' the Baron said, a manic smile appearing on his lips. 'And when this Ceridwen's Cheese is mixed with Mathonwy's Chutney, whoever eats it becomes an all-powerful wizard. I would have been able to take over the world and all would have fallen at my feet. It all seemed perfectly logical, don't you think?'

Aiden said nothing and continued to press the blade against the Baron's throat. 'And did you not also kidnap Queen Ophelia, leaving her locked inside a dingy cell, and without a comb?'

'Yes,' the Baron said, preceding the word with a bored sigh.

More gasps from the audience, a few boos, and a shout of 'shame on you' from the large woman with the floral hat who'd been on the tour of the palace.

'And there's more isn't there?' Aiden said.

'What do you mean?'

'You know what I mean,' Aiden said. 'And I think these people have a right to know.'

Aiden tightened his grip on the Baron's hair and pushed his head down hard on the floor. 'Oh, very well,' the Baron said, 'I do have a small penis.'

The audience took the gasping to a new level of intensity, placing it in direct competition with the rumbling, bumbling mumblings. There were also several titters and a cry of 'I knew it' from the large woman with the floral hat.'

'Actually, I was referring to the fact that you really don't like rock music at all,' Aiden said.

'Damn,' said the Baron.

A commotion by the door provided a momentary distraction from the Baron's embarrassment, as two unusual looking men entered the theatre. 'Right, then, I think we can take that as a confession,' a tall man wearing a trilby hat and a full-length sheepskin coat said.

'Indeed,' said a shorter man, also wearing a trilby hat and a full-length sheepskin coat that was so long that it completely covered his feet.

'Allow me to introduce myself,' the taller man said, producing a police badge. 'I'm Chief Inspector Buttered and this is my partner, Detective Crumpet. We've been monitoring this individual for some time now and, thanks to you, we can finally ensure that he feels the full power of the law for his crimes. The last thing that's needed around here is a despotic megalomaniac with a small penis who doesn't like rock music.'

Aiden stood up and pulled the Baron to his feet. Inspector Crumpet produced a pair of handcuffs, snapping them onto the Baron's wrists. 'I'd have got away with it too, if it wasn't for you, that dog, a possessed mixing desk, an irate wizard-chef, cats, curries, faeries, sheep and those pesky Vikings,' the Baron growled.

'You've all done your country a great service. Enjoy the rest of your evening,' Chief Inspector Buttered said, as he man-handled the Baron out of the theatre door and into a waiting police carriage, the sound of booing pigs ringing in his ears.

In the theatre, cheers rang out, followed by several farts and the sound of cheese being sniffed. Champagne corks popped in the bar and Aiden blushed as an impromptu rendition of 'For He's A Jolly Good Fellow' was started by the audience.

As the police carriage disappeared around the corner and raced past the palace, boos turned into cheers and the delirious pigs ran into the theatre, followed by Cracky, Ophelia, Humphrey and Captain Marmaduke. Cracky ran straight over to Aiden, who was already being hugged by Mara, and threw his arms around him. 'I told you that you hadn't seen everything, didn't I,' he said, ruffling Aiden's hair. 'Lunch will be on me when we get back.'

Ophelia hurtled down the aisle and dived onto the stage. Olaf joyfully embraced her and the two kissed passionately, as the audience applauded and said 'aah'.

Then Mr Kneepatcher reached into his pocket and produced Ophelia's pink comb. 'Your Majesty, I believe this is yours,' he said, kneeling before her.

Ophelia's eyes lit up as bright as a Christmas tree with an extra set of lights, and she gratefully took the comb. 'Thank you, Gilbert,' she said, holding it tightly to her chest before planting a big kiss on Mr Kneepatcher's cheek.

'Oh, my,' he said. 'You sure know how to turn a man, Your Majesty. I'm more dithered than I've ever been!'

Roisin and Mara ran to Ophelia and they hugged, screamed and danced excitedly… and then made sure Ophelia's hair was well combed.

Back at the mixing desk, a familiar figure bounded into view. 'You see, I can't let you out of my sight for a minute without you getting into bother, can I?' Humphrey said to Aiden, wagging his tail.

'Humphrey!' Aiden shouted, running over to the little dog and hugging him. 'Er, you can speak.'

'Quite. And I'm looking forward to having some interesting conversations with you later, particularly regarding quantum computing and erroneous formulae. But, for now, I have a tremendous need to lick you all over your face, if that's not too much trouble.'

As Humphrey and Aiden reunited, Smid was hoisted high by the pigs and carried around the aisles like a hero. 'This is my daddy,' Crusher said to anyone in earshot. 'And he's my hero, and a very good bass player.'

With the theatre welcoming triumphalism with open arms and giving it a glass of champagne, Olaf decided to seize the moment, and the microphone.

'Good folk of Chester, are you ready to rock!' The response was in the affirmative, and even the large lady took her floral hat off and waived it around.

'Excuse me,' the lead violinist from the Cestrian Baroque Ensemble said to Olaf. 'Would you be offended if, on this joyous day, we asked to sing with you? We have decided to abandon our instruments in favour of a more choral approach.'

'Now that would depend on whether you can actually sing,' Olaf said. 'And also if you will all sing in the key the song is being played in.'

The four members of the ensemble coughed and broke into an extremely melodious four part harmony… all singing in the same key.

'That was impressive,' Olaf said. 'So why not.'

'Now, wait one minute,' an officious-looking organiser said, as Sacred Wind and the OSO began readying themselves on the stage. 'I'm afraid we're past our curfew time now. There'll be no more music tonight, that's the law.'

Angus McSvensson picked the official up in one hand and held him above his head. 'Who's law?' he said.

'B-Baron B-B-Blacktie's, of course,' the official said.

'Well, shall we ask the Baron if, in this instance, we can bend the rules a bit?'

'We can't, it would appear he's been arrested.'

'Ah, yes,' Angus said, 'that does create a wee bit of a dilemma. I'll tell ye what, given that we live in a democracy, why don't we ask these good people here what they'd like?'

With the official still hoisted high above his head, Angus turned to the crowd. 'Do ye want abide by the curfew or do ye want to hear some more music?'

The response was noisy and unequivocally unanimous.

***

The police carriage pulled to a halt just outside the city gates, and it soon became apparent that things were not perhaps what they seemed.

'We have arranged a safe haven for you, my Lord,' Hob said, removing his trilby.

'Indeed,' said Nob. 'It will provide you with an opportunity to keep a low profile for a period of time, and give you a chance to plot your next move.'

'Excellent,' said the Baron, as Nob removed the handcuffs. 'And I already have a plan, gentlemen… and a task for you.'

'Driver!' Hob shouted, and the carriage sped off into the night.

CHAPTER 47 – ODIN BLESSES YOUR WIND

'All we desired was to play our music freely,' Olaf said to the crowd. 'But the cost of this endeavour has been great. Friends who travelled with us have sadly fallen, but their memory, their heroism and their love will live long in the memory and be told in tales for evermore. They, like us, simply wanted to undo wrongs that have been wrought upon us all, and make our land a more just and happier place; for that was, and is, the spirit of our Companionship. We supported each other in times of need; we laughed with each other in times of joy; we farted freely together; we fought with some particularly dodgy curries, and we played a very good game of charades. In the end we proved that if you stick together, and if you truly believe, you can accomplish anything. And that is the way it should be for all.'

A massive round of applause burst from the audience, shaking the rafters and scaring the bats. The combined armies of Wrexham, Mold and the Cestrian-Russians bubbled and noisily clapped their mini-poppadoms together, as they balanced precariously on the tops of seats at the back of the theatre.

'And we have learned much,' Olaf went on. 'We have learned that Welsh Vikings can have platonic relationships with English sheep. We have learned that prejudice is a rock that can be shattered if the desire is there. And we have learned that everyone, no matter how big or how small, no matter how old or how young, has a hero inside them just waiting to be set free.'

At the mixing desk, Oldfart smiled and put his arm around Aiden, as the crowd went potty. 'Thank you so much,' Olaf said, with a tear in his eye. 'This is *"Fart for Odin"*.'

Cliff put a Sacred Wind sticker on his cello, Henry raised his conducting baton into the air and the OSO began the opening bar, a crescendo of strings, brass and woodwind buoyed along by rolling tympani.

And then the stage exploded with sound and light as the orchestra, band and choir powered into the introduction. Melodies soared, drums and tympani shook people in their seats, strings pulsed with emotion and urgency, and on top of it all Grundi's lead guitar blasted notes into the stratosphere. As the introduction reached its tumultuous climax, violin arpeggios flew up and down the scale like tuneful bees before band and orchestra bolted into a thunderous crescendo.

Olaf farted loudly and Agnar broke into an intricate pattern of sixteenth notes, interplaying between his tom toms and bass drums. Smid and Cliff played beat-for-beat with Agnar, a whirlwind of bass and cello rattling up and down the necks of their instruments in unison, smoke streaming from Cliff's bow. Then Grundi and Oriana entered the fray, lead guitar and flute elevating the music by an octave, as Oriana balanced expertly on one leg.

When the song reached the driving bridge prior to the first verse, Cliff raised his arms in the air and banged his head to the music. He looked towards the rest of the OSO, beckoning them to follow suit. And they did. The stage was a delightful mixture of heavy rock and headbanging sheep. The audience was compelled to follow suit, with the large lady in the floral hat leading the charge. She whipped off her hat, took the hairpin from the bob in her hair and really let herself go.

We drop our pants for Odin
And climb upon our steeds
We pass the Sacred Wind
Until our bottoms bleed
It's all in praise of Odin
We feel him in our hearts
For he gives us our power
And we give him our farts

Fart for Odin, Fart for Odin
Raise you bottom to the sky
Fart for Odin, Fart for Odin
Spread your cheeks, spread them wide
Fart for Odin, Fart for Odin
Let your bottom burp with pride
Fart for Odin, Fart for Odin
To the circle of wind we ride

At the mixing desk, Aiden was astonished how quickly the sound had come together. It was almost as if he was getting a helping hand... particularly when some sliders started moving by themselves.

'You know maybe you should forget about the whole vacuum cleaner thing. Maybe this is your thing,' Aiden said.

'Not a chance,' said the mixing desk, as a quick blast of feedback came out of the speakers.

'Whoa,' Aiden said. 'Fair enough, vacuum cleaner it is.'

Henry waved his baton aloft again and tapped his music stand, indicating it was time for the headbanging to cease and for the accompaniment to resume for the second verse.

We hail the mighty Asgard
With fire in our veins
In all its strength and majesty
In flatulence it reigns
Oh hear this mighty Odin
From one who is so true
My rear end shakes like thunder
As I let one go for you

Fart for Odin, Fart for Odin
Raise you bottom to the sky
Fart for Odin, Fart for Odin
Spread your cheeks, spread them wide
Fart for Odin, Fart for Odin
Let your bottom burp with pride
Fart for Odin, Fart for Odin
To the circle of wind we ride

The band, orchestra and choir then moved seamlessly into the mid-section. The Cestrian Baroque Ensemble exploded into full voice and Grundi's lead guitar sent notes towards the heavens once more, seeking out their stratospheric cousins. Although this section of the song had previously been instrumental, Olaf thought the occasion demanded something more. And so, lifting his head upwards and in time with the music he said the words.

Odin I beseech thee, accept my gift of wind
It's from the heart of my bottom
It's a gift I won't rescind
I fart for all your glory; I fart for all your might
Give me the strength to not follow through
And I'll fart for you; I'll fart for you all night

As Olaf poured out the emotional last phrase and the instruments began to fade in preparation for the guitar solo, Sacred Wind grabbed their weapons, pointed them skyward and farted, one after the other.

And then the theatre was bathed in light and filled with the sound of angels. 'Now is this part of the act?' Paddy McLeprechaun asked, as Colin Mowsel shrugged again.

All eyes turned towards the source of the light and a face began to appear in a nebulous cloud. Lightning bolts fizzled and thunder showed the rumbling, bumbling mumblings what real rumbling was all about. The features of the face slowly began to sharpen; a big beard, a very shiny Viking helmet... and a DJ's microphone.

'Odin blesses your wind,' a booming voice said.

An audience that had surely gasped enough for one evening felt compelled to do so again. Oldfart sank to his knees at the mixing desk, closely followed by Sacred Wind on stage.

'All-father,' Olaf said, his words echoing in a theatre filled with an awe-inspired silence. 'We thank you for this wondrous blessing. We, your humble servants, will forever remember this glorious day. You are truly the most wise, kindly and noble of all gods. We long to serve you and—.'

'Sorry to interrupt,' Odin said, 'but I get the picture. Now will you please get on with the bloody song. I'm looking forward to the guitar solo.'

And so they did.

Grundi's dazzling guitar playing captivated the audience and the crowd sang along with zeal in the last chorus. As they powered through the finale, band, choir and orchestra were musically and spiritually aligned, as coruscating flashbombs signalled the end of the performance.

The crowd roared their approval, they got a standing ovation from the judges and Odin clapped and nodded in appreciation. 'Definitely get you lads on the show,' he said, and promptly disappeared.

Sacred Wind, the OSO and the Cestrian Baroque Ensemble came to the front of the stage and bowed. Grundi threw some guitar picks into the audience, which caused quite a scramble, and Agnar followed suit by flinging out some of his spare drumsticks. One of the General's Knights inadvertently caught one, but was quickly felled by a vicious blow from the large lady with the floral hat, grabbing the drumstick off him before he could recover. Oldfart raced to the stage and hugged anyone in reach, leaving his final hug for Olaf, who had Ophelia on his shoulders.

'Well, I think it's safe to say we've not seen anything quite like that before,' the announcer said, bounding onto the stage. 'Judges?'

'My neck's sore from banging my head too much!' Paddy McLeprechaun enthused. 'I loved all of it, especially the big guy with the beard in the cloud.'

'I liked the farting,' Shirley Divastropalot said.

All eyes fell on Colin Mowsel. He had his pencil in his mouth, popping it up and down between his teeth. 'I thought it was absolutely extraordinary,' he said, to cheers and whoops from the audience. 'And I'll tell you why it was so good,' he went on. 'It was full of passion, the singing was fantastic, the headbanging sheep were out of this world, and I agree with Shirley, I loved the farting; a fabulous performance.'

Sacred Wind punched the air and the announcer did another twirl. 'And so, now we come to the moment of truth,' he said as the lights dimmed. 'Judges, have you totted up your score cards?'

'We have,' Paddy McLeprechaun said, passing the results to a nearby organiser, who quickly ran to the stage and deposited the envelope in the announcer's hand.

'So, if we can have all of tonight's contestants back on stage now please,' the announcer said.

The remaining acts hastily ran on to the stage and nervous tension seemed to be conversing with everyone.

'Right,' the announcer continued, opening the envelope, 'the judges have awarded marks out of ten in five categories; musical talent, song choice, artistic impression, likeability and originality. And now, in no particular order, I can reveal that the following three contestants have received the most points.'

A theatrical pause was inserted for effect between each act and the audience were on the edge of their seats. 'The Knights of Flatulence... Kyleene Mingin... and... Sacred Wind!'

The audience cheered, Oldfart clapped like a maniac and Mr Kneepatcher wiped sweat off his brow with the remains of his battle cravat.

'A big round of applause for the unlucky losers, then,' the announcer said, as the downcast contestants left the stage. 'You were all marvellous and let's hope we see you back here in the future... well, some of you.'

'And now,' he continued, as the lights dimmed, with a single spotlight shining on each of the remaining contestants, 'the act with the third highest score is ... and I must say that this is a surprise...'

Oldfart held his breath and Mara and Roisin held Mr Kneepatcher up to stop him fainting.

'... The Knights of Flatulence.'

Polite applause rippled through the crowd and General Darkblast looked crestfallen. Several of the Knights were openly weeping and the keyboard player tore off his cape and threw it on the stage, before walking off with his nose in the air.

'He plays crap music and he's a sore loser,' Smid mumbled to Grundi.

Now, only two spotlights remained. Kyleene Mingin was having trouble keeping still and bounced nervously, waving at the audience with a toothy smile. Sacred Wind and the OSO huddled close together, linking arms and hooves in a sign of unity.

The announcer signalled for quiet in the theatre. 'And so, it gives me great pleasure to announce that the winner of the Cestrian Music Tournament 1987 is…'

Another dramatic pause screamed silently in the air and all eyes were glued to the announcer. Another pause began where the first left off, although it could have been the first pause in disguise crying for more attention.

'… Kyleene Mingin!!'

Fireworks erupted from behind the stage, confetti streamed down from the roof, but the audience were aghast. Boos rang out and bits of rotten fruit were hurled. The announcer ran for cover and Olaf stepped in front of a quaking Kyleene Mingin.

'Stop, I say. Stop!' he bellowed, authoritatively.

The audience calmed down, but the rumbling, bumbling mumblings barged their way back into the theatre.

'It is not this girl's fault that she has been deemed the winner,' Olaf said. 'She was awarded the most points by the judges.'

So the audience pelted the judges with rotten fruit instead. Paddy McLeprechaun was hit in the chest with a rotten tomato, Colin Mowsel had cauliflower in his V-neck sweater, and Shirley Divastropalot hid behind her seat, just after a carrot had parted her hair.

'Stop!' Olaf roared again, banging the hilt of his huge sword on the stage. 'The judges have simply done their job as they saw fit. Do not vent any wrath upon them. Although we may be disappointed not to win, we feel blessed that we have been able to play here, and have been accompanied so marvellously by our friends. This is a time for celebration, not conflict. Blacktie is vanquished, my Queen is safe and we can fart freely.'

The audience looked embarrassed and dropped their heads in shame, the rumbling, bumbling, mumblings becoming contrite whispers.

'So, I say, show your appreciation for Kyleene Mingin,' Olaf went on. 'She performed heroically, if a little oddly, and we wish her well. She is welcome to fart with us anytime.'

Sacred Wind and the OSO began a round of applause and the crowd joined in with bashful enthusiasm.

'Er, can I just say something,' Colin Mowsel said, brushing cauliflower out of his V-neck sweater. 'There was actually only one point difference in the scores between the winner and the runner-up. Based upon that, and based upon the fact I thought Sacred Wind were fantastic, I have a proposal.'

'Ooh,' said the crowd.

'Now, although the tournament rules state only the winner will receive a record contract with Dee Records, I would hereby like to rip up those rules and extend that prize to the runner-up as well.'

Oldfart dashed towards the judge's box and waved. 'Hi, I'm Oldfart Olafson, the manager of Sacred Wind. Are you offering us a record deal, Mr Mowsel?'

'I am, and please call me Colin.'

Oldfart fainted and the theatre erupted once more. The fireworks and confetti resumed and the rotten fruit went back into brown paper bags for next year. 'And another thing,' Colin Mowsel said, as Oldfart got to his feet, 'I want the internationally-renowned producer Mutt Allomrock to work with the band; and we need to get you out on the road, beginning with a national tour.'

Oldfart fainted again, before being picked up by Olaf and carried onto the stage to be embraced the band. Roisin grabbed Agnar and kissed him full on the lips, causing his face to go several interesting shades of red.

Amidst the joyous celebrations, Aiden looked down at the mixing desk and tapped it affectionately with his hand. 'Thanks for your help,' he said, as he got hugs from Mara and Mr Kneepatcher.

'No problem. Just don't forget the vacuum cleaner.'

CHAPTER 48 – DRAGON SHIPS AND WOMEN'S HIPS

For the trip back to Llangollen, Ethel was filled with happy hearts and sore heads. Colin Mowsel had arranged an after-tournament party at the plush Chester Groovier hotel, including free food and drink, and rooms for all.

In an atmosphere of joyous insobriety, old enmities were temporality forgotten and even the keyboard player from the Knights of Flatulence joined Sacred Wind in some celebratory farting, along with Colin Mowsel and Paddy McLeprechaun. Shirley Divastropalot invited Ophelia, Mara and Roisin to her forthcoming super-duper-mega-ultra-celeb birthday party, and Mr Kneepatcher was presented with a commemorative cravat from the hotel, with the Groovier logo on it.

As Ethel passed under the arch of the Iron Bridge of Alford, they were met by cheering pigs. The front of The Pig's Trotters was festooned in bunting, with a large banner on the roof that simply said 'Odin Blessed Your Wind'. Most of the pigs were wearing imitation Viking helmets, much to the delight of Oldfart.

Smid had insisted Crusher, Chopper and Percy were invited to the party and travel back with the band, so Ethel was temporarily moored to let them disembark. As Smid and Crusher embraced, Oldfart promised Archie Backrasher that Sacred Wind would return next week for an acoustic gig.

They encountered no pirates or dodgy curries on the journey home and arrived back in Llangollen around mid-afternoon. News had obviously travelled fast and the banks of the river Dee were filled with waving people and sheep. Flotillas of boats accompanied them towards the quay and a brass band blared out its own rendition of 'Fart for Odin'.

Cracky insisted they all went to the diner for what was now a late lunch, and he took great delight in preparing a variety of new dishes he'd been working on, including Beef Medallions of Merriment, Cod of Conviviality, Shindig Salad, and Ice Cream Whoopee Wafers for dessert.

'Cracky, this cod is delicious,' Aiden said. 'What's in the sauce?'

'You don't want to know,' Cracky said.

Unsurprisingly, Maurice had arranged a party at The Sheep's Stirrup for the evening and had insisted that Sacred Wind play. The band readily agreed and Oldfart asked if he could set up a merchandising stall outside.

Aiden retired to his room and flung himself on the soft bed. Humphrey joined him, as he always used to, and they both drifted off into an untroubled afternoon nap, readying themselves for the night ahead.

They awoke to the sound of fireworks and a sun that was already halfway below the horizon. Downstairs, Maurice had decked out the pub in as much Viking paraphernalia as he could get his hands on. Swords, shields, axes and hammers adorned the walls, little wooden Viking longboats had been placed on serviettes on every table, and charming Viking figurines were sat like little guards on the windowsills.

'May Odin bless your wind,' Maurice said, his oversize Viking helmet nearly covering his eyes.

'And may Odin bless your wind also,' Aiden said, laughing.

'Well, I won't be needing this anymore,' Maurice said, removing the flatulence license from behind the bar, and letting out a little fart in the process.

'I was very sad to hear about Charles,' he added. 'He was a lovely old sheep.'

'He was,' Aiden said with a sigh. 'I can't think of anybody that won't miss him.'

'And I heard about the King and Queen, that was a very noble sacrifice,' Maurice said. 'I hope nobody thinks ill of us, but Blanche has prepared two special curries in their honour. I'm going to give them a special place on the buffet table… with a sign that says "Do Not Eat".'

'I think that's very appropriate, actually,' Aiden said, patting Maurice affectionately on the hoof.

No sooner had Aiden taken a sip from his glass of orange juice when Cracky arrived. He was wearing what appeared to be a brand-new full length cloak and a hat as pointed as a sharp nail. 'My, we are dressed for the occasion,' Aiden said.

'Well, we're sort of celebrities now, so I thought I should make the effort. Why are you drinking orange juice?'

'If we're in for a long night I want to enjoy it. I'm still not properly recovered from yesterday.'

'Good for you,' Cracky said. 'And although I feel I should follow your lead I'd like a pint of Riggley's Piddle, please Maurice.'

'Coming right up,' Maurice said.

It wasn't long before The Sheep's Stirrup was packed to the rafters. Sacred Wind and the OSO were given a hero's welcome when they arrived, with Roisin perched on Agnar's shoulders and Ophelia carried aloft by Olaf.

'Where's Mara?' Aiden asked, as they joined him at the bar.

'Oh, she's helping Mr Kneepatcher get ready,' Roisin said. 'They should be here soon.'

Angus McSvensson had to duck low to get through the door and soon found himself surrounded by adoring sheep, much to his embarrassment. 'Och, they seem to have really taken to me,' he said to Aiden at the bar. 'That one over there with the blond fleece extensions has been giving me the eye ever since I arrived. I may have to sneak out the back later.'

Mara burst through the door with a huge grin on her face. 'Please put your hands together for the man whose battle cravat served us so well, it's Gilbert Kneepatcher!'

Mr Kneepatcher jumped, ballerina-like, into the pub and did a pirouette. His knee-length brown boots joined seamlessly with his tartan jodhpurs, and his matching plaited tartan jacket was set off by a bright red cravat. On his head he wore a tartan deerstalker hat.

'Why, that's the McSvensson tartan!' Angus exclaimed, as Mr Kneepatcher milked the applause.

'You'd better believe it, big boy,' he said, with a wink.

'Now I really will have to sneak out the back later,' Angus whispered to Aiden.

By the time Prince Theo, Captain Marmaduke and Half-blind Ron arrived, the party was in full swing and the cats were welcomed with open arms and saucers of milk. 'And I have something for you, little fellow,' Cracky said to Half-blind Ron, pulling out a full roast chicken from a carrier bag.

Half-blind Ron's face lit up and he purred profusely. 'All for me?'

'Why, don't you think you deserve it?' Cracky said.

'Deserve it! After fighting witches, ferrets and nearly being killed dead, I reckon I does deserve it. If that's alright with you, Majesty, Princeness?' he said, with an appealing look towards Theo.

'Oh, you deserve it alright,' Theo said, licking one of Half-blind Ron's ears. 'Just don't make too much of a mess.'

As the ale flowed and spirits began to soar, thoughts turned to music. 'We'd better get on and play some tunes before I forget which way round I'm supposed to hold my drumsticks,' Agnar said to Olaf, as he finished his second tankard of ale.

'You have a good point, my friend. Smid, Grundi, shall we play?'

'Why not,' said Smid, as Grundi nodded in agreement.

They opened with 'Hurricane Ass', the lyrics representing Olaf's feelings on Ophelia's kidnapping… and Grundi's powerful rear end. Sheep danced on tables and Mr Kneepatcher incorporated his new penchant for ballet on the last chorus.

Harold and Greta had arrived and were doing their best not to look solemn, but their sadness at the loss of the King and Queen was still etched on their faces. They held General Lamb Korma-Saffron Rice and General Beef Madras-Wholegrain Rice aloft, who sang along merrily, emboldened by the significant quantities of lime juice supplied by Maurice.

'And now, we'd like to make a very special presentation,' Olaf said, as the applause died down. 'Without this splendid fellow, I'm not sure whether we'd all be here tonight. He certainly won't sing his own praises, so I'll sing them for him. Please give it up for our friend and mixing engineer, Aiden Peersey.'

Aiden's face reddened as Olaf beckoned him to come forward and Grundi hastily disappeared through the dressing room door, returning with a large wooden box. 'We'd like you to accept this by way of thanks,' Olaf said, handing him the box. 'And, obviously, we'd be honoured if you'd continue to be our mixing engineer.'

In the box was a beautifully-crafted broadsword with an ornately-carved gold hilt. The inscription on the blade said, 'To Aiden Peersey, Honorary Member of Sacred Wind.'

'I don't know what to say,' he said, holding it aloft, as his eyes filled up and The Sheep's Stirrup cheered.

'Well, that pocket knife was beginning to look a bit embarrassing, you must admit,' Grundi said, patting him on the back.

It began as a disconcerting rumble, causing the entire pub to go quiet. Above Agnar's drum kit the air rarefied and a soft white glow began to expand. Lightning bolts shot through the air as only lightning bolts can, and the sound of angels filled the room.

'Hello there,' Odin said, waving. 'I just thought I'd pop in to say well done. You really kicked some ass last night, including Blacktie's!'

'All-father, we are blessed again,' Olaf said, as he and the band dropped to their knees.

'Oh, please get up,' Odin said. 'As much as I appreciate the gesture, let's keep it informal. This is a celebration, after all. And, also, there's someone here who wants to say hello.'

Another figure appeared next to Odin, fuzzy and indistinct at first, but slowly resolving into a shape that could be discerned… it was the shape of a sheep… of a sheep with spectacles… and a trumpet.

'Well, bless my clacky hooves,' Charles Corriedale said, as Odin put his arm around him.

'Uncle!' Cliff yelled.

'Oh, hello my boy, how are you all?'

'Er, we're fine now, how are you?'

'Well, apart from being dead, I feel absolutely splendid. Odin's been a great host. Your Auntie Betty and I are to be guests of honour at a big bash in Valhalla later. And they've asked me to play a trumpet concerto for them, so I may have to take it easy on the cider.'

'That's fantastic,' said a beaming Cliff.

'How's Oriana, by the way? She looks lovely tonight,' Charles went on.

Cliff held Oriana's hoof and smiled warmly. 'She's fine uncle. We were going to announce it later, but now seems to be much more appropriate; she's agreed to be my wife.'

'Well, bless my clacky hooves again, what splendid news,' Charles said, clapping his hooves together as The Sheep's Stirrup roared their approval.

'Oh, and I have a message for Grundi from Frigg,' Charles added. 'She sends love and kisses and would love some private guitar lessons.'

Grundi went a very bright shade of red, until Agnar nearly sent him flying with an enormous pat on the back. 'Hey, you're in there!' Agnar exclaimed, as Odin tutted, saying 'that goddess is such a flirt' under his breath.

Odin then raised his hands in the air to restore order. 'One more thing before we go. Now, there are times, when particularly noble deeds have been performed, that I deem it necessary to interfere. True, I'll probably get a right telling off at the next Bi-Millennial Deity Conference, but in this instance I'm just going to tell them to stick it where the sun don't shine.'

He held out the palm of his left hand and pointed it towards the buffet table. A golden beam of light issued forth and engulfed the two curries created in honour of Vindy and Tikky. 'Goodbye for now,' Odin said, as he and Charles waved. 'I bless your wind, and may your ale always be served by buxom women, may your poppadoms ever be crispy, and may your curry never be blighted by watery rice.'

As the vision faded, all eyes turned to the buffet table. Both curries glowed gold, then there was a blinding flash and the light disappeared. At first, nothing happened. But then, slowly, each of the plates started to wobble, with little wisps of steam rising into the air.

'Tikky, is that you?' Vindy said, puffing his rice.

'My darling Vindy, is that you? Tikky replied.

'It is, my Queen. But you look so young and luscious. I've never seen your meat look so tender, your rice so fluffy.'

'And you, my King, why your beef is so well pronounced and your sauce, it's so thick and splendid.'

'Maurice, have you still got that tinfoil!' Vindy shouted.

Harold and Greta ran over to the table for a joyous reunion. General Lamb Korma-Saffron Rice and General Beef Madras-Wholegrain Rice, decidedly worse for wear on lime juice, celebrated the occasion by regaling the King and Queen with a rather bawdy curry song about saggy poppadoms.

'Oh, stop it, Saffy, you're making me blush,' Tikky said.

'Well, now we seem to have even more reason to celebrate,' Olaf said, as he slung his guitar around his neck. 'So we'd like to play a song that perhaps befits the occasion. This is "Dragon Ships and Women's Hips".'

Dragon ships and women's hips
Make me feel alright
I've got the wind in my sails
Headin' for the shore
Headin' for my baby

When we're far away
I know that I long for the day
When I can steer my ship
Towards your hips
And dock it in your bay
Because when we are far apart
I feel an aching in my heart
My axe don't feel the same
There's no flame
Even when I fart

You're in my heart and soul
For all time now
I see you waiting for me
And I know that

Dragon ships and women's hips
Make me feel alright
I've got the wind in my sails
Headin' for the shore
Headin' for my baby
Dragon ships and women's hips
They've been in my dreams
They put a smile on my face
Headin' for the shore
Headin' for my baby

'I think you need a little bit more top on the vocals,' Humphrey said, as he watched Aiden at the mixing desk.

'Okay, thanks Humphrey.'

When the seas are rough
And I feel that I've had enough
I think of your sweet face,
Our special place
And your hips in the buff
Because you are my faerie queen
You are the reason that I'm clean
I've had a real good scrub,
In the pub
And now my helmet gleams

You're in my heart and soul
For all time now
I see you waiting for me
And I know that

Dragon ships and women's hips
Make me feel alright
I've got the wind in my sails
Headin' for the shore
Headin' for my baby

I see you now on the shore
I'll soon be back in your arms
And your hips
Cause I love you

Grundi's guitar solo was accompanied by the entire OSO, playing air guitar. Mr Kneepatcher grabbed Angus by the hand and dragged him onto the dance floor, and even Cracky and Oldfart put up little resistance as Roisin and Ophelia cajoled them to join in.

Dragon ships and women's hips
Make me feel alright
I've got the wind in my sails
Headin' for the shore
Headin' for my baby
Dragon ships and women's hips
They've been in my dreams
They put a smile on my face
Headin' for the shore
Headin' for my baby

'I'm really pleased for Cliff and Oriana,' Mara said, as she linked arms with Aiden. 'They make a lovely couple, and I'm sure they'll have beautiful little lambs.'

'Me too,' Aiden said. 'I couldn't be happier for them.'

'You know, perhaps it's time I settled down and got married,' she said, her eyes indicating this was a question as much as a statement.

Then Aiden's phone rang. It was Tom. 'I just need to take this call,' Aiden said, touching Mara on the cheek as he walked out the pub.

'Well, hello there,' Tom said. 'Been up to anything interesting while I've been away?'

'You could say that,' Aiden replied. 'How did your enquiries about getting me home go?'

'Ah, now there's the thing,' Tom said. 'I may not have been entirely honest with you.'

'Meaning?'

'Do you remember when I said that my role is to guide you on your way and help you make the right decisions; the decisions that are best for you?'

'Yes.'

'Well how do you think you ended up here in the first place?'

Aiden's mouth dropped open and he was lucky there were no flies around. 'Hang on; are you saying all this was meant to happen?'

'Absolutely,' Tom continued. 'Just think about the things in your life you've always dreamt of. All I needed to do was push you in the right direction. Where do you think that the idea for the QC Nova phone came from?'

'Well it just sort of came to me one day when…oh my, that's astonishing.'

'Not really,' Tom said, 'not if you think about it. Don't forget, the Multiverse works with us all the time. We feed it with thoughts, emotions, all kinds of stuff. And sometimes, particularly if those feelings are strong enough, we find out it's actually listening. How cool is that.'

'Well, what would happen now if I used the QC Nova phone to navigate back to Wrexham?'

'I think that depends entirely upon you; it's your choice. As Odin said, that's why we've got freewill.'

Mara appeared at the door and waved. 'C'mon back in, you're missing all the fun. Mr Kneepatcher's serenading Angus with a rose between his teeth.'

'You know, I think I may just hang around here for a bit,' Aiden said, as he waved back at Mara.

'Good choice,' said Tom.

'Will I speak to you again?'

'Oh, I would think so. Remember, I do sort of know what can happen next, depending on your decisions, of course.'

'But you're not going to tell me.'

'And spoil the fun, are you serious?'

'Thanks for everything, I suppose,' Aiden said.

'You've very welcome,' said Tom. 'Goodbye for now.'

'Goodbye Tom,' Aiden said. And he clicked the end call button on the phone.

'Who were you talking to?' Mara asked, as they went back inside the pub.

'An old friend. He just wanted to make sure I was alright.'

'What did you say?'

'I would have told him I've never been happier, but I think he already knew.'

Some members of the OSO had set up their instruments and were playing a lively jig. Mr Kneepatcher was dancing around a very confused looking Angus McSvensson and Agnar seemed to be doing an interesting variation of 'The Twist'.

'Would you care for a dance, Mr Aiden Peersey?' Mara said.

'You know, I believe I would.'

The End…? I very much doubt it.

Andy Coffey

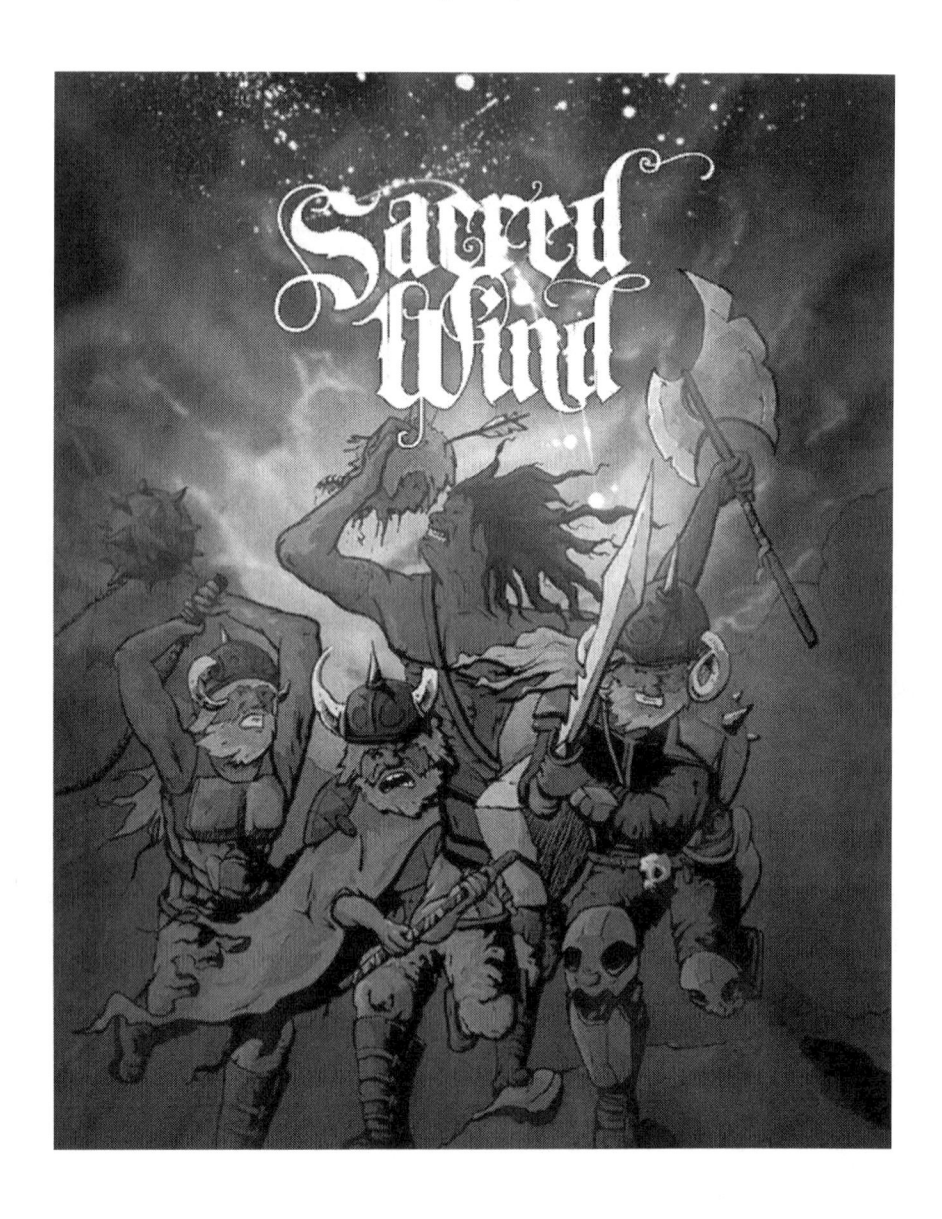

EPILOGUES

The ancient stones of the Circle of Wind still stood firm against the elements, as they had for millennia. Tonight the air was still, the stars were bright and the only sound was the chirruping conversations of crickets.

Two figures appeared from over the nearby hill, teetering along like two crabs wearing particularly ill-fitting shoes. They appeared to be singing, but the song could not be discerned at this distance. As they got closer to the Circle, the song could still not be discerned. Not because it was an ancient song spun from some arcane language; not because it was a song from a faraway land, brought home after years in the wilderness; no, it could not be discerned because neither figure seemed to know the words or the melody.

'Dish ish deh plache!' Grundi the Windy said, lifting his arms to the heavens.

'Itsh very nicshe,' said Henry Fluffywool, hiccupping loudly.

'So, what we need to do ish take down our troushers,' Grundi said, 'and bend over like thish, see.'

'Like thish?' Henry said, copying Grundi.

'Thatsh it! Thatsh perfect.'

'What now?' asked Henry.

'Why, fart of courshe,' Grundi said.

'But I haven't got any fart in me,' Henry appealed.

'Courshe you have, you jusht need to push hard. You'll soon let one go. Remember, itsh for Odin.'

Henry concentrated hard and pushed... and pushed... and pushed... until.

'Oh, dear,' Grundi said. 'I shink Odin got a little more than he wash exchpecting then, but never mind, itsh the thought that countsh.'

**

The interim Supreme Ruler of North Wales, Chester and the Wirral sat on his gold and marble throne reading, as his Chief Courtier entered the room. 'My Lord, there are papers for you to sign and also a decision you must make about General Darkblast,' Pimple said, handing over the pile of papers.

The Baron read through each one carefully before signing his name. He passed them back to Pimple, who placed them in his briefcase. 'Thank you, my Lord.'

'You're welcome, Pimple.'

'And General Darkblast, my Lord?'

The Baron stood up and walked around the throne, leaning on the back. Pimple waited patiently while the Baron mulled over the options in his head. 'Grunt has decided that General can continue in role of General,' Baron Grunt said.

'Thank you my Lord. The General will be very relieved, and he asked me to personally convey his assurance of loyalty to you.'

A scream from a nearby room echoed through the palace and Pimple turned his head towards the door. 'Oh, you'll have to excuse me, my Lord; one of the cleaners appears to be having some sort of breakdown. The poor, deluded woman seems to think the vacuum cleaner is out to get her. Only this morning she said it was levitating and speaking in tongues.'

'Grunt excuses Pimple.'

'Thank you, my Lord. I'll be back momentarily.'

Pimple ran into the room to find the woman cowering in the corner and the vacuum cleaner standing silent. It was switched off, but still plugged into the wall socket.

'There, there now,' he said, as he unplugged the vacuum cleaner. 'See, everything's fine, I'll put it back into the cupboard for you.'

'No you bloody won't,' said the vacuum cleaner. 'Cause I've got a message for you.'

Baron Grunt lifted his head and shook it slowly, as two screams echoed through the palace. Then he picked up his book and continued to read.

***

Saturday night at Billy's Chippie was always eventful. Once the nightclubs had emptied their sozzled customers onto the street they did a roaring trade, with the queue extending out of the shop. The quality of the food was actually considered edible, and this led to Billy being given the 'Scouseland Chippie of the Year' award, which he proudly displayed in a frame on the wall.

'Gimme a portion of scallops, a fish and a carton of gravy,' a staggering man in a leather jacket said.

'Do you want salt and vinegar on that?'

'Yeah, oh and throw in a couple of sausages as well.'

'What size?'

'What size? Sausage sized.' the staggering man said.

'Look, we have regular sausages, large sausages and super-size sausages. It's really quite simple. Even someone with your limited intellectual prowess should be able to grasp that.'

'Ay, are you taking the mickey, pal?'

'Oh, I doubt I could do that. You look far too stupid.'

Scuffles broke out over the counter and Billy rushed in from the back of the shop. 'Calm down, Calm down!' he said, pushing the staggering man away.

'Look, I'm sorry, Tony,' Billy went on. 'Dis lad's new and he's still learning deh ropes. 'Ave a free pie,' he added, handing a pie to Tony.

Tony staggered out of the shop and Billy's face transformed from a congenial smile into a furious scowl. 'You get in deh back now,' he said, marching into the kitchen.

'He was an imbecile and he was obnoxious.'

'Look, I don't care what religion he was,' Billy said. 'A paying customer is a paying customer, you got dat?'

'Yes, I suppose so.'

'Good, cause otherwise instead of getting a payslip with Bart Blacktie's name on it at deh end of deh week you'll be getting a letter of dismissal and a boot up the arse.'

***

Deep in the passages of the Great Pyramid of West Kirkby the incessant darkness was interrupted by three small torches. 'This is the way gentlemen; no-one but me has been down here for over a thousand years. Yes, only I, Mustapha Haircut, know how to navigate these tunnels.'

'We are honoured to have found such an erudite and hirsute guide. Both Mr Tattle and I are most appreciative.'

'Indeed, Mr Tittle speaks the truth,' said Mr Tattle. 'It is an honour.'

A small gust of wind momentarily threatened to extinguish the small flames on the torches and the three men held their breath. 'Ah, we are here,' said Mustapha Haircut. 'Look gentlemen. Look at something that no man on this earth has seen before.'

Mr Tittle and Mr Tattle held their torches against the wall in front of them and turned towards each other with amazement. A smile formed on Mr Tittle's lips.

'We must get a message to the Baron,' Hob whispered to Nob. 'He was correct. The Great Pyramid of West Kirkby does indeed have an "On" switch.'

APPENDIX 1 – A QUICK GUIDE TO QUANTUM COMPUTING

The workings of quantum mechanics are wacky. Let's not beat around the bush here, Niels Bohr, who won the Nobel Prize for Physics, said 'Anyone who is not shocked by quantum theory has not understood it'. Another Nobel Prize winner, Richard Feynman, said 'I think I can safely say that nobody understands quantum mechanics'. So these guys were baffled by it and they were really clever.

Quantum computing is, perhaps unsurprisingly, computing that harnesses the bizarre workings of quantum mechanics and, depending upon what you read, can be met with the same degree of obfuscation. So, anyone who really isn't bothered how it works and is quite happy to accept that it's simply wacky and uses other dimensions to assist in computations, good for you. For those of you who are slightly more curious, or those of you who have a technological masochistic propensity, please read on.

Now your normal, everyday computers, when you really get down to it, all work on the principal that little switches on silicon chips or suchlike are either on or off. And to denote something as either being on or off, binary numbers are used at the lowest level of programming. You see, whereas we can count in base ten, e.g. 1, 2, 3, 4 etc. up to 10, computers can't. They have to translate everything into a mixture of 0s and 1s (if computers had ten fingers and ten toes maybe things would be different). So, thousands or even millions, of tiny, tiny, tiny, tiny little, itsy bitsy transistors (basically little switches) on a silicon chip are either 'on', which may denote 1, or 'off', which may denote 0.

And that's basically it. In theory, simple; in practice it can get pretty complicated otherwise we'd all be at it. Computer languages effectively tell these little switches which of them should be 1 and which should be 0, based upon the instructions written in the higher language of the program, which is translated by the computer down to low-level languages and eventually into binary instructions; at which point the computer says 'Aha, now I understand!' and goes off about its business.

So, if a computer has to do everything in 0s and 1s, how does it count you may ask? Okay, let's take the number 5 as an example. In binary this is represented as 101. Because in binary the natural steps of multiplication aren't 10s, 100s, 1000s etc. they are 2, 4, 8, 16 etc. Have a look:

Binary number	1	0	1
Decimal integers	1	2	4

So, 101 is one number 1, no number 2 and one number 4 = 1 + 0 + 4 = 5.

Confused? Okay, here's the number 9:

Binary number	1	0	0	1
Decimal integers	1	2	4	8

So, in decimal this translates thus, 1 + 0 + 0 + 8 = 9.

And the number 52 (just to get really adventurous):

Binary number	0	0	1	0	1	1
Decimal integers	1	2	4	8	16	32

No number 1, no number 2, one number 4, no number 8, one number 16 and one number 32 = 0 + 0 + 4 + 0 + 16 + 32 = 52!

Hopefully you've now got the picture, although why they didn't just create computers with ten fingers and toes in the first place is probably the question we should all be asking.

Now, in general computing terms a single switch is called a 'bit' and can be either 1 or 0. Eight bits make a 'byte' (which could be 10010011, for example), hence the term 'megabyte' (a million bytes), 'gigabyte' (a thousand million bytes) and 'terabyte' (oodles and oodles of bytes).

So, let's take an imaginary computer that only has two bits and can, therefore, only have the following states: 00, 01, 10 or 11

Okay, so it can have the above four states but only one state at a time, as the switches are either 1 or 0 , and obviously not both as that would be impossible... or very wacky; which leads nicely into an explanation of a qubit and something called 'superposition'.

A qubit (or quantum bit, to give it its full title) is a single quantum switch that could be, say, an electron. And electrons are entities which exist in atoms, so as you can see we're really getting to a whole new level of tiny here. Now, electrons have this property called 'spin', although it should really be called 'point' as they can be either pointing up (spin up) or pointing down (spin down). So you now have a really, really, really, really, really, tiny, itsy bitsy, cute little switch, where up could be 1 and down could be 0. But, and here's where the wackiness really kicks in with a vengeance, in the quantum world entities like electrons can be in what's known as a 'superposition' of states, which means that in the right conditions they can be both 'on' and 'off' at the same time. No wonder the scientists are still baffled.

And before any of you start shouting, 'aha, I've got an electricity switch in the house that behaves in the same way', can I just say that this is not the same thing.

So, in order to have a regular computer display the states 00, 01, 10 and 11 simultaneously you'd need four pairs of bits. But in a quantum computer you'd only need two qubits to do the same task, as they can be in all four states at the same time!

Ok, that's quite cool, you may think, but it gets cooler the more qubits you have. Eight qubits is called a 'qubyte' (no surprise there). A normal byte can be in 256 different states (e.g. 00000000 and all variations up to 11111111), but can only be in one of these states at a time. However, a qubyte can store all 256 states AT THE SAME TIME!

'How does it do this?' I hear you ask. Easy, each state is a probability that exists in a different dimension.

APPENDIX 2 – THE BI-MILLENNIAL DEITY CONFERENCE

The Bi-millennial Deity conference is a grand event where Gods, Demi-Gods and mystical figures from all the major, minor, fledgling and even non-existent religions meet to discuss the current state of the Multiverse, changes and improvements to policies, upcoming mystical events, and who has the most statues. The event is hosted on a rotating basis and minutes and records are closely guarded and stored in the Principal Akashic Library. However, following a major lapse in security, the library systems were hacked by an undercover journalist and the partial records of the 15,876th meeting were, for a short time, made publicly available.

The Official Records of the 15,876th Bi-Millennial Deity Conference
Location – Valhalla
Host – Odin

Primary Attendees (Deities): Zeus, Hera, Hercules, Uranus (Greece), God (Christianity), Jupiter, Juno, Mars, Neptune, (Roman), Vishnu, Brahma, Kali (Hindu), Odin, Frigg, Thor, Loki, Tyr (Norse), Pangu, Si-wang-mu (Yin), Mu Gong (Yang) (Chinese), Osiris, Isis, Thoth (Egyptian), Buddha (Independent), Quetzalcoatl (Aztec), Anu, Ea, Damkina, Ishtar (Babylonian), Izanimi, Izanagi (Japan).

Attendees (Non-deities, guests of honour and interested parties):
Confucius, Lao Tzi, King Arthur, Bernard and Dennis (fledgling religion for The Brotherhood of Alligator), Elvis Presley, William Shakespeare.

Apologies for non-attendance: Prophet Mohammed, Horus, Mother Theresa.

Agenda:

1. *Welcome and registration*
2. *Opening speech - Odin*
3. *Freewill debate - God*
4. *Coffee/Ale break*
5. *Guest Speech: The generation of peace and harmony throughout the Multiverse - Buddha*
6. *'Icon of the Year' presentation - Zeus*
7. *Tea and biscuits/Ale break*
8. *'Vision of Honour Raffle' - Vishnu*
9. *Closing speech - Odin*
10. *Evening meal/Ale and entertainment – including Mozart/Beethoven piano battle*

(Partial transcript from 'Welcome and registration')

'Well, fancy seeing you here, you old bugger! How are you?'

'I fare well, good Odin,' replied Zeus. 'And you?'

'Not so bad, really. I did hit the ale a little too hard at the pre-conference party last night, though, so I'm suffering a bit. You really don't want to have a drinking competition with the Egyptians, you know. I never knew old Osiris had it in him. And the language out of Isis! You wouldn't believe such a sweet mouth could utter such words. Very funny jokes though.'

'Did she tell you the one about the phoenix, the priest, the scarab, and the assorted candles?' Zeus enquired.

'Laughed so hard I nearly shat myself,' said Odin

'Anyway,' he continued, 'is your good lady attending today?'

'Hera? Yes, she's over there chatting to Aphrodite and Kali. I'll call her over. Hera, Hera,' Zeus shouted, in the direction of his wife. 'Look which old scallywag I've bumped into.'

'Hello, you old dog,' Hera said to Odin, running over and planting a kiss on his bearded cheek, 'lovely to see you.'

'Likewise, of course, my lady, it is rare that Valhalla is treated to such beauty. And may I say that your wonderful dress serves well in displaying your most exquisite charms.'

'Oh, stop it Odin,' Hera said, blushing.

'Indeed, though,' Odin continued 'the cut is most complimentary. You must congratulate the designer, as he or she no doubt understands to perfection how to amplify the effect of the bosom of my favourite goddess, as to set my heart racing and my blood coursing.'

'Will you stop looking at my wife's cleavage you randy old fool!' Zeus admonished.

'Oh, Zeus, he's only being playful,' Hera said, 'and anyway, I find his ways very charming,' she added, fluttering her eyelashes.

'Why thank you, kind Hera,' Odin replied, with a sideways smile at Zeus.

'You can take that smug look off your face right now, my old friend,' Zeus growled. 'You won't look so smug with a lightning bolt up your arse, I can tell you.'

(...the transcript then moves on to reveal part of the 'Opening speech'...)

'Fellow Gods, guests and those of you who bribed the doormen, I extend a warm welcome to you all for this our 15,876th conference. You will be relieved to know that I will keep the speech short and will ensure that the ale remains readily available throughout the day.'

(Laughter and applause)

'And please make sure you get your raffle tickets for the 'Vision of Honour' Raffle' later. This event's winner will get a chance to provide the vision of his/her choice to one of our carefully selected planets. And don't forget all proceeds from the raffle are distributed to worthy causes throughout the Multiverse, after the standard reductions required for administration and distribution. And please remember to write your name clearly on the back of your ticket before placing it into the ceremonial bucket when the girls bring it round later. Also, our evening entertainment includes the long-awaited piano battle between Mozart and Beethoven, which promises to be a lively affair given the taunting and arguments that took place at the weigh-in and press conference yesterday.'

(...the transcript moves on the guest speech from Buddha...)

'My friends, the Multiverse today requires our earnest attention. Division is rife and it is our responsibility to restore balance and harmony, so as to perpetuate an everlasting flow of good karma...'

'You know, I really like Buddha but he can be a bit melodramatic at times,' whispered Hercules, son of Zeus.

'Indeed,' responded Thor, the Norse God of Thunder, 'he dost often delveth into the most sacred of matters and canst become immersed in their profundity.'

'Why are you speaking like that?' said Hercules. 'You sound like a right pillock.'

'I hath been taking archaic elocution lessons to enhanceth my image.'

'Art thou taking the pisseth?' Hercules laughed. 'Wait until Mars hears this. Hey, Mars,' he called to the next table, 'Thor's started speaking like a right fop. He thinks he's bloody Shakespeare or something.'

'Get thee hence, uncouth barbarian. Dare thee not to seek to make my personage blameworthy in this matter,' William Shakespeare said from the opposite table.

'Ooh, get Willy there, will you. Keep your wig on, mate,' Hercules responded.

'Will you please be quiet,' Neptune the Roman God of the Sea chided. 'I'm trying to listen.'

'Can you smell fish? I can smell fish,' Hercules said.

'Very funny,' said Neptune. 'You better watch yourself next time you're at sea, you over-muscled, egotistical halfwit.'

'You watch who you're calling "egotistical", gill features.'

'Ssssshhhhh,' Uranus, the Roman God of the Sky hissed. 'Buddha's saying something significant here. Stop being so ignorant, Hercules.'

'Oh, don't be such a party pooper, Uranus,' said Loki, the Norse God of Mischief. 'Hercules is only having a bit of fun.'

'Yeah, thanks Loki,'

'And anyway,' Loki added, 'he's hardly likely to take the advice of someone who's named after somebody's bottom, is he?'

'Well I never!' said Uranus.

'Well maybe you should,' said Loki, 'and then you'd lighten up a bit!'

'Good one, Loki!' said Hercules.

'Now look here,' Thoth, the Ibis-headed Egyptian God of Wisdom, said, with exasperation. 'Will you all please just pack it in. Most of us would like to listen to Buddha and believe he has an important message. It is vital that we encourage universal peace and harmony, lead by example and ensure that this message of love is inculcated throughout all life forms in the Multiverse.'

'Oh, shut it, bird-face,' Hercules said.

'Right, that's it,' Thoth said, standing up, 'bring it on then you gormless, Greek delinquent. I'll peck your bloody eyes out.'

(Scuffles break out in the Great Hall)

'Please, please, my friends,' Buddha pleaded. 'Is it any wonder our beloved Multiverse is filled with torment and suffering when we who should be the most compassionate of beings cannot settle our differences amicably?'

'Sorry about this, Buddha,' Odin said jumping onto the rostrum, 'but it'll calm down in a minute. They really should show you more respect.'

'Thank you, kind Odin, but I do not desire respect,' Buddha replied, 'for that is merely a facet of ego. And ego blocks compassion. I have thankfully attained peace of mind and have long since abandoned the need for attachments of that nature.'

'Well good for you,' Odin said.

'Anyway,' Buddha said, pointing at his chest and shouting at the scuffling crowd below, 'who's got the most statues, eh?!'

(...the transcript moves on to the 'Vision of Honour Raffle'...)

'Ok, it's now time for the raffle,' Odin announced, 'and I'd like to invite our great compatriot, Lord Vishnu, to the stage to draw the winning ticket.'

(Warm applause as Vishnu makes his way to the rostrum)

'Right, then,' said Vishnu, as he put one of his four hands into the bucket.

'Make sure you just pick one, Vishnu,' Odin advised. 'It got pretty nasty last time out.'

'And the winning ticket is... why it's none other than the king himself; it's Elvis Presley!' Vishnu announced.

(More applause as Elvis makes his way to the stage)

'Ah, I'm glad he's won,' said Hercules, joining in the applause. 'I love listening to him.'

'Yes, it doth warmeth my heart and doth provideth sustenance to my loins in these most testing of times. Verily, his fetlocks art replete,' Thor replied.

'Have you any idea what you're actually saying, Thor?'

'Er, no, not really. Sounds good, though, doesn't it.'

'No, Thor, it doesn't.'

'He's from our home town, you know,' Dennis, High Priest of The Brotherhood of the Alligator, shouted over, pointing at Elvis.

'Is he, now?' replied Thor. 'Have you met him?'

'Well, we visited his grave once and said hello, but he must have been out,' Bernard, High Priest of The Brotherhood of the Alligator, replied.

'Have you two been sacrificed recently by any chance?' asked Hercules.

'Indeed,' answered Dennis, 'we were told we had been specially chosen by Arthur, our Lord Alligator.'

'Yes, I can see why.'

'Anyway,' Hercules continued, 'after the last vision debacle with Tiahuizcalpantecuhtil I'm sure that Elvis will do a much better job.'

'Why, what happened?' Thor asked.

'Well, he went to a planet in the Dyslexia-Prime system and gave them a morning prayer that included saying his name 47 times. Most of the population died out in the first week.'

'And so, it gives me great pleasure to present this year's Vision of Honour prize to Elvis Presley,' Vishnu said, handing over the commemorative scroll.

'Thankyuhverramuch,' said Elvis.

Addendum – 'Vision of Honour'

On the tiny planet of Weyweydoun word had got out and a large crowd had gathered on the plains of Extrixieth. Priest Milliwopple had had a dream, so it was said, and this dream foretold that a wonderful vision would appear today in the sky at 12:03 pm, and would speak of love, hope and unity. Everyone was very excited and the souvenir vendors were already rubbing their hands with glee.

12:03 pm arrived and the crowd turned their eyes skyward. 'Speak to us, our Lord, as was prophesised, we await your blessing,' Priest Milliwopple exhorted to the sky.

Almost imperceptibly at first, the light appeared. It grew rapidly in incandescence, its brilliance illuminating the field below until it soon shone brighter than the sun… and then…

'Way, Way Down', sang Elvis.

'The Lord speaks to us!' Priest Milliwopple cried, turning to the crowd.

'Ahh,' said the crowd.

'By what name are you known, oh Lord?' he continued, shaking as he spoke.

'I am the king,' said Elvis.

'Oh, our King, we are forever blessed!' cried Priest Milliwopple.

'We are forever blessed!' cried the crowd.

'Are you known by any other names, oh King?'

'Elvis,' said Elvis.

'All praise King Elvis!' shouted Priest Milliwopple.

'All praise King Elvis!' shouted the crowd.

'Oh, King Elvis, we have waited for your coming for countless ages. You have brought light and hope into our lives!'

'I'm all shook up,' sang Elvis.

'He is all shook up!' cried Priest Milliwopple.

'He is all shook up!' cried the crowd.

'Oh, King Elvis, we feared we had been abandoned and that no one was watching over us.'

'You were always on my mind,' sang Elvis.

'Praise the King!' said the crowd.

'But, King Elvis, where have you been all this time?' Priest Milliwopple asked. 'We have felt alone in the darkness, with no one to guide us.'

'In the Ghetto,' sang Elvis.

'Ah, and now you have finally come to us, your people. We will worship you always!'

'You don't have to say you love me.'

'Oh, King Elvis, but to worship you will fulfil our lives and allow us to honour your magnificence. How shall we do this?' Priest Milliwopple implored.

'Love me tender,' crooned Elvis.

'We will love you tender!' cried Priest Milliwopple.

'We will love you tender!' the crowd shouted, adoringly.

'Please let me through, let me through,' a woman pleaded, pushing through the assembled throng.

'Oh, King Elvis, I have sinned. In order to feed my family I have sold myself to men, women and cattle for their pleasure. Could you please find it in your heart to forgive me so I can once again feel at peace with myself?'

There was silence and the crowd sighed.

'That's all right mama,' sang Elvis.

'She is forgiven, she is forgiven!' the crowd shouted.

'King Elvis,' a man called out, 'some of us have been enticed by the Great Fido, the canine deity of Poochbarkia. Why should we now worship you?'

'He ain't nothin' but a hound dog.'

'All hail the King!' yelled the crowd.

'Wise King Elvis,' another man shouted, 'we have been at war with our neighbours, the Pisspithians, for many years. Now they say they want peace, but we do not know if we can trust them. We have a meeting to discuss a truce tomorrow, what shall we say?'

'We can't go on together with suspicious minds.'

'Praise the King!' shouted the man.

'Praise the King!' shouted the crowd.

'How would you have us live our lives so that we can serve you, oh noble King Elvis?' said another.

'Don't be cruel,' Elvis crooned.

'We will not be cruel!' the crowd cried.

'Great King Elvis, we wish to be recognised as your people wherever we go. Shall we wear any particular vestments or apparel in your honour?' Priest Milliwopple asked.

'Blue, blue, blue suede shoes,' sang Elvis.

'We will wear them always, for we love you King Elvis!'

'We love you King Elvis!' sang the crowd.

'I can't help falling in love with you,' sang Elvis.

And with that the light started to diminish in intensity, slowly fading back into the azure sky.

'Oh, great King Elvis we, your people, will forever remember this day of all days and will try to live as you have instructed. You have enriched our souls and we are forever grateful!' cried Priest Milliwopple.

'Praise King Elvis! Praise King Elvis!' the crowd cried.

Thankyuhverramuch,' said Elvis.

And so Elvisolothism was born on Weyweydoun and soon swept the entire planet. A truce was declared with Pisspithians, the Great Fido was put in a kennel and the Plains of Extrixieth now house the largest manufacturer of blue suede shoes in the Multiverse.

APPENDIX 3 – THE FROTHY ALE TSUNAMI OF '87

And so it was that in the year of the Great Beetle, 1987, a cataclysm of proportions not seen since the Bucket of Water Dropping of 1960 engulfed our world. It had been predicted in the Ancient Book of Fleas that a deluge like no other would cover the land, and that this liquid would change the lives of all forever. And so it was so. And then some.

Although there is no one alive to tell the tale now, it was handed down through the generations by word of mouth, until it was finally recorded in the Book of Catastrophes version 2.1.2.2. This has now become the accepted version, although many feel it has been overly embellished and that, unlike version 2.1.2.1, is no longer a true representation of the monumental events experienced that day. Nevertheless, scholars of the religious texts have verified it as genuine. The following is an abridged extract:

'And the Great Beetle came before the woodlice and said, "Unto ye I now give warning. There are waters above that will soon be on the ground, and these are waters like ye have never seen before. For they are golden in colour and are frothy". And the woodlice genuflected before the Great beetle and thanked him for letting them know.

Then, one of their order, a brave woodlice by the name of Gnawer, stood tall and asked "Oh Great Beetle, what are we to do when the waters come? How are we to be saved?"

And the Great Beetle let out a mighty sigh…

"The waters will engulf all of thy land. No creature will be able to escape the mighty tides, and anyone caught in its frothy waves will surely perish."

"Then surely we need to be above the waves, in some kind of receptacle, say," Gnawer said to the Great Beetle.

And the Great Beetle looked down upon Gnawer and said "Dost thou not think that I hath not considered that, you cheeky little beggar?"

The other woodlice sensed the Great Beetle's chagrin at Gnawer's temerity, and genuflected even more. But Gnawer stood tall and said "Actually, no, I don't think you did".

And the Great Beetle went off in a huff.

Then Gnawer stood on the Sacred Peanut and shouted at the top of his voice "I will gather little bits of wood and straw, and some sticky stuff, and I will build for us a boat. This boat will carry us to safety when the frothy waters come. And I will call this boat 'Gnawer's Ark'."

And all the woodlice went "Ahhhh."

And so it was that Gnawer's Ark was built, and all the woodlice, plus two each of the other insects in what was known as "Barland", climbed aboard and waited for the waters to arrive.

Then, on a particularly noisy night, a lookout on the Ark peered up into the dusty sky and saw a shining light, and heard a booming voice, which said "Oh, bugger, I've dropped it."

And then the waters came, a massive torrent from above. And the sky was filled… until the waters hit the ground, and then the ground was filled.

Gnawer shouted down to the insects in the Ark "So it was foretold, and so it is! But we will be safe here in the Ark, for the waters will lift it up and carry it and all of us to eventual safety!"

And all the insects cheered and gave praise to Gnawer.

However, not all of the insects managed to get to the Ark and they were swept away by vast, frothy tidal waves. As many ingested the waters and began to drown, they went mad. Some sang silly songs; some tried to copulate; and others floated off, vainly in search of a Kebab shop.

But the Ark rode the mighty waves with ease, with Gnawer steering the tiller as if the Great Beetle himself had given him the power of ten wood lice… or five wood lice, if they exercised a lot.

And soon, land came into view. "We will come to rest on that mountain!" Gnawer shouted. And so it was so.

And as the Ark came to rest on the mountain known as "Mount Arrowroot Biscuit", the waters receded and there was much rejoicing. But, this was sadly short lived. Suddenly the sky became dark once more and all of a sudden a mighty forest came into view.

"Oh, look, an enchanted forest," shouted one.

"Ah, yes," said another. "And it appears to be heading this way!"

"And look over there," shouted yet another. "The land has become like metal, and is angled upwards to the sky! We are doomed! The Great Beetle is angry and he has turned his wrath towards us. We must pray!!"

And so they all prayed to The Great Beetle, but he answered them not. He was still in a huff.

And the forest met the land and the Ark was rendered into pieces. But, so it was told, the insects survived and began a new life in a wonderful new place, filled with exotic foods and strange landscapes. They named it "Binland".

To this day, many do not believe that Binland exists, for none have been able to find it. Nevertheless, many still believe.

And so it is and so it shall ever be.'

APPENDIX 4 – HISTORY OF THE CESTRIAN MUSIC TOURNAMENT

The Cestrian Music Tournament was first held in 1887, at the 'Prancing Parson' pub in the centre of Chester. It was sponsored by a local fishmonger, Ely Slapflipper, who took great delight in singing to his fish while he gutted them. His singing soon attracted other like-minded fishmongers (and one recalcitrant florist), who were inspired to sing by the aroma of fish. And so was born 'Ely and the Gills'.

Following accusations of lip-synching from the local tailor, Sigmund Stitchit, and his group of singing tailors, 'The Trouser Wafters', Ely sent out a challenge to any musical group in Chester to meet them in a tournament that would decide who really was the best.

Word of the challenge spread and feverish excitement gripped the city. The owner of the Prancing Parson, Ivor Bigbottle, offered his establishment as a venue, and the 'Chester Trumpet' newspaper ran a plethora of articles and advertisements.

The list of contestants grew, with the final line-up as follows:

Ely and the Gills - *Vocal harmony group (featuring Hilda Ribber on fish bones)*

The Trouser Wafters - *Vocals and rhythmical zipping*

Stan Anvil and the Pots - *Instrumental percussion (a group of ironmongers who are credited as the founders of heavy metal)*

Penelope Poodle's Parsnips - *Lady's quartet of musical vegetables*

The Cheesesniffers - *Musical cheese sniffing* and cheek slapping*

Wally Washboard's Scrubbers - *High-energy melodic clothes-cleaning with three-part harmony vocals*

Brassy Bill and the Bottlers - *Tuba and bottle-blowing*

* *Cheese sniffing was not considered a crime in 1887.*

On the night of the contest the city was wild, the Prancing Parson was packed, and the first ever merchandising stall was opened by Timmy Tout. A raffle was held to select the judging panel, with controversy infiltrating events not for the first time. Objections were raised and some mild protests descended into scuffles, but it was agreed that the results of the raffle stood. And so, John Firmudder-Curlyfleece became the first sheep to ever sit on a judging panel of a music competition. He was joined by the Policeman, Bob Copbobby, and the Fireman, Andy Allablaze.

And so as the tournament got underway, the city bore witness to some astonishing music and some sterling cheese sniffing. After all seven acts had performed, the judges deliberated earnestly before selecting Wally Washboard's Scrubbers as the winners. However, the decision was tainted with controversy when Ely Gill accused the judges of accepting bribes by way of free clothes laundering. This was hotly refuted at the time, although rumours continued to circulate, particularly when a consignment of washboards arrived at the local Police and Fire Stations the following week.

Such was the popularity of the tournament, it was agreed by a select group of sponsors that it would be held again the following year. And so it has been ever since. Over the years there have been many success stories, and also much heartbreak. Worldwide stars have been born and some musical careers have been shattered. For every million-selling artist, such as Hoochie Coochie and the Coos, there are also sometimes painful stories of the losers, such as the tragic tale of Dick Down's Delicates, where defeat was met with disbelief, many tears and the public shredding of their stage underpants.

The Tournament is now recognised as the largest and most prestigious in the land and is beamed live across the civilised world, and also to Scotland.

Notable Recent Winners:

The Bonsai Brigade (1985) - A punk rock band consisting of Bonsai trees, they wooed the audience and the judges with their eclectic style and multi-coloured bark. As their music is transmitted on a completely different level of consciousness, the listener is required to wear specially-adapted transducer leaves (one for each ear to get the true stereo effect).

Sid Skiffle and his Crooning Spider (1980) - After emigrating from Scouseland to Denbigh, Sid hooked up with Sammy the Spider and a legendary act was born. Sid's banjo playing was a perfect accompaniment to Sammy's dulcet tones, and they were clear winners on all of the judge's scorecards. They went on to record three hit albums and would have surely recorded more, if not for Sammy's unfortunate accident with an open plug hole and running cold water bath tap.

Melanie Fleecetickler (1975) - The first sheep to ever win the tournament, Melanie delighted everyone with her angelic baaing and dexterity on the acoustic guitar. She has since retired from music and now manages a successful chain of Shearing Salons.

Barnaby Humpypoke (1970) - Much was made of the rivalry between Barnaby and Tam James, and indeed the pair had come to blows in a trouser-tightness competition the year before. Despite barely being able to hear Barnaby's singing due to the screams of ladies in the audience, the judges were unanimous in their verdict, with extra points being awarded for multiple pant-splitting.

Tam James (1968) - 'The Singing Dwarf' was already a star in his native South Wales and his entry into the tournament was considered by many to be controversial and inappropriate. However, Tam argued that wearing pants as tight as his gave the other contestants an advantage. On the night, his brilliant rendition of 'Delia's Deli' was performed without any pant-splitting and received top marks from all the judges.

Felicity Floss and the Dentists (1967) - Considered to be one of the tournament's most unusual winners, with their mixture of flowery pop and rhythmical drilling not being to everyone's tastes, the group nevertheless had a massive hit with 'Open Wide Now'. Although the original line-up broke up in 1972, Felicity retained the rights to the name and re-launched the band in 1974. They still perform to this day, with their spectacular live shows including robotic dentist's chairs and multiple root-canal surgery.

Charlie Cobbler's Sole Brothers (1964) - With their intoxicating brand of soul music with hobnail boot tap dancing, it's safe to say that Charlie Cobbler's Sole Brothers were one of the most popular winners ever. They also further endeared themselves to the audience by throwing out 'two-for-one' shoe repair vouchers at the end of their act.

Chucky Plum and the Gooseberries (1956) - Drawing upon the rock 'n' roll revolution of the 50s, Chucky dazzled the crowd and judges with his all-energy show, including his now-famous 'Pigeon Strut'. His sheer presence and astounding guitar playing on 'Ta Ta Jimmy' had the audience dancing in the aisles. Chucky went on to have an extremely colourful career and has served as a guest judge on the panel many times, even after being pronounced acutely deaf.

ABOUT THE AUTHOR – BY OLDFART OLAFSON

Andy Coffey has been called many things; short, bald, barking mad, cute, a creative genius (… actually, I think he calls himself that). But, it is true to say that without Andy, Sacred Wind may never have made it into your particular reality. And we thank him for that.

After a brief foray into music journalism, and an attempt at rock superstardom in the late eighties, Andy eventually carved out a successful career in something called 'IT' for the best part of twenty years, attaining a Senior Management position in a company dealing with software production and IT service management. He tells me that he was a bit of a guru, by all accounts. However, the music bug never really left him and, in fact, he recorded two albums with his band, 'The Quest', in the nineties (he tells me that the second one was really good). Oh, he plays drums, and apparently his drum kit is nearly as big as Agnar's. He also developed an interest in music technology and composition. This initially caused him some confusion as he had to learn to play keyboards, discovering that hitting them with drumsticks didn't really achieve the desired results… and was more expensive.

We first managed to cross the dimensional barrier to communicate with Andy about Sacred Wind in late 2010 (your time). Having voices in his head was a bit of a shock for him at first, but he soon got used to it. So, after working with him closely for the past few years, he's now produced the Sacred Wind books and debut album, for reading and listening pleasure in your reality.

He lives with his partner, Jo, and their cat (Theo) in a little town called Frodsham, in the UK. Apparently they can fart whenever and wherever they like. He has a son, Adam; a step-daughter, Zoë, and a step-son, Johnny. He's a good lad but he needs a bigger weapon… (that pocket knife will never do).

Yours fartily, Oldfart Olafson (Manager - Sacred Wind)

Made in the USA
Charleston, SC
13 September 2015